STRANGER

OTHER BOOKS BY RACHEL MANIJA BROWN

All the Fishes Come Home to Roost: An American Misfit in India
A Cup of Smoke: Stories and Poems

OTHER BOOKS BY SHERWOOD SMITH

Crown Duel
A Stranger to Command
The Spy Princess
Sartor
A Posse of Princesses
Lhind the Thief

RACHEL MANIJA BROWN
SHERWOOD SMITH

WITHDRAWN

STRANGER

VIKING

An Imprint of Penguin Group (USA)

VIKING
Published by the Penguin Group

Penguin Group (USA) LLC
375 Hudson Street
New York, New York 10014

USA ▪ Canada ▪ UK ▪ Ireland ▪ Australia ▪ New Zealand ▪ India ▪ South Africa ▪ China
penguin.com
A Penguin Random House Company
First published in the United States of America by Viking,
an imprint of Penguin Group (USA) LLC, 2014

LIBRARY OF CONGRESS CATALOGING-IN-PUBLICATION DATA
Brown, Rachel Manija.
Stranger / Rachel Manija Brown and Sherwood Smith.
pages cm
ISBN 978-0-670-01480-4 (hardcover)
[1. Science fiction.] I. Smith, Sherwood. II. Title.
PZ7.B816684Str 2014 [Fic]—dc23 2013044551

Printed in U.S.A.

1 3 5 7 9 10 8 6 4 2

Designed by Kate Renner

Penguin
Random
House

This book is dedicated to the kids and teenagers
of the Virginia Avenue Project, past, present, and future.

STRANGER

1

Ross

ROSS JUAREZ RAN DOWN THE GULLY. WALLS OF EARTH and stone sheered high on either side, close enough to touch.

Something flickered at the edge of sight. He jammed his heel into the dirt to stop himself, scanning warily. Stone. Dust. A hardy sprig of tarweed fluttering in the breeze. Maybe that had been it.

A black claw slashed at his eyes, its serrated edges glinting with oily poison. He threw himself backward. A segmented leg emerged from a shadowy fissure; then a large, black-furred tarantula squeezed out and landed with a thump, sending up a puff of dust. Its mandibles, as long as the blades of Ross's knives, clicked together at knee height as the spider lunged at him.

Ross snatched up a loose piece of granite. No point wasting one of his precious daggers. The throw hit the tarantula in its furry abdomen. It curled up, chittering angrily.

He edged past, then picked up speed until the gully curved ahead, out of sight. When he reached the rocky outcropping, gravel and dry weeds crunched under his feet.

Crystal chimes rang sweetly.

Now, *that* was scary.

The gully dead-ended about thirty feet ahead in a grove of singing trees. Razor-edged leaves, faceted branches, and translucent seedpods sparkled in the sun, turning the parched earth into a kaleidoscope of colored light. Exposed roots glistened like veins of jasper and smoky quartz. Behind the trees, an ancient concrete wall towered above the top of the gully.

His first impulse was to run. But he reminded himself that the trees' farthest range was twenty feet, so he was safe. Which way now? He could climb out of the gully, but then he'd be visible to pursuit from above.

Sweat trickled into his eyes. As long as he kept moving, he could forget how hot and thirsty and tired and scared he was, but once he stopped, all he could think of was water. He couldn't help reaching for his canteen and shaking it, though he knew he didn't have a drop left. He had to get out of this bone-dry arroyo.

He took a cautious step, listening for the chime that usually preceded a barrage of crystal shards from the exploding seedpods. There was no wind, but the glassy leaves struck together, ringing out a threat. He was still safely out of range, but not by much.

Another step past the outcropping revealed a rock fall that had shattered a brilliant purple tree. The others in the grove were colored by the fur of the animals they had killed and rooted in: yellow brown for coyotes, dark brown for raccoons, gray for javelinas, white for bighorn sheep. But those trees that grew from humans usually took their color from the dyes in clothing. He wondered who had died to create that purple tree.

One of the boulders lay beside a hole in the cement—an open pipe. It might be big enough to wriggle through, if he took off his backpack and was willing to risk it.

He wasn't willing. He hadn't seen the bounty hunter since the day before, when he'd taken refuge in the maze of arroyos. It ought to be safe to retrace his steps; if the tarantula went for him again, he'd use a knife.

The concrete wall stretched for miles in both directions. But once he got around it, extracted water from a fishhook cactus, and snared a rabbit or quail for dinner . . . then what? He'd lost most of his supplies, and you couldn't make a shotgun and prospector's tools out of tumbleweeds. The obvious answer: he had to hit the nearest town and sell something.

For once, he had a genuinely valuable find.

Ross adjusted his backpack. He wasn't sure he wanted to give up the prize before he'd figured out its secrets. And as precious as it was, what if the potential buyer decided to steal it instead?

A shadow fell across the weeds at the lip of the gully. Ross dropped to the ground as a shot rang out.

He rolled, reached for his boot knife, and threw it.

"Dammit!"

A hit. But not good enough to take the guy out, if he could yell like that. Ross scanned frantically. He had no cover, unless he risked venturing into the trees' range to reach the boulder or the pipe.

He took another knife from his belt. The hilt slipped in his hand—his palm was slick with blood. He glanced down. His shirt was soaked all along the right side. He hadn't felt the bullet, and it didn't hurt. Yet. He scrubbed his hand and the hilt against his jeans, then pressed his forearm tight against his side to try to stop the bleeding.

All Ross saw above the gully's edge was brilliant blue sky, but the man yelled, "Let's make a deal."

"Go to hell!" Ross's voice cracked. Now he felt the burning pain, and a stab every time he inhaled. He peeled his shirt from his side. The bullet had left a furrow along his ribs—not fatal, just bloody.

He hoped the bounty hunter was starting to feel whatever damage he'd managed to do with his knife. As he squinted up into the blinding light, the shadow of a hawk fell across his face and was gone.

The bounty hunter shouted, "Listen—"

"No!" Ross yelled. Then he reconsidered. Every minute they spent talking was a minute he could figure out how to escape. "What do you want?"

"I thought I could take you in less than a day."

"So?" If he ran back, the man would follow and shoot him from above. Ross's knives didn't have a twentieth of the range of the rifle.

"That was six days ago. I respect that."

I bet. Ross pressed his arm tighter against the wound, which just made it hurt more.

"I respect it enough to offer you a deal."

Stall. "What's the deal?" No way forward, no way back, the bounty hunter would shoot him if he tried to climb out. . . .

"You've given me enough trouble already. I don't much want to spend the next six days dragging you back to Voske. Give me the book, and I'll let you go."

With his free hand, Ross patted his backpack and found the reassuring jut of the book. "It's mine!"

"I don't care. Voske wants it, and he wants you—"

"He wants to put my head on a pole," Ross muttered.

"—but he wants the book more."

I know he does, and I know what he'll do with it, Ross thought. He clutched the backpack tight.

"Turn it over and walk away free, or I sit here and wait for you to change your mind. How are you doing on water?"

Ross didn't believe for an instant that the bounty hunter was planning anything other than dragging him back to King Voske. Or killing him. That was what bounty hunters did.

A pebble rolled down from the gully's edge. Ross hurled a rock with his left hand and heard the man scrabble back out of range. He made sure his remaining knives were loose in their sheaths.

The bounty hunter kept silent. Ross knew it was to give him time to think about how hopeless his situation was: wounded, without water, trapped, and exposed in the sun. And it was working. The minutes passed, and Ross was painfully aware of his dry mouth, his burning side, and his throbbing head. Was he getting sunstroke already? The desert heat could kill him as surely as a bullet.

"I'm not going anywhere!" the man shouted.

The words stirred up first anger, then a sense of calm that washed through Ross's body like cooling water. He refused to surrender, and he refused to sit there and die.

You should have kept your mouth shut, Ross thought.

He might be able to cram his shoulders through the pipe in the concrete wall. But if he was wrong—he glanced down at his shirt and jeans—he'd become a white-and-blue tree.

He measured the distance, calculating how many steps he'd have to take while within the nearest tree's range before he could reach the cover of the boulder. Even one was too many. But it was a chance. And if he died, he and the book would become a singing tree, and the bounty hunter and Voske would never get either of them.

He sheathed his knife and rummaged through his backpack. The closest he had to a shield was his second pair of jeans. Holding his breath to ease the pain, he folded the jeans and slid them under his shirt to protect his back, then tucked his shirt into his belt to keep them in place.

Ross checked the distance once more. To his shock, he was closer than he'd thought. The trees against the wall shone like topaz and moonstone, but there were telltale shimmers in the air mere paces away. Some had shifted to transparent crystal in the hope of luring him in.

And it had worked.

He stood up slowly, using the backpack to shield his face and throat. The trees chimed as if they knew what he was thinking. Ross sucked in a breath. He'd move faster if he could relax his muscles, but his entire body was quivering like a stretched wire.

"You're crazy," the bounty hunter yelled. "Those things will kill you!"

"Better them than you!"

He ran. The ringing stopped, replaced by a sound like shattering glass. Ross passed the boulder and flung himself into the pipe. He pushed his backpack in front of him and wriggled on his elbows, squeezing his shoulders together to avoid getting stuck. The pain in his shoulders and side took his breath away, and he lay still in the chilly darkness.

He'd made it. He'd actually gotten past the singing trees. He'd heard a few shards hit his backpack, but unless they struck something living they quickly dissolved into sand.

There was no way the bounty hunter would be able to fit into the pipe, even if he managed to get past the trees. All Ross had to concentrate on now was getting through the pipe and finding water once he was free.

He began to inch forward. His left wrist stung as if he'd crawled over something sharp. He tried to lift his hand, but his whole arm felt heavy.

A needle of pain jabbed in his wrist, then shot into his forearm. Ross patted it. A hard sliver moved beneath his fingers.

A crystal shard was growing under his skin.

Terror flashed through him. He jerked his right arm backward, trying to reach the knife at his belt, but he couldn't get his hand past his chest. As he struggled to work his hand between his body and the pipe, the shard stabbed farther into his flesh. It was working its way toward his heart.

Ross wriggled as fast as he could, banging his knees and elbows and the back of his head against cold metal. He didn't know how much time he had to save himself, but it couldn't be a lot.

Light glinted ahead. He threw himself toward it, pushing off with his toes. Fresh air struck his face and hands like a new-lit fire, and he tumbled out of the pipe onto sun-warmed sand.

His left arm had gone numb, hanging from his shoulder like

a dead thing. He dragged his jacket off. The brown skin was distorted by a lump that began at the base of his palm. The lump burrowed visibly toward the inside of his elbow.

Ross knelt down. Fumbling in haste at his belt, he yanked out a knife. If he wanted to live, he'd have to cut out the shard.

Bracing his forearm against his knee, he gritted his teeth and set the point of the knife against the thing in his wrist. He leaned in, intending to use his weight to make the cut, but his arm slid off his knee. As he stared in shock, the shard grew another half inch, jolting pain through his entire body.

He dropped to the sand and leaned all his weight on his elbow, pinning his forearm to the ground.

This time he put the knife point at the inside of his elbow. He'd cut off the thing's path to his heart. One deep jab got past the outer layer of his skin. The numbness blazed to white-hot agony. Holding his breath, he dragged the knife all the way to his wrist. From beneath its coating of blood, the exposed shard gleamed with its own ruby light.

Ross dug the knife point under the shard. He tried to flick it out, but it was attached by tiny rootlets. He flipped the knife around and slashed through the tendrils. They snapped like threads, and the shard dropped to the ground.

He flung himself away from it, rolled once or twice, then lay there, his arm on fire with pain. He'd have screamed, but he couldn't catch his breath.

In a daze, he watched blood pour from his arm and soak into the ground. At first the powdery dust swallowed the blood with barely a trace, but soon it began to darken the earth, and then to pool on it. Ross tried to sit up, but his body was too heavy, and the ground kept lurching under him. His backpack had a shirt he could use for bandages, but he couldn't reach it. Finally he rolled over, pinning his arm beneath his chest, and hoped the weight of his own body would stop the bleeding. The blazing sunlight dimmed to gray, then black.

Ross stumbled across the cracked earth. When he'd come to, he'd been burning up, but now he was cold again. With his right arm, he tugged his jacket tightly across his chest. His clumsily bandaged left arm hung at his side. The ache in his head and side throbbed in echo to the stabbing pain in his arm. Worse, he was leaving a blood trail that anything could track.

It fell like red rain, pattering down and sinking into the sand. The blood had still been wet when they'd found his father. Ross could feel it sticky on his hands, feel the cool skin that used to be so warm. He heard his grandmother whisper, *He's dead, Ross. We have to run . . .*

He forced himself back into the present. He had to find water, and then shelter. If he passed out again, he'd never get up. The backpack dragged against his shoulders, pulling him down. He swayed, then caught himself. *Stand there and you'll die.* He slung the pack over his shoulder and forced his feet to move.

Two steps, and he tripped over a rock and slammed into the ground. Sand scraped his cheek. A spindly thorn apple tree cast a shadow across Ross's face, a scrap of relief from the unrelenting sun. His eyes closed. *Run.* He jerked himself awake, his fingers clenching crisp weeds. There was something he had forgotten. Something important. He was in danger . . . He was in danger from the bounty hunter, because . . .

Ross pulled his pack toward him and scrabbled through it until he touched the worn cover of the book.

"Still there," he whispered, his tongue dry as leather.

He opened his eyes, squinting against the light. There was a cactus a few yards away, haloed in pulsing rings of purple and black. Maybe he could cut it open for water. He blinked hard, and the rings faded. The spines grew in hexagons: a hive cactus. There was no water inside, only more danger if he provoked its swarm.

But a barrel cactus grew a few paces beyond. He could get water from that, if it wasn't another mirage. Ross hauled himself upright, dragging his pack by the straps. The cactus didn't fade. He let go of the pack and reached for his boot knife. When he straightened up, black spots swam across his vision. He staggered, the knife slipping from his hand, and leaned against a nearby tree. He was so tired, but at least the pain had gone. He could sleep here, like he used to sleep leaning against his burro...

"Get away from that tree."

He opened his eyes and saw a woman. Long black hair, brown hand reaching out... *Mom?*

His mother was dead. He knew that. He tried to move, but his skin seemed stuck to the tree. His palms and hip and cheek stung as if he'd embraced a wasp's nest.

"Now. It's sucking your blood."

She was right. Leechlike mouth holes had opened in the bark and fastened to his skin. He yanked himself painfully away. With a popping sound, the vampire tree let him go.

He collapsed onto the hard earth. Hands gripped his shoulder and hip and rolled him over. He could feel the cool imprint of her palms. You couldn't ever touch a mirage. Ross squinted dizzily up at the woman, whose hair covered half of her face. A steel badge glinted on her leather vest.

"Who are you?" He could barely hear his own voice.

"Elizabeth Crow. Sheriff of Las Anclas. What happened to you?"

Had he lost the bounty hunter? Or was the man still on his trail? He could be aiming his rifle at Ross right now. Or at the woman who was trying to help him.

Ross couldn't let her die for his sake, after she'd saved him from the vampire tree.

"I'm being chased." He forced the words past his raw throat. "Run and get help. Armed help."

Sheriff Crow laid her hand on the pistol at her belt. "I'm armed."

Ross whispered, with the last of his strength, "So was I."

Her voice was cool, low, calm. "It was good of you to warn me."

With enormous effort, he kept his eyes open and watched her drop his knife inside his pack. As she reached for him, her hair swung back, revealing her entire face. On one side, he saw a warm brown eye and smooth brown skin, the strong-boned face of a striking woman in her thirties. On the other side, her eye was lashless and yellow, the pupil slitted like a snake's, and her skin seemed to have melted into her skull.

He sighed in relief. She was Changed. She might have some power she could use to protect herself, and him, too.

She lifted Ross with no more effort than she'd used to pick up his pack, then shifted him over her shoulders. Her steps gathered speed until she was running faster than a deer. He peered past the swinging curtain of her dark hair at the scrub oak flashing by.

The last thing he heard was her sharp order: "Lockdown!"

2

Mia

MIA LEE WAS ON TOP OF THE WORLD. AT LEAST, SHE was on top of her world. Crouching on the sentry walk on the wall that surrounded Las Anclas, she stroked the 1,344-pound portcullis of the main gate. She'd loved working on it as an apprentice, but now that she was the town mechanic—the youngest in the town's history—touching it felt different. It was hers now.

That beautiful work of engineering was a major piece of their defenses. Mia knew she was supposed to feel solemn about the responsibility, but secretly she was thrilled.

At her appointment ceremony, her old master, Josiah Rodriguez, had shaken her hand and said that now he could retire with a clean conscience, and everyone had applauded. But the best part had been when he'd taken her aside and said, "Every generation tinkers with the main gate, since it's every town's weak point and the first thing to get attacked. You're the new generation, Mia. Tinker away."

She adjusted her glasses and tried to examine the gate as if she had never seen it before. "Preconceptions are the death of creativity," Mr. Rodriguez always said.

The manual winch they used as a backup to close the gate if the generator failed took the strongest people to crank it—people who would be needed elsewhere if the town was attacked. If she put in a differential chain block, even someone her size could operate it. But she'd need to find the space. She couldn't move the housing over the gate, with its drop holes to dump boiling or corrosive liquids onto attackers. And she couldn't put chains and counterweights into the space needed for the defenders. But maybe—

A sharp pain shot through her hand. Mia yelped and yanked it away. A pink eater-rose was straining upward, bumping up against the wall where she'd absentmindedly let her hand drift down.

Mia shook her hand, watching the rose dart to catch the drops of blood. Then she opened her lunch box and tossed down the leftover chicken bones and her dad's revolting chicken-liver mousse. The flowers ravenously crunched up the scraps. It was too bad Las Anclas couldn't plant eater-roses along every inch of the city walls, instead of just around the gates. But they didn't have enough water and meat to support 320,612 square feet of carnivorous plants.

Mia tried to return to her meditative state, but before she could, three sentries her age came wandering along.

They were too noisy to ignore. Meredith Lowenstein strutted as if to prove to the world that she might be short, but it had better not mess with her. Henry Callahan clattered a stick along the wall's shields, his blond hair flopping around his sun-reddened face. Brisa Preciado moved gracefully, almost skipping, making her chubby body look light as a soap bubble—but the rhythmic beat of her footsteps was distracting. Mia couldn't ever stop herself from noticing patterns.

"I hope he's young," Meredith said.

"I hope he's a she," Brisa retorted, laughing. The ribbons in her four pigtails fluttered in the hot breeze.

Mia had no idea what they were talking about. Then she remembered Mr. Riley telling Sheriff Crow that he'd seen a stranger in trouble, out in the desert beyond the cornfields.

Meredith polished her glasses on her shirt, then put them back on and peered over the wall. The others did too, but Mia didn't bother. Mr. Riley was Changed; no one else could see that far without field glasses.

"I hope whoever it is stays long enough for us to have a welcome dance," said Meredith wistfully. "It's been ages since the Year of the Pig festival."

"I thought you wanted a fight," Henry said.

"I'd love a fight." Meredith pushed her sleeves up her muscular forearms. "You can't train every day and not wonder what it would be like to do it for real. But a dance would be fun too."

Brisa's black pigtails swung and her crossbow jiggled against her back as she tapped out a heel-toe rhythm. "I'd rather have a dance. I've been dying to show off my routine with the backflips and the—"

"Bor-ing," Henry sang out, his freckled face shiny with sweat and aloe salve. "Anyway, that guy's probably a bandit. Bet the sheriff kills him."

Mia calculated the odds against a fight at about a hundred to one. They'd had alerts for "stranger in trouble" five times that she remembered, four for travelers who'd run out of water or into dangerous wildlife, and one for Yuki Nakamura. But no attack had ever followed. Mia opened her mouth to say so, but Brisa spoke first.

"Want an excuse to miss the dance?" She picked up a pebble, clenched it in her fist, and made to drop it down Henry's shirt. When he yelped, she giggled and flicked the pebble over the wall. It exploded in midair with a tiny pop and burst of flame.

Mia wished she had the power to make rocks explode.

Henry and Brisa began mock sparring, Henry protesting. "All I'm saying is, you don't have to dress up for a battle."

"I love wearing my fancy clothes." Meredith took a swing at him. He pretended to cower in terror, which made them all laugh.

Mia felt as left out and invisible as she had at school. But she reminded herself that although she was a year younger than Henry, she had graduated and was officially an adult, with a full job, important responsibilities, and voting rights, while the other three were still apprentices. Would an adult be bothered that she'd been ignored by teenagers? No, an adult would be paying attention to her adult job.

She concentrated on the gate again. If she put a tripod—

"Horseplay on duty?" Ms. Lowenstein, the chief archer, stepped into view.

The sentries leaped into stiff "alert" positions.

Ms. Lowenstein eyed them. "You are sentries on watch. If someone had tried to climb these walls, they would have cut your throats by now."

Henry muttered, "No, the eater-roses would have cut their throats."

Brisa examined her fingernails, which she'd stained pink with crushed flower petals. Meredith twitched guiltily, then straightened up to face her mother's yellow cat-eyes. For once Mia was glad to be ignored.

The chief archer let an awful silence build. "Nothing else to add? You're all getting an extra watch tonight. Want to make it two?"

The three sentries fled back to their stations.

New sentries came running up the steps. Defense Chief Preston strode behind them, big and scowling. He was followed by his daughter, Felicité Wolfe, in a hat with a lace veil and a matching dress in white and blue. She reminded Mia of a summer cloud floating behind a thunderstorm. Her hair was dyed the rich yellow of ripe wheat. Her golden rat, Wu Zetian, trotted at her heels, as elegant as the ancient empress who was her namesake.

Felicité's hair now matched her rat's fur. Only Felicité!

Every sentry snapped alert at the sight of Mr. Preston. Mia could hear the soft cheeping of the sparrows that had descended to peck up crumbs. She got to her feet; she didn't want him to catch her squatting like a duck.

Only Ms. Lowenstein seemed unruffled. "No sign of the sheriff as yet."

"Thank you." Mr. Preston turned to the sentry captain, who picked up his slate and read out the reports for the watch.

"Shall I write them down, Daddy?" Felicité asked.

"Stand by." Mr. Preston smiled at her.

Mia couldn't imagine calling the defense chief "Daddy." It was like calling a giant tarantula "Baby." And nobody said "Mommy" or "Daddy" past the age of ten.

But Felicité went her own way. Who else would wear a veil on the sentry walk? Mia'd heard her say that as council scribe, it would be disrespectful for her to show up in work clothes, and sometimes council meetings were held on short notice. Mia estimated the price of that blue-dyed lace at forty of her own work hours.

She would hate to always have to look respectable. She patted the pockets and loops she'd added to her overalls so she wouldn't have to rummage around in a toolkit whenever she needed something.

While Felicité read the slate, Mr. Preston gazed out with a pair of field glasses. "He came from the Centinela Pass. That leads straight to Voske's—" he began, then snatched up the bullhorn and shouted into it, "Stand by to close the gates!"

It was a rare chance to observe an emergency gate closing. Mia swept up her tools and scrambled back. Brisa and Henry jumped.

"Mia!" Brisa said. "I didn't see you."

Mia gave her a wave. On the wall, the other sentry teams

readied their weapons. Below, four strong people dashed to the gate winches, in case the electricity failed.

She almost never got to see Sheriff Crow run full-out, and estimated her speed at about fifty miles per hour. Dust feathered out behind her as she sped across the sun-baked path between the irrigated crops.

Meredith gasped. "Look at the guy! I think he's our age!"

Brisa shaded her eyes. "Ew. He's all bloody."

Las Anclas already had plenty of teenage boys, so Mia didn't see why she should get excited over one more. But if he was injured, maybe her dad could use her help. During Lockdown, her position was at the surgery, anyway.

She yanked off her smeary glasses again and tried to clean them on her filthy overalls, but it was hopeless. She crammed the glasses back on and squinted at the body slung over Sheriff Crow's shoulders, and caught a glimpse of a boy's dark face and curling hair as the sheriff shot through the gates, yelling, "Lockdown!"

Mr. Preston shouted through the bullhorn, "Lockdown!" Then he clicked open his pocket watch. "One thirty-one, Lockdown. Get the rest, darling."

"First sighting at one twelve . . ." Felicité recited the records as she wrote them in her notebook. She'd already memorized everything on the watch captain's slate.

Mia envied Felicité's perfect memory. It would be so handy! She could remember numbers, but other things— especially things she shouldn't forget, like whether she'd left her lights on—fell out of her mind as if it were a sack with a hole in it.

"Lockdown!" echoed from team leader to team leader, all along the walls.

The bell in the tower began to ring out the Lockdown pattern in a steady toll. Some little kid was getting the thrill of a lifetime. Nine years ago Meredith had been on bell duty during a Lockdown that actually went to Battle Stations, when a gang of outlaws led by a fire-throwing woman had burned down half the northern plantation.

Mia had never gotten to ring the bell for a Lockdown, though there had been one when she was at school and another when she was asleep. She was briefly jealous of the bell-ringer, then reminded herself that her own job was fun every day rather than only during emergencies.

The sentries scrambled into defense positions as the field workers bolted for the gate. The person on wall-feeding duty, no doubt someone assigned drunk-and-disorderly community service, hastily waddled inside. It was impossible to recognize anyone through the top-to-toe protective gear. Too bad the padding did nothing to block the reek of giblets and gobbets of rancid meat.

Mia grinned as Alfonso Medina veered away from the gate and ran alongside the wall until he was past the area covered by eater-roses. He leaped at the wall, the gecko pads on his fingers and bare toes splayed out, and rapidly scuttled upward. She loved watching him climb. It looked like so much fun.

Then she caught Mr. Preston's lip curling in revulsion. Everyone knew what the defense chief thought about Changed people, but it never failed to annoy Mia when she actually saw it. It was so hypocritical. No one in town refused to be treated by her father. They'd let him save their lives, then justify it by saying that he "wasn't like other Changed people," or that "at least he wasn't a monster," like Sheriff Crow or Alfonso.

Mia glanced at Felicité, but she was giving Alfonso the same bland, polite gaze that her mother, the mayor, used. Perhaps the entire Wolfe-Preston household despised Changed people, but at least Mayor Wolfe treated everyone the same.

The last of the field workers passed through the gates. There was no sign of pursuit, which was no surprise. Most Lockdowns turned out to be false alarms.

"Close the gate!" Ms. Lowenstein shouted.

The portcullis screeched a metallic protest as it lowered, followed by the boom of the gates. It seemed slow. Mia made a mental note to test and clock it later.

Everyone assigned to secondary support began arriving on the ammo platforms. She was in the way.

Mr. Preston said, "Felicité, report to the town hall command post. I'll be there shortly."

Felicité tucked her notebook, quill pen, and ink bottle into her embroidered carryall. "Shall I have Wu Zetian send any messages?"

"No, keep her with you for now." Her father took out a clean, pressed handkerchief and polished his glasses, then hurried down the steps and vanished beyond the armory.

Felicité followed him. Tall Tommy Horst adjusted his crossbow so he could lean over and whisper to her.

"Not now, Tommy." She spoke with mock reproach, softened with a smile. Several boys nudged him and snickered, while others petted Wu Zetian as she passed by.

Felicité's rat is more popular than I am, Mia thought glumly.

Meredith poked Brisa. "Did you see the guy? Definitely our age!"

"Who cares how old some dead bandit is?" Henry laughed.

"He's not dead," said Meredith. "Sheriff Crow wouldn't bring back a corpse."

Brisa added, "She wouldn't bring back a bandit, either."

All three peered around guiltily, but Ms. Lowenstein was talking to the watch captain. Mia headed down the steps.

"Mia!" She jumped. Meredith was leaning down, her red

curls glittering in the sun. "Brisa and I want all the details on the stranger."

The ribbons in Brisa's pigtails lifted in a gust of hot wind. "*You* want all the details, Meredith. Now, if it was a girl . . ."

"Come on, Brisa, you know you're curious. We haven't had a stranger in town since those traders in April."

"Becky can tell you about him," Mia called up.

Meredith made a dismissive gesture. "Becky isn't into boys."

"And she's very focused," Brisa added. "She won't notice anything but gross medical stuff."

"All right," Mia said. "I'll take a look at him for you."

Meredith gave her a playful salute, then hastened back to her post.

So Mia wasn't invisible all the time. They saw her when they wanted something fixed, or some news. But she didn't mind, especially if it was people like Meredith and Brisa. Neither was a close friend, like Jennie Riley, but they were . . . friendish.

As she hurried past the armory, she thought about how excited Meredith was about the prospect of a new boy in town. Shouldn't she be excited too? She tried imagining a girl instead, but that didn't make any difference.

Practically everyone her age had already had at least one serious romantic relationship. Mia had been on one date in her entire life, and she hadn't even kissed the guy. Worse, she hadn't wanted to kiss him. What was wrong with her?

Blood rushed to her face when she remembered her dad's talk after her depressing night out with Carlos. She'd confessed that she'd only gone out with him because she didn't want to turn eighteen without having ever had a date, and her dad had tried to make her feel better about being such a freak by telling her that some people never had any interest in romance, and that was "perfectly normal."

She kicked at a tumbleweed. *Normal for freaks like me.*

She stomped onto the porch outside her father's house, kicked off her shoes, and padded past the empty infirmary, toward the surgery. She nudged aside Spanner, Phillips, and Fluffy as she opened the door. The cats were banned from the surgery, but they were still convinced that if they waited by the door, someday someone would let them in.

She stepped into clean surgery slippers as she closed the door behind her. Her father, his shy apprentice Becky Callahan, and Sheriff Crow bent over the unconscious boy on the examination table. They had taken off his leather jacket, exposing a tattered, blood-soaked shirt and a clumsily bandaged gash in his left arm that ran from elbow to wrist. Becky was nervously avoiding eye contact with the sheriff as she cut off the boy's shirt with a pair of shears.

Mia's dad glanced up. "He's lost a lot of blood. Mia, give me a hand with the ropethorn?"

"Sure."

She followed him to the shelf of potted surgical plants. The ropethorn's green tendrils lashed out when they sensed body heat, extending their thorns to pierce skin and drain blood. Mia picked up the implement she'd designed as a catch-and-shield, a giant spatula with a hole in it. She held it to the thrashing plant, blocking it, until a single tendril poked through the hole. Her father deftly grabbed it behind the thorn at its tip, pulled it taut, and snipped it off at the base.

"Good catch," Mia said. He often got stuck by the thorn, but he didn't like to use tongs for fear of damaging the delicate tendrils.

He handed it off to Mia, who held it stretched between her hands to keep it from whipping against her arm. Then he set out a basin of saline solution, wiped down the back of the boy's right hand with alcohol, and nicked the vein with a scalpel. He taped the cut end of the ropethorn to the boy's vein, and put the thorn end in the basin. Fooled by the warmth and salt content, the vine swelled as it began to suck the liquid from the bowl and transfer it into the boy.

Mia's dad gave Sheriff Crow a bemused look. "What happened to him? He looks like you picked him off a battlefield."

"All I know is that he said someone was chasing him. When I found him, he was already bleeding and sunstruck and trying to keep himself standing by hanging on to a vampire tree." Sheriff Crow indicated the bloody bites that marred the boy's upturned palm. "He had to be pretty far gone not to notice that the bark had mouths."

"That's the desert for you," Mia's dad said, tightening the bandage he'd applied to the boy's arm. "Once you're injured and not thinking clearly, everything you do gets you in worse and worse trouble. Becky. Treatment for vampire tree bites?"

Becky's soft voice was confident here in the surgery, as it rarely was outside. "The sap prevents blood from clotting. Wash out the sap and apply yarrow leaves to stop the bleeding."

At his approving nod, she headed for the surgical plants. A ropethorn tendril grabbed a lock of blonde hair that had escaped from her hair net, and she jerked away.

Mia remembered her promise to Brisa and Meredith, and examined the boy for the details she knew they'd be interested in. Because everyone knew Mia wouldn't be interested. But that was *perfectly normal.*

His face was turned aside, but faces were hard to describe anyway. He had overgrown wavy hair that was as black as the sheriff's where it wasn't matted with blood. His body was thin but muscular, his ribs and collarbone sharply etched, and he had a lot of scars for someone his age. Mia bet each one came with a thrilling story.

Her father sponged at the drying blood on the boy's side. "That's odd. This is a gunshot wound. But this . . ." He indicated the bandaged gash in the boy's arm.

Sheriff Crow inspected it. "Looks like a defensive wound. Gun battle *and* knife fight?"

"Maybe he fought one bandit at close range. Then the other bandit shot him."

"Or he was shot, and dropped. When the bandit got close enough to rob him, he fought back, and got knifed. Either way, he put up quite a fight." Sheriff Crow pushed her hair back. "But he still warned me. Actually told me to leave him and return with armed backup. Take good care of him, Dante."

Ever since she had won her place as sheriff, Elizabeth Crow had seldom used first names, and corrected anyone who forgot and used hers. The boy must have made quite an impression on her, to cause her to forget that she was the sheriff for a moment. Mia was impressed too. She wondered if she'd have been willing to risk her life for the sake of a stranger.

"I will." Mia's dad bent over the boy's injured arm. "Though he may need some difficult surgery. It looks like there's some damage to the tendons that control the fingers. This will be a good one for you to watch, Becky."

Becky nodded as she applied yarrow leaves to the boy's cheek.

"Do your best." Sheriff Crow straightened up. "Well, I'll search him for weapons, and then I've got to run."

"Did you have a chance to speak to Tom Preston?" Mia's dad asked.

"No, I ran straight here. I'm sure he'll be on me to know whether or not the boy is Changed."

Mia double-checked to see if she'd missed any tentacles or feathers. There was nothing, unless it was a Change that a pair of ripped-up jeans would cover. Of course, he could have a cool nonphysical power, but Mr. Preston seemed less bothered by Changes he couldn't see.

Sheriff Crow continued. "All the defense chief will get from me is that I checked for weapons."

She shook out the leather jacket, confiscated a knife from the boy's boot, then slid his belt from his jeans. Another knife and a marvelous array of tools hung from it: two beautiful screwdrivers, a set of lock picks, a miniature pry bar, a folding blade, and even a tiny crowbar. Mia coveted them all, but especially the screwdrivers. Sheriff Crow took the blade and the knife, but left the rest alone.

"Prospector's tools," Mia said longingly. "Could I search his pack for you? We haven't had a real prospector here for ages."

"Well, that makes sense. Prospectors are always targets for bandits." She tossed Mia the boy's dusty backpack. "Have a treat. If you find any weapons, you know where to bring them."

As Sheriff Crow started to leave, Mia's father called, "Don't forget to drink some water and have a good meal. You ran nearly a mile in the sun carrying this boy."

"He doesn't weigh much." With the half smile that was the only one she could make now, she added, "I could have carried him that distance before I Changed. Maybe not running. But thanks, Dr. Lee." She nudged Fluffy away with her foot, then closed the door behind her.

Mia took the sheriff's place. Now she could see the boy's face. He had very long black lashes and straight black eyebrows. His skin was smooth medium brown where it wasn't smeared with blood and dirt, with an underlying pallor that would go away once her father got him back on his feet. The delicate skin under his eyes looked bruised, as if he hadn't slept in days. His mouth was . . . just a mouth, but Mia liked its shape. She leaned closer, half-tempted to trace it with her finger. Her glasses slid down her nose. She shoved them back up absently.

"Mia."

"Huh?"

"Take off," her dad said with a smile. "Have fun with the backpack."

She kicked off her surgery shoes and walked to the kitchen, where the usual smells of vinegar, soy sauce, and garlic were overlaid with something strange. Not only were the regular jars of cabbage and radish kimchi present, but there was disturbing evidence of experiments with non-traditional goat-cheese kimchi. She made a face. Pickling cheese was just plain wrong.

She opened the window to air the place out, sat down at the table, and eyed the young prospector's pack. It was like being a prospector herself. Anything could be in there!

Prospectors charged high prices for luxury goods like ancient jewelry and art, and for usable mechanical parts. But they also sold scrap metal, cloth and clothing, plastic items, and objects of no clear use. Mia collected those. The last had been a paper-thin metal disc stamped with a woman's name and numbered phrases like bits of poetry. The prospector had laughed when she asked who bought that sort of thing. "Dreamers," he'd said.

Her heart thumping with anticipation, she opened the pack.

The first thing she found was a blood-smeared knife, which she set aside for Sheriff Crow. Under that was a strip of bloodstained jerky with a stainless-steel bolt and a tiny plastic dog stuck to it. Mia gingerly detached the finds, then tossed the jerky into the mulch bucket.

An inner pocket held a pouch made of the slippery ancient cloth that melted when it burned, containing a pair of tarnished silver earrings set with moonstones. Beneath those were three matching stainless-steel forks. It was all valuable. But the real find was the plastic cup with a screw-in lid that had a tab that could be slid back and forth to create an opening. How clever!

Another inner pocket held calculating devices: an abacus and a slide rule. She barely glanced at those, or at the empty canteen, crowbar, chisel, flint, and candle stubs, or the half-full can of oil. Then she found an intriguing object like a plastic clamshell. She worked her nail inside and flipped it open, revealing a mirror and a shallow container. A whiff of perfumed dust rose and vanished. She liked the tiny mirror. That would come in handy if you glued it to something long and flexible, to use for seeing around corners.

She reached down farther. A coil of rope, a coil of wire, and a purple plastic comb. A folded sheet of flexible plastic to make a solar still to extract water from the ground. A handful of ancient coins in a clear plastic box, a pair of scissors with a bright orange plastic handle, and three chunks of steel pipe that could be melted for scrap.

Not a bad set of finds. Mia was already mentally sorting her own stash of trade items and duplicate tools as she reached inside again. But when she touched the last thing in the pack, everything else fell out of her mind. Carefully, reverently, she pulled out a rectangular object swathed in more of that slippery cloth. She unwrapped it, revealing . . .

A book.

A precious, ancient book. It was battered, like everything from the ruins, but unlike most prospected books, it was intact. It was handwritten in beautiful script, but in an alphabet she didn't recognize.

The second page had an incomplete diagram for a crossbow that could shoot six arrows; the blank spaces had notations in those unreadable letters. Why hadn't she thought of a multi-arrow bow already? She bet she could fill in those blanks and make a prototype.

Excited, she turned the pages and found more diagrams. Some were enigmatic, but others seemed to be for defense or weapons. If everything in the book was this useful—including the pages and pages of unreadable text that came after the diagrams—Mia understood why someone had tried to kill for it.

3

YUKI

A FLASH OF SILVER DISTRACTED YUKI NAKAMURA AS his patrol rode below the foothills east of Las Anclas. A lizard that shone like molten metal skittered out from between Fuego's hooves and darted into a crack in a scrub oak. Intrigued, Yuki leaned out to take a look. His rat, Kogatana, left her saddle perch and climbed up to his shoulder, as if she, too, was curious. He scratched behind her ears, and she rubbed her furry gray face against his fingers.

Paco Diaz reined up next to him. "See something interesting?"

"A silver lizard."

The angles of Paco's face sharpened with interest. Sidewinder, his buckskin gelding, neatly pivoted on the narrow path and stepped closer to the oak. Paco's horsemanship was a beautiful thing to observe. He never had to give verbal commands but relied solely on the subtle movements of his body and the animal's response. Yuki shifted his weight forward and to the right, and Fuego moved obediently to the side.

He slipped from his saddle. Paco's feet hit the ground with a soft chuff.

Paco smiled, his brown eyes narrowed. "My mom and the other Rangers were patrolling here the other night. She said she saw a mutant shape-shifting reptile."

"Really?"

"It looked like a snake, but then it grew legs and ran away.

Since she saw it in the dark, I'm thinking it glowed. Might be the same thing. If it's settled down in there, maybe it's pulled its legs back in."

Yuki sent a silent message of gratitude to his mother for assigning Paco to his bow team after Paco had passed the archery test. They'd never talked much at school. But while patrolling together, they'd discovered that they both sought out new discoveries. Like this snake-lizard—anyone else would ignore it, except maybe to avoid it in case it was poisonous.

"I'll take a look." Yuki took his glasses out of his pocket so he could see up close, then unsheathed his knife and angled it to reflect sunlight into the crack.

Paco didn't push his way forward; when Yuki nodded, he stepped in closer, his muscular shoulder touching Yuki's. The "lizard" had indeed turned into a silver snake. It hissed when the light struck it, then extruded legs and scrambled up the interior of the trunk.

"What's going on?" The patrol captain, Julio Wolfe, rode toward them.

"A shape-shifting reptile," said Yuki, knowing exactly what Julio would say next.

Sure enough: "Did it attack?"

Paco shook his head. "It grew legs and ran."

Yuki waited for Julio's bored eye-roll, and he wasn't disappointed. It hadn't been that long since Julio had been in school with them, flirting with the girls and forgetting his homework. Now he was a Ranger, always talking about his "life of adventure." But to Julio, that meant training and fighting, not exploration or discovery.

"Move along, Prince." Julio clapped Yuki on the shoulder.

Yuki couldn't help stiffening. By now he should be used to the way people in Las Anclas were constantly, unnecessarily touching one another, regardless of whether they'd gotten any signal that it would be welcome. But even after five years the gesture felt as intrusive and rude as it ever had. And Julio knew perfectly well how much Yuki had grown to hate the word "prince."

Mrs. Callahan rode up behind Julio. The dressmaker's face was sun-reddened. "My son, Henry, would never lollygag about on a patrol. Why do you always waste your time staring at useless bugs and worms?"

That was another thing: the way nobody minded their own business. When a lot of people were crammed into a small area, it was natural that everyone knew what everyone else was up to. But on the *Taka*, they had understood that it was only common politeness not to mention your knowledge unless you were invited to do so.

"I'd think your adoptive mother would have taught you better," Mrs. Callahan added.

The nagging was annoying, but "adoptive" stung. It had been a long, hard journey for Yuki to truly feel that the people who had taken him in were his family, but he did.

Yuki pocketed his glasses and rode out ahead, with Paco right beside him. "I know she wasn't trying to be rude," he said, trying to convince himself.

Paco chuckled. "Nah, I'm pretty sure she was. Mom warned me that Mrs. Callahan hates patrolling. Puts her in a terrible mood every time. Don't let her get to you. Blood doesn't matter. Family is family."

"Thanks."

"Hey, Yuki . . ." Paco cleared his throat and spoke in Japanese. "How do you say 'lizard' in Japanese?"

His inflection and pronunciation were so perfect that homesickness pulled at Yuki like a riptide. He steeled himself not to reveal his feelings, but Kogatana sensed them and nuzzled him, her soft whiskers tickling his chin.

When he spoke, he made sure his voice sounded casual.

"*Tokage.* Snake is *hebi.*"

"So, lizard-snake would be *tokage-hebi*?"

Yuki nodded. "You're a natural. I've only been teaching you for a month, and your accent is already better than Mom's or Meredith's ever was."

"I listen to the rhythm and timbre of your voice, not only the words. It's like learning a piece of music." Paco drummed out a beat on the saddle. "Do you speak Japanese with your family?"

This time Yuki was prepared for the question. "No. Not for years. Mom thought I'd learn English and Spanish better if I practiced at home. And . . . I didn't try very hard to teach them."

When he fell silent, Paco asked, "Because you didn't think you'd be here long?"

"As soon as I can find a prospector who'll take me on, I'm leaving. A reliable prospector," he added bitterly.

"Yeah, that was bad luck."

"It was a bad decision. My bad decision," he admitted.

"No, come on," Paco protested. "That guy took in the entire town."

Yuki scratched Kogatana's ears, hiding his face. "I should have known he was too good to be true."

He felt as angry and humiliated as if it had happened last week, rather than last year. That smooth-talking prospector, Mr. Alvarez, had seemed like the answer to his dreams. Sure he needed a smart, reliable boy for an apprentice. Absolutely he would teach Yuki everything he needed to know in return for a year of his work. Of course he'd show Yuki the world.

It had taken some persuading, since Yuki still had a year of school left. But he'd convinced his mom and the council that this chance was worth interrupting his education. He'd been saving scrip from his job helping Mrs. Riley train horses, and he got himself fitted out with tools and supplies. His mom and the Rileys had pitched in to get him a horse. He'd said his farewells, promised to come back in a year or so, and set off with a dizzying sense of infinite possibilities.

Mr. Alvarez, if that was even his name, broke out his favorite herbal tea to celebrate their partnership once they made camp. Yuki woke up the next afternoon with a splitting headache. Mr. Alvarez was gone, along with Yuki's horse and all his belongings but the clothes he wore. At least Kogatana had managed to evade him. She was licking Yuki's face when he woke up.

Yuki had tracked the prospector till nightfall, burning with fury, then reluctantly gave up. The man was long gone, and Yuki couldn't survive long in the desert without weapons or water. He'd been forced to walk back to Las Anclas, feeling like a fool with every step, and then had to face crowds wanting all the humiliating details.

He'd had to return to school, he still hadn't finished repaying his mom and the Rileys, and the only prospector to visit since had arrived in a full suit of blue armor, claiming that the reflective paint she'd formulated would make her invisible to the deadly crystal trees that surrounded the distant ruined city.

Yuki had desperately hoped that she was an eccentric genius rather than desert-crazy. He'd even let himself indulge in fantasies about exploring the city in his own suit of armor. But of course, as everyone had warned her, she hadn't been invisible at all. Now a new sapphire tree grew at the edge of the crystal forest.

Fuego balked, and Yuki consciously relaxed his body. The red-gold gelding moved onward.

"Prospecting's not the only way to see the world," Paco said. "You could sign on to a trading ship, the next time one comes around."

Trading *boat*, thought Yuki, but didn't correct him. No one in Las Anclas had ever seen a real ship.

"You swim like a fish," Paco continued. "And you fight like—like a Ranger. Traders always have guards to protect their wares. You could be a guard."

"Yeah, but . . ."

Even to Paco, there were some things Yuki couldn't talk about. His throat tightened at the thought of living on a boat, smelling the salt air and rocking on the waves, and never losing sight of shore. Being constantly reminded of the true deep ocean in a craft that could never get there would be like dying of thirst with a full canteen just out of reach. It was hard enough living on the coast, with the ocean breeze blowing straight into his bedroom window.

"Traders don't explore," Yuki said. "They only go back and forth along the coast, buying and selling the same goods at the same towns. I want to see new things. Find new things."

Kogatana nuzzled him again. Paco glanced at her, and Yuki could practically see him decide to change the subject.

Paco fished in his pack and held out a tamale, still wrapped in corn husks. "From Luc's. He handed them out last night after we finished playing."

"Thanks. Sorry I missed it. I had to help Mrs. Riley with Tucker. He got his hoof tangled in the fence, and he was panicking."

"I figured it was something like that. We're playing again on Tuesday."

"I'll be there."

Yuki liked music, but he loved watching Paco. Most people dedicated themselves to work and training, and thought of things like music as something to squeeze into their spare time, if they had spare time. But while Paco worked and trained without complaint, he poured his heart and soul into his drumming. Watching him play was like watching Paco's mom, Sera Diaz, sparring, or his own mother shooting, or Paco's apprenticeship master, Mr. Ahmed, blowing glass: observing a master at work.

Yuki choked down the tamale. Five years since he'd been shipwrecked at Las Anclas, and he still hadn't gotten used to having his mouth and throat burned by chili peppers. But since Paco was watching, he said again, "Thanks," and added, "it's good."

The reverberating toll of a bell cut through the desert air—the signal for Lockdown.

Yuki jerked his head up, the tamale falling from his hand. He halted Fuego and squinted against the lowering sun at the town walls half a mile away. His distance vision was as sharp as his close-up sight was blurry. He made out the sentries looking back and forth. Whatever the problem was, they obviously couldn't see it either.

Julio rode up beside him. "Let's go to high ground. We'll have a better view."

Near the top of the hill, they entered a copse of juniper, eucalyptus, and copper-barked manzanita. A few shrubs had black leaves with glowing yellow veins. As Fuego brushed against them, the "leaves" took flight, leaving the shrub a bare gray skeleton. A citruslike scent filled the air, masking the pungent smell of eucalyptus. When Yuki glanced back, the butterflies had settled back down, and the illusion was complete again. Yuki had never seen this before, nor the brightly colored scorpions nearby that seemed to guard a pulsating blue fungus.

He lifted his scrutiny past the walls of Las Anclas that rose up like bars in a cage, to the plains and hills and maze of arroyos that made up the desert. Someday he'd be out there, away from the crowds and the sameness and the reminders of everything he'd lost. Just him and his horse and his rat, exploring ancient ruins, discovering fascinating relics, and studying the ways of strange animals and plants. Every step would be into new territory.

"Rein up," Julio ordered.

Everyone dismounted. They'd reached the top, but it wasn't quite high enough to see inside the town walls.

Yuki indicated the tallest tree, a thick juniper. "Shall I climb it?"

"Do it," said Julio.

"Kogatana, stay." She twitched her pink nose at Yuki, but stayed on her perch.

He climbed, shoving past the pungent needles until he could see. There was no fighting in the streets, and nothing seemed to be damaged. From this perspective, Las Anclas appeared insignificant, a small part of a far larger world.

He started down. About ten feet from the ground his palm punched through the bark as if it were paper. Something gave an ear-scraping screech, then a line of pain slashed across his palm. Yuki jerked back instinctively, and lost his grip. He twisted in the air and landed in a crouch, his teeth banging together.

Owls launched out of the hollow, slicing down with their talons and the razor-sharp quills at their wingtips.

Yuki's sword and crossbow were still on his horse. He made a dash for Fuego. But before he got there, an owl dove at Sidewinder, claws tangling in the horse's antlers. The owl screeched, and Sidewinder squealed and bolted. Every horse followed, stampeding into the woods.

He watched in dismay as Fuego galloped off, Kogatana clinging to her perch. He drew the only weapon he had left, the knife at his belt. The useless knife—owls swooped overhead, easily evading his reach.

Paco snatched up a fallen branch and swung at an owl striking at Julio's eyes. It veered away, then grabbed the branch in its talons. Paco tried to shake off the owl, but it held fast, flapping its wings and screeching. He flung down the branch and went to grab another. An owl dove at Paco's unprotected back, its wingtips slicing down. Yuki lunged out with his knife, knowing he'd be too late.

A crossbow twanged. The owl thumped to the ground. Mrs. Callahan had managed to grab her bow before the horses bolted.

"Fall back!" yelled Julio. "They're protecting their nest."

The patrol ran into the woods. The owls didn't pursue them. They found the horses in a glen, clustered around Fuego.

Belatedly, Yuki reported, "I didn't see anything going on in town."

"It's probably a false alarm. But let's play it safe." Julio began pointing at patrollers. "You three stay with the horses. You two come with me. And you . . ." Yuki's elation when Julio pointed to him and Paco dissipated when Julio's finger moved to include Mrs. Callahan.

He sent them to a boulder-strewn promontory. "Keep watch over there. Stay low, and don't create a silhouette for someone to shoot at."

Yuki sat in a narrow niche between two boulders, the only place that offered both cover and a view of the plains below. He pointed to a smaller promontory higher up. "Kogatana, watch."

The rat scurried off.

Paco settled down next to him, and Mrs. Callahan plumped herself down on his other side. She wriggled into a comfortable position, shoving him against Paco. Yuki gritted his teeth, embarrassed, then forced himself to relax. He felt Paco vibrate with silent laughter.

"Are you okay?" Paco's breath was warm on his ear. "Your hand is bleeding."

"It's fine."

Mrs. Callahan snapped, "What were you thinking, Yuki, sticking your hand into an owl's nest?"

He shrugged and twisted his handkerchief around his palm. How much more of a signal could he send? On the *Taka*, people had often been in tighter quarters than this, but that only made them more mindful of not intruding on each other.

Mrs. Callahan was still going on about Yuki's careless-ness, and he tried to shut her out. It wasn't hard, when he could focus on the press of Paco's arm, his body so close that Yuki could inhale his scent of clean sweat.

"That nest was perfectly camouflaged, and he was climb-ing down," Paco pointed out. "You wouldn't have seen it either."

Mrs. Callahan ignored him. "Yuki, you should have sent Kogatana to scout. Isn't that what you have her for? Your problem is that you only make an effort with things that you care about. Take that garden of yours. I saw four giant tomato worms munching away yesterday."

Yuki pretended to examine the slash across his palm. Of course she'd been watching his garden. Everyone watched everything. If he locked himself in his room, pulled the cur-tains, and coughed, the next morning three people would offer him honey and lemon juice.

"And dandelions everywhere," she went on. "Isn't the weeding your—"

"Mrs. Callahan!" When she stopped talking, startled, Paco said, "Thank you for shooting that owl."

She looked slightly abashed. "Oh, well, don't mention it. Anyone who had their crossbow would have done the same."

As silence fell, Yuki felt Paco shift his weight. Strong brown fingers took the handkerchief from Yuki's hand, where he'd been twisting and twisting it. Paco untwisted the handkerchief, then rewrapped and tied it securely. "I should have asked," he said softly. "Sorry. I know you don't like that."

Yuki shook his head. "I don't mind."

With Mrs. Callahan listening, he couldn't add, *I don't mind when it's you.*

4

Jennie

JENNIE RILEY PROWLED ALONG THE SENTRY WALK at the back wall, crossbow loaded and ready. Her neck twinged as she scanned from the golden hills to the east, across the fields of corn and vegetables, to the desert sands that dropped away toward the thin line of the ocean, glimmering silver in the midday sun.

She spotted a wisp of dust rising up, and tensed even more—someone coming around for a flank attack? But it was only a deer, taking advantage of the deserted bean fields to munch on the crops. Except for the honey-birds darting back to their hive in a mesa oak, all else was still.

Though nothing had happened for hours, her muscles were still locked for action. The Rangers said that waiting for battle was harder than fighting. She bet that they were right, but she wouldn't find out today. Even if the Rangers were ordered to ride out, Jennie would stay behind, stuck on the wall. Waiting.

She spotted a rock lying on the sentry walk, ready to trip someone. She held out her hand, tensing slightly as she pulled with her mind. The rock leaped up to smack into her palm, and she tossed it over the wall.

When Lockdown first rang, her blood had fizzed like ginger beer, but after hours' worth of boredom, it had gone flat. So had everyone else's, apparently. All along the wall, people were chatting, wiping sweaty faces, and watching the hawks circling lazily in the sky.

If I were King Voske, this is when I'd attack.

That was the one thing she wouldn't prefer to waiting. One of her grandfathers had been killed when Voske had first tried to take Las Anclas, eighteen years ago. Jennie had been a baby.

She pushed her thoughts in a more cheerful direction—they had a stranger in town, and that was always interesting. Maybe she could interview him for next week's *Heraldo de Las Anclas*. Jennie loved it when Mr. Tsai, the printer and librarian, used one of her stories in the one-page newspaper. "You always manage to find an interesting angle," he had told her. "Better than the usual 'Six-Eyed Mutant Goat Spotted by Mill!' or 'Whistling Zucchini Sprouts in Olive Grove, Dogs Howl!'"

Jennie's little sister Dee appeared, in company with her two best friends. They were on duty to fetch and carry ammunition, but you'd never know it from their bored expressions. The weaver, Ms. Salazar, also looked like she wished she were somewhere else, with her aura of glittering light illuminating how awkwardly she held her bow.

To Jennie's amusement, the Terrible Three arranged themselves in order of height. They were nothing alike—Dee with her hair clipped into a cap of tight black curls, Nhi Tran chewing on a long brown braid, and Z Kabbani flicking a dead leaf from her red-brown bangs—and yet the way they all looked hopefully at Jennie made them seem more similar than different.

"Do you need more arrows?" Dee asked. "I could run and get some."

"We all could," Z said.

Nhi nodded so hard that her braids bounced against her skinny body.

Jennie tried not to laugh as she hefted her crossbow. "Not till I've shot some of the ones I have."

Nhi let out a dramatic sigh. "I thought a Lockdown would be more exciting. But I bet it's exciting where the Rangers are!"

Z said sarcastically, "At their training grounds, waiting for orders?"

Dee poked Jennie in the ribs. "Is that where they are?"

Dee and Nhi fixed her with expectant gazes. Z scowled at the adobe floor as though a secret message was carved into it.

"Probably." Jennie waited for them to get to the point. In her experience both as a sibling and as the interim teacher, younger sisters were not exactly subtle. Or patient.

Z scowled harder. So she was the one with the problem.

Nhi lifted her chin high. "The day I turn sixteen, I'm going straight to Sera Diaz to say, 'Captain, I'm ready to start Ranger training.'"

"You better hope you don't Change first," retorted Z.

Jennie stepped in. "I'm Changed." A flurry of sparks arose as Ms. Salazar sent a sharp glance her way. "I've been training with the Rangers for two years, and not once have they said anything about it."

"See?" added Nhi. "Captain Diaz isn't prejudiced."

Z muttered, "*She* isn't. But everybody knows that Defense Chief Preston is. And he's the Rangers' boss." She sucked in a breath and glared at Jennie. "I don't see why you have to be a Ranger. You were going to be a teacher. You're good at it. You're the best teacher we ever had."

Jennie said gently, "That's not very fair to Grandma Wolfe."

"Grandma Wolfe was boring," Z informed her toes.

Dee grinned. "It wasn't boring when she set the schoolhouse on fire!"

"Not funny, Dee," said Jennie.

At first Grandma Wolfe had been able to rush outside when she sensed a hot flash coming, and the uncontrollable new power that had come with her menopause had harmlessly set fallen leaves and tumbleweeds aflame. Then, three months ago, her desk had exploded in a fireball.

No one was hurt, and the kids were thrilled. But by nightfall, Grandma Wolfe—who had taught generations of Las Anclas kids, and loved it—had been moved outside the walls, into the house of nonflammable adobe that had been built generations ago, for a different person with a similar, out-of-control Change. And Jennie had been asked by the council to postpone joining the Rangers and take over teaching until Grandma Wolfe's other apprentice, Laura Hernandez, was ready.

Z sniffed. "Laura is even more boring."

"I like Laura," Dee said instantly.

Nhi nodded. "I think those black claws of hers are cool."

Z crossed her arms. "I didn't say she wasn't nice, or that her claws aren't cool, I said she's boring. And bossy." She stared accusingly at her friends.

"Laura's only sixteen," Jennie said quickly. "Give her time."

"You were never bossy. Anyway, I don't see why you want to be a Ranger when you know Defense Chief Preston hates Changed people."

Jennie reached beneath her leather armor to pluck at her sweat-soaked shirt, wishing she was with the Rangers. "People change." She lifted her voice so Ms. Salazar could hear. "And I don't mean in the 'get powers' way. I may be the only Ranger candidate with a Change power, but Mr. Preston invited me himself. Once Laura's ready to teach, they'll swear me in."

Z sniffed. "You think so? Look how quick Mr. Preston was to kick his own mother-in-law out of town!"

Jennie kept her voice even. "Grandma Wolfe was not kicked out. She agreed to go. If she ever learns to control her power, she'll be back."

She let out a sigh of relief when Dee pointed over the wall, shrieking, "Oh! Oh! I see something over there!"

The three rushed to peer recklessly over the shields. The vines groped for their toes, and a tendril that had escaped trimming grabbed Nhi's dangling braid and yanked. They began squealing in mock terror and excitement.

A machete whistled down, slicing off the tendril. Nhi's shriek was entirely real as she jumped back. Jennie grinned up at her boyfriend, Indra Vardam, as he slid his machete back into its sheath.

The heat made her feel grubby and sticky, but Indra's sheen of sweat only made his black hair glisten and his shirt cling to the muscles of his chest and upper arms. She couldn't wait till they were both off-duty. Maybe they could get some time alone at the beach before the sunset bell called everyone back inside the gates.

"Nhi, Z, Dee, get back to your station," Indra said sternly. But the crinkles at the corners of his eyes gave him away.

As Z followed the other two back to the ammo platform, she fired a final, muttered, parting shot: "She only joined the Rangers to be with her boyfriend."

Indra waited until they were out of earshot, then said, "That would take some doing, considering that we were Ranger candidates for almost two years before we started dating."

"Z wishes I'd stay as her teacher," Jennie said. "It's no big deal."

His glance was searching. "'But'? Do I hear a 'but'? You're not regretting your decision, are you?"

"No! I love teaching, but I want to be a Ranger more."

She wondered if Indra had overheard the part about Changed people. Jennie knew that Indra agreed that the Rangers themselves were more important than whatever prejudices their boss might be harboring. Indra's own father was Changed.

"Glad to hear it." He sounded like he was trying not to laugh.

"What are you doing here, anyway? Not that I'm not glad to see you. Are the Rangers riding out now?"

"Soon." He shook his head, sending his long braid swinging. Jennie couldn't resist giving it a tug. He grinned. "I came to fetch you. Mr. Preston is sending us out to search for whoever attacked that stranger. He wants you to come with us. We're swearing you in now."

"Now?" Jennie's uncertainty vanished. "Let's go!"

Indra held out his hand. They ran down the stairway. Then he stopped, leaned against the wall, and glanced up. Jennie followed his gaze, knowing what he was thinking. No nosy little girls were watching. She stepped into the heat of his body and tilted her head back, sending the beads that tipped her braids clattering. He bent to kiss her, then stopped short. His breath was like the lightest of kisses as he whispered, "We can celebrate tonight."

Jennie pulled him down for a real kiss. His mouth was hot as the sunlight burning down on them. She held him tight, sliding her arms slowly down his back. Then she reluctantly extracted herself. "Tonight."

"Assuming we're back by then," Indra added wryly.

She shrugged. She'd be as happy spending the night searching the desert with Indra and the other Rangers, on her very first mission. They could always celebrate later.

As they ran down the dusty street, she thought of a headline: "Former Schoolteacher-Candidate Jennie Riley Appointed Ranger in Emergency Ceremony!" On second thought, that was too long to fit. "What do you think about the headline 'Surprise Ranger Ceremony Shocks Town!'"

Indra laughed. "If you wait till tomorrow, maybe you can get 'New Ranger Singlehandedly Captures Bandit Chief!'"

Jennie laughed too.

They skirted a burro pulling a cart full of tomato seedlings, and came to Mia Lee's cottage. Jennie tugged Indra to a halt. "Wait. I have to tell Mia!"

The door was closed, and the curtains were drawn. Jennie knocked, and was disappointed but not surprised when Mia didn't answer. She was either asleep after working all night on a particularly interesting or dangerous project, or she was awake and absorbed in a particularly interesting or dangerous project. Jennie wondered what it could be. Mia had long since stopped staying up all night to work on her flamethrower. But if it was something new, she would have told Jennie what it was.

Or would she? Jennie guiltily counted up how many days it had been since they'd talked. Lately she'd been so busy with Ranger practice and teaching...

"I guess I'll tell her later."

She and Indra hopped a low fence. Grandma Thakrar stuck her head out of the brewery window, calling, "Any news?"

"Not from the back wall," Jennie replied as she raced by.

They found the defense chief pacing on the town hall's veranda. Along with Jennie's father, Mr. Preston was one of the few people in town so big and imposing that he didn't seem dwarfed by the huge double doors.

He stopped when he saw them. "Sera is on her way." In a rare note of apology, he added, "I hate to rush you through something so important, Jennie, but rules are rules."

"I don't mind at all. I'd much rather miss the ceremony than the mission."

"That's the attitude." Mr. Preston gave her a friendly clap on the shoulder. "You'll be a fine addition to the team."

Jennie considered his smile, so bright in his craggy, dark face. She was once again conscious of being the first Changed person invited to join the Rangers since a group of Changed people—including two Rangers—had left Las Anclas ten years ago.

His heavy brows lifted as he added forcefully, "I wish we had two of you, as well as two of Indra. Three! We need every one of you."

It was like he was trying to convince someone that he accepted her even though she was Changed. Himself, maybe?

"Congratulations, Jennie." Felicité Wolfe's voice, instantly recognizable, always reminded Jennie of caramel. She stepped daintily up, leading—

"Ma!" Jennie exclaimed.

"I'm so happy for you." Her mother's puff of graying hair was flecked with hay and horse hair; she must have come straight from the stables. Jennie hugged her.

"I thought you'd like to have your mother here, Jennie," Felicité said, turning so Jennie's ma could read her lips. "I'm sorry your father couldn't come, but he rode out to guard the pipeline."

Mr. Preston patted his daughter's shoulder, more gently than the thump he'd given Jennie. "That was very thoughtful, darling."

"It sure was. Thanks, Felicité," Jennie said.

"I remembered how important it was for me to have my parents there when I became the town scribe," said Felicité.

Her pretty rat stood up on her hind legs. Her silk bow matched Felicité's veil, blue as the summer sky. "You wanted to congratulate Jennie too, didn't you, Wu Zetian?" Felicité crooned, twirling her fingers.

The rat dipped her head, bowing. Indra laughed and petted her. Jennie did too, wondering why she felt so sour. Felicité had done her a kindness, but around Felicité and her father, she sometimes felt like she had a fever coming on, as if nothing she heard or saw was quite real.

"Jennie, I am so glad!" Sera Diaz ran up, strong hands outstretched, gray-flecked hair rumpled. Jennie's unease vanished as the Ranger captain enfolded her in a fierce hug. "That is, glad for us, but I'm sorry this is so slapdash. You deserve a full ceremony."

The other Rangers crowded up. The entire team was there, with the exception of Julio Wolfe, who had been leading a patrol at Lockdown.

Jennie's heart thumped against her ribs as Sera went on. "We followed the boy's tracks, and found a lot of sated blood lizards. They churned up the ground, so we couldn't find any tracks but his. Once you're sworn in, we'll do a wide perimeter search."

They headed inside, where Mayor Wolfe waited in a gown of dark-blue silk, composed and elegant.

"This deserves a fresh page in the record, don't you all think?" Felicité said in a sprightly voice. Wu Zetian rose on her hind legs to reach Felicité's outstretched hand. "Do you want to lead the ceremony, Wu Zetian, sweetie?"

Jennie couldn't help a flash of irritation at how Felicité was making herself the star of the show. Then she pushed it away. The important thing was that Jennie was going to be a Ranger at last.

Her gaze skimmed past Felicité, to her ma, Indra, the Rangers, Mayor Wolfe, even Mr. Preston. They all wished her well...

... and they were all Norms, except for Jennie. And possibly her ma, though no one knew whether her knack at communicating with horses was a Change or merely a talent. What would happen if Jennie were to reach out with her mind toward the pen on the desk, and pull?

The Rangers gathered in a circle, their faces solemn. They wanted to make her one of them. They wouldn't care whether she walked over and picked up the pen or pulled it into her hand from across the room. As long as they accepted her, it didn't matter what Mr. Preston might think.

Defense Chief Preston said, "Captain Diaz, will you do the honors?"

Sera had mentored Jennie every step of the way. It felt right that she should be the one to administer the oath. She raised her right hand, and so did Jennie. Sera's dark gaze settled on her as she said, "Repeat after me. *'On my honor...'*"

"On my honor ..." Jennie's voice started to tremble, but she made herself speak precisely, so her mother could understand. She sensed Indra behind her, a supportive presence. Jennie's ma smiled at her, loving and serene.

"I will uphold the laws of Las Anclas..."

Jennie knew the oath by heart, but as she spoke it, she felt that for the first time, she truly understood it.

"... *protect the citizens of Las Anclas even at the cost of my own life...*"

"... *have the courage to hold myself and others accountable for our actions...*"

"... *and I will never leave a fellow Ranger behind.*"

As she spoke the last line, all the Rangers joined with her: *"I swear to protect, defend, and serve."*

Jennie's eyes stung as her ma hugged her, whispering so only she could hear, "Pa and I are so proud of you, sweetheart."

"Welcome to the Rangers, Jennie," Sera said. When she spoke again, it was to them all. "We've got a mission waiting. Let's go."

5

Felicité

ON HER SIXTH BIRTHDAY, FELICITÉ HAD BEEN allowed to play with a necklace of golden coins that her daddy had given her mother as a wedding gift. The sound of gold on gold made a lovely chime.

This was the sound that Felicité heard inside her head when she paid compliments. Each compliment was a coin of gold that would return as a vote when she was ready to run for mayor. Those that took the most effort—that disguised how she truly felt—rang the sweetest.

"Congratulations! Have a safe journey," Felicité said to Jennie, but her smile was for Indra as the two clasped hands and ran out with the Rangers.

Clink!

Jennie and Indra. Now, there was a pairing that was wrong in every way. Indra was a Vardam, the second wealthiest family after the Wolfes. And a Norm, of course. Her daddy had said Indra was one of the most promising of the younger Rangers. He could become captain someday, when Sera retired. Later, he might be elected defense chief. That made him the perfect match—for Felicité.

When Felicité's father had been both sheriff and defense chief, he'd unquestionably been the most powerful man in town. He still was, even after Elizabeth Crow had used her Change to steal his position as sheriff. Felicité's parents represented the marriage of military and civil power, far stronger together than each would have been separately.

Felicité intended to marry someone who could stand beside her in the same way.

As her mother always said, a first attraction seldom lasts. Indra was bound to get tired of Jennie Riley. They hadn't a thing in common, except for the Rangers.

Felicité chirped to Wu Zetian, who leaped up to perch in the crook of her arm. She straightened the rat's bow, and noticed with dismay that it was already wilting. She'd have to talk to the maid about cornstarch—

"It's also possible that he's a spy. It looks like he came down the Centinela Pass, and that leads straight into Voske's territory."

Her daddy's voice was sharp. Felicité glanced up. He sat with her mother at the Lockdown command post, where the council held open meetings. Despite his best efforts to instill discipline, everyone was roaming around. If the Lockdown went to Battle Stations, they'd all have to take their positions. But until then, anyone who wasn't on duty was free to drift on over and voice their uninformed opinions.

"Some spy, collapsing half-dead in the arroyo," scoffed Mr. Nguyen. As if a furniture maker knew anything about spies! "If Eagle-Eye Riley hadn't spotted him, he'd be completely dead. Can't do much spying then."

"Trust Voske to be the first to put ghosts in the field," joked Grandma Lee. Everybody laughed.

Everybody but Mrs. Hernandez. "Maybe he's a trader, and he was attacked by bandits."

"All alone? Traders always travel in groups, because of bandits."

Mr. Horst blared over everyone's heads, as if he was in his forge and needed to shout over hammering: "I'll wager there's a war party sent by Voske, hot on his trail. Why aren't you ringing Battle Stations, Preston? You're the one always complaining we don't have proper discipline."

"If the Rangers find any sign of a war party, we'll go to Battle Stations." Felicité's mother didn't raise her voice, but everyone shut up. It was one of her maxims: If you always demonstrate self-control, people will accept your authority.

Never forget that you are a Wolfe, she said. And nobody else will forget.

More mayors had come from the Wolfes than from any other family.

Felicité's mother said to Mrs. Hernandez, "Where were we? The street signs in Sunset Circle, was it not?"

"And who'll repaint them," Mrs. Hernandez added. "Valeria, you know I'm not one to make trouble, but . . ."

She went on—and on, and on. Her daughter, Laura, also rambled when she taught. Felicité was so glad her next birthday would be her eighteenth, and then she could graduate. Six more months.

She missed her *grandmère*. If only she hadn't Changed— Felicité jerked her thoughts away from that subject.

At least Jennie Riley's Change was invisible. It was irritating to see a ruler fly across the classroom—so unnatural—but it could be worse. Felicité buffed her shiny nails, wondering how Mrs. Hernandez felt seeing her own daughter's monstrous, catlike claws every morning at the breakfast table, wrapped around mugs or scrabbling to pick up a spoon.

"Look at that golden hair." Mrs. Hernandez sighed. "Laura keeps pestering me to buy that pricey dye the next time traders come round, but her hair is fine as it is, an honest black, and who'll do the extra work to pay for it?"

"I wish my hair had beautiful blue highlights like Laura's," Felicité said in her best imitation of her mother's diplomatic voice. "But mine isn't true black. It's plain dark brown. Laura is so lucky."

Mrs. Hernandez sniffed, but her mouth relaxed. Felicité's mother smiled.

Clink!

Felicité found a corner where she could listen, unnoticed, and secretly practice Wu Zetian's codes. Her parents usually included her in political talks, but sometimes they sent her off, saying, "You're only seventeen." Well, if they could keep secrets, so could she. Not even her daddy knew what Felicité had taught Wu Zetian.

She understood the importance of discipline. And the importance of knowledge. The best kind of knowledge was the kind that other people didn't know you had.

As time wore on, tempers sometimes wore out, and people started revealing things they didn't mean to. The carpenter and the ironmonger clearly had a personal conflict. They kept taking opposite sides, even when the talk came around to the worry that the entire town shared: not if, but when, King Voske would attack again.

Mr. Nguyen made a dramatic gesture. "It's a sad state of affairs when a single bandit can throw the entire town into such an uproar."

"Bandit! It's Voske! For all we know, Voske's invisible son is right here in this room!" Mr. Horst bellowed.

Her father didn't raise his voice, either, but like her mother, he commanded attention, as Mr. Horst had not. "Feel around for him, Horst, if that's what you believe. The way people rush around in this town, someone would have run into him by now—if he exists."

Felicité clutched Wu Zetian close to her chest. That was one secret she was sorry she'd learned. The council knew from questioning traders that Voske's eldest son, Sean, had a Change power that allowed him go unnoticed unless you consciously searched for him. The traders had added that everyone in Voske's empire was constantly peering over their shoulders and jumping at shadows. The council had decided to keep an eye out for him themselves, but not to confirm the rumors. As her daddy said, "Alertness is good, but in an armed town, paranoia can kill."

As far as anyone could tell, Sean had never attempted to spy inside Las Anclas. But Felicité's father scanned for him every day, and so did she. Whatever Voske's methods, he knew things. No matter how prepared a town was, he always attacked at the exact moment when they'd dropped their guard.

Mr. Horst startled Felicité by thundering, "Far as I'm concerned, we ring the bell and everybody goes to fight, the way we drove Voske off eighteen years ago. But it's quite another matter if certain people are using 'the military' as a cover to pilfer nails for their own projects!"

"Listen here, you jackass—"

A rustle of silk, a waft of lemon verbena, and Felicité's mother was at her side. "Run to Jack's saloon and order sandwiches and drinks, will you, dear? Mayor's budget."

Felicité ran, controlling her impatience. She was dying to hear more. Mr. Nguyen had plenty of business. If he was stealing . . . why?

The saloon was nearly empty, because of Lockdown. Jack Lowell made sandwiches of fresh-baked buns and braised rabbit, and set glasses and jugs of tamarindo in a small wagon. "Whose charge?"

"Mayor's budget." Felicité loved saying the words. She was sure she'd love it even more when it was her own budget.

Back at the town hall, everyone called her an angel and suggested that she get a medal. Felicité poured out the tamarindo and waited until their attention was firmly on one another.

Then she walked by Mr. Nguyen, carrying Wu Zetian and a jug, and casually chucked the rat twice under the chin: the signal to learn his scent. Wu Zetian hopped down and stood up on her hind legs, and Mr. Nguyen reached down absently to pet her.

Felicité topped off everyone's cups, then took Wu Zetian aside. She took the rat's paw and traced the initials "SN," for Sebastien Nguyen, on her own palm. She repeated it until Wu Zetian squeaked, signaling that she knew it.

The westering sun was streaming through the windows when the Rangers strode in. Jennie wasn't with them. She must be putting away the horses and equipment.

Excellent.

Sera reported that they had found evidence that a single person had been pursuing the boy, and had been wounded doing it. "I'll send a team to ride the far perimeter. But there's no one in attack range now."

"Do that," her daddy said. Louder, he announced, "Ring the Stand Down."

The messenger on duty ran out.

Felicité walked up to Indra, who was as handsome as ever, even dusty and tired and smelling of sweat and horses. "Would you like some tamarindo?"

"Thanks, Felicité."

As she smiled up at him, she heard his breathing change. That signaled some alteration in emotion. Attraction, perhaps?

She refilled the mug he'd emptied in three gulps. "Now that you're back, would you like to go to Luc's with me?"

His smile tightened to politeness. "I'm in a relationship right now."

"I didn't know it was exclusive," Felicité replied, hiding

her disappointment. When had that happened? And how had she not known? "Congratulations! I'm planning a party. You and Jennie should come."

His smile relaxed again. "Sure. Let us know when, okay?"

"I certainly will." Felicité's mind was racing. Now that Jennie was a Ranger as well as interim teacher, her schedule would get complicated. It would be easy enough to schedule the party when Jennie had duty. Then Felicité could see how serious that "exclusive" was. Maybe Jennie was pushing Indra into a serious relationship before he was ready.

Once everyone was gone, Felicité picked up Wu Zetian's paw and used it to trace the initials "SN" on her own palm.

"Follow," she whispered.

Wu Zetian would track the carpenter while seeming to wander around town. She was as clever as her namesake, the empress who was one of Felicité's several royal ancestors. When she reported back, Felicité would learn the truth.

6

Ross

CHIMES RANG AS ROSS SET THE KNIFE AGAINST HIS ARM, aimed at the wound on his wrist. He bore down with all of his weight, methodically cutting down, exposing the growing shard. It gleamed a rich ruby red. He tried to pull it out, but it was as slippery and smooth as glass.

As he braced himself to try again, the shard melted into his body. He tried to run, but his feet were rooted to the ground. Cold red crystal crept up through his body, paralyzing him.

Triumphant chimes rang around him. He and the ruby shard were one—

Ross fell to the ground with a thump, smothered in something soft. He thrashed, desperate to get it off. A heap of blankets dropped beside him, leaving him sprawled on a cool wood floor.

He clutched his left arm. The skin was soft and human. A long scar remained, but the terrible pain had faded to a dull ache. He flexed his fingers. They moved, but he couldn't close them into a fist, and it hurt when he tried.

Ross looked around. He lay beside what appeared to be a real bed. He touched a polished wooden leg. It was a real bed.

He wasn't dreaming anymore. He'd cut the shard out. He was still alive, and he wasn't going to turn into a tree. The Changed sheriff must have brought him here.

He put his hand on his side, where the bounty hunter's bullet had clipped him, and took a deep breath. There was no pain, only the raised edges of a scar. Then, puzzled, he examined his hands. He always kept his nails clipped, but they had grown out. His hair seemed to have grown too. How long had he been unconscious?

A soft blue-green glow came from a bright-moth cage on a stand. Someone had selected only the most restful colors, but he knew better than to think he was safe. Still, he recalled all the times he'd lain awake in the desert, watching their rainbow hues against the dark sky, and couldn't help but feel slightly reassured.

The familiar lump of his backpack was beside the bed. He grabbed it and felt inside. The book was gone.

He leaped up and ran to the door, bare feet skidding on the polished floor. Then caution took over. He cracked the door open and peeked out. No one was on the landing outside. Okay, that was one good thing: he wasn't a prisoner.

Or at least not in this room.

Ross closed the door again. Except for the narrow bed, the bright-moth cage, and a bed table with a glass of water and a folded set of clothes, the room was bare. He reached for the glass eagerly, then paused. Who knew if it was really water, or what might have been added to it?

The windows were paned with glass, free of all but the smallest streaks and bubbles. This had to be a wealthy person's house. The closest window revealed a huge square partly sectioned into gardens, with an enormous two-story building on the other side. They had electricity there—floodlights silhouetted a sentry patrolling on the roof. He dropped down, out of sight.

Then he tried the other window. The closest structure was a cottage, its curtained windows golden with a steady light. That light illuminated a treasure trove of prospecting finds in the yard and on the flat roof—and not even guarded. It was obviously the home of another prospector.

Bet whoever lives there has my book, he thought. *They're probably nosing through it right now.*

Ross checked his pack again. His knives were gone too. He upended it on the bed. Everything he could possibly use as a weapon was missing. His right hand clenched, and pain shot through his left wrist as those fingers locked, unable to close. He relaxed his hands. Some towns required visitors to surrender their weapons. It didn't necessarily mean they meant him any harm.

He searched under the bed for his boots, finding nothing but a three-eyed spider wrapping a cricket in luminescent silk. There was nothing he could improvise into a weapon that would give him more of an advantage than his own hands and feet.

It was harder than he would have imagined to dress with only one useful hand. How long would it take to heal? he wondered. How well could he fight when it took him several tries to button his jeans? How much harder would it be to survive in the desert?

I'll figure it out, he thought, dragging on his leather jacket. He'd met plenty of people who'd been disabled by Change or injury and were surviving just fine. There was the prospector whose right hand was a bird's wing. She'd worked so smoothly that it had taken him several minutes to notice that the feather brush she used to clean her finds had grown from her wrist. If she could manage, so could he.

He hefted his pack and opened the door again. Something warm and furry collided with his ankles, nearly tripping him. Before he could pull back, his foot propelled the thing off the landing.

The creature splayed out in midair. Flaps of furry skin stretched and arrested its fall, and the tabby cat glided down to the ground floor. It glared at Ross and let out an indignant meow.

"Sorry," he muttered.

He walked more cautiously down the stairs—stepping over

a calico cat and skirting a black one—and into a parlor flooded with moonlight. Near the front door, he found a shoe rack with his boots.

He pulled them on, impatiently stuffing the laces inside rather than trying to knot them one-handed, then straightened. A door opened to a room with a big table and medical equipment. The tabby cat made a run for it, but Ross shut the door first. Had the people there healed him? Didn't matter anymore. They'd taken his prize and weapons, and he'd get them back, even if he had to fight the thief to do it. The fact that King Voske had sent a bounty hunter to retrieve the book only proved its value.

Ross ran to the house with the treasures in its yard. He used the sheets of metal and the sound of the humming generator as cover as he made his way to a gold-lit window. Pressing close to the wall, he peered inside.

It was a one-room cabin, half of it crammed with prospected parts, broken machines, and tools. The other half was very clean, organized around a burner, a water pump, a sink, and a table covered with glass bottles and containers.

A narrow bunk had a complete engine resting on the patchwork coverlet. A side table was piled with yellowed pages out of old manuals. A prospector could spend his entire life searching and never find half this stuff. He couldn't see the entire room from where he was, but he spotted part of someone's back. He moved to get a better look.

A teenage girl crouched over his book like a vulture.

He charged around to the door and flung it open. "Give me back my book!"

The girl blinked up at him. She didn't move to defend herself, or even to protect the book. "Hi," she said cheerfully. "Do you know how to read this?"

Ross breathed hard, trying to contain his anger. "It's mine."

"I know." She patted the air between them, as if that would

make everything okay. "I know! I'm not stealing. I'm only looking. I meant to return it before you noticed it was gone. My father didn't think you'd wake up till halfway through tomorrow."

"Who else knows about it?" he demanded.

The abacus and slide rule on the girl's belt rattled as she clutched the book. "No one! Not even Dad." He reached for it. She didn't let go but turned it around so they both could see it. "Here, check this out." It was open to a diagram that had also intrigued him, of a crossbow that shot six arrows at once.

His anger died away. She seemed excited but not greedy. He waited.

She smiled back from a round face framed by short black hair. Friendly brown eyes examined him from behind square wire-rimmed glasses. "Isn't it wonderful? I wish I knew how to read that script. Can you?"

The back of his neck itched with embarrassment. Obviously she could read every scrap of paper in the room. No way would he admit that he couldn't.

Instead, he changed the subject. "Are you a prospector too? It looks like there's great pickings around here." He paused. "Uh, where is 'here'?"

"Las Anclas. The last town before you hit the ocean."

"Oh, what the maps call World's End."

"Well, I'm the chief mechanic of World's End." She smiled proudly. "But really, I'm an engineer."

Usually Ross told little about himself. It was safer that way, and most people didn't care. But he'd never met an engineer his age, and the urge to talk to her was irresistible. He tapped the book. "I almost got killed by people trying to get this thing. Do you know what it is?"

"Not exactly, but I'd love to find out. Do you know how rare it is to find a complete book with diagrams?"

"Yeah. I'm a prospector."

"I know! I saw your tools." She sighed with envy. "You must see cool stuff all the time."

"Not really. A good find is always exciting." Ross indicated the engine on the bed. "Like that. That's complete, isn't it? I've never seen one in such good shape."

The girl beamed. "You noticed!"

"It's a treasure. Does it work?"

"It will when I'm done with it," she assured him, giving the engine a familiar pat. "That is, if I can find the right kind of fuel." She picked up a yellowed page from the table. "Here's part of the schematics. Have you ever seen another manual for internal combustion engines? Or even a piece of one?"

Ross tried to sound out the first few letters, but hundreds and hundreds of letters followed those. It was hopeless. He raised his eyes to find her watching. She knew what he'd been doing. His face heated up. But she didn't mock him, or even give him a look like she thought he was stupid.

"My name's Mia Lee," she said. "What's yours?"

"Ross Juarez. Do you have my weapons?"

"No, Sheriff Crow took them. Don't worry, she'll give them back."

"Point out where she is. I'll get them on my way out."

Mia flapped her hands frantically. "No, no, no! I have to study your book some more! Please don't go! Do you have somewhere you need to be?"

Ross had never in his life had somewhere he needed to be. "I have to take my book and go." *Before someone decides to keep my book and get rid of me,* he finished silently.

"How's your arm?"

"Fine."

She offered him a wrench. Confused, he held out his right hand to take it.

She shook her head. "Left hand."

His shoulders tensed. She knew he couldn't use it. She could turn that to her advantage if it came to a fight. He said warily, "What do you care?"

"Sheriff told us how you warned her. My father can help with your hand, if you stick around a while."

"But they wouldn't let me stay here . . . would they?"

"Sure," Mia said cheerfully. "That's why we put you in the guest room. Why not?"

"There's this guy after me. The one who shot me. How long was I out, anyway?"

Mia pursed her lips. "One night."

His hand went to the scar over his ribs.

"Dad healed you," she explained. "Whoever's after you, no one's seen them, and no one can sneak into Las Anclas. And if you stay, we can have a dance! The mayor always holds a dance if someone new comes."

Ross had considered a number of possible outcomes as he'd headed for the cottage, several involving his own death. This was not one of them. "I don't know how to dance."

"You'll learn." Mia smiled. "Hey. About learning. We've got a schoolhouse here. And my best friend's the teacher."

"You have a school?" He couldn't keep the longing out of his voice. It had been years and years since his grandmother's lessons; all he could remember was her teaching him, not what she'd taught.

"A library, too. It's got three hundred and nine books, and twenty-two of them are artifacts. Not all of them are complete, though. But you could sit there and read all you liked, once you learned how."

Ross felt as if he'd tunneled into some unpromising-looking rubble heap and found a treasure trove.

"Well?" Mia asked. "Would you like to go to school?"

"I guess so," he said slowly. "But I don't want people to know about my book. Don't tell anyone about it."

"I won't," she assured him. Her brown eyes widened hopefully. "If you stay, will you let me look at it? You could keep it here, at my place."

That roused his suspicions. On the other hand, the easiest way to get the book would have been to simply let him die and take it. But her father had healed him instead. Still, it didn't feel right to walk out the door, leaving his book behind.

"You can take it back with you, if you like," she offered. "But unless you carry it all the time, it's safer here. And if you do take it, everyone will wonder why you're always hauling your backpack around."

She had a point. Besides, it would take seconds to search the room he was staying in, while her cabin was full of hiding places.

"Let's make a deal," he said. "If you don't tell anyone, I'll let you look at it as for long as I'm in town."

"Deal," Mia said formally, holding her hand out flat.

Ross laid his palm against hers. She had calluses in the same places he did. "Deal. Guard it for me."

She smiled radiantly at him and then at the book. "Why don't you go back and get some rest? Got a big day ahead of you tomorrow."

Ross next woke to the pale light of early morning. He drank the water by the bed, then went downstairs. He could smell tortillas and savory aromas that he didn't recognize.

A man stood cooking at an iron stove as the mewing cats wove around his ankles. He was short and solid, with salt-and-pepper hair in a ponytail and a round, pleasant face like Mia's.

"I didn't expect you to wake up so soon. That is, good morning. I'm Dante Lee, the doctor." Dr. Lee's smile was like Mia's too. "Welcome to Las Anclas."

"I'm Ross Juarez."

Mia wandered in, her eyes bloodshot and her hair standing up in tufts. She stepped out of her shoes, leaving them by the door.

"Good morning, Mia," Dr. Lee said. "Yesterday's clothes, I see."

"They are?" Mia blinked at her overalls in vague surprise.

"Been up all night continuing your passionate affair with the generator?"

"Nope." Mia gave Ross a mischievous glance. "Found something new."

Her father laughed and waved his spatula. "Ah! Young love." He returned to flipping tortillas.

Ross had never seen a father and daughter talking like that. Was this how families normally behaved? His last memory of his father alive was a view from up high, as he'd sat securely perched on his father's broad shoulders and clutched handfuls of his rough black hair.

"Ross?" He jumped, the voice startling him out of memory, his good forearm coming up in a block.

"The silverware?" Mia pointed to a basket on the sideboard. "Sooner the table is set, the sooner we eat."

His face burned. But no one commented as he helped set the table, watching Mia carefully to see how everything was supposed to be laid out.

Dr. Lee brought over a platter of food. He had rolled scrambled eggs—eggs!—beans, fresh tomatoes, and salsa up into burritos. Ross's mouth watered. Wild birds usually either laid poisonous eggs or nested on branches too thin to bear a predator's weight. Months earlier, he had managed to get a gamy roadrunner egg. He hadn't had a fresh hen's egg since... The image of his father came to him again, though no memory came with it. Since he was a little kid, he supposed.

"I have trade goods," he began.

Mia shook her head vigorously. "You're our guest."

Dr. Lee gave his daughter a surprised glance, then smiled at him. "Welcome to Las Anclas," he said again.

"Thank you so much for the eggs, Dr. Lee. Oh. And for saving my life," Ross added hastily.

Dr. Lee accepted his thanks, then tapped the platter with his fork. "Dig in."

It was the first hot meal Ross had had in more than a week. He was too hungry to savor it until he'd wolfed down half his burrito. But after that, the eggs were as good as he'd imagined. So were the warm biscuits with fresh butter and sweet, nutty mesquite syrup. The side dish of tangy purple stuff was delicious too. As he polished it off, Ross had the sense that he was being stared at. He met Mia's fascinated gaze.

"What?"

"You liked Dad's eggplant–goat cheese kimchi?" She indicated the purple stain on his plate.

"Fantastic."

"Our guest has good taste," Dr. Lee observed triumphantly.

"Dad likes to experiment." Mia looked down at her own kimchi. "Want another helping?"

"Sure you don't want it?"

"More fun to watch you eat it." Giving a teasing look to her father, she tipped her kimchi onto Ross's plate.

Ross inhaled half of it before he remembered that there were other important things beside food. "Dr. Lee, is whatever you used to heal me something I can trade for?"

"Unfortunately, no."

He paused, a forkful of eggplant halfway to his mouth. Dr. Lee seemed to be hinting at a Change power, and the sheriff had been Changed. Still, it would be safest to let the doctor himself mention the word—or not.

"It's my Change power. But it's not exactly a healing power, if you've come across something like that before."

"Yeah, I met someone once who had kind of the opposite

of that. She could make people sick." Ross crunched a clove of pickled garlic. "She said she Changed when she got pregnant."

"Did she lose her baby?" Mia asked, suddenly serious.

"I don't know. I met her at a trading camp. Never saw her again."

She pointed to a painting on the wall, of a laughing woman with curly black hair and Mia's small nose. She said softly, "My mother Changed the second time she got pregnant. She died. So did my baby brother."

Ross had no idea what to say, but Mia was watching him as if she expected a response. He muttered, "I'm sorry."

"Pregnancy is the most dangerous time to Change." Dr. Lee's voice was low and gravelly. He was looking at the picture, not at Ross. Then he coughed and wiped his face with a napkin.

When he turned back to Ross, his voice was brisk. "The Change is set off by chemicals in your body called hormones. Women have hormonal surges when they get pregnant or go through menopause, so they can Change then if they were born with that potential. When babies are born Changed, it's because their mother's hormones affected them during pregnancy. And, of course, both men and women can Change during puberty, when hormone levels rise."

Mia scooped up a purring calico cat. "Dad, I'm sure Ross knows all this already."

"I don't," Ross said. "I mean, I knew when people can Change, but not why. What did you mean, 'born with that potential'? Some people say you inherit the Change, but you can have two Changed parents and still be a Norm."

"Well, you don't inherit the Change, per se," Dr. Lee explained. "You inherit the potential to Change. But that doesn't mean it'll happen. Plenty of people could Change, but never do. And unless both of their parents are Changed, there's no way to tell in advance whether or not a person has the potential."

He went to the windowsill and brought back a potted tomato plant dotted with green fruit the size of olives. "As for my own Change, I was born this way, and that's why I trained as a doctor."

He poured his glass of water into the soil, then touched the plant. Tiny leaves unfurled and stretched out, and the little fruits swelled and blushed red.

"Ow." Dr. Lee winced, then rubbed his forehead. He took a deep breath, and his face relaxed. "I can speed up time for living things. What I did for you was age your body to the time when your wounds would have healed. That's the good news."

Ross looked doubtfully at the tomatoes, now ripe and scarlet. The cat in Mia's lap batted at them. "There's bad news?"

She pushed the cat to the floor and began to pluck the tomatoes. "You're two months older than you were yesterday." She put them in a basket. "We didn't miss your birthday, did we?"

"I don't know," Ross admitted. "I don't know when I was born."

Mia went on, "Dad, you were right about his hand. He can't grip a wrench."

Feeling a strange sense of shame, Ross turned his wrist over to hide the scar. But Dr. Lee was looking into his eyes, not at his arm.

"Some healing needs more than the passage of time," he said. "I can give you a set of exercises for your hand. Do them every day, and you should get some of your strength back."

Ross's heart sank. "Only some? How much?"

"Ross, I wish I knew," said Dr. Lee. "Sometimes it's harder not to know than to hear bad news. I think you'll be able to use it again, but I doubt that it'll ever be as strong as it was."

Though the doctor's expression was grave, Ross felt better. "Not as strong as it was" wasn't so bad; he'd been pretty strong before. As long as he could grip and strike with it, he'd be fine.

"How long before I can make a fist?" Ross asked.

"Could be a while. Be patient. So, what brings you in this direction? Anything interesting going on in the wider world?"

"I'm a prospector. I don't go to towns much."

"Found anything worthwhile?"

Ross sneaked a look at Mia, to find her giving him an equally furtive look. "Nothing special."

Mia began stacking plates with so much force Ross expected them to chip. "Great burritos today, Dad!"

"Where do you come from?" Dr. Lee inquired.

Questions made Ross wary. But Dr. Lee sounded so mild, and Mia's face showed only curiosity, not suspicion. He decided that he didn't mind if they knew a little more. "All over. After my grandmother died, I apprenticed with different prospectors, and they travel. A couple years ago I decided I could survive on my own."

Dr. Lee remarked, "You very nearly didn't."

"Yeah, well." Ross was trying to think of something polite to say when the door opened and a man walked in.

Mia's chin came up, and her father rose. Ross eyed the new-comer, a big, tough-looking man whose blue eyes gleamed pale and startling in his brown face. He looked wealthy, with his silver-rimmed glasses, crisp new shirt, and shiny boots.

"There's a doorbell, Tom," Dr. Lee said.

"Oh, really, Dante? Didn't notice it." He helped himself to Mia's chair.

As the doctor sat down again, he said, "Tom, this is Ross Juarez. Ross, this is Defense Chief Preston. Tom, what brings you here?"

Mr. Preston put his elbows on the table and examined Ross, eyes narrowed. *There* was the suspicion. "What news can you tell us?"

That was often the first question people asked in a town. Ross edged his chair back, wary of the man's intense stare.

"Nothing" was certainly going to be the wrong answer, but it was the only one he had.

"Been alone for a long time," he began.

The stare turned into a squint of disbelief. "Are you Changed?" demanded Mr. Preston.

In Ross's experience, if that was the second question, it meant the town was either all Norms and hated the Changed, or all Changed and didn't welcome Norms. This had to be a Changed town. Stalling for time, he asked, "What's your Change?"

Judging by the anger that tightened the defense chief's face, Ross would have made a better impression if he'd slugged him. He grabbed the chair arm, ready to run.

"I'm normal, and I'm asking you," Mr. Preston snapped.

Dr. Lee laid a hand on Ross's shoulder. He flinched. The doctor removed his hand, but stayed close. His voice was calm and deliberate as he said, "Ross, you don't have to answer. Unless the sheriff asks."

Mia, standing by the door, nodded firmly.

They're on my side, he thought. It was a strange feeling, but not a bad one.

Mr. Preston glared at all three of them. "She'll be asking soon. You may as well answer me now."

Mia joined her father beside Ross's chair. "Ross is our guest. That means he's got guest privilege."

Mr. Preston got to his feet. "Are you sure you want to invoke that? You don't know anything about this boy."

Dr. Lee folded his arms across his chest. "I know that my daughter invited him. That's good enough for me." He turned to Ross. "Would you like to stay in Las Anclas?"

He had only just met the Lees, but he already liked them. He did want to learn to read, and it would be a good idea to live in relative safety until he could use his hand, at least a little. Maybe he could let Mia study his book for the week or two that

should take. He didn't usually stay anywhere that long, but—
fresh hen eggs! "Sure, I want to stay."

"Then we need to get you to school. Come on." Mia moved
toward the door.

Glad to leave the scowling defense guy behind, he followed
her. "Thanks for the breakfast, Dr. Lee."

As he left, he heard Mr. Preston say, "Dante, we have rules
for a reason."

Ross and Mia walked to a busy intersection marked with
signs he couldn't read, where they stopped for a cart pulled
by armor-skinned bullocks. There were people everywhere, so
many that it was impossible to keep them all safely within view,
and they all either openly stared at him or pretended they
didn't. Children nudged one another and pointed. His shoulder blades crawled with the need to get a wall at his back.

"How big is this town?" His voice was soft, but everyone
within earshot stared.

"Population one thousand sixteen," Mia said with visible
pride. "Including our newest citizens, Enrique and Esteban
Carrillo, age three weeks."

His attention was caught by a couple in pants and shirts the
color of desert sand, walking quickly and with purpose. They
bristled with weapons. Ross glanced enviously at the machete
hanging from the belt of the teenage guy with the long braid.
The woman with the rifle and bandolier was older, with gray-
flecked hair, but from the way she moved, she was clearly just
as dangerous. They glanced at him but didn't break stride.

Ross waited until the pair had vanished around the bell
tower, and the crowd had thinned out a bit. "Who were those
people?"

"Defense Rangers." Mia kept her voice low. "They used to
be the sheriff's Rangers. That guy who was bullying you, Mr.
Preston? When he first came to Las Anclas, he and the two
people he brought with him joined the Rangers—the woman

you saw, Sera Diaz, and a man who got killed a while back. A couple of years later, there was trouble in town, and some Changed people were forced out, including two Rangers. Mr. Preston got himself elected sheriff, and he took charge. The Rangers are completely loyal to him. They're all Norms, of course. If Mr. Preston had his way, this would be a Norm town."

Ross stepped aside for a man in a wheelchair, and was almost run over by three kids chasing a rainbow-striped bright-moth. Cries of "Catch it, catch it!" faded behind them.

Mia went on. "He set it up so the job of sheriff wasn't decided by election, like the rest of the important jobs. Since he was the sheriff *and* the defense chief, he had two votes on the town council. Between his votes and the mayor's vote—did I mention his wife is the mayor?—he made it so sheriff is decided by duel."

"Only sheriff?" Ross had heard that in Voske's kingdom, duels determined every major position that might require fighting. Otherwise this town wasn't like anything he'd seen there.

Mia nodded. "You saw how strong Mr. Preston is. I thought he'd be sheriff forever. But a couple months ago, Elizabeth Crow Changed. She challenged him and she beat him, fair and square. Well, maybe not fair by his standards." She chuckled. "It was great. We all came to watch, right in front of the town hall."

"She picked me up and ran me all the way here, didn't she? How long did it take her to beat him?"

This was clearly one of Mia's favorite memories. "However long one jump takes. She slammed him down on the ground, and pinned him so all he could move was his left hand to tap out."

"Wish I'd seen it."

The path was lined with pocket gardens overflowing with thriving vegetables and pungent herbs, surrounding the rows of low adobe buildings. There was no way Las Anclas was maintaining all these lush green gardens by squeezing water out of cactuses.

"Where do you get your water?" he asked.

"Off the hills." Mia pointed eastward. "It took generations to build the pipes. There's a couple of lakes at the highest point, and underneath us we've got a water table that fills every winter."

"But it was desert outside your walls."

"If you'd gone west instead of south, you'd have walked right into our cornfields."

The thought that he could have easily saved himself and hadn't disturbed him more than the fact that he'd nearly died. "All I had to do was go west?"

"Well, up a slope and west. You were walking along the bottom of a ridge. You can't see the fields from where you were."

"No," Ross said slowly. "I wouldn't have gone uphill. Not unless I'd known something was there."

Animals tended to drift downhill when they were wounded or exhausted, instinctively taking the easiest course. Ross had often used that knowledge while hunting mule deer and javelinas and bighorn sheep. No doubt the bounty hunter had used it to track him.

Though he was sure he'd lost the man, he couldn't help glancing around. He was reassured by the sight of the sentry wall rising above the jumble of buildings. "Did you say you have cornfields outside the walls?"

"And beans and squash and lots of other things," Mia said proudly. "For ten years now. I keep having to repair the irrigation. But it's a marvelous engineering project."

Ross could see from the houses and fences how everything in Las Anclas was repaired and reused, but those luxurious gardens made it look prosperous.

"Don't you get attacked for your crops? Don't you worry

about someone trying to take the town for himself?"

"Sure, we worry. King Voske tried before I was born. He tried again ten years ago too, but not with a full army. We've been attacked by bandit gangs and outlaws, but no one's ever gotten inside the gates."

Voske! Ross wished he'd never hear that name again.

7

Jennie

JENNIE WATCHED MOTES OF CHALK DUST SWIRL IN rays of morning light over the pale wood of the new teacher's desk, incongruous before the battered desks that had been old when the present students' great-grandparents had been children.

If she didn't have to teach, she'd be on a Ranger mission now, side by side with Indra.

Jennie stretched out her hand and pulled with her mind. The worn slate that used to be Mia's spun through the air and smacked into her hand.

I'm here.

There was no use wasting time thinking about what she wasn't doing when she had plenty to do right now.

Beautifully articulated black cat claws pulled the door ajar, and Laura Hernandez poked her head in. "Hi, Jennie. Congratulations on your promotion." Before Jennie could thank her, Laura added anxiously, "You're still going to teach, aren't you?"

"Don't worry—this just means that now I can patrol with the Rangers on weekends."

"Good." Laura let out her breath. "I'll put out the practice mats."

The door closed. Jennie gazed out the window, rubbing her thumb over the diagrams Mia had carved into the frame of the slate, back when they'd been students themselves.

As if summoned, Mia appeared from around the bell tower,

her glasses winking in the sunlight, with a guy Jennie had never seen before. The mysterious stranger!

He stopped at the edge of the schoolyard. Mia kept walking, then noticed that he was hanging back and beckoned. He hesitated before following her. The way he moved, wary and light on his feet, reminded Jennie of a wild creature: not a herd or pack animal, but something solitary—maybe the bobcats she occasionally spotted on early patrols, with their watchful readiness to either fight or flee.

The students crowded around, and Alfonso Medina scurried halfway up a wall to get a better view. Jennie stepped onto the porch, hoping the school's welcome wouldn't scare the skittish boy.

The girls at the forefront had broken out their best clothes for the occasion of a stranger in town. Felicité was in the lead, wearing a particularly elegant sapphire dress. At her side was Sujata Vardam, in wine-red dimity and golden lace. Becky Callahan's pink-and-white linen, trimmed with leaf-green ribbons, was her mother's latest creation. Matching ribbons tied the bonnet she wore so she wouldn't burn in the sun.

But it was tiny compared to Felicité's broad-brimmed sun hat. Her skin was the same sun-friendly brown as her father's, but she was obsessed with protecting her precious hair (and, Jennie suspected, her precious hair dye).

Jennie recalled her ma saying, "Felicité is a law unto herself."

Her pa had added, "Her great-grandmother, the mayor before Brad Gutierrez, was a snappy dresser. I remember her from when I was a kid. She set a fashion for Chinese-style embroidery. My own pa had a waistcoat with dragons on it."

Felicité was saying in her caramel tones, "Oh, you're the new boy! I'm glad to see you out of the infirmary. Welcome to Las Anclas. I am Felicité Wolfe." Had Jennie imagined the faintest emphasis on "Wolfe"?

Mia's voice rose to a nervous squeak. "This is Ross Juarez. Our guest."

"Hello, Ross." Sujata's sleek black hair shone as she stepped out of the shadow of Felicité's hat. "I'm Sujata Vardam. If you're getting a tour, be sure to stop at our orchards. You might meet my grandmother. She's a judge and a member of the town council."

Jennie listened in amusement, wondering if some rivalry had developed between the two school leaders.

Meredith Lowenstein elbowed between them, unconcerned with social hierarchies. She and Mia had always been small for their age, but while Mia had hidden behind schoolwork or Jennie, Meredith had learned to push back.

She smiled at Ross. "I saw Sheriff Crow bring you in. Where did you come from?"

Yuki Nakamura appeared behind his sister, his long ponytail like a fall of black silk against his unbleached cotton shirt. It was odd how tiny Meredith, with her challenging saunter, took up so much more space than tall, powerful Yuki, who moved so economically.

The prince. Jennie had trained herself not to think of Yuki's old title. But sometimes he got angry, or needed to get people's attention. And then—still without making a single unnecessary movement—he seemed to tower over everyone. That was when she remembered that he'd been raised to rule.

"Is it true that you're a prospector?" he asked, his expression not giving anything away.

Before Ross could speak, everybody was jostling to be heard.

"Were you in a gunfight? Pow!" Will Preston made a shooting gesture. "That's so cool!"

"Wasn't it a knife fight? Even cooler!" Jennie's sister Dee squealed.

"I rang the bell for you!" exclaimed little Hattie Salazar.

"Did you meet anyone on the road?" called Alfonso, ten feet off the ground.

"Where's your family?" asked Carlos Garcia.

Felicité raised her hand to adjust a fluttering ribbon. Ross sidled away as if he thought she would hit him. He reminded Jennie of a colt unused to the training rope.

Mia touched Ross's arm. He flinched, and she pulled back. "That's the schoolhouse," she said, her voice calm. "And here's Jennie."

Ross followed Mia onto the porch, pursued by a swarm of little kids.

Now was the time to interfere, thought Jennie. Before Ross either got pulled into pieces or smacked someone in sheer self-defense.

She raised her voice. "I see a lot of eager volunteers to clean the windows."

The kids stampeded. Felicité obligingly beckoned the older students away, giving Ross space.

To Jennie's surprise, Becky Callahan stayed. Her voice was so soft, it was almost inaudible. "They're only crowding you because you're new. Once they get used to you, they'll stop." It was fascinating how a stranger could stir people up. Becky rarely spoke, much less to anyone she didn't know well.

Ross nodded cautiously, and Becky darted away, almost colliding with Brisa Preciado.

"What did you say to him?" Brisa asked curiously. Becky's lips moved, but Jennie didn't hear her answer. "Oh, is he shy?" Brisa sounded disappointed. "Are you sure? I won't bother him then." She patted Becky's pale arm. "It was sweet of you to notice."

On the other end of the porch, Felicité seemed to have missed this entire exchange. "Shall I throw a party to welcome Ross? Paco, when is your band playing?"

Paco Diaz was drumming on the railing. His eyes were closed, and his hands moved so fast that the sticks left blurry trails in the air. It seemed impossible that such an intricate piece of music could be created by one boy with two sticks and a fence post.

"Paco?" Felicité called.

"He's gone," Henry said. "Just forgot to take his body."

As everyone laughed, Jennie spoke. "Come inside, Ross." She stood back so she wouldn't seem like yet another threat.

He surveyed the ceiling as if enemies might be lurking in the support beams, then examined the rest of the room. Finally, he came in. That was odd. Even the older Rangers, who tended to check any room they entered, didn't often look up at the ceiling.

"Ross," Mia said, "this is Jennie Riley, the teacher."

His eyes were on the floor, the windows, the chalkboard, anywhere but on Jennie. Though he was terribly thin, he was also one of those boys who made girls jealous with their foot-long eyelashes. His hair was black as soot, and his broad shoulders made her wonder how much muscle he'd put on if he ever got enough to eat.

"I thought you'd be older," he said, then blushed.

She spoke quickly, so he wouldn't feel awkward. "I'm not that young—I'm eighteen. In some towns, I've heard, teachers start at sixteen. How old are you?"

That seemed to make him a hundred times more awkward. He hunched his shoulders and muttered, "Don't know exactly. About eighteen. I think."

Jennie couldn't think of a reply other than "I'm sorry," which she suspected he would hate. She was trying to think of a better response when Mia took her by surprise.

"Jennie, Ross wants to come to school."

He stared down as if his shabby boots had his future written on them. Behind him, Mia flapped her hands and mouthed some words that Jennie couldn't figure out.

She was dying to ask him for any news he'd picked up—maybe she could put it in *El Heraldo!*—but she could see how tense he was. She kept her voice friendly and casual. "So, where'd you leave off when you were last in school?"

Ross glanced up for half a second before mumbling, "Never

really started." He gave her an even briefer look. "Where do the little kids sit?"

Jennie had always thought "heart-wringing" was merely an expression, but she actually felt something twist inside her chest. And she suspected that half of what was making him so self-conscious was the thought that people were pitying him. "I'll bet you know more than you think you do." She was rewarded by a glance of a full two seconds. His eyes were very dark brown, almost black. "A prospector is a kind of engineer, like Mia."

Mia blinked. "You're right. I hadn't thought of it that way before."

Ross's expression eased into genuine interest. Encouraged, Jennie went on. "Mia designs and builds things, and prospectors . . . what do you do? How do you get into those ruins? How do you even find them?"

"Maps. Old stories." He spoke slowly, but with a tentative confidence. "If you get up high, you can see ruins, sometimes."

"Go on," Jennie said, smiling.

Ross flicked a glance at Mia, who nodded encouragingly. "But even if they're buried, the way the plants are growing can show you there's something underneath. As for getting in, you can dig if they're not too deep. If it's a collapsed structure, you have to shore it up so it won't fall on you. Sometimes you have to blast your way in."

"How do you do that without blowing up the whole thing, or making the collapse even worse?" she asked.

Behind Ross, Mia automatically raised her hand, then quickly lowered it, embarrassed.

"See what the structure is made of," said Ross. "Look for a wall that isn't the sole support of anything. To figure out how much explosive you'll need, you have to calculate the overpressure."

As Jennie had suspected, however spotty the guy's overall knowledge was, he knew a lot about his own field. "How do you do that?"

Mia caught her hand halfway up, then sat down abruptly on the little kids' bench, trapping both hands under her thighs.

"With a slide rule," he replied.

"I see," said Jennie. "Ross, there're only three or four people in town who know how to do that, and two of them are here in the room with you."

Mia extracted her hand to tap the slide rule dangling from her waist.

"How much can you read?" Jennie asked.

Ross ducked his head. "Only numbers. Well, a couple letters you use in math."

"What about history?"

"I don't know anything. I just wonder. How the things I find got there. What people used them for. Why all the cities were destroyed."

"I know that one!" exclaimed Mia before Jennie could answer. "According to the accounts we've found, it was a natural disaster. There was a storm on the sun, and it released radiation. Do you know what that is?"

"No," Ross muttered, embarrassed.

Jennie wished she could tell him that she'd never heard Mia this eager to talk to anyone but her father, her old master, Mr. Rodriguez, and Jennie herself. However had Ross gotten Mia to trust him so quickly?

"It's a sort of energy," Mia went on. "Like light. It changes living things. Some animals and plants died, and some mutated. Some people died, and others got the Change. Also, the solar storm caused a geomagnetic storm on the Earth. Not a storm with rain. It was a change in the Earth's magnetic field."

Ross glanced up. "That's what makes a compass work, right?"

Mia's head bobbed enthusiastically. "Yes! Exactly. And back then, nearly everything was mechanical. When the magnetic field changed, most machines stopped working. People had to leave the cities and start farming, and eventually the cities got overgrown and knocked down in earthquakes and storms. And then singing trees started growing around them, so no one could get back in."

Ross pulled his left arm in across his chest, rubbing it as if it hurt. "The books. Tell me what happened to the books."

Under his direct gaze, she fiddled nervously with her glasses. "Maybe Jennie could explain it better."

"You go on. You're doing great." Jennie winced inwardly once the words were out. She sounded like she was talking to a little kid.

But Mia didn't look insulted. "Back then, most books were machines. I don't understand how that worked. But all the book-machines were destroyed in the geomagnetic storm. That's why so much knowledge was lost."

"Were they destroyed, like smashed to bits?" Ross asked. "Or did they stop working?"

"Stopped working," said Mia with a sigh. "And never started again. We're not even sure what they looked like."

Ross indicated Mia's old slate. "Can I draw on that?"

"Yes!" She shoved a piece of chalk at him. "Do you know what the book-machines are?"

"No, but there's some artifacts I find a lot. They're made of black glass and plastic." As he spoke, he sketched rectangles and squares and ovals, using shading to give them dimension. He was no artist, but, like Mia, could draw accurately.

"If you take them apart, there's more plastic and metal parts inside." He drew some of those parts as he went on. "They're the right size to hold in your hands. They could have been book-machines. They were obviously something, or I wouldn't find so many of them. But like you said, they've stopped working. I don't even pick them up anymore. No one buys them."

Mia stared intently at the slate, then whirled to face Ross. He slid backward, his left hand coming up in a block and his right hand going to his hip for a weapon that wasn't there.

"It's okay!" she exclaimed.

Ross dropped his hands, his brown skin darkening with a deep blush. "Sorry."

"I was going to say, I never get to talk to anyone like this," she continued. "I mean, other than Dad and Jennie."

Jennie barely caught Ross's mumbled, "I don't either."

Jennie had been writing out math problems while Mia and Ross had been talking. Now she set the slate and abacus on a desk. She was sure he would be relieved to take a break. "Ross, can you try these?"

The haste with which he did so proved her right. He handled the abacus so awkwardly that she was puzzled—surely he didn't only use a slide rule?—until she remembered that he'd been injured. Finally, he gave up trying to use the abacus with his left hand, and began switching between it and the chalk with his right.

"What did you give him?" Mia asked softly.

"I have no idea how he'll do with non-practical math," murmured Jennie. "So I started with arithmetic and finished with some calculus and physics from our last academic decathlon."

"Those were so fun," said Mia wistfully.

Jennie laughed. "They were fun because we always won."

Mia looked disappointed. "Was that why you liked them? I liked them because it was you and me against the world."

"You and Me Against the World." That had been their motto, back when all it took to be best friends was being the two smartest kids in their age group. Jennie had forgotten.

Mia was only a year younger than Jennie, but in a lot of ways she still seemed like a kid. She'd moved into Mr. Rodriguez's old cottage right across from her father, and Dr. Lee still cooked all her meals. She still blushed and talked too much when she got nervous, and social situations made her nervous even though she'd known everyone her entire life. She'd never had a boyfriend or girlfriend, or even wanted one, though she had confessed to Jennie that she wanted to want one.

Jennie wished none of that mattered. But recently she'd found herself talking about certain subjects with Indra or Meredith, not Mia. Without Jennie even noticing it, they'd drifted apart.

A burst of cheers rose up from outside. Glad for a distraction, she looked out the window. Yuki Nakamura, bow in hand, stood before a target with an arrow in the exact center of the bull's-eye.

It was too bad Yuki didn't want to be a Ranger. He shot as well as his sister Meredith, and he was the best of the guys his age with a sword or hand-to-hand. But he tolerated rather than enjoyed working in a team, and the Rangers relied upon teamwork. She remembered Sera commenting, "Anyone who'd want to be a prospector wouldn't make a good Ranger."

Ross's glossy black hair hid his face as he worked. Mia was hovering anxiously, as if it were her test. From the way he twitched every time she moved, he didn't like people lurking in his peripheral vision.

What turned someone into a prospector, traveling alone in the dangerous world? Trading, she could understand. Traders were usually families, people you'd trust to have your back. Like your fellow Rangers . . .

Ross put down his chalk. "I'm done."

"Already?" Jennie hoped he hadn't given up halfway through.

Mia snatched up the slate. "I knew it," she exclaimed in glee. "If this was a decathlon, he'd be a real challenge for us."

"Mia's right." Jennie examined the awkwardly written numbers. "When it comes to math and physics, you could teach the class yourself."

Ross gave her a doubtful glance.

"Seriously. And if you're handling explosives, you have a head start on chemistry. I'll help you catch up on reading, writing, history, and literature. Maybe biology, depending on what you already know."

She had to lean forward to catch his muttered, "But reading. Aren't I too old?"

Jennie shook her head. "Absolutely not. You watch. By the end of tomorrow, I'll have you reading entire sentences."

"You can do that?"

"*You* can do it," she said firmly.

Ross took a deep breath, those amazing lashes lifting. He touched the line of writing on her teacher's slate as if the words themselves were precious. For the first time since she'd begun Ranger training, Jennie remembered the joy that had first drawn her to apprentice to Grandma Wolfe—the joy of teaching someone who loved learning as much as she always had.

"Welcome to school, Ross," Jennie said. "Now, let's go outside. We always start the day with drill. Ever done any fighting?"

8

Ross

THOUGH MIA HAD SAID JENNIE WAS HER FRIEND, ROSS had assumed the teacher would be an adult who would make him feel ashamed of how much he didn't know—or worse, laugh. He hadn't expected another teenage girl, let alone a nice one. Let alone a pretty, nice one.

And they were as different as two people could be. Mia's skin was light, while Jennie's was nearly true black. Mia's hair was clipped into a raggedy bowl cut, while Jennie wore hers in a lot of little braids decorated with colored beads. Jennie was taller than Ross, Mia shorter. And Jennie was much, much curvier. But he liked how they both smiled: Mia in sudden wide grins, and Jennie with her lips barely parted, and the left side a little higher than the right. They kept smiling at him.

Like everything in Las Anclas, Jennie had been a surprise. A pleasant one, this time, but Ross was unnerved by how hard it was to predict what would happen in this town. At least with the scavenger gangs that roamed the desert, he always knew where he stood.

The students outside had split up according to age and size. The younger kids wore padding and masks.

Jennie called out, "Ten-and-unders, follow Laura." Ross noticed the girl's cat claws as she beckoned to the kids. "Mia? Want to practice with us?"

"I have to get back to work," Mia said hastily. "Pick you up at lunch!"

He joined the warm-ups, though he had to sit out the ones

that required the use of both hands. The others eyed him curiously, and the guy with the ponytail gave him a suspicious stare. Ross had seen that look when he had accidentally wandered onto another prospector's claim. He wondered what he'd done to annoy him.

"Seniors, line up by height and fold around," Jennie ordered. They formed two lines facing each other, and she partnered with him. "I can see from your stance that you've trained before. Good! We'll go easy on your left side."

He was unfamiliar with some of the moves, and others had different names from those he'd learned. But it was basic stuff: kicks and punches, slides and blocks.

"Free sparring," Jennie announced.

The tall boy headed straight for Ross, who put up his hands and kept himself light on his feet.

Jennie swept the guy's arm aside with an open-handed block. "Yuki, I want you to spar with Henry. He's been dropping his fists. Pop him on the nose if he doesn't get those blocks up in time."

A boy with sand-colored hair and freckles clutched his nose in mock agony.

Jennie smiled at Ross. "We'll start slow and light, okay?"

They began to circle. Ross watched her for an opening. She didn't have any obvious weaknesses. Her balance was excellent. She bounced lightly on the balls of her feet, one muscular arm forward and one held back. He snapped out a jab to test her defenses. Rather than blocking, she slid back, braids swinging, leaving him fully extended with his fist one inch short of her face. She was teasing him.

Then she threw a jab, careful of his left side. Unlike his testing move, hers was a fake. Her thigh muscles bunched under her pants, signaling a sweep, and Ross leaped up. Her foot swung through the empty space where his ankles had been.

He grinned at her, and she grinned back, on the verge of

laughter. He could feel as well as see that she loved sparring as much as he did.

"Okay, maybe not so slow and light," she said.

And she lunged. Ross knew he was good. He had to be, or he'd have been dead a long time ago. But Jennie was right there with him. She knew moves he'd never even seen—spinning kicks, leaping kicks, deceptive moves to lure an attacker off balance, joint locks, throws. He clipped her cheek with an open-handed strike, and when he paused to see if he'd hit her too hard, she grabbed his right wrist and threw him down, then waited for him to roll and leap to his feet. He stopped worrying about hurting her. He wasn't sure he could, anyway.

At least he was making her sweat. Her skin gleamed like obsidian. He blinked salt out of his own eyes. She seemed to be laughing at him.

He lifted his right hand in challenge. "Come on! That all you got?"

Then she did laugh. Whether she took his bait or didn't believe that he was her match, he didn't know, but she charged exactly as he'd hoped she would, coming in fast with her arms twisting to grab. Rather than dodging, Ross dropped low and tackled her.

They hit the ground rolling, each struggling to gain control. Strong legs clamped around his and flipped him over on his back. He pinned her left arm with his right. Inches above him, her deep brown eyes gazed into his. Warm breath brushed his cheek. It smelled like peaches. A drop of her sweat fell into the hollow of his throat.

Neither moved. A flash of light drew his gaze upward, past Jennie's face. The entire school had circled up to watch them.

"That's what I call a good match," she said breathlessly, and leaped to her feet.

9

Mia

MIA WAS IN THE HALLWAY WHEN SHE HEARD A muffled explosion, followed by swearing. She scooped up the sand bucket and burst into the kitchen, where she found her dad slapping a wet dishcloth at a pillar of green flame rising from a frying pan. Mia tossed the sand onto the fire and watched in satisfaction as the flames died. An acrid smell rose up from the pan, making her eyes water.

She wrinkled her nose. "What were you making this time?"

Her father gave a rueful sigh. "You know the seaweed that gels liquids, the one I use to make pills? I used it to solidify some chicken broth, and then I cut it into noodles, coated them in flour, and tried to fry them. I was hoping they'd be crispy on the outside and liquid on the inside."

"That is disgusting, Dad. Who'd eat that?"

"I would." Ross appeared at the door. "Sounds interesting." Mia could actually see when the fumes reached him—he rocked backward and rubbed his eyes. "Unless it tastes like the smell in here. What happened?"

"An unfortunate chemical reaction when chicken gelatin made contact with hot oil."

"Let's all go to Jack's," Mia said, knowing how happy the suggestion would make her father. "We can invite Anna-Lucia."

"Excellent idea." He picked up a piece of chalk. "I'll leave a note for Becky to join us. She's checking on Grandpa

Wells. And I'll take along some of my latest kimchi for Anna-Lucia. She has good taste."

"Who's Anna-Lucia?" Ross sounded distinctly alarmed.

"My girlfriend," Mia's dad explained. "She manages the saloon and she's the best baker in town. Luckily, I have the wherewithal for all of us—and even dessert." Mia fished some scrip from the basket while he wrote a note on the slate by the office.

As they walked out, Ross asked, "Those strips of colored paper are scrip, right? What's it based on?" He sounded more suspicious than curious.

"You earn it at your job," she explained. "The guilds and the council decide how much an hour of your particular skill is worth. Or you can trade. What's scrip based on where you've been?"

"Silver's the most common. Ore. I heard of a town up north where it's gold. But there's worse things." Ross said the last under his breath, scanning the square as if it might conceal some predatory animal.

"Like what?" Mia remembered a story that had given her nightmares when she was small. "Like . . . human heads?"

"What?" Ross exclaimed.

"What?" Her dad turned to stare at her.

"A trader told us King Voske keeps human heads on pikes. I figured if he had them already—"

"Those are a deterrent." Her dad smothered a laugh. "Not a form of currency. They don't keep well."

Mia eyed Ross. "So . . . like what?"

"Some places, they hand a trader or traveler some scrip and make it easy to buy on credit. Before you know it, you're in debt. Then you have to earn your keep, but your earnings are never as much as the scrip is worth. So you end up working your whole life, and you never pay it off."

"Sounds like you speak from experience," Mia's father said.

"It's all right for me. I can always run. But some people . . ." Ross's voice trailed off unhappily.

"The guilds and the council balance each other here, to make sure things are fair," Mia assured him. "No one will rip you off."

She knew he didn't believe her.

"I'm not trying to say things are perfect." Her father waved the scrip emphatically. "The other day, I thought the entire council was about to challenge each other to duels."

"Mr. Preston thinks we should be making more weapons and ammunition," Mia explained. "But I'd like better electricity. And so would Dad, for the surgery."

Ross did not look reassured. She couldn't figure out what was still bothering him. It was an ordinary day. People streamed in through the back gate, returning from the fields. The smiths were closing up the north forge. Sentries paced unhurriedly along the wall; Mia spotted Meredith's red curls. These were everyday patterns, comforting in their lack of danger, but the way Ross was acting, Mia thought that if she dropped her abacus, he'd bolt for the hills. Or reach for the empty sheath on his belt.

"We haven't talked about a trade yet," he said abruptly. "For my bed. My food. Most of my goods got stolen, but I can show you what I have. Or I could take it out in work. Though I don't know how useful I'll be with one hand."

Mia opened her mouth to say that he was a guest, not a boarder. She was about to explain guest privilege when her father caught her eye and shook his head.

"I'd like to take a look at your trade goods," he said. "But you could also help Mia. Our generators run on used vegetable oil, and you could collect it for her. Also, I have some little jobs around the house: leaky faucets, sticky door handles, squeaky floorboards . . ."

Mia again opened her mouth. That was her department.

But Ross nodded, looking a lot less worried. "Sure. I can do that."

She had begun collecting oil for Mr. Rodriguez when she was ten. She'd meant to find and begin training a helper—some kid who loved mechanics—but since Ross wanted to work, or didn't want to be beholden, she could use him instead.

He straightened, sniffing at the air. "What's that smell?"

"That," Mia's dad said, "is Jack's Saloon. The best food in town."

Mia hoped the prospect of good food would help Ross relax. If he liked Las Anclas, maybe he and his book would both stay. "No, Luc's has the best." To Ross, she added, "And Luc's has music and dancing." To her disappointment, that didn't seem to enthuse him.

Her dad opened the back door, releasing a burst of chatter and laughter. Ross backed away, shoulders tense. Mia was puzzled. The smell of spices, roasting meat, and baking bread was even stronger with the doors open. Then she remembered his wariness at the schoolyard and wondered if the problem was large groups. Mia didn't care for them herself.

"There won't be a crowd in the back," she said.

Ross squared his shoulders and stepped inside.

Jack Lowell came up with a steaming basket of bread. His cheeks were flushed and his blond hair was damp from the heat of the kitchen. "Welcome to my saloon," he said to Ross. "And welcome to Las Anclas. Here, have a piece of garlic bread. On the house."

Ross took a bite, and his eyes widened appreciatively.

Mia looked hopefully at Jack until he gave her a piece too. "Last year we voted Jack's garlic bread one of the ten best foods in town," she said. "Though Luc's has four of those places. I can take you there."

Ross swallowed his huge bite, his eyes watering slightly. "Thank you," he said to Jack.

"Anna-Lucia can join you, if you like," Jack said. "I'm about to turn it over to the evening shift."

"In that case, why don't you join us too?" Mia's dad held out the scrip.

"Thank you, Dante. Don't mind if I do." Jack put it in his pocket. "We have sweet-corn tamales tonight," he added.

At a quiet corner table, Mia watched Ross watch the tamale platter as Anna-Lucia brought it out of the kitchen and over to them. She tried not to laugh; it was as if it might leap off the tray and run out the door. Anna-Lucia sat beside Mia's dad. Beads of sweat gleamed on her high forehead and on the dark skin visible between the short twists of her hair. Mia turned her attention to the flower vase in the center of the table when they leaned into each other. She was glad he had somebody to kiss, but it was embarrassing when it was your father, and it went on right across from you.

In the meantime, Jack had joined them. "Ross, I understand you went to the school," he said. "How did your first day go?"

"Fine." Mia watched Ross's gaze switch back and forth between Anna-Lucia, who had one hand on the platter, and her dad, who had picked up the serving spatula.

"What's going on in the outside world?" Jack asked with a friendly smile.

"Been traveling alone." Ross pressed his back hard into his chair.

Mia wished she could signal *Drop it,* but Jack got the message. "I hope you'll enjoy our town."

Her father had been smart to avoid the front of the saloon; Ross would have been mobbed for sure. Jack's questions had made it clear that the adults were as interested in Ross as the students had been.

Jack served Mia's dad first, as he was the oldest at the table. Then he took pity on Ross and heaped his plate with sweet corn tamales, refried beans topped with goat cheese crumbles, cactus sautéed with tomatoes and onions, steamed mussels with chorizo and chilies, and her dad's own extra-spicy zucchini and pumpkin kimchi.

Ross fingered his fork and spoon like a horse at the gate. Jack picked up his own silverware and began to eat, a typically kindhearted gesture. Mia hoped meeting Jack would make a good enough impression on Ross to overcome that dose of Mr. Preston.

"Dante, do you need any supplies for your guest?" asked Anna-Lucia.

Everyone gazed at Ross, who was oblivious to everything except tamales.

Mia's dad shook his head. "Ross can probably fit into some of my old clothes."

Ross froze with fork poised and mouth open. When he saw everyone watching him, he ducked back down and returned to eating.

"We can work out a trade later," Mia said, and was rewarded by a mumbled "Yeah."

Anna-Lucia tried again. "How are the kimchi experiments? Do you think you'll ever go back to turnips now that you've discovered the joys of . . ."

Mia whispered to Ross, "Everything that doesn't taste good in vinegar." She scowled at the latest experiment as the adults began discussing avocados and squash blossoms.

Ross whispered, "I love this stuff." At her dubious look, he added, "Shouldn't I?"

"If you like Dad's cooking, he'll chain you to the kitchen."

The back door opened, and Sheriff Crow entered. Ross's fork clattered to the table.

"Come in, Elizabe—Sheriff," Jack said.

Mia stared down at her plate; her dad and Anna-Lucia were also carefully not looking at Jack. It had been the talk of the town, behind closed doors, when Elizabeth Crow had broken off their engagement after she Changed. It wasn't uncommon for relationships to end if one person Changed, but it was nearly always the Norm who ended it.

Jack set a chair beside his own. "Have you eaten? We have tamales."

"For those, I always have room." She sat down and leaned toward Ross. "When we first met, you warned me that you were being chased. Who was chasing you?"

His tension made Mia's own body constrict in sympathy.

"Sheriff Crow, might these questions wait for the end of our meal?" her dad asked gently.

"Perhaps a bit after the end of the meal?" Jack suggested. "I have apple crumble waiting."

The sheriff turned her brown eye toward him. Neither spoke, but a message passed between them. Then she sat back, saying, "My favorite." She helped herself as everyone resumed eating. Ross did too, but he kept sneaking peeks at the sheriff.

"Do you want to ask her something?" Mia whispered. "Go ahead. She won't bite."

"No." Though Mia had barely heard his reply, everyone else turned. Ross set down his fork. "Sheriff Crow. I wanted to thank you. For saving my life."

She gave a little nod. "Just doing my job." But her voice was friendly.

The meal continued in a lighter atmosphere. But as Jack brought out the apple crumble, the door between the saloon and the back room flew open. Becky Callahan dashed in, blonde hair clinging sweatily to her face. "Dr. Lee, it's the mayor! She's looking for you."

She turned to flee but nearly collided with Mayor Wolfe.

Becky spun around, almost tripping over her own feet, and stumbled farther into the room, trapped like a rat between the mayor and the sheriff. Her blue eyes went wild with alarm.

"Becky, please join—" Mia's dad began, but Becky remembered the back door and ran out, letting it bang behind her.

Though Mayor Wolfe wasn't much bigger than Mia, sometimes—and this was one of those times—she seemed taller than the town hall. Maybe it was her upswept hair, or the extravagant arch of her brows above her dark, tilted eyes. Or the high-necked formal dress with a hundred polished stone buttons down the perfectly fitted front. Mayor Wolfe only brought out the Button Dress when she was on the attack.

"Good evening, Sheriff Crow." The mayor didn't sound happy. She gave Mia's dad a look of equal disapproval. "I did not think it would be necessary to remind you, Dr. Lee, that it is customary to bring visitors to us first."

"'Us'?" echoed the sheriff.

The mayor shrank to a mere twelve feet. "To me."

"Are you here as mayor or as citizen?" Sheriff Crow asked.

"I'm here to question the newcomer." Mayor Wolfe looked from Ross to the sheriff, who tilted her head to regard the mayor with her yellow snake eye. Some people flinched when that happened. Mayor Wolfe's lips twitched.

"That's the sheriff's job," said Sheriff Crow.

"Tom and I always performed this task together," the mayor replied. "Perhaps this would be more appropriate in private."

Sheriff Crow said agreeably, "I don't mind doing it here."

Mia considered fleeing the polite battle being waged across the table, but then she'd be abandoning Ross, whose dark eyes flicked back and forth nervously. Anna-Lucia broke into the duel by aggressively serving the apple crumble—without setting a plate for the mayor. Mia's father picked up his fork. He was controlling his expression, but Mia knew he was annoyed.

Ross reluctantly pushed away his plate. "Go ahead and ask your questions."

The noise from the saloon seemed be getting louder. Mia wondered if that was her imagination, but Jack tipped his head, listening. "I'll go get the coffee."

"Why don't you?" Anna-Lucia said, with extra emphasis.

Sheriff Crow gazed at Ross. "When we first met, you told me to run. Who shot you?"

"And why?" the mayor added.

He glanced nervously from the mayor to the sheriff. "Some bandit."

"Why?" asked Sheriff Crow.

Ross flung out his hands. "Because he was a bandit!"

"How many of them were there?"

"Just one."

"When I found you, you seemed to think he was right behind you. Was he?"

Ross shook his head. "No . . . he was long gone. I don't remember what I told you. I was out of it. But I know I lost him."

The sheriff said, looking at the mayor, "This bandit seems to have lost the Rangers as well. Quite some bandit."

The mayor had grown two hundred feet tall again. "I can assure you that the Rangers searched quite thoroughly. There is no bandit."

"In that case, I wonder who shot this boy."

Ross was frozen like a rabbit between two coyotes.

"I wonder too. And I wonder why." The mayor studied Ross. "Are you Changed?"

Sheriff Crow slammed her hand down. Plates of apple crumble jumped.

Jack called from the doorway, "Early warning! Concerned citizens on the loose."

"You and I will have a private talk later," the sheriff told Ross.

The mayor tapped her fingernails on the table. Mia could tell she didn't like that idea. Only three months ago, "private" talks with the sheriff had always included the sheriff's wife.

Jack was shoved aside by a bunch of townspeople, who all began talking. Every single one was a Norm. *Oh, not this again*, Mia thought in disgust.

Sheriff Crow stood up. "One at a time. You know the rules. Mr. Horst?"

The huge ironmonger glowered down at Ross. "My son told me that new boy's too strong for a Norm. He's Changed."

Mrs. Garcia broke in. "I knew that boy was Changed! We don't want any more—"

Sheriff Crow swept her hair from the Changed side of her face. The pupil of her snake eye contracted in the light. "Yes?"

The Norms backed up, then began to slink out. Mrs. Callahan, the last to leave, paused in the doorway, her freckled face ruddy with anger. "I shouldn't have to remind you of the importance of keeping this town safe, Sheriff Crow." She marched out.

Under her breath, Sheriff Crow said, "Don't let the door hit you in the ass."

Ross, the only person still eating, nearly choked. Mia avoided looking at him. She was afraid if he smiled she'd let out the laugh ballooning in her stomach; she caught a look from her father and bent over her plate. Only yesterday, he had reminded her that Mrs. Callahan was undoubtedly still upset because her husband had left Las Anclas—and her—last year. Mia didn't recall the woman being any nicer before he'd left.

Before the door could slam shut, another delegation

entered. To Mia's total lack of surprise, this one was Changed. Indra and Sujata's father, Mr. Vardam, was first. As he left the doorway, his right hand, which had shifted to match the color of the oak door, slowly paled to the dun of his clothes.

Sparks glittered in the air as Ms. Salazar entered, with the chief archer, Ms. Lowenstein, right behind her, yellow cat eyes gleaming.

Mr. Vardam addressed the mayor. "Valeria, I'd like to assure the concerned citizens gathering in the square that the newcomer will be treated fairly. Whatever he is."

"Of course he will be," Mayor Wolfe replied.

"My daughter Meredith says you fight well," Ms. Lowenstein said to Ross. "Are you planning to stay?"

Ms. Salazar's aura had the soft glow of candlelight as she asked kindly, "Are you Changed, young man? My son recently—"

Mrs. Callahan barged back in, glaring at the Changed adults. "Norms have rights too, you know!" she cried, jostling the table.

"Watch the apple crumble!" Jack rescued Sheriff Crow's plate as it began to slide over the edge.

The sheriff clapped her hands for silence. "I will interview the newcomer. When I'm done, the council will meet—"

"Tomorrow," said the mayor.

"—at their weekly meeting in three days. Unless I find it necessary to call a special meeting."

"Will this be a closed or open meeting?" Mrs. Callahan demanded.

"Closed," said Mayor Wolfe.

"Open," said Sheriff Crow.

Mia held her breath. Her father said in his peace-making voice, "Speaking as a council member, I encourage you to consider an open meeting, Mayor Wolfe." He smiled. "Not having to repeat our conclusions will be a great time-saver."

The mayor gave a stately nod. "Wise counsel, Dr. Lee. So it shall be."

"You heard the mayor," said the sheriff. "Go on home. Tell your teenagers they'll have to run the afternoon patrol, since most of their parents will want to be at the meeting."

She followed the mayor and the remaining citizens out. Mia's sigh of relief blew a daisy out of the vase.

Before anyone could speak, the door opened yet again, and in came—Mia blinked in surprise—Brisa Preciado. Then she saw the napkin Brisa was holding to her palm. "I cut myself."

Mia's dad examined her. "How exactly did this happen?"

Brisa gave him a rueful glance. "Juggling."

"Juggling knives?" exclaimed Mia.

"I'm not reckless. Wine glasses."

"You break it—" Jack began.

"You pay for it. I know," Brisa finished with a sigh. "Do I need stitches? Again?"

"Becky can do them," said Mia's dad. "You'll find her in the surgery. Make her come back and have dinner when she's done, will you? Tell her the mayor and the sheriff are gone."

Once Brisa left, silence fell. "That meeting," said Ross at last. "It's about me, isn't it?"

"Yes," said Mia's dad. "But I'm on the council, and I'll speak up for you. Mia, is your flamethrower ready yet? You could bring it on patrol."

Mia shook her head sadly. "I'm having some control issues." She perked up. "But I could test it."

Jack handed Ross the serving dish of apple crumble. "Take the rest. You look like you could use it."

10

Ross

ROSS WOKE UP GASPING FOR BREATH, HALF-SMOTHERED in a tangle of sweat-soaked sheets. This time, rather than dreaming that he was turning into a singing tree, he'd dreamed that he'd always been one—a tall, blood-red tree, waiting for human prey.

Needles of pain pulsed behind his eyes, and his jaw throbbed from clenching his teeth while he slept. His muscles had locked with tension. He had to force them to relax, limb by limb, before he could move.

He rolled onto his back. His entire body ached like he'd been beaten. The ceiling loomed above his head, threatening to cave in on him. He'd never had nightmares when he'd slept outside. That was the worst part about sleeping inside houses. Ceilings.

He got dressed and went downstairs, deliberately not looking up. The hallway smelled temptingly of fresh eggs. He had to admit there were some good things about houses.

Dr. Lee was busy at the kitchen stove, and the sheriff sat drinking coffee at the table.

"Good morning, Ross." The doctor peered at him, melted butter dripping to the floor from a forgotten spatula in his hand. "You look tired. Did Mia keep you up all night?"

"We collected oil for a few hours after dinner. I'm fine."

"Will you join us for breakfast, Sheriff?" Dr. Lee asked.

"I want to have a talk with Ross. He'll be back before the

eggs get cold." She hefted her mug. "Let's go back to your room. Sound carries outside."

In his bedroom, the sheriff leaned against the wall, sipping steaming coffee. Ross sat on the bed. Sheriff Crow wasn't a big woman and she wasn't even armed, but she seemed to take up a lot of space. Between her and the walls of the small room, he felt more trapped than ever.

"What brings you to Las Anclas?" she asked.

"I told you, I was chased by a bandit."

"No—I mean, where were you going before the bandit chased you?"

Ross shrugged. "West."

"Why?"

"I heard life was better there. I wanted to see the ocean."

"All right." She sipped more coffee. "Where were you when the bandit started chasing you?"

"I . . ." He'd be gone long before he could draw Voske's attention to the town, but he didn't want to get thrown out on his ear just for mentioning Voske. "In the desert, out east. Between the mountain ranges."

"And there was just the one bandit?"

"Yes."

"What did you have that he wanted?"

When he didn't reply, she said, "Look, I know you prospectors don't like revealing exactly what you find and how much it's worth. If it's something good—something valuable—I won't tell anyone else about it, and I won't try to take it from you. All I want to know is if you were attacked in a robbery, or if it was for some other reason."

Under her intent gaze, it took conscious effort not to glance out the window, in the direction of Mia's house—and his book.

"As long as it isn't something that could explode or release poison or otherwise be dangerous to the town," she added, "I don't care about it."

"It's not. It won't."

The sheriff nodded. "And how long was this bandit chasing you for it before he shot you?"

"Six days."

The eyebrow on the normal side of her face rose. The other side, with its wasted muscles, didn't move. "Six days to the east is the border of Voske's kingdom. What were you doing there?"

"Prospecting. My map said it was open territory outside of some town called Rio de Hierro."

"Not anymore. Voske attacked Rio de Hierro and took it over. He wants to turn his kingdom into an empire, and he's well on his way to doing it."

"I was trying to stay out of his territory, but I didn't realize how big it had gotten."

"Where were you when you got shot?"

Her jumps from topic to topic were obviously designed to catch him in lies—and it was working. He'd already lost track of what the last few questions had been. It seemed safest to answer honestly. "An arroyo that dead-ended in a cement wall and a bunch of singing trees. I crawled through a pipe and came out somewhere in the desert. Mia said it's by your corn-fields. But I went downhill."

She nodded. "Okay. I know where that is. So how did you get that gash in your arm? Your bandit's work?"

"I had to cut out a shard from one of the trees."

"Really?" For the first time, he seemed to have surprised her. "Let me see."

Ross reluctantly pulled up his sleeve. He hadn't even been able to really look at the scar himself, let alone show other people, and the thought of someone touching it was even worse. Reflexively, his right hand made a fist, and the fingers of his left ached as they tried to do the same.

She bent over his arm but didn't touch it. "Tilt it a bit to the left." She indicated a discolored spot on his wrist that he hadn't even noticed before. "You're right. There's the entry wound."

He shook his sleeve back down.

"Have you ever killed or hurt anyone accidentally? Hit some-one too hard and they died? Or have you ever lost control of a power?"

"No."

"Have you ever killed or hurt anyone for any reason other than a fair fight or a battle, or defending yourself or others?"

"No."

"You're done."

He was startled. No threats? "That's it?"

The sheriff tilted her mug to get the last drops of coffee. "I told you, I don't need to know everything. Just what concerns the safety of the town."

He followed her back to the kitchen. With a tip of her hat to Dr. Lee, she headed out the door. Ross sank into the nearest chair. He felt like he'd been through a fair fight, but he didn't know who'd won.

"Tell you what, Ross," said Dr. Lee. "While the beans finish cooking, I'll teach you some exercises to strengthen that hand."

11

Jennie

JENNIE DUSTED HER FINGERS AND SET DOWN THE last slate. Cutting up a plum to explain fractions to the eight- and nine-year-olds definitely worked better than Grandma Wolfe's method of drawing pictures on the board. Letting the kids eat the fractions after they solved their problems was a bonus.

She stretched out her arms. Her left shoulder ached from the joint-lock Ross had put her in that morning. Someone had taught him well. He must have had some bad experiences, the way he always sat with his back to a wall, and hunched over his desk. From the shadows under his eyes, it looked as if he hadn't slept since he'd come to Las Anclas. But he'd been showing up all week, though there were times when he seemed poised to bolt like some wild thing.

She tried to dig her knuckles beneath her shoulder blade, but she couldn't quite reach the sore area. She'd have to get Indra to massage it out before training.

Indra! Training! By the slant of the sun outside, she was already late.

By the time she had changed, grabbed her sword, and run to the training grounds, the Rangers were well into warming up. Indra was sparring with Julio Wolfe. His braid swung out as he stepped in close for an elbow strike. Julio dodged, blocked, and the two of them broke apart. Then Indra saw her. His eyes widened, his lips parted—and Julio darted in for a hip throw, slamming him to the ground.

Julio laughed. "Jennie, you should always come late when

I'm working with Indra. It's good for him to take some falls."

Everyone chuckled as Jennie laid down her sword beside Indra's machete, Sera's rifle and bandolier, Julio's rifle with bayonet, and Frances's paired short swords.

When she'd finished her stretches, Sera beckoned. "Come spar with me." The pale tracks of crow's feet crinkled around her brown eyes as she smiled. "I hope chasing ten-year-olds isn't slowing you up."

"Try me." Jennie's mind went immediately to Ross. For some reason, her face heated up, and she shook herself. *Concentrate.*

They squared off. Sera was a defensive fighter, moving as little as possible to conserve energy. But her control of distance and timing was so perfect that Jennie's blows always ended one or two inches short. She didn't even see Sera's foot move when a sweep knocked her feet out from under her, and landed her sprawling on the ground.

Sera pulled her to her feet. "You should have seen that coming."

"I was watching your hands."

Sera nodded. "I like some of your moves. Who have you been working with? You slipped in some interesting blocks there."

"The new guy, Ross."

"How's he fight?"

Several of the others glanced their way; Jennie felt Indra's eyes on her.

"Let me put it like this," she said. "The first time we sparred, he took me down."

Sera's eyebrows rose. "Think he'd be interested in becoming a candidate?"

"I don't know if he's staying that long. Anyway, he's not eligible. He has a pretty bad injury to his left hand. He can't use it at all."

"Jennie!" Sera shook her head with exaggerated sorrow. "He took you out with one hand? The schoolhouse is making you lazy. . . . I know! You can carry Indra through the obstacle course." She raised her voice. "Everyone, line up!"

Jennie stood beside Indra, at the junior end of the line. She could feel the heat coming off his body. Jennie had wondered if that biological quirk of his was a minor Change, but she'd never suggested it to him.

"Go!"

They raced for the rock wall. By the time they reached it, their breathing and footsteps were synchronized. Jennie loved that—it felt so intimate. She vaulted up the wall and swung her legs over, balancing on her hips as she reached down to clasp his forearms. He leaped, she tugged, and he was up beside her. They jumped off the wall. Indra lay down in a deliberate sprawl, making himself look even bigger.

He grinned up at her in challenge, and she prodded him in the belly with the toe of her boot. "How many of Luc's tacos did you eat today?"

"No more than fifty. Maybe sixty."

"All right!" Sera yelled. "Your partner's gone down, but you never abandon another Ranger! Pick them up and get them to safety!"

Jennie wrestled Indra into position, and hauled him up over her shoulders. His body draped over her like a very heavy blanket, reminding her of when he slept next to her.

"Lift with your legs," he whispered.

"You're unconscious."

He relaxed into dead weight, one arm swinging lifelessly at her side. Jennie stood, then set out at a brisk pace, weaving around the rock markers.

"The kids have slowed you up," Indra whispered.

Jennie snorted. "Kids? I haven't forgotten Yuki dumping you on your ass when he was barely sixteen."

"I let him have it."

"Yeah. Right. Paco is fast, when he tries. Your sister, too, when she tries. Brisa's fun. Even Henry—" Jennie abruptly recognized the Ross-shaped hole in the conversation.

"Move your feet, slowpoke!" Sera called.

Jennie concentrated on her breathing—in through the nose, out through the mouth—as she lengthened her strides. Ten . . . six . . . two more rocks to dodge.

"And the new guy?" Indra prompted. "What's he doing at school at all? Is he stupid?"

"No. He's been on his own for a long time. He fights . . ." Jennie's throat rasped. She shouldn't be talking.

Indra shouldn't be talking. What did he care about Ross?

"Yes?"

"Can't talk," Jennie gasped.

She let out a breath of relief when they rounded the last rock, and headed toward the mud pit.

"Mud," Indra said. "Don't you dare." He shifted his weight, trying to hook his legs over her shoulder to keep himself clear. It nearly knocked her off balance.

"Back to sleep," she ordered.

Indra flicked his braid safely over her shoulder, and kept himself curled away from the mud.

"Taking root?" Julio called. He'd already finished, but he'd only had to carry Frances.

"My dead guy talks too much." Jennie scooped up a handful of mud and tossed it over her shoulder into Indra's face.

"Hey!" Indra protested.

She laughed as she clambered out of the pit and started back toward the rock wall. Her breathing was too shallow; she gulped in more air.

"Going to camp there all night?" Sera called.

The Rangers obliged with a chorus of snores from the other side of the wall. Great. Jennie and Indra were last.

Everyone began calling encouragement. She grabbed the wall with mud-slick hands, regretting that handful she'd tossed onto Indra. Halfway up, all her muscles began to tremble—she'd lost her rhythm. She clung to the wall, trying to force her legs upward. Though Indra cooperated by staying absolutely still, her legs wouldn't move. Her breath burned her throat.

"Jennie," Sera shouted. "There's always one more drop of lemon juice. Squeeze!"

She made a tremendous effort, and heaved herself to the top. She lay there, gasping.

Indra spoke softly into her ear. "If we moved in together, we could do this every morning before breakfast."

She froze, then realized that he had to be joking. With a slightly forced laugh, she leaped down, barely catching herself, and thankfully pushed Indra off her shoulders.

He landed as lightly as a cat, so graceful for such a big guy. She never got tired of watching him move. He smiled at her, and her emotions swooped like a bright-moth caught in the wind.

"Let's do that again," Sera said. "Indra, carry Jennie. You can recite the Ranger oath while you run."

Jennie tried to keep her mind on practice, but she kept coming back to what Indra had said. Of course he had been joking.

After Sera dismissed them, he fell in step with her. "What do you think? There's open apartments at Singles Row."

His skin glowed warm in the last light of the setting sun, and his whole body seemed to radiate hope.

"I'm only eighteen." Jennie winced at how defensive she sounded.

"You're a Ranger now, a voting citizen." His gaze was steady and serious.

She fumbled for words. "In my family, we usually don't move out. We add another room."

"So let's add a room." Indra flicked one of her braids back, his thumb gently stroking from her ear to the curve of her neck.

She leaned into his touch, then pulled back, trying to gauge his expression in the rapidly gathering darkness. "I like my room. I like things the way they are—"

"Am I interrupting anything?" Felicité's sweet voice startled Jennie. "I'm on my way to Sunset Circle to take peach turnovers to Grandma Chen; she's still recovering from her fall. I'd like to invite you to a party at Luc's, tomorrow at eight, to welcome Ross Juarez to Las Anclas."

Jennie exclaimed, "Ross is coming to a party?"

"I couldn't find him to ask, but Dr. Lee promised to pass on the invitation. Please come."

"Sure," Jennie said. Indra nodded enthusiastically.

"Good night." Felicité walked on.

"I just realized," Jennie said. "My schedule got changed so I can ride with the Rangers. I'll be on the wall tomorrow night. But you go. Tell me all about it!"

"If you can't go, I won't either," Indra said.

"Seriously, go," she urged. "We don't have to do everything together."

Indra didn't reply. Only then did she remember what they'd been talking about before. She wondered if she should explain that she'd meant the party, but then they'd have to return to the subject of moving in. It was too sudden—she was too young. He was too young. They'd only been dating for six months.

They walked on in a tense silence.

12

YUKI

YUKI'S SENTRY DUTY ENDED AT SUNSET. HE STOWED his weapons at the armory and loped up the path to the west harvest barn. Paco used it as his practice space. Yuki loved watching Paco drumming. Or watching Paco sparring, or riding, or even just sitting at a desk, his dark head bent over a slate.

The rhythmic tattoo reached him, and he slipped inside the barn. Paco was alone. He had a rule against people crowding in to watch him practice, but Yuki was the one exception. "Because he's quiet," Paco had said.

Yuki walked softly across the dirt floor. The air inside the windowless barn was stifling hot. Paco stood at his tall drum, shirt off, sweat dripping down his bare back. The only illumination was a single lamp on a bale of hay. Golden light flickered across the sharp planes of his face and his damp black hair. Paco moved like a dancer, like a fighter, fluid and controlled at once, immersing his entire self in the rhythm. His eyes were closed, but Yuki was sure Paco knew that he was there.

Yuki leaned back against the rough wall. He could feel the vibrations in his entire body, as if the drum were making his heart beat to its rhythm. Paco played on, his head bent, his profile like a finely carved statue. Yuki's gaze followed those angular lines to the taut curves molding Paco's shoulders and arms, and from there to his long-fingered hands. They'd sparred together that morning, and Yuki found himself reliving the moment when Paco had caught him in a grappling hold, the imprint of Paco's fingers on his wrist and shoulder.

He wanted to be touching now. He wanted to walk right up and put his hands on Paco's shoulders, wanted it so badly that he felt like he might not be able to stop himself from doing it.

The drumming stopped. Paco opened his eyes, his gaze arrowing straight to Yuki for an endless moment. Yuki was sure that Paco could see everything that he felt, as clearly as if it were written on the heated air.

Then Paco moved. Yuki stumbled toward him, and they were kissing.

Yuki had no idea how much time had passed before he thought of anything other than Paco's lips and hands and skin. Then he blinked in sudden darkness.

"The lamp burned out," Paco said, breathless with laughter.

"Do we need one?" Yuki asked, laughing too, light-headed and almost dizzy.

"No . . . yes. I'm due at Luc's at eight. I don't think it's eight yet. Come with me."

Yuki had known for weeks that this would happen, just not how or when. But he hadn't imagined anything past the two of them together.

When he'd dated Dan Valdez, all of Las Anclas had to comment. It happened to everyone. Kids in the street made kissy noises if you so much as looked at each other, and if you broke up, what seemed like half the town would offered condolences the very next day. Yuki grimaced, imagining Paco's band members winking, and Meredith teasing, and the gossip about "the prince and the drummer boy."

"Do you mind if we don't tell anyone yet?" Yuki asked. "At least, not the whole town? Everyone in Las Anclas knows the number of tomato worms in my family's vegetable patch. I'd like to have one thing that only the two of us know."

Paco stroked his back. "Sure. We'll go separately, but you sit up front. After I play, we can go to my house. My mom's out with the other Rangers, and she said they'll probably be gone for a few days. Oh, hey—what do you think about Ross Juarez?"

Yuki looked away. "I don't know if I trust him. And he looks younger than me. Even if he's not a con man, he can't be very experienced."

He felt Paco shake his head. "I didn't mean you should try to apprentice yourself to him. But he might have some interesting stories. Maybe he could tell you some routes to take, when you go out yourself."

Yuki blinked. "'When'?"

"You said you wouldn't wait around forever. I figured if you can't find someone to apprentice to, eventually you'll leave and teach yourself."

"Yeah, that's my plan," he admitted. "But everyone says if I haven't been trained properly, I won't last two days alone in the desert."

"You lasted two days when Alvarez ditched you," Paco pointed out. "And you didn't have weapons or supplies or even water. I think you could do it."

"Thanks." Yuki leaned back against Paco's chest. The one person who believed he could make it by himself was the one person Yuki would take along if he could.

13

Felicité

FELICITÉ KNELT ON HER BEDROOM FLOOR. WU
Zetian traced "SN" and "GN" on Felicité's palm, then, in
small letters, "su." Sebastien Nguyen and his wife Grace, at
the surgery.

"Very good, darling." Felicité kissed the rat's pink nose,
then gave her a salted almond.

All Wu Zetian could report was where people went and
who they were with. She was an exceptionally bright rat, but
she was still only a rat. However, Felicité knew enough about
Las Anclas to be able to extrapolate a lot—and what she
couldn't extrapolate, she could find out via careful checking
in person. Mr. Nguyen was not stealing, just trading nails in
exchange for help turning his attic into a room "for boarders."

She knew what that really meant. Many women found it
hard to get pregnant and easy to miscarry. So they might fix
up a room, but they'd say it was for boarders or visitors, in
the hope of avoiding bad luck. And now the Nguyens were
visiting Dr. Lee. Grace Nguyen was pregnant.

Felicité dusted salt off her fingers. It was surprising how
many people carried on secret arrangements without their
guild chief knowing. She was glad that her daddy handpicked
the Rangers, who would never go behind his back.

She peered out the window. There was no sign of rain, so
she decided not to bother with a veil. Instead, she draped a
carmine silk scarf around her throat to set off the brilliance
of her ivory dress.

Wu Zetian trotted into her rat house and curled up on the pillow. Clever Wu Zetian! She'd recognized Felicité's dancing dress, and knew she wouldn't be coming along.

"Felicité?" Her mother's voice came from below. "Are you ready? Your friends are on the veranda."

She gave her reflection a last glance. Her figure was much more elegant than Jennie Riley's. Jennie's was all the same—big breasts, big hips, big butt, big everything. Felicité's had contrast, which made each part stand out more. She ran her hands from her gently rounded hips up to her slender waist, then cupped her breasts in her hands. She didn't have as much cleavage as Jennie, but it was more impressive because her torso was willowy.

She wondered again about what she'd seen the other night between Jennie and Indra. It was easy to fool oneself into seeing what one wanted to see. But, for the first time in six months, they had walked without being glued to each other's side, and Jennie's hands had been as tense as Indra's shoulders.

Felicité had been right to pick a night when Jennie couldn't come. All she wanted was a chance to see Indra in a social situation, alone. If he seemed interested, then she would be justified in pursuing her own interest.

As she passed the office, she saw her mother seated at her ebony desk, reading Felicité's minutes from the last council meeting.

"Mother, they'll all ask about the visitor's dance."

Her mother laid down the record book. "I'm afraid your father and I are not inclined to permit that boy to stay. There are too many unanswered questions, and you know how careful we must be. No word of that to your friends: the council hasn't voted yet. But there can't be a visitor's dance if there is no visitor."

Felicité suppressed a frown. Poise and control. "But you

always say that celebrations are good for a town. They keep up morale. Can't we have a dance anyway? There must be something to celebrate."

"There's a great deal of work involved, and we already have so much to do." Her mother indicated a stack of papers.

"Then let me take the responsibility, Mother," Felicité said. "I'd enjoy it—the whole town will enjoy it. The only work you'll need to do is put on your best dress, and be the guest of honor."

Her mother paused, then smiled. "When you put it that way, darling, it sounds like an excellent idea. Very well. I'm sure you'll do a wonderful job. And don't think you have to stay behind the scenes. You'll have plenty of time for dancing with someone special."

"I was thinking of Indra Vardam." Felicité wouldn't have said that much if she hadn't seen the tension between him and Jennie. It might not be anything, but why not try out the idea on the person who knew best?

"An excellent choice, my darling. Indra is a responsible young man from a respectable family." She paused. "But he is a young man and you are a lovely young woman. You know that the Wolfe women have proved to be more fertile than many families. I trust that if you do go together, you will use contraception."

Felicité recalled the briny scent of the kelp condoms at the back of her drawer. They had appeared, along with a set of menstrual sponges, once she'd started getting her period. Her maid replaced the condoms every few months, before they could grow brittle, but Felicité had never used them. "If Indra turns out to be the One, I will. Until I'm sure, I'd rather wait."

"You are such a romantic, dear! It runs in the family." Her mother kissed her cheek. "Now, don't be late to your own party."

Felicité slipped on her scarlet dancing shoes. Everyone was waiting on the veranda. She paused a moment before she joined them, framing herself in the doorway. Then she showered them with sweetly chiming compliments, piling on extra for unfortunate choices. Sujata Vardam wore crimson velvet, which was lovely, but she'd soon be unpleasantly sweaty. Pale, yellow-haired Becky in a yellow dress looked like a jaundiced ghost.

"You remind me of a jonquil," Felicité said.

"Really?" Becky said doubtfully. "I think I look like sour milk, but Mama has a lot of this cloth to get rid of. The dye was supposed to be gold."

Felicité said, glad to be able to tell the truth, "That drape on the bias looks so sweet on you. Maybe it will start a new fashion."

"That's what Mama hopes."

Tommy Horst pushed forward. "Well? Are we having a visitor's dance?"

"Yes, and I'm in charge."

The girls squealed gleefully. Tommy tried to elbow past Henry, undoubtedly intending to ask her out. Felicité had no intention of getting stuck between Tommy, with his ham hands and jug ears, and Henry, the class clown, who had been asking her out once a month since her quinceañera. Indra came first.

Stepping neatly in front of Tommy, she linked arms with Sujata and Becky. That used up the width of the path, forcing the rest to follow all the way to Luc's. Light and music floated out the open door. Sujata started dancing on their way inside.

The band formed a half-circle around Paco Diaz, who wore only a vest and black trousers as he pounded on his tall drum, hair spiked with sweat, the hard line of his cheekbones gleaming under the lights. Felicité hurriedly averted her gaze from Laura's hideous black claws strumming the guitar, and toward the older Norm guys playing the qeej and flute.

Luc's was already hot and crowded. Everybody their age had jammed around Yuki, who sat at the table closest to the band. His sister Meredith was dancing, flinging her arms out so wildly that she nearly hit Felicité.

The others offered her the best table under the window. Felicité looked around for Indra. Fat Brisa Preciado crowded up in front of her, blocking her view. Felicité was about to politely ask her to step aside when Brisa asked Becky, "May I have this dance?"

With a squeak of delight, Becky jumped up, and they hurried to join the dancers, Becky's yellow skirt clashing unfortunately with Brisa's bright pink. The ribbons in her pigtails trailed behind her like a banner.

Felicité eyed the glass of lemonade Brisa had left behind without even a coaster, making a ring on the table. She was about to have a waiter take it away when Sujata said, "That's the happiest I've seen Becky look in a long time."

Felicité set the glass back down. Becky did look happy. Brisa wasn't the girl Felicité would have picked for her, but it could be worse. Brisa was Changed and from a poor field-worker family, but at least her Change wasn't visible.

Indra finally appeared, his blue-black tail of hair soaking wet, with several fresh-scrubbed younger Rangers. They all stopped by the kitchen.

Felicité said, "I'll order us a jug of lemonade."

When she neared the kitchen entrance, the waiter came out with a pitcher and a tray of glasses. She smilingly took them, saying, "Tonight's my party, remember?"

"Sure, Felicité." He vanished back into the kitchen.

She set the pitcher and tray on a nearby table, and offered

Indra a glass of lemonade. "Have you been training? You must be thirsty."

"Thanks. You're always taking care of people, every time I see you." He held up his glass in salute.

What to say to that? *It's the way I was raised.* No, that was pompous. "I like seeing people happy." So he wouldn't think she was fishing for compliments, she added, "How was practice?"

"Sera works us hard. It's great." Indra downed half his glass.

The fiddlers had slowed down to a slow, sad song, accompanied only by the flute player. Brisa and Becky waltzed slowly, holding each other tight.

"I love this song," Felicité said, as a hint.

There was a commotion—the guest of honor, Ross Juarez, was standing in the doorway, blocking everyone trying to get in and out.

Felicité called encouragingly, "Welcome, Ross! This party is for you."

Instead of looking grateful, let alone thanking her, Ross blanched like he was about to be hanged. What was wrong with him? She'd noticed how jumpy he was at school. She hoped it wasn't guilt over being a criminal on the run. If he was, she hoped he'd be out of Las Anclas before anyone ever found out that she'd thrown a party for an outlaw.

At least he cleaned up well, with gorgeous black hair falling softly over the collar of one of Dr. Lee's good linen shirts. Mia, who stood at his shoulder, had made a typically Mia sort of effort—she had traded her usual grubby overalls for riding trousers and another one of her father's good shirts.

"You look great, Mia," Felicité called, hoping to extract them from the doorway.

"Hi, Ross." Indra held up his glass. "I'm Indra. Want a drink?"

Ross stayed in the doorway like he was glued there. It reminded her of Rabbi Litvak—he lived outside of town, because he couldn't shut off his ability to sense emotions. Every Friday evening, as he walked through the town gates, he had to brace himself. Perhaps this was Ross's Change.

Mia urged him, "Come on—I promise, the tacos are worth the crowd."

Felicité gave him her best smile. Reluctantly, led by Mia, he edged into the room.

When Ross was a few feet away, a music stand onstage fell over with a crash. Ross jumped backward and whipped out his arm like he was blocking an attack, knocking a glass of pomegranate juice out of Meredith's hand. Cold liquid splashed Felicité from head to toe. Ross lunged toward her to catch the glass.

"Get away from me, you mutant!" Felicité cried.

She snatched a napkin from the nearest table and hurriedly wiped off her face and hands. But though her hat brim had shielded most of her face, and her layers of petticoats kept her body dry, bright red juice dripped from her hat—her beautiful new hat!—and splattered the ivory gown.

The entire room had gone silent. Everyone was staring at her and Ross. Instead of apologizing, he bolted for the door.

Mia glared at Felicité. "He didn't do that on purpose. And I can't believe you used that word!" She hurried after him.

"I am so sorry—" Felicité began.

Meredith didn't let her finish. "What a hateful thing to say! Some party!"

The threat of tears burned Felicité's eyelids. "I didn't mean—"

"You did mean it," Meredith interrupted.

"Give it a rest, Meredith," Tommy shouted. "You call people names all the time."

"Not that one." She turned on him, looking like a flea challenging a wolf. "You think I'd ever call a human being a mutant? My own mother is Changed!"

"What do you expect?" the qeej player commented. Even the band had stopped playing to witness her humiliation! "She's Preston's daughter—she probably hears that kind of language every day at home."

"I didn't mean it, I didn't mean it," Felicité repeated, her brain frozen with horror. "Indra. It's not something I believe. It slipped out."

"Does it slip out whenever you see my father?" Indra turned his back and stalked away, to the Rangers' table.

Felicité faced a room full of whispers and nudges. "I am truly sorry."

For a long, painful moment, no one spoke. *This is what happens when you lose control. Remember it.*

Brisa spoke up, for once not smiling. "Seems to me it's Ross you should apologize to."

"Yes." Felicité heard how breathless and shaky her voice was. "I intend to do that right now. The rest of you, enjoy the party. It's still my treat."

She had to tell her parents before they heard about it from someone else. While her mother never discussed her feelings about Changed people in general, neither would she refer to them with a slur. And both she and Daddy would be disappointed at Felicité's lack of control.

She longed to go home and get it over with, but she had to keep her word. So she forced herself to walk to Dr. Lee's in a ruined dress that looked like she'd been murdered, just to be told that Ross and Mia weren't there.

Felicité knew that she would never be able to look at him again without being reminded of her humiliation. But luckily, soon the council would meet, and then he would be history.

Until then, she had her reputation to protect among those who mattered.

She'd apologize tomorrow. At school. In front of everyone. *That will be better, anyway. They will all see how sincere I am.*

14

Ross

ROSS JERKED AWAKE, GASPING. HE TRIED TO SIT UP, BUT his head banged against something hard. He was trapped!

He opened his eyes. Wooden slats loomed over him. Oh. He'd thrown himself out of bed and rolled underneath it. Dim blue light illuminated the room, and he caught a whiff of the pungent incense that Dr. Lee burned when he meditated every morning before sunrise.

Ross got dressed, afraid to go back to sleep in case he fell back into that dream of bleeding to death on the sand while the pool of his blood hardened to crystal. He slipped out and paced around the darkened town, but it was a long time before his heart stopped pounding.

When the sun rose, he returned to his room and did the exercises for his hand. They seemed to be working. Three days ago, he couldn't even hold the leather ball Dr. Lee had given him, and now he could dent it.

He wished there were exercises for nightmares.

When he came down for breakfast, he found that there were burritos again, with fresh eggs and spicy chicken sausage. And cheese. He'd miss that when they threw him out of Las Anclas. Since the council would meet today, he decided to make the most of what he had, and ate an extra burrito.

Dr. Lee covered a full plate with a napkin, and handed it to Ross. "Looks like Mia stayed up all night again, communing with one of her machines. Will you drop this off on your way to school?"

Carrying the plate in his right hand, he knocked on Mia's door, but there was no response except for a clink he figured was not directed at him. He knocked again. Then once more. Finally, he opened it. She was bent over an interesting-looking device on her worktable. The engine was still on her bed, but it had been joined by an array of tools and several gallon jugs of oil.

"Do you ever sleep?" he asked.

Mia jumped. "Oh, hi, Ross. Knock before you come in. Sometimes I work with explosives."

"I did knock."

"Oh."

"Several times."

"Oh. I guess you should knock louder." She probably wouldn't have heard him if he'd blown up the door. Mia shoved her glasses up her nose, leaving a streak of grease, and picked up a screwdriver with her left hand.

"Are you left-handed?" Ross could have sworn she'd had it in her right hand when he'd walked in.

"I'm ambidextrous," she replied. "Both-handed. Dad says it's rare."

"What are you working on?"

Mia held the contraption up, beaming proudly. "It's a flamethrower."

Ross eyed it. "Can you shoot that thing all the way from the sentry walk?"

"No, the flame wouldn't reach the ground. It's for the singing trees. Melting's the only safe way to destroy them. If you blow them up, shards go everywhere. Have you ever seen them kill an animal? Ugh!"

"Yeah, I have." Ross rubbed his scar. Since he'd already told the sheriff, he might as well tell her, too. "Actually . . . that's what happened to my arm. I was only hit by one shard, or I'd be a tree right now. I had to cut it out. It was already growing roots by the time I got my knife out."

"Wow." Mia stared at his arm, and even though his sleeve covered the scar, he resisted the impulse to pull it to his chest. "You're the first person I've ever heard of surviving a hit. Of course, I've never heard of anyone only getting hit by one shard. How did that happen?"

"I was mostly behind cover." He deftly changed the subject, pointing at the flamethrower. "Are you testing it?"

"Yeah," she replied, easily distracted. "I'm taking it along to try out today. There's a lot of those singing trees between us and the big ruins."

"Big ruins?" Ross asked, the old prospecting itch waking up.

"Huge. Enormous. Gigantic! But they're surrounded by those trees. They got the last prospector who came to town." She patted the flamethrower. "I'll test it during the school-house patrol. Should be fun. Usually we go with Mr. Riley's patrollers, but they'll all be at that council meeting about you."

Ross hated the idea of being talked about almost as much as he hated crowds. Or situations like the day before, when Felicité Wolfe had been waiting for him at school like a cougar concealed in the undergrowth.

His blood had run hot and cold and hot again when she'd apologized in front of everyone. He'd rather have had her call him a mutant again—at least then he wouldn't have had to stand there and take it. By the time he'd managed to stammer out, "I'm sorry I ruined your dress," he'd felt like he was being stabbed by invisible knives.

The school bell began to toll.

Ross remembered the plate in his hand. "Here's your breakfast."

"I'll walk you over. I need some air." Mia set it on top of the engine on her bed and opened her door.

"Aren't you going to eat that?"

"Oh, yeah." She ate the burrito as they walked. He could tell her mind was on her flamethrower, and she wasn't appreciating her father's cooking at all.

"The problem is, the oil burns too fast." Mia licked a drop of salsa from her finger. "I get a big burst, but it's over in seconds."

"Use a bigger canister."

"Then it weighs more than you do."

"Oh. Right. Put it on wheels?"

"That's a thought," said Mia. "Though it'll limit maneuverability. Jennie's been researching other fuel, but—I have to get back to work!"

She took off, to Ross's confusion. Then he spotted Felicité walking up, arm in arm with her friends Becky and Sujata, followed by a bunch of other girls. Felicité's scarlet hat and dress reminded him of his nightmare of blood and crystal. He edged away, trying not to look at her.

"Ross," Felicité called. "I hope you're well today?"

How was he supposed to answer that? "I hope you are, too," he mumbled, and fled into the relative safety of the schoolhouse. Behind him, somebody giggled.

Jennie gave him a genuine smile. "Hi, Ross. I've got some exercises in verb conjugation for you this morning. They're written out on your slate."

He exhaled in relief, and got to work as the rest of the students wandered in and sat down.

An odd, rhythmic clicking caught his attention. It seemed to be coming from Felicité's desk. She peered inside, then leaped up with a scream. A roach the size of a man's hand slowly dragged its bloated body out from under a pile of chalk. Crumbs of white chalk stuck to its grinding mandibles, and its eye stalks switched back and forth. Armor plates clicked together as it moved.

Then its eyestalks stiffened. Its wings spread, and with a hiss it leaped into the air—straight for Felicité's head.

She threw up her hands, crying out, "My hair!"

Henry Callahan lunged out with a slate in both hands. He slapped the roach out of the air, then slammed the slate down, crushing it to the floor.

Instead of a squish, there was a loud crack. Henry lifted the slate. The roach lay still. Then one eye stalk popped up, followed by the other. The roach zipped away and vanished under a storage box.

Felicité frantically brushed herself off as if she were covered in roaches.

Henry flicked little Hattie Salazar's braid. "Is that another one?"

A pack of little kids started screaming, and another pack began racing around, slamming slates into imaginary roaches.

Rico Salazar shoved Henry. "You scared my sister!"

He shoved back, knocking Rico into Yolanda's desk. She lifted her hand, and a gust of wind blew slates off desks and into Henry. Next thing Ross knew, half the school was in a shoving, yelling match. He moved out of the way, wondering if he should ignore it or try to break it up.

A crossbow flew from its mount on the wall and smacked into Jennie's palm. The students settled down, though Felicité stayed in the aisle.

"I'm so sorry," she said to Jennie. "You know I can't stand it when things get in my hair."

"We all know that. I assume that's why someone thought it would be hilarious to put a roach in your desk." There was complete silence as she walked around the room. "Henry?"

"I have no idea how it got there. It was just one roach."

"There is never 'just one roach,'" said Jennie.

He shrugged. "I didn't put it there."

"I heard what you said to Hattie. I saw you tickle her too."

"I was kidding. It wasn't my fault everyone went crazy."

"Fine." Jennie smiled a hard, thin smile. "Then instead of morning drill, we're doing Lockdown drill."

"Oh, hell," Henry said to Yolanda. "See what you did?"

"Me?" Yolanda glared. "Who's the jackass that put the roach in Felicité's desk?"

Groans and complaints drowned out the bickering as the students began passing out armor, weapons, and ammunition.

Jennie beckoned to Ross. "Everyone has their place, and they know their orders. Until you get some, you can take a break."

As Laura led the little kids outside, Sujata pulled Henry aside. "That is not how to get a girl's attention. Let me give you a tip..."

Ross asked Jennie, "What happens now? Everybody goes to the walls?"

"Yes. I'll come around on inspection after they've been wearing full armor in the sun for a while. Then we come back, work until the bell, and then we'll go out on patrol. If you'd like to go with us, come back at the watch change."

Ross went back to Dr. Lee's for his wagon and started collecting oil. As he walked, he thought about Jennie—she was about his age, but she was in charge of sixty or seventy people. He'd never been in charge of anyone but his burro, Rusty. And he hadn't even been able to save Rusty from being stolen by Voske's soldiers.

He turned down the main road and started to glance past the signpost, when the sign itself caught his eye. LA TIJERA. He could read it!

He'd always navigated by landmarks and constellations, adding drawings to his maps. As he worked his way past the longhouses on the west side, some painted bright colors, others old and patched, he sounded out the street signs. An entirely new part of the world had revealed itself to him, as if he had Changed and could suddenly see like a hawk or track scents like a dog. It was amazing.

At the north forge, a huge man stepped out in a waft of

heated air that smelled like metal, blocking his path. He was one of the people who had shoved their way into Jack's back room, demanding to know if Ross was Changed. The sheriff had called him Mr. Horst.

"I want a word with you, boy." Mr. Horst snapped his fingers at Ross, beckoning him to come closer.

Ross stayed where he was, eyeing the man warily. He had no plans to get anywhere near those strong blacksmith's arms.

When he didn't move, the man took a menacing step toward him. "Are you Changed?"

Ross edged backward.

Mr. Horst gave him a contemptuous look. "Too scared to admit it?"

Even if he said he was a Norm, he couldn't prove that he didn't have a power, and the man had clearly already made up his mind.

Then he whipped out his right hand, but Ross was out of striking distance. He didn't flinch.

Mr. Horst scowled and dropped his hand. "Are you counting on all two of your Changed friends on the council to talk the others into keeping you here?" He snorted. "We've had enough trouble with you people. The last thing this town needs is another damn mutant!"

He shouldered his way back into the building and slammed the door.

It was hardly the first time Ross had been called names or threatened, and he usually let it roll off his back. But between the nightmares, the aching arm and hand that he still couldn't use, and being called a mutant twice in two days, the joy in his newfound ability to read had vanished.

He unloaded the oil in Mia's yard, then walked quietly into the cottage. He discovered Mia asleep on the floor, curled up in a ball with her head pillowed on folded oilcloth. She reminded him of a kitten, or maybe a raccoon pup—something small and cute. Her hair fell loose across her round cheeks, and her eyelashes were like dark half-moons.

It was obvious that Mr. Horst was right about one thing. Even if the sheriff voted with Dr. Lee to let him stay a little longer, the two of them would be overruled by the five Norms on the council. *I don't want to leave,* he thought as he watched Mia sleeping. *Ceilings and all.*

But he hadn't left yet. He hunted around and found a blanket for Mia, but when he scooped up the gears piled on it, the sound woke her. She stretched and blinked. Her face was different without her glasses, her eyes even wider when she strained to see. She patted around on the floor. Ross picked up the glasses and put them in her hand.

She smiled at him as she settled them on her nose. "Patrol time?"

Ross explained about the Lockdown drill as Mia strapped her flamethrower across her back. He took the extra oil canisters and walked her to the school, where they found tired, sweaty students in leather armor.

"I wish I could go along, but I'm due at town hall. Enjoy the patrol," Felicité said sweetly, rising from her seat.

Jennie said, "Ross, there's extra gear in the bin."

He picked out a pair of well-honed and balanced throwing knives. It was good to have weapons again, even if they were only borrowed. The heavy, cumbersome armor was made from the hide of armored cattle. He turned away so no one would see him wrestling with the stiff straps and buckles.

At the door, Jennie separated two younger girls from the crowd. One looked like her, but had dense, close-cut black curls. The other had lighter skin and a mop of red-brown hair.

"No, Z," Jennie said. "Your thirteenth birthday isn't till next month."

"That's not fair!" yelped the redheaded girl. "One month!

You're letting your sister go, and she's only two months older than me, and I can shoot as well as her!"

Jennie's sister chimed in, "Please, Jennie. You know we're good shots."

"Dee, rules are rules." It was clear Jennie said that a lot. "The cutoff has to be somewhere. Z can come with you next month."

Z stomped back into the classroom, and Dee stomped outside. Jennie cast a rueful look at Ross. He thought she was doing a good job of being fair, though it was clear Dee didn't agree.

Armor buckled on, he went to help Mia with her flame-thrower, tucking an oil canister under his arm. "I didn't know Jennie had family in the school."

"She's got lots. Two younger brothers and a younger sister, and another sister too young for school."

"From the same mother?" Ross had never heard of someone having five children before. A woman was lucky to have three.

Mia nodded. "Amazing, isn't it? But the Rileys are different. They're almost all Changed. They never get big powerful Changes, but they always get useful ones, without any nasty side effects. Riley men father lots of healthy children, and the women in Mrs. Riley's family are all fertile and never die in childbirth."

Mia glanced down, and Ross remembered how her mother had died. He had the impulse to comfort her somehow, and reached out to touch her shoulder. Then she raised her chin, and he jerked his hand back.

"I'm not done with Jennie's family," she said, the cheer back in her voice. "She also has three foster sibs. And me."

"What? You two are related?"

Mia laughed. "Not by blood. Her father's ex-wife is my mother's sister. I guess you'd call us half-stepcousins."

"How can you keep track of all that?"

Mia looked surprised. "It's not hard remembering important stuff. What's more important than family?"

Everyone in Las Anclas was always talking about family—what their mother thought, what their grandfather always said, what they had to make sure their sister knew. The thought of a whole bunch of people knowing everything about him made Ross feel like he was in a tunnel with the walls closing in. But here, it seemed to make people feel cozy.

Experimentally, he thought to himself, *My grandmother used to say . . .*

It took a moment, but he found a memory. They had been sitting at a campfire, making tortillas. "Make the dough into a ball the size of a plum," she'd said.

He'd asked, "What's a plum?"

He hadn't noticed then, but now he thought that his question had made her sad. She'd reached out and closed his chubby kid fingers. "Make it into a ball the size of your fist."

He couldn't remember anything more.

"Ross?" Mia said. "The stables are—"

A gray rat the size of a terrier came scuttling up—a rat, in broad daylight! It was going straight for Mia.

"Rat!" Ross yelled, dropping the oil canister and grabbing his knife. Before he could make the throw, someone slammed into him, knocking them both to the ground. The knife skittered across the dirt.

"She's *my* rat," Yuki snapped, getting to his feet and dusting himself off. "What the hell is wrong with you?"

Ross rose on his elbows, blinking against dizziness. The rat was winding in and out of Mia's ankles, like a cat.

"Yuki? Ross? What happened?" Mia asked, stooping to pet it.

"Come." At Yuki's call, the rat turned with trained precision and ran to Yuki, who scooped it up and cradled it against his chest. Then he turned to Ross, making an effort to control his anger and explain. "We breed working rats here. This is Kogatana." He traced a symbol in the air, then stopped, as if he hadn't meant to do it. "She usually doesn't come with me to school, but we're going on patrol. She'll ride with me in case we need her to scout."

His face burning, Ross scooped up the canister and hastily followed Mia to the stables. So rats here were working animals, not vermin. Yet another thing Ross hadn't known—another way for him to make a fool of himself in front of everybody.

At the stables, he had yet another unpleasant surprise: horses. The ones in Las Anclas had been cross-bred with deer. They were small and slender, and half of them had antlers. The animals moved restlessly, unlike his burro Rusty. Ross hoped he was all right. Surely even Voske wouldn't harm a good working animal.

He lowered his voice. "I don't know if I can ride these."

"Sure you can," said Mia. "You've ridden *something*, right?"

"My burro, when I was a kid."

"Think of them as burros with antlers. Grip with your thighs. Walk the horse like it's your legs. When you want to go faster, move your hips like you're running, and the horse will run. Like the burro, right?" Ross nodded doubtfully. "Great!" Mia ran off toward Jennie.

Yuki stepped forward, still clutching his rat protectively. "You don't know how to ride?"

Ross's ears burned. "Of course I do."

The tall boy's eyebrows shot upward. Then, without a word, he shook his head and walked away.

Henry indicated a speckled gray horse. "How about Old Betsy? If you don't mind going slow. See how gray her coat's gone? She's getting up there."

"Slow is fine," said Ross, relieved. At least Old Betsy didn't have antlers to jab him.

He glanced around, hoping Mia or Jennie would come back. Yuki was staring at him. Ross watched some students load their weapons and mount up. He copied them. Mounting was harder than it looked.

Old Betsy sidled under him, muscles quivering. Ross grimaced. Rusty hadn't bounced around, and he'd been much lower to the ground. And it had been years since Ross had been small enough to ride him; he'd mostly used the burro to carry his packs.

The left rein kept sliding out of Ross's hand, so he was forced to use his right hand for both. The horse seemed to dislike that. She bobbed her head and shifted her rear end back and forth, like she wished she could shake him off.

"Everyone ready?" Jennie called. "Ride out!"

The horses headed for the main gate, except for Old Betsy. She whipped around, mane flying, and trotted determinedly toward a large saguaro. Ross clutched at the reins, then pulled, but she put her head down and sped up.

"Whoa! Stop!" Ross yelled.

Old Betsy stopped. But first she scraped Ross against the saguaro, and tumbled him to the ground with spines stuck all along his right side.

15

YUKI

FROM HIS PERCH ON HIS HORSE, YUKI WATCHED ROSS pick himself up. He was immediately swarmed by teenage girls, pulling out cactus spines and commiserating. He didn't look like he was enjoying the attention.

Yuki ticked off what he knew about Ross Juarez: He'd been dragged into town half-dead, which didn't speak highly of his survival skills. He'd warned Sheriff Crow of pursuit, which might mean he had some honor, or might just mean he had been sunstruck and delirious. He fought brilliantly, even with one hand. He knew nothing about horses and couldn't ride. It was like a handful of puzzle pieces that didn't fit together.

Jennie rode up to Yuki and Paco. "How did Ross get Reckless, Yuki? I thought you were going to give him a training horse."

"It was one of Henry's pranks."

Jennie frowned. "And you didn't stop him?"

"He was going to kill Kogatana."

Paco leaned out and petted the rat, who nibbled delicately at his fingers. "Wild rats will creep up while you're sleeping and rip your throat out. He didn't realize she was tame." Then he gave Yuki a look as if he could see right through him. "It isn't Ross's fault that he had chances you never got. Don't take it out on him."

Yuki felt exposed. "Jennie, are you letting him patrol? He doesn't know how to ride."

Jennie gave Ross a quick, searching glance, then faced Yuki. "Yes, I am. You've seen how he fights. He'll be fine as long as he isn't on Reckless. Switch horses. And you and Henry can both clean out the stables tonight."

Reluctantly, Yuki rode over to Ross. "Here, take Fuego. He won't give you any trouble." As he handed over the reins, the red-gold gelding gave what Yuki could swear was a disappointed look. "Sorry," he muttered to the horse.

Reckless had her ears laid back, clearly in a terrible temper, but he stroked her until she was calm enough to mount.

"You all right, Ross?" Jennie called.

"Isn't the first time a plant's gone after me." Ross jerked a last cactus spine from his shoulder, then awkwardly hauled himself into the saddle.

Jennie cupped her hands around her mouth. "Form up! By twos. Listen up! The watch captain has gotten reports that someone, or something, is raiding crops. It might not be as harmless as raccoons, so keep alert."

"A tomato eater," said Brisa to Becky, knotting up an unraveling blue ribbon. "That's terrifying."

Becky let out an unexpectedly loud giggle, then ducked her head.

The line rode out, Yuki taking up his usual position at the rear. Outside the walls, he could see clear to the horizon line, but that taste of freedom had a bitter tinge. He felt like a stallion penned up in a corral. A horse bred in captivity wouldn't mind the fence, but a wild horse, born in the desert, would never stop longing for its true home.

Still, he was only a few months away from graduation, when he'd become a legal adult. Then, he could leave, with or without a guide.

Yuki thought about how Paco had encouraged him to strike out on his own. Everyone said prospecting was far too dangerous without proper training, but someone must have been the first prospector. He'd already taught himself as much as he could in Las Anclas. Like a taunt, the ruins of an untouched city were barely a day's ride away from Las Anclas—but they were ringed by an impassable band of singing trees.

Ross was his age, and somehow he'd become a real prospector, making his way through dangerous wilderness and tunneling into ancient ruins. So why not Yuki?

Meredith, Brisa, and Becky dropped back to ride with him, peering at the fields to the south.

"Looks like we'll be picking corn soon," Brisa was saying to Meredith. "Boring! Unless we get attacked by bandits. That would be cool. It's been forever since we've been attacked by anything. Except boredom." She grinned at him. "Hey, Prince—oops. Yuki, aren't you bored?"

Yuki shrugged. "No more than usual."

Brisa laughed, and she and Becky trotted ahead. Brisa's clear voice carried back. "I owe you for stitching my hand. Shall I knit you a pair of socks? I have some nice orange and gray yarn, like a sunset."

He couldn't hear Becky's reply, just a pause and then Brisa saying with a giggle, "No, of course not! I'm just accident-prone. But seeing you is a bonus."

Meredith rode in closer. "You know Mr. Preston and Mayor Wolfe might get the council to kick Ross out, just to spite Sheriff Crow. If you want to find out what it's like where he came from, now might be the time to ask."

Yuki hesitated. He could ask, but how could he know whether Ross was telling the truth? His sister said coaxingly, as if she were offering him a gift, "If he came from the south, he could tell you about the Saigon Alliance. And if he came from the east, then maybe Voske's kingdom isn't as tough as everyone says."

"Maybe later." At the very least, he wouldn't approach

Ross in front of all the same people who had witnessed how Alvarez had tricked him.

Henry pulled out a slingshot. "Want me to get his attention? Bet I can make him fall off again."

Meredith rolled her eyes. "Idiot. Let me do this." She trotted up the line. Yuki heard her voice clearly in the still air. "Hey, Ross. You came from the south, didn't you?"

"East."

"What's it like?"

"Hot."

"Everywhere is hot. What else is it like? Any good prospecting?"

"No."

"What's Voske's territory like?" asked Meredith. "Is it true about the heads?"

Yuki barely heard Ross's "Yeah."

"Well, what's past his kingdom? Anything worth the risk of getting your head on a pole?"

That seemed to annoy Ross enough to provoke entire sentences. "What you have here in Las Anclas is as good as it gets. Who cares what it's like anywhere else?"

"That's strange coming from a prospector," Meredith retorted. "There's nothing to prospect here—at least, nothing you can get at."

She rode back, but didn't bother to lower her voice as she said to Brisa, "Okay, I'm officially uninterested. Ross is hot, but I've already got one sulky prospector at home." She shouted, "Hey, everyone—let's go to Luc's when we get back. Paco's drumming tonight."

"I'm in," Yolanda said, and others echoed her. The bristly-haired girl stretched out her hand, calling up a breeze to cool her sweaty face.

"Some for me, please?" asked Meredith. Yolanda obligingly sent the wind to ruffle her coppery curls.

Yuki shot a glance at Paco, and caught him grinning. Was he thinking about their date after the show?

"What's so funny?" Henry asked.

"Nothing," Yuki and Paco spoke simultaneously, and Paco laughed.

Dee Riley and Nhi Tran reined in and leaped off their horses. Squealing, they pointed at a ball of white fur with huge, wistful blue eyes. "What is that?" Dee cried. "It's so darling!"

"Watch this!" Henry hefted his slingshot and expertly let loose a pebble, which struck the furball straight on. It let out a pathetic squeak and leaped into the air.

Dee caught it and hugged it to her chest. She glared at Henry. "You hurt it!"

Nhi pouted. "It's only a helpless little . . ."

". . . what?" Dee studied the creature.

"It's a long-haired rat." Nhi flung back her dark braids in Henry's direction, then lifted one of the creature's paws. "Or something."

"It can be my pet." Dee clutched it tight. "Henry wounded it."

"I barely touched it," he protested.

Meredith reined in. "Put that thing down, whatever it is, and catch up."

The girls moved closer, squishing the furball. It squeaked in protest.

Yuki put on his glasses and examined the creature. It was not a rat of any kind—more like a furry slug with paws. Interesting.

Dee turned pathetic eyes on him. "Yuki, you understand. You like new creatures."

"Wild things should be left in the wild. No matter how cuddly it is now, it won't bond with you like a rat will."

Meredith nodded. "Once it matures, it'll forget all about you and run away. Put it down."

"N-o-o-o-o!" the girls shrieked.

Yuki peered along the line of horses, to Jennie at the lead. She obviously hadn't seen any of this, and neither had anyone but Meredith, Henry, and him. "Oh, put it in your pouch and come on," he said, pocketing his glasses. "Remember, you have to take unknown creatures to quarantine first if you want to bring them into town. And make sure it eats. If it doesn't, you'll have to let it go, or it'll die."

They trotted up the road. Yuki could understand the girls being intrigued, but rather than trying to figure out what the creature was and how it lived, they were more interested in giving it the most nauseatingly cute name possible.

"Fluffy?" Nhi cooed.

"Boring. Snowball!"

"Snowflake."

"No, even prettier. Cloud."

"Oh! Oh! Princess Cloud."

Princess Slug, thought Yuki.

The squash harvest had begun in the southern fields. Some workers were roasting one for lunch, sending the sweet, acrid smoke drifting on the western breeze. Yuki glanced through the haze at Paco, who had his reins in one hand, and was tapping out a rhythm on his saddle with the other. No matter how much he wanted to get out of town, when he thought of Paco, the idea of being alone out in the desert seemed lonely.

"What were you thinking?" Paco asked.

Yuki glanced around. Henry had ridden ahead to talk to Tommy and Carlos. This was as much privacy as he was likely to get. He lowered his voice. "Would you ever consider leaving Las Anclas?"

Paco raised a hand to shade his eyes. "Sure. Musicians are welcome wherever they go. If I had a band to travel with . . ."

"How about a prospector?" Yuki asked casually.

"Dig by day and play by night? Sounds good to me."

"Really?"

"Really." Paco's dark gaze was serious. "I'd want to come back here sometimes. But if you'd do that, I'll come with you. You're not the only one who'd like to see more of the world."

Yuki grinned, his future rearranging like a kaleidoscope. He'd be free and independent, but he'd have Paco, too. If they ran into trouble, they'd fight side by side. That should satisfy some of his mother's worries about him getting ambushed by bandits, or having no one to help him if he got sick or injured.

Paco added, "I've always wondered if my father was a traveling musician. Mom didn't really know him. They were both just teenagers. We might even catch up with him someday."

Yuki longed to drop his arm around Paco's shoulder, but five thirteen-year-olds were riding twenty paces away, and Henry could be more annoying than all of them. "Where is your mom? The Rangers are still gone, aren't they?"

Paco nodded, his grin flaring. "I have the house to myself all night."

The horses began to descend toward the canal. At the bridge, Fuego started dancing around, head tossing, ears flat. Yuki leaned forward to see Ross sitting rigid in the saddle, gripping the reins to his chest and dragging Fuego's head back. Mia tried to get Ross's attention, to no avail.

Yuki hated to think what damage he might be doing, and hurriedly crossed the bridge to rescue the gelding.

Mia's voice rose above the others, "What's wrong, Ross?"

Ross leaped off Fuego. Still holding the reins, he began running along the ridge that formed the eastern border of the fields. Yuki urged Reckless closer, leaned down, and yanked the reins from Ross's hands.

"What the hell?" Yuki demanded.

Jennie reined in beyond Ross and scanned the slope. "Get back!"

Below them, a blood-red column of branching crystal rose up from the bleak desert sands. It was a singing tree, closer to Las Anclas than any he'd ever seen. Though there was no wind, the leaves began to tremble, then to gently tap each other. They caught the sunlight and sent dancing glints to dazzle the eyes. A melodic chiming reverberated through the air.

Everyone scrambled back, even Yuki, though at the top of the ridge they were well out of range. Everyone, that was, except Ross. He stood as rigid as the tree, staring into nothingness, as if he was witnessing something horrifying that no one else could see. His thin face had blanched to a mottled gray.

"That's the tree Pa was talking about," said Dee. "It sprang up a few days ago."

Mia flung herself down and pulled the latest incarnation of her flamethrower from her saddle pack. "Let me run down there and blast it."

Ross spun around so fast he fell to one knee. Then he scrambled up to block her. "No!"

"No? Those things are killers. Hey. How did you know it was here?"

"I didn't. I—" He looked around, then seemed to see where he was for the first time. He backed up quickly, dragging Mia with him. "I—I've been here before."

She shoved her glasses back up her nose. "Oh. That's *your* tree."

"His tree?" Jennie echoed.

Mia patted Ross on one bony shoulder. He jumped like

she'd stuck him with a cactus spine. "Go on. Show her the scar."

Ross crossed his arms across his chest and shook his head.

He was making such a scene that Yuki wondered if he was doing it deliberately, to get attention or as part of some elaborate con, except that no one could make their face go that gray. But if singing trees scared him that much, why make a mad dash to get a good look at one?

"He got hit by a shard coming here. Cut it out of his arm with a knife." Mia drew her forefinger from her elbow to her wrist. "Down to the bone. That's why he can't use his left hand." Her voice rose with the thrill of discovery. "So the trees don't need to kill someone to grow! That one came from the shard Ross cut out of his arm. See? It's blood-red."

"Eeeew," Dee shrieked.

Henry eyed Ross. "With a knife?" He whistled. "Damn!"

"I don't want to talk about it." Ross got back on Fuego even more awkwardly than before. Mia tried to show him how to hold the reins. He could barely manage them; his hands shook. Fuego shied and balked skittishly. It made Yuki uneasy.

The patrol resumed, everyone chattering.

Paco rode up beside Yuki. "What do you make of that?"

"He's starting to remind me less of Alvarez and more of the prospector who thought blue paint made her invisible."

Paco shook his head. "It made me think of something I saw when I was a kid. I must have been seven or eight— way before you came here. King Voske sent a strike force of thirty soldiers to Las Anclas. Mom thought the plan was to sneak over the walls, assassinate the council, and take over. The Rangers spotted them twenty miles out of town. They got reinforcements from town, rode out, and fought them.

They killed some of them, and the rest retreated. Some of our people were killed, too."

Yuki had heard this story, but never from Paco. "Anyone you knew well?"

"Not really. But the Rangers all came back to our house afterward. Mom sent me to my room, but I peeked out. Uncle Omar was sitting at the kitchen table, not saying a word, looking a lot like Ross did just now. Something about it scared me, and I went back to bed."

It was hard to picture that haunted expression on the boisterous man whom the entire town had called "Uncle."

"So, you're saying there's nothing wrong with Ross?" Yuki asked doubtfully. "He's shaken up, not crazy?"

"I'm saying I wouldn't look for blue paint just yet." Paco idly tapped the saddle in an intricate rhythm, then lowered his voice even more. "I'll tell you this, though, Yuki. That was when I stopped wanting to be a Ranger when I grew up."

They had passed the mill and were headed for the back fields. In the distance, below the bluffs, lay the ruins of the great city, surrounded by a forest of singing trees. Most of the trees were gray or tawny, the colors of coyotes and jave-linas, but a few had brighter, man-made hues. Yuki spotted the sapphire tree, and couldn't hold back a shudder.

The sweet scent of the bean fields perfumed the air. Jennie set a faster pace as the afternoon shadows length-ened. Thanks to Ross, they'd have to hurry to make it back by sunset.

"Yuki," Dee said, riding up close, her little nose lifted smugly. "Princess Cloud ate a biscuit."

"That's nice."

His sarcasm didn't register. Triumphant, she and the furry slug returned to Nhi.

The patrol was rounding its northwest corner when

Kogatana squealed a warning. A rattle arose from the shrubs on the left.

"Rattlesnake!" Jennie yelled.

"Kill it?" Henry shouted hopefully.

"No. We don't know how big it is. Leave the road. We'll swing around these bushes. Go."

The line turned northward. Since that took them into the scrub beyond the tilled field, they were now out of Las Anclas's bounds, and the standing orders were to ready arms. Yuki unslung his crossbow and slapped an arrow into it. Gripping Reckless tightly between his knees, he began to crank the bow.

"Snake on the right!" Sujata shouted.

An enormous head reared up from behind a boulder. It was the biggest rattlesnake Yuki had ever seen—the length of a grown man. Maybe longer.

Reckless tried to rear, but Yuki settled his weight down to control him. Yolanda sent a gust of wind into the earth, directing a spray of gravel into the snake's eyes. It dropped down behind the boulder.

"There's another one!" A frightened-looking Becky pointed left, at an ominously rustling shrub. "It's huge!"

The snakes were blocking the most direct route back to Las Anclas.

"Ride out!" Jennie ordered. "Straight west!"

As she began to gallop, another giant snake rose up before her, fanged jaws gaping. Her horse reared, whinnying shrilly.

Yuki clapped the crossbow tight against his side, gathering the reins in his free hand. None of the snakes were in his range. "Meredith!"

"On it!" His sister shot three times in quick succession. The snake dropped with an arrow in its head and two in its body. "Ten points."

"Ten to you," called Brisa.

Despite the danger, Yuki almost laughed. "Are you girls still doing that?"

Jennie got control of her panicking mount and waved her arm. "North!"

"But that's away from town," Sujata protested. "We'll be nearing the bluffs, and we're losing the sun."

"We have to get around these—"

A boy screamed. Two snakes popped up on the left, one close enough for Yuki to see the diamond markings on its back. He leveled his crossbow.

The arrow whizzed past the snake as Reckless danced, head tossing. Yuki slapped in another arrow and cranked hard. *Sight and fire*—the bolt crunched through the snake's head.

"Cool!" Grabbing his slingshot, Henry loosed a rock at a snake slithering out from under another boulder.

Dee and Nhi began shrieking. Their horses whinnied in panic.

"Hold on," Yuki shouted. "Hold them."

He waited for Jennie's next order, but she had dismounted to grab one of the younger boys, who was off his horse and trying to run.

"If you run, you're dead!" Jennie shouted. "Get back on!"

Despite Jennie's orders, the younger kids were breaking the line in panic. The patrol had disintegrated into chaos. A row of hissing snakes rose up between them and the town. But none had struck, though they'd had many chances, as horses sidled restlessly, always retreating northward—

Northward, into the scrub. And all the snakes were on the south.

"Jennie!" Yuki shouted. "We're being herded!"

Her head lifted, then snapped northward. "Paco, scout!"

Paco rode away, circling through the scrubby bushes.

"The rest of you, in line!" Jennie pointed. "Meredith and José, ride the line as rovers. Brisa, give us some covering fire."

Brisa reached into the sack of fist-sized rocks by her saddle. She grabbed one, concentrated on it, and threw it at the nearest snake. Its tail lashed, knocking the rock aside. The rock hit the ground and exploded, and the snake slithered off.

"Oops." Brisa frowned. "Should've aimed at the head. Let me try again." This time she scored a direct hit. "Ten points! That makes eighty!"

Paco rode back, his tension evident only in the sharp-cut angles of his face. "I didn't see anything but grass. No sign of snakes."

The horses were as nervous as the patrollers as they began another wide circle to the north. Yuki's skin prickled with apprehension. He'd rather face the snakes than whatever unknown thing they were being herded toward.

"Jennie, can I try with Kogatana?" he asked. At her nod, he pointed northward.

"Kogatana, scout."

Kogatana ran, nose down. Yuki urged Reckless behind the racing rat, who was no more than a ripple in the tall grass. Then she rose on her haunches, squealing in warning. Yuki saw nothing but dirt and scrub, so he dismounted to investigate. Kogatana instantly darted up and pressed herself against his boots.

Yuki froze. The rats were trained to do that as a signal to their partners: *Take one more step and you're dead.*

He unsheathed his sword and prodded the ground in front of him. The point touched dry earth, then broke through into nothingness. Yuki twisted the sword, levering up a piece of earth woven through with grass and something that glistened like slug slime. His hand jerked involuntarily, jostling another fragment. The entire field crumbled before him.

Reckless scrambled back, nickering in fear. Yuki stared down into a huge funnel carved into the ground. At its bottom, the powdery earth stirred and he saw a glint of something sharp and white.

"Shit!" Adrenaline spiked. He jammed the sword into its sheath, grabbed the rat, leaped into the saddle, and galloped back, shouting, "Get back! Get back! It's a pit mouth!"

Several younger kids screamed in terror.

Gasping for breath, he added, "It's the biggest one I've ever seen. That thing could swallow all of us."

"Meredith!" Jennie shouted. "Take your bow team, and clear those snakes. Paco! Brisa! Yuki! Reinforce them."

Mia leaped off her horse and unstrapped her flame-thrower. Clutching the hose in both hands, she directed a blast of flame at the nearest snake. With a high-pitched hiss, it retreated into the tall grasses. "Fire in the grass. Help me stamp it out."

"José!" called Jennie.

He knelt down and placed both palms flat on the earth. A ripple of disturbed grass spread outward until it reached the flames. The fire sank into the earth and vanished.

José stood up and was almost trampled by Fuego. Ross struggled to control the horse, but Fuego was trying to get to the front, as he'd been trained to do. Ross dropped the reins and grabbed his sword. When Fuego began to charge, Ross lurched awkwardly. His left hand fumbled at the reins, and he dropped the sword in order to use his right.

Yuki wished he'd argued harder with Jennie over letting Ross come on patrol. He was endangering himself, Fuego, and everyone around him.

"Ross!" Yuki shouted. "Get out of the way! Go to the rear!"

This only confused Fuego, who danced sideways. Yuki

drove Reckless forward and slapped Fuego on the neck, commanding him to retreat.

The younger kids began shooting wildly, creating a whole new danger.

"Aim, *then* shoot!" Jennie shouted.

Meredith's sword whistled, and a snake head bounded away in the dirt. Grimly, she scanned for another, the counting game forgotten.

"There must be ten of them!" Paco scythed his sword at another. Despite his lack of enthusiasm for fighting, his technique was perfect. A scaly head thumped to the ground.

Yuki urged Reckless into the gap where José had been. A snake slithered down a juniper branch, dangling by its tail, so close that he could see a drop of venom glistening on one fang. He cocked his shoulder back and turned in the saddle. Reckless shifted to help him balance. Then he brought the sword around in a whistling arc. The snake dropped headless to the ground.

From behind came the whistle and crunch of another snake decapitation. Ross scrambled up from the dust, recovering from a backswing as the head bounced into the bushes.

José got to his feet beside Ross. That explained how he had managed to kill a snake—José had trapped it in the earth.

Jennie's horse shied as she bent over its withers. "We have two people down! Henry, Brisa, get Paco."

Paco! Jennie shouted more orders, but Yuki couldn't hear. He scanned frantically. Paco was rolling silently back and forth on the ground, hands clutched near an arrow in his knee. Yuki leaped down. "Paco." He caught Paco by the shoulders. "It's me."

Paco opened his eyes but didn't speak. Yuki could see he was clenching his jaw so he wouldn't scream. The arrow had sunk in behind his kneecap. It wasn't bleeding much, but the pain had to be terrible. Yuki picked him up, careful not to let the arrow touch anything.

Henry and Brisa helped him lift Paco onto her horse. Yuki knew he ought to get back to Reckless, but he didn't want to leave Paco.

Jennie clapped her hands. "Mount up! We need to get out of here."

Mia reached up to hook the flamethrower back in her saddle pack. A scaly tail swished out from the bushes, knocking her off her feet. The tip, as wide as a man's arm, wrapped around her ankle and jerked. Her body slid a few inches in the dust. The snake was trying to drag her away. As Yuki ran to help, Mia stopped trying to kick free and whipped her flamethrower's nozzle around. Her other hand scrabbled at the canister.

A jet of fire shot out, but the flames vanished into the air as the snake jerked her in another direction. Glasses askew, Mia flung herself onto its tail, angled the nozzle at the thick body, and ignited the flamethrower. The snake released her with a hiss and writhed away. She aimed a final blast, but the flamethrower stuttered and stopped, out of fuel.

Yuki turned around. Mia's horse had stampeded. Ross had managed to get back on Fuego. They halted next to her.

Ross fumbled with the reins and dropped his sword *again*. It lifted as if kicked by the earth, and Jennie caught it by the hilt. Ross extended his hand to Mia, though he was seated so precariously that she'd pull him down if she took it. Luckily, she had the sense to mount by herself.

Meredith's bow twanged as she shot at a pair of snakes. One thumped to the ground, twitching. The other vanished into the underbrush. "No more in sight. We can ride right through here."

"Do it," Jennie ordered.

Yuki took one last look at Paco, then hastily mounted. The line galloped behind Jennie. A couple of the small kids were whimpering, and one moaned in pain.

Yuki hadn't been this scared since he'd first come to Las Anclas. Being endangered by a creature that no one had ever seen, other than its mouth at the bottom of the pit, was more terrifying than any number of snakes.

The sun had sunk past the distant line of the sea when the patrol reached the western fields, where the exhausted horses forced them to slow. The smell of fertilizer from the giant compost worms drifted on the breeze. They could see the sentries now—which meant they could be seen. Yuki counted under his breath. Six seconds, and the bell began to clang the alert.

"Jennie, should I take Nhi ahead?" Dee called. "She broke her arm."

"Stay together. Once we get inside, take the wounded to the infirmary."

Yuki caught up with Paco and Brisa. Paco leaned against her, pale and sweating, but he didn't make a sound. He was more stoic with an arrow lodged behind his kneecap than that useless Ross had been just looking at something that scared him.

Yuki laid a gentle hand on Paco's shoulder. "I'll stay with you."

Paco shook his head, a tiny movement, but it made him wince. "Go check on the others," he muttered, then closed his eyes.

"I've got him, Yuki." Brisa sounded exhausted. Even her ribbons drooped.

He fell back. A few of the younger kids bragged to one another, their laughter loud and sharp with reaction nerves. "Did you see that big snake I killed?"

"All you did was scream until you scared off the snake."

"At least you didn't drop your sword," said Henry.

Tommy laughed. "Who dropped their sword?"

"Cactus boy here." Henry gestured at Ross.

"He killed a snake with one hand," Mia snapped. "How many did you get, Henry?"

Henry held up his hand, five fingers splayed. Then he turned earnestly to Ross. "But really, I have to thank you, Ross."

"What for?" he asked suspiciously.

Henry made sure he had an audience before he went on. "If you hadn't fallen off your horse, landed on a cactus, and lost your mind on the bridge, we wouldn't have been out so late, and I wouldn't have had the chance to rack up a snake count. They only come out at dusk, you know."

Ross's face darkened. Mia, who was usually so shy, was the one who spoke. "You put him on Reckless on purpose, didn't you?"

Henry gave a blithe shrug. "Testing his riding skills, to see if he was fit to patrol. He failed."

Henry might be a jackass, but he had a point. If Yuki hadn't been distracted trying to get Ross out of everyone's way, maybe he would have spotted whoever had been shooting wildly before they hit Paco. Now Paco was looking at months of painful rehab—and if the tendons behind his knee had been severed, he might have a permanent disability. Would he still be able or willing to venture into the desert then? Yuki saw the dream they'd had started to build together dissipating like smoke.

Fuego whinnied sharply. Ross was holding the reins so tightly that the gelding was forced to bend his neck at an awkward angle or hurt his sensitive mouth.

Yuki shouted. "Ross! Let go of the reins! You're hurting him!" Ross did, but Yuki was still angry. "You should have told us you can't ride. Putting your pride ahead of everyone else's safety isn't courage, it's selfishness."

Jennie reined in beside him. "If you don't like the way he rides, do something about it. I want him using a sword on horseback by the end of next month. Teach him."

Ross's look of alarm was a perfect mirror of Yuki's dismay.

Hooves thundered through the gate. Riding in perfect formation, Defense Chief Preston, Sheriff Crow, and Yuki's mother led a heavily armed team toward the patrol.

The council meeting to determine Ross's fate must have already happened. Yuki couldn't help hoping he'd never have to teach that lesson. Regardless, he had more important things to deal with. He rode to check on Paco.

16

Ross

MIA'S WARM BODY TENSED BEHIND ROSS. "UH-OH." HER breath tickled his ear.

Defense Chief Preston's voice carried to the back of the group. "You're late. What happened?"

Jennie rode forward. "We were attacked by at least ten large rattlesnakes beyond the creek along the back fields. They herded us north. Yuki and Kogatana scouted and reported a giant pit mouth. We engaged the snakes and rode home. There were half a dozen injuries, three serious, and Midnight ran off."

The riders in Mr. Preston's group began talking.

The defense chief raised his hand for silence. "At dawn tomorrow, we'll locate and destroy the pit mouth. Mia, prepare the explosives. Yuki, you'll lead us to it. Jennie, you'll accompany us. Everyone else, the debriefing's tomorrow afternoon. Dismissed."

"They'll blame Jennie," Mia whispered, as they rode to the gate.

"She did fine," Ross protested. "No one got killed. Except snakes."

Some of the others glared at him. They'd all heard what Henry and Yuki had said. The worst part was, they were probably right.

Sheriff Crow and Ms. Lowenstein edged their horses up beside Jennie's.

"Come to my office, Jennie," the sheriff said. "Soon as you can."

At the stables, Ross was relieved to finally dismount. His entire body ached, especially his useless left arm. Mia spotted him wrestling with the saddle buckles and came over to help, which only made him feel more incompetent. He could barely bring himself to return the weapons he'd checked out, and after he had, he felt completely unprotected.

As soon as they walked into Mia's cottage, she dropped her flamethrower with a clatter, picked up a box that was connected to the wall with black cord, and pushed a button. A lamp hanging from the ceiling lit up. Ross was too tired and angry to be impressed.

She sat down, looking as exhausted as he felt, and leaned against the bed. He sat beside her; the floor pressed painfully against his bones.

"I realized something," Mia began. Ross stood. She blinked up at him, then went on. "When Yuki told you Kogatana's name, he drew letters in the air. He used to do that more when we were younger, when he was still learning Spanish and English. I recognized what he drew. Your book's in Japanese."

"So?"

"So, there's other people in town whose ancestors came from Japan, but that was in ancient times. They don't speak the language anymore." She paused. "Yuki is the only one in Las Anclas who can read your book."

Every muscle in Ross's body tensed at the thought of letting yet another person see it—and Yuki, too. During the ambush, he fought with sword and bow as easily and gracefully as if he and his horse were a single creature. Ross had been useless, and that made his shame burn even hotter.

"Don't tell him about it!" The words came out louder than he'd intended.

"Okay!" Mia gave him a wary look. "You don't have to shout."

He took a deep breath. None of this was her fault. "Sorry. I just don't want anyone else to know about it."

Mia pushed her glasses absently up her nose. "Even Jennie?"

"Could she read it?"

"No, but she'd love to see it. And she'd keep it secret."

Ross was ready to grab his book and run, assuming that the council hadn't already voted to kick him out. "Where is it?"

She tapped one of the stacked boxes. "Safe and sound. Let's go eat."

Ross's gloom lifted a little when they reached the kitchen, which was warm and smelled like spices.

Dr. Lee had already set the table. "I need to finish up with the wounded kids. Dig in. I'll join you as soon as I'm done."

At her first mouthful, Mia closed her eyes in ecstasy. "Noodles with black bean sauce. Lee family secret." She noticed another dish. "Oh! My favorite—fish dumplings!" And then another. "Normal kimchi instead of some weird experiment." She bit into a pickled radish with a loud crunch. "Dee-licious." Her voice was muffled. "Can't get food like this in the desert, can you?"

Dr. Lee returned before Ross had even finished a plate of noodles. He pulled up a chair. "Paco told me what happened."

Mia hastily swallowed. "How is he?"

"The arrow missed the tendons, so there shouldn't be any permanent damage. Once I gave him some painkillers, he made quite a passionate case for me to heal him, what with the possibility of a dance coming up and the band playing. I'm not convinced that one night of fun is worth months of his life." He glanced at Mia. "I gather the fight was chaotic."

"It was the most scared I've ever been. By far. Rattlesnakes! A pit mouth! Kids shooting every which way!" She stabbed at a dumpling with her fork, then shot a glance at Ross. "What did the council say?"

Dr. Lee rubbed his chin.

"Did they argue? Spit it out, Dad."

"It was a four to three vote, but the sheriff and I managed

to persuade the judges that the town can always use another productive citizen. Ross, you've been accepted on probation. After a time yet to be determined, you can become a full citizen. But for now, you can stay as long as you like."

Mia jumped up from her chair. "That's fantastic!"

"Wait, what?" Ross asked. "I thought you were arguing over whether or not I could stay for the next few days."

"No, no! I thought you knew! I thought you wanted to stay for good! Don't you?" When he didn't reply, she said coaxingly, "This is great. Better than you hoped for, right? Don't worry about the probation. I'm sure they'll vote you in as a full citizen. You were a big help in the fight."

"No, I wasn't." The rush of blood started at his face, then spread until his whole body was uncomfortably hot. Sweat prickled at his temples. "I fell off my horse. I dropped my sword. Twice. That was the worst I've ever done in a fight."

"See, that's why you should stay!" Mia grabbed him by the shoulders.

Ross was so startled that he almost knocked her away. He slid his chair back until she was forced to let go, but she kept on talking. "If that was really your worst ever—well, it was still better than a lot of us did. Anyway, I'm sure you fight much better on foot. That's what you're used to, right?"

Her voice was making his ears ring. And she was so close. She could easily put a knife through his heart at that distance. He was trapped with too many people in a hot, enclosed space whose heavy adobe walls and ceiling could collapse and bury him at any moment.

Ross got up and started backing toward the door.

Dr. Lee held up his hand. "Mia, why don't you give him—"

Mia darted to the door and stood with her back to it. "Ross, you can't leave. You can't use one hand. You won't make it."

"I can't make it *here!*" Ross knew he was shouting, but he couldn't seem to stop. "I can't deal with all these people. I can't fight. I can't sleep. Every time I lie down I feel like the ceiling's falling on me. I keep dreaming of that singing tree—and that tree! It's *here!* I can't live here with that thing right outside the walls!"

Dr. Lee stepped between Ross and Mia. "It's a beautiful night. Why don't we talk outside? We'll go to our vegetable garden. I need to pull some weeds."

He passed Ross's full plate to Mia and took the other two himself. Gently moving his daughter aside, Dr. Lee left the house.

Ross hurried after him. Once he was out under the night sky, he felt a little less trapped.

Mia grabbed a lamp. It swung in her free hand as they walked past a golden-lit longhouse. He heard bits of conversations from open doorways, and smelled hot chili and frying tortillas. He breathed in slowly, trying to calm down. Dr. Lee was no threat, and Mia was a friend.

As he passed a pocket garden jeweled with tomatoes and strawberries, he spotted a vague green shape, more like the idea of a plant than the thing itself. Once he gave the blob his full attention, the illusion faded, replaced by a cottontail rabbit gobbling down feathery green shoots. Ross had always wondered if rabbit illusions worked better on other animals than they did on people, or if coyotes found them just as unconvincing. Two little girls dashed out of the house, waving their hands and shouting. A bush beside the rabbit wavered and disappeared, and two rabbits stamped and bolted.

Families and friends. Ross sighed.

"That one rabbit was pretty good," Mia remarked. "Its bush had leaves and everything." She was keeping her distance, and Ross could hear how hard she was trying to be casual.

He wished he hadn't yelled at her. She hadn't done anything to him. What had made him feel like she was a threat? Why hadn't he been able to stop himself?

They stopped at a fenced plot in a patchwork of gardens. Here and there a few people worked by lamplight. Ross could hear voices, but no words.

"This one is ours." Mia hung the lamp on a pole, then reached down to disengage the heat-sensitive bean tendrils that had wound around the bare skin of her ankle.

Dr. Lee set the plates on a bench and squatted by a row of green shoots. "You two finish your dinner. I'll weed these turnips."

Ross sat down. Mia joined him and began eating, her elbow digging absently into his side. His heart pounded like someone had drawn a gun on him. He tipped his head back. No ceiling. Stars, sky, the same sky he saw when he slept out in the open.

Mia jerked her arm away and hunched over her plate, her hair swinging forward to hide her face. Ross's panic cooled to regret.

He liked the Lees. They were good people. What was wrong with him? Why was he trying his best to make them hate him?

Dr. Lee pulled up a weed. "Mia, you'll be happy to hear that I'm thinking of devoting these turnips to regular kimchi."

She laughed. "You won't mash them up with goat cheese, pickle them, and then fry them? Good choice, Dad!"

He said to Ross, "My daughter is the tragic victim of my cooking and gardening experiments. I get bored doing the same thing the same way. I like to try new things. Not just with food—I grow medicinal herbs here too. Of course, I'm much more careful with those experiments."

He kept weeding. Ross felt like Dr. Lee was waiting for him to talk, so he took a bite of dumpling. Its initial wash of heat was followed by a tangy aftertaste.

"I've been a doctor here for a long time," Dr. Lee continued. "It was the obvious job because of my Change. I apprenticed when I was much younger than Becky. I've patched up a lot of people after fights. Sometimes the battle isn't over after the wound heals."

He worked his way to the end of the row. Ross reached for another dumpling, and discovered that he'd eaten them all.

Mia nibbled on a piece of kimchi. His muscles slowly began unknotting. He wondered what would happen if she moved closer, or if he did: if it would feel better, or if he'd want to run.

Dr. Lee paused in his work, kneeling in the dirt before them. "When a wound heals, you still have a scar. When something happens to you, you still have a memory. After something very painful happens, it's normal to have feelings that are strange to you—that feel like healing wounds. You were almost killed when you were hit by that shard. That sort of thing has an effect."

Ross wondered if anyone else had ever had a nightmare come true. One moment he'd been riding along, and the next he was standing on the hill, staring at the singing tree that had haunted his dreams, with no idea how he'd gotten there.

He set aside his plate, though he had some noodles left. His appetite was gone. "Do you mean other people have nightmares while they're awake?"

"Yes." Dr. Lee's tone reminded Ross of Jennie's, when a student solved a difficult problem. "That's exactly what I'm talking about."

"When I went up that ridge, I didn't even know what I was doing," Ross confessed.

"You tried to save my life," said Mia. "I was so excited about trying out my flamethrower, maybe I would have gone too close."

At the time, it hadn't even occurred to him that she might be putting herself in danger. He'd stopped her because . . . Why had he stopped her? Well, he'd been confused. Maybe he had been worried, but didn't remember it. Or maybe he'd wanted to destroy the tree himself.

"But these things heal," she said softly. "Like your arm. It takes time. You can stay here with us. We won't let anything happen to you."

"She's right." Dr. Lee began on another row. "Also, you're not trapped here, even if you do decide to become a citizen. This isn't like Voske's kingdom, where no one leaves without his permission."

Mia picked up the plates. "I'd better get my explosives ready. Then maybe I'll play my flute. Ross, you're always welcome to come in. But knock first. Or maybe kick." She started to reach out, then dropped her hand, gave a sad flicker of a smile, and walked away.

Ross helped Dr. Lee collect the dishes. "I didn't know Mia played an instrument."

"She doesn't play like most people do, to entertain friends. You could call it her own form of meditation. I don't think most of the town even knows."

Ross had seen that expression, simultaneously inquisitive and perceptive, when the doctor had examined his arm and again just now, when he'd spoken about memories like scars. It was as if Dr. Lee knew something about Ross that he himself didn't.

So Mia had told Ross a secret. Why? He'd endangered the patrol, and then he'd yelled at her for no reason. He wanted to listen to her music that no one else got to hear, but it scared him to think that she trusted him that much.

He made himself help Dr. Lee clean the kitchen, then went to his bedroom. He tried pulling back the curtains, but it still felt like one of the spaces he'd prospected: a dangerous place to work in, with one eye on the exit.

He was grateful for the comfortable and clean bed, but he always woke with a pressure on his chest like the ceiling had already caved in, his mind crowded with frightening images: the glowing shard, the ruby tree, his own blood pooling on the ground. Once he'd liked scarlet. He'd even searched for it in ruins, as unfaded colors brought good prices. But he was beginning to hate bright red.

He hurried outside. Dr. Lee's house faced the town square. Ross breathed more easily in that open area. He dodged around the pocket gardens, looking up at the stars, and passed the dark town hall.

The night air carried the tart and spicy scent of apples and pastry from Jack's saloon, which had one window lit, in the back. Without meaning to, Ross drifted closer and closer.

"Ross?" He started. It was Jack Lowell, the saloon owner. "Will you work for crumble?" The man came outside, two lanterns in hand, and gave him a friendly smile. "Hot weather like this, everyone seems to want my cold brews. Mia hasn't finished fixing the wiring for our cold storage in the town hall basement, and I could use a third hand to hold a lantern."

Ross held up his right hand. "I've got one right here. Especially for crumble."

Jack laughed, and led him into the hall. The interior was so huge that he didn't feel too trapped.

"How big is this place?" he asked.

The golden light of Jack's lanterns reached the far walls, thick adobe framed around pine logs. "We can fit the entire town, if need be, and defend from the roof. But don't worry. We've seen attacks over the years, but no one's ever gotten inside."

The thought of being trapped inside this building, surrounded, made even the huge room seem confined and threatening. Ross's shoulders tightened.

"Basement's this way." Jack handed him a lantern, then unlocked the iron-reinforced door.

"What needs locking up?"

Jack smiled. "I don't want anyone siphoning off my beer." He led Ross down a ramp to a cool basement with barrels stacked against a wall. "Hold the lantern close, please. These labels are hard to read."

The barrel sloshed as Jack began rolling it up the ramp. Ross looked around as he waited for the saloon-keeper to return. Adobe buildings tended to collapse into a solid mass when they fell. But this basement, with its strong reinforced timber, reminded him of the few he had been able to prospect in. He imagined what it would be like if the rest of the building collapsed. The barrels would be smashed, but there would still be a little pocket where the structure was strongest....

He headed for the one place that would stay intact even if the roof fell in, which was piled with bunting, painted columns, and other festival decorations. In the center of the ornaments and barrels was a broken wagon draped in moth-eaten fabric. Something like that was always repaired or broken up for spare parts, but instead it just sat there, covered with dust.

It didn't belong—it didn't fit.

That was the signal of a potential prospecting find.

He heard Jack's quick footsteps and backed away from the wagon, bending to inspect the barrels, each labeled in chalk with a date.

"Two more should do it," Jack called.

Ross waited until Jack had vanished up the ramp again. Then he hurried to the wagon, lifted the fabric, and held up the lantern.

A trapdoor! It was painted to blend in with the floor, but you could see it if you were looking for it. Ross set the lantern down. Wedging his fingers into the crack, he pried the door open, then used his shoulder to lift it all the way up.

Holding it open against his back, he picked up the lantern. Rough steps led down to darkness. Another basement? The walls and floor were plaster and brick, smelling like dust and old moss. Cold air whispered along Ross's cheek: not a hole, but a tunnel.

He hastily closed the trapdoor. When Jack returned, they left with the last barrel. Ross wondered if he knew about the tunnel, but didn't ask. He'd learned that people didn't like stray prospectors discovering their secrets.

Jack took him into the back room of the saloon. "Help yourself, Ross."

A plate of crumble was already dished up and garnished with a chunk of cinnamon stick. Ross reached for it.

"That's for someone else," Jack said quickly, then smiled. "Here, I'll give you a bigger one."

Being full made Ross sleepy at last. Under the gleaming stars, he made his way to Mia's house. The open windows were as bright as always. Ross could hear clinking and sifting, and smelled the rotten-egg stink of sulfur. He knew exactly what she was making, and thought of knocking—or kicking—at the door and asking if he could help. Maybe he'd ask her about the tunnel, too.

But he was so tired, and there was a cozy space out of view of the main square, between an aluminum barrel and a pile of scrap metal. He lay down. His aches eased away with the firm support of solid earth, and the sight of nothing but stars overhead.

A flight of green bright-moths swooped toward the windows, attracted by the light. He watched them dancing in looping circles as the sound of a flute reached him, so soft that he almost thought he was already dreaming. He had never heard music like it before, sometimes eerie, sometimes plaintive. Like the stars, the bright-moths, and the earth beneath his body, it calmed him, and he slid into sleep.

And dreamed of the blood-red tree.

17

Jennie

"MORNING, JEN. BREAKFAST?" JENNIE'S FATHER greeted her.

"No thanks, Pa. I'm not hungry."

"Hurting?" he asked in sympathy.

Jennie sighed. "You've been there."

Her pa tucked his dreadlocks behind his ears and handed her a warm corn muffin. "I have. Eat. We've got to deal with this pit mouth first, and you don't want to pass out halfway through the debriefing."

She almost laughed. "I think I'd enjoy it more if I was unconscious."

He sat down at the table across from her. "It's always hard after a major action. That time Voske's gang tried to conquer the town, when you were a baby? The debriefing took days. The same when Gabrielle Bell lost the election, and families who'd been here for generations packed up and left. Everyone blamed everyone else. Remember, they're all scared. Running into a pit mouth, especially one teamed up with snakes, would have shaken anyone." He pushed a dish of peach preserves at her. "Eat."

Jennie crumbled an edge of the muffin. "They'll kick me out of the Rangers and the schoolhouse. I can see the headline now: 'Rattlesnake Fiasco Forces Dishonorable Discharge.'"

"'Tenacious Teacher Brings Endangered Patrol Safely Home.' They'll rake you over the coals, but they won't demote you."

"Sure about that?"

Her father smiled ruefully. Jennie knew she hadn't been the only one unable to sleep. She'd heard her parents talking all night. "Where's Ma?"

"She'll meet us at the stable."

Jennie had wrapped up the muffin and some bacon before she registered the "us." At least she wouldn't be facing down a pit mouth and Defense Chief Preston alone. "Let me get my weapons."

Blue-green light flared under a door; Tonio was playing with his luminescence—or practicing, she hoped. As she passed Dee's room, she heard through the closed door, "Oh, aren't you pretty, Princess Cloud! Hold still, I have to comb your be-yooo-tiful fur."

At least Dee had recovered from her tantrum the night before. Jennie was glad Dee could distract herself with Princess Cloud, who had to be the fluffy white kitten from Tansy's latest litter. That made four cats, six kittens, three dogs, nine ferrets, and a wounded hawk. If Dee decided not to apprentice with their mother, she should consider the veterinarian, Ms. Segura.

Jennie went into her own room and sat on the bed she hadn't been able to sleep in. Her weapons flew into her hands. She only wished that she had problems that could be vanquished in a good fight.

At the stables, her pa rapped three times on a support post, making the wood vibrate. Her ma glanced up and greeted them. "Saved a nice horse for you, Jennie." She indicated Sidewinder, a buckskin gelding with a magnificent rack of antlers.

Jennie stroked his velvety nose, then turned so her mother could read her lips. "Thanks, Ma."

Her pa had already mounted Spot, a huge pinto mare. He settled his sword across his back and slung his fighting staff into its holder. Her ma handed up his rifle. He checked the chambers and pocketed his ammunition. By then the rest of the patrol had gathered, and Mia's barrels of explosives had been packed into a cart.

Mia patted the nearest ox's armor plating. "I saw Ms. Lowenstein and the sheriff close in on you last night. How did that go?"

"Rotten," Jennie began, then stopped. A step, a rustle of silk, and the aroma of rose water. She turned reluctantly, knowing who was there.

Felicité was immaculate in eggshell blue, from her ribboned sun hat to her fingerless gloves and walking shoes. Jennie couldn't help remembering Indra's description of her splattered in pomegranate juice, nor could she help wishing that she'd seen it.

Usually she felt guilty for thinking mean, small thoughts about Felicité, but the girl had called Ross a mutant. She'd sounded sincere when she'd apologized before the entire schoolhouse, but Jennie suspected that Felicité had rehearsed it all, down to the regretful tilt of her head. *Every time she tells me how pretty I look*, Jennie thought, *she has to be thinking "for a mutant."* It was like they were all acting in a play, with Felicité Wolfe in the leading role. And she was the only one who knew her lines.

On the other hand, they still had to live with each other.

"Hi, Felicité." Jennie forced herself to smile.

"Jennie, a delegation of kids came to me before breakfast. Your sister Dee was one of the ringleaders."

"I didn't know that," Jennie admitted, intrigued.

"It was a conspiracy among the thirteen-year-olds," Felicité said. "They've asked me to speak for them before the council. I agreed, but I wanted to hear your thoughts first."

Jennie tried to be fair. Felicité was not making the disaster her own issue—she was listening to all the sides, just as Jennie herself would have done.

"My parents told me what happened yesterday. Would you

recommend keeping the patrol age at thirteen, or raising it back to eighteen, as my parents want?" Felicité asked.

"Since everyone sixteen and up did well, I'd make the age sixteen," Jennie said slowly. "Meredith Lowenstein might have taken the blame for Paco being shot—she did the most shooting—but I'm certain she placed every arrow where she wanted it to go."

"Thank you, Jennie. As it happens, that's what the sheriff said too, after speaking to Yuki and Paco. I'll carry your words to the council."

As Felicité left, Jennie faced Mia. "Those thirteen-year-olds went berserk. Chely got a saguaro spine in the eye! It was such a disaster, I wonder if some of them will still be useless when they reach sixteen. But if I get kicked out, I won't have to worry about that, will I?"

Mia polished her glasses on her shirt. "I bet Mr. Preston will find some way to blame everything on the Changed kids."

Jennie didn't want to think about that possibility, let alone talk about it. "Hey, how's Ross doing? He must be so relieved to have gotten probation."

To her surprise, Mia shook her head. "Not really. He thought the vote was for him staying a couple of days. I don't think he even considered living here permanently. He doesn't like buildings any more than he likes crowds. I ran into him in my yard this morning, and he jumped like I was attacking him. I have no idea what he was doing there. He sure didn't want to get near me."

"Maybe he was shook up over the fight," Jennie suggested. "Give him time. He'll come closer."

Mia's eyes were huge behind her glasses. "I'm not trying to get him to come closer! Anyway, he runs away any time I touch—I mean, get near him. But that's fine. He can keep his distance."

As Mia continued to babble about exactly how much she didn't want to get near Ross, Jennie thought, *She really likes him.*

What kind of "like"? Jennie scratched Sidewinder's withers

as she tried to define her own "like." Whenever she and Ross sparred together, she felt a connection—more than a connection, an attraction. Though they were fighting, they were also completely in tune, aware of each other's bodies and movements to an intense degree. And though he was painfully embarrassed about his lack of education, he asked intelligent questions. He made her heart beat faster, and he made her think. It was an irresistible combination.

When she'd started dating Indra, they'd agreed that they were free to date others. But neither of them had. And until a few days ago, they hadn't had "the talk" about where the relationship was going. They'd never needed to; it just *was*. Until now.

Jennie shouldn't even think about another guy until she figured out what was happening with Indra. And she certainly shouldn't if Ross was someone Mia might be interested in too.

"Is Ross planning to leave, then?" Jennie was relieved at how casual her voice sounded.

Mia shrugged unhappily. "I don't know. If Dad hadn't talked him out of it, I think he would have taken his stuff and gone. He was really upset."

"Over Henry's stupid prank?"

"More about that singing tree we found."

"Think he'd feel better if we burned it for him?" Jennie suggested.

"We can't. I used the flamethrower on a snake, remember? The range was only twelve feet. The hottest point is halfway along the flame—"

"You were calculating the range in the middle of a fight?" Only Mia! Even now, with everything going wrong, being with her made Jennie . . . not exactly happy, but happier. "Hey, I'm taking the Terrible Three for a beach picnic next Saturday. How about you come too, and bring Ross? He said he wanted to see the ocean."

Mia's beaming smile was answer enough, and Jennie smiled

back. A pang of guilt accompanied the thought, *It's been too long.*

"Mount up," her pa called.

Jennie mounted Sidewinder, and Mia hopped into the cart with her explosives. Yuki was waiting outside, between Sheriff Crow and Mr. Preston. Kogatana perched on the back of his saddle, cleaning her whiskers. The rat was the only member of the party who seemed pleased to be there.

The riders reached their destination first. While they waited for the cart, Mr. Preston examined the hoofprints, scuffed footprints, and winding tracks. Jennie heard someone counting up the dead snakes. That made her feel slightly better—until Mr. Preston called her over.

He pointed to a stab mark in the dirt. "There's no snake track here, so no one killed a snake. But someone dropped their weapon point-down."

"Ross Juarez," she admitted. "He's never fought on horseback before, and he can't use his left hand."

The defense chief stared at her incredulously. "And you let him ride with you?"

Jennie felt like a fool. "He's a match for me when he's on foot," she protested. "He killed at least one snake."

"One." Mr. Preston raised his bushy eyebrows. "I hear he panicked over that singing tree."

"He didn't panic." If Ross wasn't getting snubbed for being a stranger and poor and illiterate and maybe Changed, he was getting accused of being a coward. Jennie couldn't help leaping to his defense. "He almost got killed by one of those things. Of course seeing it upset him. A bit."

"Sounded like more than a bit, the way I heard it. Sounded like he might be unstable. Might even be dangerous."

Jennie folded her arms and kept quiet. Defending Ross was obviously only making things worse.

Disapproval radiated off Mr. Preston as he followed a trail of footsteps to a scuffed area. "What happened here?"

The trampled earth didn't reveal anything special. "I don't know," she was forced to admit. "I don't remember this spot."

He knelt carefully, placing one knee into one scuff mark, the other knee in the one beside it, and finally putting the heel of his hand into a gouge in the earth. "Looks like someone fell down." He flicked a finger at a patch of brown-stained grass. "And bled. I'm guessing Paco was here. You didn't see it?"

"I was too busy killing snakes." *And trying to keep the kids from killing one another.*

Sheriff Crow called to them, "We're up to fourteen."

Mr. Preston got to his feet and dusted his knees. "Fourteen snakes, one lost horse, and several wounded kids. And we haven't found this supposed pit mouth."

Supposed. Mr. Preston wasn't ranting about Changed people; he was disappointed. In her. For the first time ever—and only days after she'd been inducted into the Rangers. Jennie's stomach churned.

He shaded his eyes, observing the cloud of dust of the approaching oxcart. "Let's spread in a line. Mia! Stay behind me. Team Leader Riley, take the right wing. Sheriff Crow, please take the left. Yuki, show me this pit mouth."

Jennie fell in behind Yuki, sick with humiliation and anger. It was obvious what had happened once Mr. Preston had interpreted the marks. She'd studied tracking for years, but she'd never before had to read the scene after a fight, with the man standing in judgment over her.

She wished Sera were leading the expedition instead. Sera never made her feel intimidated, but the Rangers hadn't yet returned from investigating a possible bandit sighting. They were off being heroes, while Jennie had stayed behind to lose control of a bunch of little kids and get Sera's son shot by friendly fire.

Yuki peered at the grass. "There's no tracks. But I know I rode out from here. There's that big juniper that the snake dropped out of."

The moment was vivid in Jennie's memory: the snake, the screams of the little kids, the juniper with a black streak from a lightning strike. "Yeah, this is the place."

Yuki scooped up Kogatana. "Mr. Preston, can I go on foot with Kogatana? Maybe the tracks are too faint for me to find."

"Hoofprints are too faint to find?" Mr. Preston asked.

"Can *you* find them?" Sheriff Crow retorted.

The defense chief waved at Yuki. "Go ahead. Send the rat."

Yuki set Kogatana down. "Track me." Kogatana set out northward, sniffing constantly. Then she stopped and let out a loud squeak. "It's here," Yuki said.

Mr. Preston ran up, almost bent double. "But there's no prints."

"It's right here. Watch this." Yuki jabbed the trackless ground with the tip of his sword.

The earth crumbled into emptiness. Then cracks spread out, not only before him, but beside him.

Jennie watched in horror as Yuki scrambled backward. His feet broke through into empty space as a gust of rot spread through the air. Yuki threw himself full-length on the ground, and clutched at earth that fell away under his hands.

Mr. Preston lunged out, grabbed Yuki by the collar, and yanked him onto solid ground.

"Kogatana!" Yuki yelled.

"She's right here," Jennie called.

Mr. Preston shook his head, his expression solemn. "I have never seen one that big. And snakes herding you kids to be devoured."

He shook his head again as Mia stepped up, rubbing her hands. "It's my turn now."

Jennie's headache had reached thunderstorm proportions by the time she reported to the town hall. She fought it with relaxation breathing during the debriefing and the resulting vote, but her head still throbbed when she and Felicité were released to return to the schoolhouse.

As they walked through the plaza, sounds jabbed at Jennie like cactus spines, unnaturally loud: Felicité's mincing steps, the rustle of her skirts. Even the smell of her expensive lemon verbena soap was nauseating.

Jennie took a deep breath. Everything had turned out fine. Both the defense chief and the mayor had been unstinting in their praise of her handling of the disaster in light of what they'd discovered. As the mayor put it, "for keeping a cool head under extraordinary circumstances." To which the defense chief had added, "This is exactly what I expect of a future leader."

Felicité had smiled as she noted it for the record, but Jennie wondered if that was yet another part of her act. Who was the real Felicité Wolfe—the considerate girl who did everyone favors, or the mean-spirited bigot who had called Ross a mutant? Jennie wished she'd been there, if only to hear what Felicité's voice was like when she wasn't . . . performing.

"Do you want to announce the result, as representative of the kids' delegation, or shall I?" Jennie asked.

"I think as teacher, it is your place," Felicité said.

Which was only fair.

Jennie winced as a splash of sunlight reflected off sheet metal in Mia's yard. Maybe she was holding an unfair grudge about the "mutant" remark. It wasn't as if Jennie had never said something in anger and regretted it later.

Then Jennie remembered Felicité's quinceañera. She'd stood in the decorated town square, accepting her presents and greeting everyone in her sparkling dress and tiara. Alfonso Medina had brought her a rarity, a huge conch shell that he must have dived deep to find. Felicité had smiled her perfect smile and thanked him prettily, but she had indicated a table for him to set it on, rather than touching his gecko fingers. And when she'd gone home, the shell had remained. Nothing had ever been said, but Jennie had not forgotten the hurt in Alfonso's eyes.

On the other hand, that had been two years ago. People changed.

The trouble was, you never knew what Felicité really felt. At school, she ended up reading history when she ought to be tackling physics, explaining, "Mother says I need to know history for my job." On hot mornings, rather than training, she'd organize the little kids, whom, Jennie had to admit, Felicité managed better than Laura. But she never actually said, "I hate studying physics and getting sweaty, so I won't do it."

With the people Jennie liked best, what you saw was what you got: Mia, Sera, Indra, and her parents. But Henry was like that too, unable to take anything seriously, and so was Tommy Horst, dropping his father's opinions like an anvil on your head. Neither of them hid their true feelings, but sometimes she wished they would.

Ross, now . . . Jennie couldn't figure out where to place him. He seemed straightforward by nature, and yet so much about him was a mystery. Where had he come from? Why had he been attacked? She'd seen his scars when they'd been sparring, and they weren't all recent. Were they from accidents or tangles with wildlife, or were some from battle? Had he ever had to kill another human being?

She didn't even know if he was a Norm or Changed, and that was no accident: she'd heard the kids trying to figure that out, via subtle and less-than-subtle questions, and he'd resolutely refused to say.

Not that Jennie blamed him. She liked to think of herself as honest and up-front, but she knew she hid many of her feelings. Maybe her real problem was that she and Felicité were too much alike. There was an unpleasant thought.

She wondered what Felicité thinking now, while she waved

at Mr. Nazarian propelling his wheelchair with his strong arms, on his way to mend fishnets.

Felicité seemed to feel her gaze, and smiled brightly. "I'm having a party tomorrow night to choose the music for the dance. Since my mother's the guest of honor, the band's going to play songs popular when she was our age. I want to make sure they're still danceable. Everyone gets a vote. I've already invited Sujata and Indra, and if you come, maybe he will too. I know he likes to dance. Please come."

This was the first time Felicité had invited Jennie to one of her exclusive Hill parties. *She's certainly not thinking mean thoughts about* me, Jennie thought, and said, "We'll be there, thank you."

At the schoolhouse, they found Ms. Lowenstein supervising a reenactment of the snake battle. Older teens were the snakes, armed with sponges dipped in beet juice, while the thirteen- to fifteen-year-olds defended themselves. Jennie didn't know whether to be pleased or depressed that the defenders were doing better under the chief archer's cat-eyed gaze than in the actual battle.

Ms. Lowenstein clapped her hands to end the drill, and pointed out the students who were splashed with dark red. "You're dead... you're dead ... you might live for two days in the infirmary. You lost that arm. Ms. Riley? They're all yours."

"Inside." Jennie's throat was dry.

Ms. Lowenstein thumped Jennie on the shoulder. "Remember. Hindsight is always a hundred percent after a battle. In the heat? Any of us could have done what you did. If you want to talk about it some more, why don't you join us for Shabbat dinner this Friday?"

Inside, the students sat quietly for once. Each would tell his or her parents what Jennie said. She had to choose her words carefully. "Okay, here's what we did right. We killed fourteen huge rattlesnakes, even though we never trained to fight more than one snake at a time. We located and evaded the largest pit mouth anyone has ever seen—even Mr. Preston. And nobody was killed."

She stopped when a few began to whisper. The voices instantly ceased.

"Here's what we did wrong. Nearly everyone under sixteen forgot their training and panicked. Some tried to run. Three were wounded, one by someone's arrow, and three lost control of their horses."

The younger teens began protesting. Jennie lifted her voice. "I know that some of you sent a delegation to Felicité Wolfe, and she spoke to the council on your behalf. But they've decided that from now on, patrol age is sixteen and up."

The protest was louder this time.

"Other people panicked, but I was okay!"

"That's not fair!"

She slammed a slate on her desk. It sounded like a rifle shot; Ross wasn't the only person who jumped.

"Quiet." She lowered her voice. "Things change. When our parents were young, patrolling age was eighteen. Train hard, and they might change their minds. But if you act like little kids, they might go to twenty."

"Then *you* won't go." Tommy's whisper was calculated to reach Jennie.

She turned, ready to annihilate him. But every other face was somber. Dee whispered, "Thanks for trying, Felicité."

Jennie forced her shoulders to relax. "Now, let's break into study groups, and review—"

The bell began to clang: two short tangs and a long one.

Stranger at the gate.

18

Felicité

FELICITÉ SWEPT HER SKIRTS TOGETHER. SHE loathed wall duty, but she loved to watch her father in command, and it was important to observe how he did it.

Jennie Riley still frowned, even though she'd been completely exonerated. What more could she want? She said in her teacher voice—which Felicité had to admit was quite authoritative—"Those on wall duty for 'Stranger,' go."

People grabbed their weapons, and Felicité got her bow. Henry paused in the doorway. "Let's run! Mr. Preston will be timing us."

The students tore after him, Felicité following more sedately. When they reached the wall, sure enough, her daddy clicked his beautiful old stopwatch. But he didn't praise their speed.

The sheriff stood beside him, hands on her pistol grips. The Rangers were back from their mission, lined up and ready; Jennie wasn't even out of breath as she raced to join them on the ammo platform.

Felicité's attention shifted from Jennie to Indra. The sun gave his hair a blue sheen and glinted off the machete at his belt. She wished she could enjoy the sight, but she recalled the painful visit to the Vardams' to apologize.

At least Indra had been pleasant and friendly when he forgave her. She'd been relieved that she hadn't burned any bridges. But unfortunately he'd had to rush off to Ranger training, leaving her alone with his Changed father and the rest of his family.

Sujata had been equally pleasant, though quiet. The elder Vardams had been gracious but stiff, offering her manzanita cider and a warm chapati spread with the latest jam from their orchards. Each bit of polite talk she scraped out to fill the awkward silences was a reminder of what happened when one lost control. Felicité was certain that she would never again enjoy pomegranate jelly.

I'm so glad I thought of asking Jennie to my party, she thought now. Indra had changed his mind about coming, as she'd hoped, once he found out Jennie was invited. Felicité could work on recovering lost ground.

On the wall, Indra and Jennie stood shoulder to shoulder, both alert and full of authority of which they weren't even aware. Their attention was solely on the stranger striding through the shimmering heat waves and dust.

Popular teacher—skilled patrol leader—Ranger. Jennie could do no wrong. Though the Rileys didn't live on the Hill, they were respected by Norms and Changed alike. *Sooner or later, she's sure to end up on the council,* Felicité thought.

And where would that end? Indra and Jennie stood there like the town leaders of the future. Felicité's heart twisted.

The sentries readied their weapons. The approaching stranger was a tall man in a long black duster, a rifle slung across his back. He carried a staff. His broad-brimmed hat hid most of his face, until he paused about twenty paces from the gates. Then he lifted his head, squinting against the sun.

He was about her father's age, tough and weather-beaten. He laid down the staff, then stood, holding out his empty hands. The sleeves of his coat slid back, and Felicité saw the edge of a bandage on his right arm.

His gaze flicked from her father to Sera Diaz. Finally

he examined Sheriff Crow's hideous skull face. Then he addressed Daddy; he knew who the real leader was.

"Your town has something I want."

An hour later, Felicité dipped the steel nib of her pen into the inkwell. Her mother gave a nod of approval before scrutinizing the bounty hunter. Since the stranger had refused to give his name, Felicité was abbreviating him as "B. H."

"Yes, I shot that boy," the man said. "Winged him as a warning. He jumped a claim and I'm bringing him back for the bounty."

"A claim jumper?" The sheriff's snake eye narrowed. "That's a serious accusation." No wonder Ross Juarez was so twitchy. "Whose claim did he jump? And who are you bringing him back to?"

"A private individual." The man's voice was deep as a gravel pit. He leaned toward the sheriff as he spoke, as if the mutated side of her face didn't repulse him at all.

The normal side of Sheriff Crow's mouth pulled down in annoyance. "I'm finding it very difficult to take anything on faith from a man with no name."

"I'm also a private individual," said the bounty hunter. "That boy is dangerous, Sheriff. Better let me take him off your hands."

"Which brings us to the real question," said Felicité's mother. "Do we surrender Ross Juarez or do we not?"

"Not. At least until the council reconvenes." The sheriff shot a look at the man, her hair swinging back from her skull. "You stay away from him until then. You can sleep outside the walls with your weapons, or inside without them." She held out her hands.

The bounty hunter's eyes flicked from her hands to her face and back to her hands, as seconds ticked by.

Sheriff Crow didn't move.

The man reached over his shoulder and pulled his sectional staff from its harness. In a surprisingly formal gesture, he held it out with both hands. With the same formality, she accepted the staff, and then his rifle and his pouches of bullets and gunpowder.

Felicité saw her mother's eyes narrow. The sheriff and the bounty hunter seemed to have made a wordless truce without consulting her. "As Mayor of Las Anclas, I accept you as a guest of the town," she said graciously.

The sheriff added, with no grace at all, "You can get a room from Jack Lowell at the saloon."

"My husband wished me to invite you to stay at our house," Felicité's mother cut in. "I believe you will find it more comfortable and far less noisy."

"Thank you," the bounty hunter said.

Felicité tried to see her home as a stranger would. The bounty hunter showed no signs of appreciating the roses that lined the walkway, but he did pause in the foyer to look around the parlor—from the Mexican piano handed down through generations of Wolfes to the Chinese screen, also handed down for generations, and upward to the French crystal chandelier, whose tapers were lit only on holidays.

"I'd better dust off my coat, Mayor Wolfe," he said finally.

Felicité's mother gave him her most gracious smile. "You may remove your boots here. If you would like to avail yourself of a hot bath, we have the means. We will dine when you are ready."

Wu Zetian scampered up to greet Felicité. Seeing the stranger's curious gaze, she explained, "We've had trained rats in Las Anclas for forty years, ever since Tatyana Koslova came here with four breeding pairs. They're mostly reserved for official use, running messages and scouting and so forth. But a boy who wants to be a prospector has one, and I do too, as council scribe."

The bounty hunter let Wu Zetian sniff his boots but did not pet her. "You tie messages to their collars, like carrier pigeons?"

"Yes, exactly. They're even trained to deliver them to specific people or places."

"Very clever."

Unnerved by his shrewd gaze, Felicité wished she hadn't gone on about Wu Zetian. But everything she said was public knowledge.

"I'll take that bath now," he said. "Thank you, Mayor Wolfe. Felicité."

When he was gone, and they heard water gushing into the heating cistern, her mother said, "Felicité, tell the cook to have dinner at eight. You and I can take your father's to him on the wall."

The door banged open, and in pounded Felicité's little brother Will—with his shoes on. "Mother! Rico said you've got that bounty hunter here!"

"Will, please remove your shoes," Felicité asked as pleasantly as possible.

He jerked up one shoulder. "I'm going right out again."

"William," their mother said, "you must demonstrate better manners than these. If you want to meet our guest—"

Will flung his shoes into the cubby. "Is he gonna arrest Ross Juarez? Did Ross shoot somebody? Is he gonna shoot someone here?"

"William, dear—"

"Ross is cool! He killed a snake one-handed!"

Their mother patted his cheek. "Take our guest's boots to Clara to clean and polish."

He scampered off. Felicité and her mother collected a packed dinner from the cook, then headed for her father's command post.

A couple of passersby asked, "What's going on?" and one, "Is the council meeting again?"

Her mother answered them all without stopping, and no one dared hinder her. Felicité memorized her tone and gestures. She needed to learn how to express authority just as naturally. *Jennie Riley will not take my place*, she thought.

At the wall, Daddy grinned in welcome, looking like a grown-up version of Will. "My two favorite ladies in the world!"

As she unpacked the basket, her mother recounted the interview.

"So is the boy Changed?" her father asked, his heavy brows furrowing. "I knew we shouldn't have had a council vote before that was determined."

"The man was careful not to say," Felicité's mother replied. "I invited him to stay with us, as you requested. The sheriff did not like that. But she conceded."

"She'd figure I'll keep a personal eye on him. And she'd be right."

"I trust he will open up more to you. He told us very little, not even his name. What is it?"

He smiled. "Ah, Valeria. Can't tell you everything. A man's got to have a few secrets."

Felicité couldn't resist. "You don't know, do you, Daddy?"

"You got me." He laughed. "I never learned much about him. He's a very dangerous man. We've always had agreeable interactions—he keeps his word—but I confess I'll be relieved when he takes that boy and leaves."

Felicité nodded, thinking, *I can train Wu Zetian on his boots. He won't go anywhere in this town without my knowledge.*

Her mother shook her head. "Only if the man is legally entitled to him. If not, keeping the boy might not be such a bad alternative. He is a strong young man, and you know how much we need healthy young folk."

Her father retorted, "If they're healthy and *normal*."

It always upset Felicité when he got that tone in his voice.

"Thomas," her mother murmured.

He glumly eyed an open container. "Dearest Valeria, I hate sardines. You know that."

Felicité averted her gaze from the silver-scaled fish, their bulging eyes and their hideous, gaping gill slits. "I agree, Daddy. Mother, can't we have them banned from the kitchen?"

"Felicité, you used to love pan-fried sardines," her mother said with gentle reproof.

"When I was twelve. Whole fish are revolting."

"They're good for you, my dears. Plenty of calcium."

As they returned home, Felicité wondered if Ross really was a claim jumper. She recognized she wanted him to be one, only because life would be simpler if he was gone. Every time she saw him, she remembered her humiliating loss of control and the shock in everyone's faces.

Maybe if Ross chose to leave on his own? There were a lot of people in town who—quite rightly—loathed the idea of claim jumpers. She smiled. Sometimes the best way to make people believe an accusation was to insist that it couldn't possibly be true.

Most important of all, she had to make certain that Felicité Wolfe would be the female half of the most powerful couple in Las Anclas's future.

19

Mia

"TEN!"

Mia made sure everyone was crouched down and out of range of the shock wave.

"Nine . . . eight . . . seven . . ."

She gripped the plunger, smiling to herself. Two explosions in three days—first the pit mouth, and now blowing up ancient sewers for scrap metal. She hoped something interesting would turn up so Ross would want to stay.

"Six . . . five . . . four . . . three . . . two . . . *one!*"

Mia shoved the handle down. She felt more than heard a dull thump. Then the blast kicked up a satisfying cloud of dust and debris. The shockwave rocked her back on her heels and filmed her glasses with powdery earth. In the distance, it rained metal.

Mayor Wolfe rose gracefully. "An excellent detonation, Mia. The raw materials will be much appreciated."

People moved into the hanging cloud of dust to collect the scrap metal and cement.

Julio Wolfe gave her a high-five as he went by. "Not bad for the youngest mechanic in history."

By the time Mia got back to town, it was late afternoon. She ran down her list of outstanding jobs. She didn't look forward to a hot, boring walk to the broken spigot at the farthest end of the cornfields. Why not get in some shooting practice instead? It was the one kind of drill she enjoyed.

She found nearly the entire teenage population of Las

Anclas at the range, instead of at their apprenticeships. Then she remembered: the monthly archery tournament was approaching. They'd practice all week and make up their work time later. But the only people actually training were Yuki and Meredith, and Ross, all alone on the other side, struggling with a crossbow, his profile frustrated and angry. Everyone else stood around in a clump, talking.

Becky was saying to Felicité, "I'm honored, of course, but a presentation with everyone watching? To the mayor? I couldn't! Ask Brisa. Nothing scares her."

Brisa grinned. "What if I did it with you?"

Felicité adjusted her hat. "Certainly. I'll order another bouquet. I want this to be special, since it's my first community celebration."

"Oh, I'd love to do it. Come on, Beck, if we're together it'll be fun."

Becky eyed Brisa as if it was the least fun thing she'd ever heard of, then reluctantly said, "Okay. But only if you're with me."

"Nothing easier, since we're going together!" Brisa gave Becky's shoulder a squeeze. Becky smiled doubtfully.

"Thank you both," Felicité said pleasantly. "Jennie, since I'm never any good at the tournaments, do you mind if I get on with my chores? What with our guest, the investigation, the preparations for my celebration . . ."

Investigation?

"Of course, Felicité." Jennie's manner was tense. Something was up.

Becky said, sounding troubled, "Oh, I hope it's not true about Ross."

"What about Ross?" asked Mia, glancing across the range, where he let fly an arrow that missed the target entirely, then wrung his left hand.

"That stranger says Ross is a claim jumper," Sujata

explained. "Felicité doesn't believe it, but her parents want an investigation."

Henry laughed. "I hope he is! That would be cool."

Will Preston shoved forward, glowering. "Claim jumpers are not cool."

"Who says he's telling the truth?" José demanded. "That guy looks more like a claim jumper than Ross."

"My dad says there's something suspicious about Ross," Tommy Horst added.

Meredith stalked up, bow in hand. "Who cares what your dad says?"

Sujata said earnestly, "Why would a bounty hunter be chasing Ross? They're paid to catch criminals."

"He might be after Ross's finds," Mia said.

That caught Henry's attention. "I thought he showed up with nothing but his own blood, and the clothes on his back."

She quickly backtracked. "Nothing special! He had some stuff in his pack. Earrings and stainless-steel forks and tinfoil. Stuff like that."

"A bounty hunter chasing a guy down the Centinela Arroyo after tinfoil?" Henry retorted incredulously. "Not a chance. Ross has to be some kind of outlaw, or there's no reason for that guy to be here. I think that's cool. I mean, it's interesting."

"Pa Riley says bounty hunters are nothing but thieves themselves," said José. "They steal people. And sell them."

Henry smirked at Yuki, who was still determinedly practicing. "Looks like Ross is another Alvarez. Did you sign up to travel with him, too, Prince Yuki?"

With an icy edge in his voice, Yuki said, "Drop it, Henry."

He snapped a salute. "Yes, Your Highness."

Sujata nudged Mia. "If you knew anything, you'd tell us, right? Just because he's your boyfriend—"

"Boyfriend?" Henry clapped his hands to his forehead and staggered. "Mia has a boyfriend?"

The thirteen-year-olds instantly began a chorus of kissy noises and moans of "Mia's in *lo-o-o-ove!*"

Henry laughed. "I thought the only hot dates you ever had were with your crescent wrench!"

Thud! Ross's knife slammed into the bull's-eye. He threw another. *Thud!* Another bull's-eye. Henry was nowhere near, but he took a step back.

Mia's entire body prickled. "He's not my boyfriend!" She'd spoken loudly enough for Ross to hear. "And he's not a claim jumper!"

The boys laughed. She backed away hastily.

Sujata pursued her. "Hey, Mia, I didn't mean anything by it. I only—hey! We all know what the first time's like. Come back, it's okay!"

"I have work!" Mia fled.

That's what she got for avoiding that stupid spigot! She fetched her bag of tools and took the long way to the cornfields, hoping she'd feel better by the time she got there. She didn't. She sat down, the corn stalks towering over her head, and dried her eyes on her shirt.

"In love." Trust those obnoxious boys to make it sound like something to be ashamed of. What did "in love" even mean? Love songs talked about worlds turning upside down, and feeling faint, and being so overcome with fire and passion and stuff that you couldn't even speak.

She'd never been overcome with fire and passion, which had always made her feel like something was wrong with her. If anything, Ross was easier to talk to than the guys she'd known all her life. When he smiled at her, she didn't feel like fainting or bursting into flames. She felt like smiling back. Was that love? Or friendship?

The difference between love and friendship, Mia supposed, was sex. Or, at least, wanting to have sex. Did she want to have sex with Ross?

She tried to imagine Ross naked. Or should she imagine herself naked? Herself and Ross, naked together . . .

Her face heated up, but with embarrassment, not fiery passion. More proof that she was a freak.

She squatted down beside the broken spigot, hoping it would be hard to fix. A complicated problem was exactly what she needed right now.

Before she'd even finished taking it apart, she heard men's voices. *Who'd be way out here so late in the afternoon?* she wondered. The field workers had all gone.

". . . I like a nice quiet walk."

She didn't recognize the man's voice.

Then Mr. Preston spoke. "No one is out here this time of day."

Oh, great.

Mia was unsure whether to call out, or to stay still and hope they didn't see her.

The man went on, "I have to say, I never thought to find the wild and dangerous Tom Preston married and settled down." It was the stranger, the bounty hunter.

Mr. Preston laughed. "If you'd met Valeria first, you'd probably be here too."

"She would have to be some woman to get me to settle down."

"She is that. And our kids are the other thing that makes it all worthwhile. My boy is still young, but he's shaping up. Felicité is the image of her mother: a perfect lady, smart, with a will of steel."

"I did get a glimpse of them. A mighty fine family, Tom, I must say. Mighty fine."

Mia rolled her eyes as she unscrewed a bolt. Maybe she

should make some noise, so she wouldn't have to hear any more of this stupid conversation.

"So," Mr. Preston said, "you still working for Voske?"

Mia froze.

"This time, yes."

"Does it bother you?" Mr. Preston asked. "It bothered me a lot."

"And that's why you're here with your fine family now, protecting this fine town."

The two men kept moving. Leaving her tools, Mia followed, staying one row of corn over, out of sight. She couldn't believe that Preston knew that the bounty hunter was working for Voske—and didn't seem to care!

"It needs a lot of protection," Mr. Preston continued. "Bandits, coyote packs, animals mutating all the time, singing trees growing closer every year. Half the traders who come through are either Changed or turn out to be scouts for bandits. When you leave this town, with or without the Juarez boy, will you feel obligated to tell Voske where you found him?"

"No. I get paid for delivery. Not for information. But I'll give you some for free, on account of our old friendship. Six months ago Voske took over Gabrielle Bell's town and put her head on a pike."

"Well, you won't see me shedding any tears," Mr. Preston said. "Though it means he's still expanding west."

"That he is," agreed the bounty hunter.

There was a silence. Then Mr. Preston spoke. "So—for old times' sake—tell me why we should surrender Ross Juarez to you? I remember how Voske got some of his claims. How do I know he didn't jump the boy's?"

The bounty hunter chuckled. "I suspect you'd be just as happy to see Voske lose, but here's what's important. That Ross Juarez is Changed."

No way, Mia thought. *Ross would have told me.*

"That's what I keep asking!" Mr. Preston exclaimed. "I'm the only one who seems to care."

Wouldn't he?

"The Changed here sure won't care. That sheriff of yours scares me. By the way, Voske said the last he'd heard, you were sheriff. What happened?"

Mr. Preston gave a sigh. "Four months ago Elizabeth Crow was one of Rivkah Lowenstein's archers. She was engaged to our saloon keeper. When she got pregnant, she Changed. Lost the baby. Left the infirmary. Walked up to me and challenged me to a duel. Unlike previous challengers—and I've had my share—she won. Nothing more to say." He paused. "Tell me about Ross Juarez."

"He has a very interesting, oh, *talent,* I guess you'd call it. He makes people like him. Maybe you've noticed that already."

"That's it?" Mr. Preston asked.

Mia thought, *He sure knows how to work Mr. Preston.*

"Like him, trust him, do whatever he says," the man went on. "Gabrielle Bell didn't succeed in taking over your town, but this boy might. Turn him over to me, and then he'll be my problem."

"Won't you start liking him?"

"I don't like anybody," the bounty hunter said menacingly. Then he laughed. "It takes a while to work. If you haven't had a lot of direct contact with him, he probably hasn't gotten to you yet. And once he's in my custody, he won't be doing any talking."

Their talk faded as they headed for the gate. The sun was nearly down. Mia ran to retrieve her tools.

The bounty hunter was lying. Wasn't he? There were plenty of people who didn't seem to like Ross—but they hadn't spent much time with him. Mia had. She'd been teased about having crushes before, but it had only been embarrassing, or made her wish she did have a crush. Why was it different with Ross? Did it mean her feelings weren't her own?

When she'd thought he'd leave and get himself killed in the desert, she'd been frantic. Why had she cared that much about a relative stranger? But she would feel that way about anyone in the same situation. Wouldn't she?

This was horrible; not only couldn't she trust Ross, she couldn't trust her own mind.

She had to talk to Jennie.

The bell tolled for the closing of the gates for the night. Mia threw her bag over her shoulder and ran.

She slipped inside the gate behind a few people with baskets of radishes, bolted into her yard—and collided with Ross.

20

Ross

ROSS RUBBED HIS BRUISED NOSE. MIA'S GLASSES HAD hit him so hard he was surprised they hadn't broken.

She stared at him as if he were a rattlesnake, then continued backing up until she tripped over an engine. It was so weird that he felt he had to explain his presence. "Your father sent me to find you. Kimchi fried noodles!"

Mia didn't look as excited as that deserved. "I was ... working." Without looking behind her, she stepped over the engine and hurried to her front door.

Ross followed. "Do you need some help with something?"

"No. No." She shook her head a little too fast. "I'm good. I'm good. So ..."

Why was she acting like he'd attacked her? "I'm sorry I bumped into you."

"Did I hurt you?" She started to touch his face, then abruptly pulled away and backed inside, where she began picking up and setting down tools at random.

Ross edged in, still rubbing his nose. "Are you okay?"

"Sure! Yes." Mia glanced down at the hammer in her hand, then carefully laid it on her pillow. "So ... I guess you've had an easy time making friends. Around here."

She sounded as fake as a trader who was trying to fob off pyrite as a gold nugget. "What?"

"Well, people always like you. Right?"

"What people? The guy who shot me?"

Mia gave him a sideways look. "Well . . . that was from a distance."

"What difference does that make?" Ross asked. "And who are all these people who like me? Henry, who wants me to be a claim jumper because he's bored? Mr. Horst? The bounty hunter I warned you about, who's been welcomed into town anyway?"

She seemed to think about that, then let her breath out in a whoosh. "Good point. Sit down. We need to talk." She kicked the door shut, dropped her tool kit on the bed, then reached for the cooler she kept under her work table. "Want a glass of hibiscus tea? Dad made it."

Ross ignored the offer. "What's going on? What's this stuff about people liking me?"

Mia finally met his eyes. "Okay, seriously. Are you Changed?"

He'd thought she was the one person who didn't care. "Does it matter? Your father's Changed."

"I didn't mean it that way! I heard the bounty hunter talking to Mr. Preston. He said you're Changed. He said you make people like you, and I . . ." She fumbled the cooler open and pulled out a stoneware jug. "Are you sure you don't want any? Here." She poured hibiscus tea into a cup and an ancient glass jar. "See? I wouldn't share a drink with someone I didn't like. I mean, regular liking. Not creepy mind-control liking." Her hand shook as she held it out. "Right?"

Ross took the jar. He knew he ought to be angry, but instead he wanted to laugh. She'd always been honest with him, as far as he knew, and it seemed wrong to shut her down.

"I'm not Changed." Once those words were out, it was easier to keep going. "But I don't know how to prove that I don't have creepy mind-control powers. Does it feel like I do?"

When he leaned toward her, she flinched away, almost dropping her cup. Then she leaned in, and peered earnestly over her glasses. Her eyes were wide and brown, and so close he could see himself reflected in them. His palms tingled with the urge to caress her face.

He put down the jar and rubbed his hands on his jeans. If anyone had mind-control powers, it was Mia. When he was close to her, he wanted to touch her so much that he almost had to sit on his hands to stop himself. But then she'd touch him, and he couldn't help flinching.

"I guess not?" she said at last.

"My parents were Changed." Ross didn't know how to tell this story. He'd never told anyone. But then, he'd never had anyone to tell. "We lived in a town a lot like this, far as I can remember. Then..."

The memories came in fragments. His mother waking him up, whispering, "Don't make a sound." Ash falling like rain as houses burned around them. His father pushing him into his grandmother's arms. Blood on stone...

"I don't know what happened. Exactly. But the Changed all had to run. My family split up." His hands began to tremble, and then his whole body. It was hard to get the words out. "Because of me. I was only four, and I was slowing them down. My grandmother took me. My father went with my mother. She was pregnant. They got killed after we separated. We should've stayed together. If I'd been older, we would have."

"I'm sorry." Mia leaned close, absolutely still. "Ross, I am so sorry."

He couldn't bear to look at that steady gaze. He ran his finger around the rim of the glass jar. "I hate the thought of Norms being nice to me for being one of them when my parents died for being Changed. I'd rather not say what I am."

Mia picked up a screwdriver and poked at her nails. "There's a Changed town called Catalina, on an island across the bay. About fifteen years ago, a woman from there named Gabrielle Bell came to Las Anclas. Lots of people liked her, and she could mold metal with her hands—so useful! I wish I could do that."

Ross wouldn't have thought he'd be able to laugh so soon, but Mia's enthusiasm got a chuckle out of him. "Yeah, that's a great power."

"Then she ran for mayor, and said she'd only put Changed people in the government. She was going to ban Norms from the council, even though this town is two-thirds Norm. She said the world was evolving superior humans, and the Changed needed to lead the way to a better world."

"I've heard that kind of talk before," he muttered. "Though not as much as I've heard 'monster' and 'mutant.' Can't say that I like it any better."

Mia nodded. "Me neither. Anyway, Mayor Wolfe ran for office for the first time, saying that she'd treat all people equally—but she was married to Mr. Preston, so not everyone believed her. Dad says it got really ugly, on both sides. You can see who won the election. Gabrielle Bell left, and a handful of Changed went with her. Some of the other Changed were so disgusted with her *and* the Norms that they moved to Catalina."

It was a sad story, but all Ross could think was, *At least no one hunted down the Changed people who'd tried to leave. Like my family.* He cleared his throat. "And now no new Changed are welcome, huh?"

"Not by Mr. Preston." Mia looked uncomfortable. "When I was about ten, we had a terrible drought. But Catalina got hit worse. A boatful of Changed people came to Las Anclas and asked for help. Some of them used to live here. They went to the Rileys' house first—Jennie and I were having a sleepover that night. Mr. Preston showed up with the Rangers and told them get back in their boats. He said they'd made their bed and they could lie in it. Mrs. Riley was crying. It was awful. And no one from Catalina has come here since. They used to visit a couple times a year and put on plays and concerts. We all looked forward to it so much. Now we'll never see them again."

Mia fiddled with the screwdriver. Ross suspected that the real question was coming. Her expression was half worried, half hopeful. "How about the rest of the stuff that man said? He said you jumped a claim. Was that another lie?"

"Yes." That was easier to talk about. He took a sip of tart hibiscus tea. A few shreds of the flowers floated in the purple liquid. "Well, in a way. Voske's guys jumped *my* claim, so I jumped it back. All I managed to grab was the book, but it was probably the most valuable thing there. I guess Voske thinks so too."

"So the bounty hunter's really after the book, not you?"

"He's after both. Voske wants to prove that nobody crosses him and gets away with it. Voske's lieutenant told me that anyone who steals from him gets his head cut off and stuck on a pole. He wasn't kidding. I saw them on the city gates."

Mia grimaced. "I think we'd better talk to my father. Is that okay?"

He fingered the jar. Weird, how ready he was to say yes. It *was* as if Mia was mind-controlling him. He tried to think of reasons to say no, but all he could come up with was habit. "Okay," he finally said.

As they crossed the road, an object came whistling through the air. Ross tackled Mia to the ground, shielding her body with his own. He grabbed for his knives, and found only empty belt loops. But he could throw back the knife that had been thrown at him . . .

A small rock rolled along the road. It wouldn't have done more than bruise him.

"Ross?" Mia squeaked.

He scrambled off her. "Sorry. Someone threw a rock at me." She stared at him. Feeling like a fool, he muttered, "I thought it was a knife."

Mia glanced around wildly, though whoever had thrown the rock had to be long gone by now. "Was it the bounty hunter?"

Though his heart was still pounding wildly, he almost laughed. "No. Some of the boys have been doing stuff like that. Throwing rocks when I collect the oil. Giving me practice crossbows with damaged strings so they snap in my face—"

"Who?" she demanded, outraged.

Ross shrugged. "I don't know all their names yet." It was mostly true, and he didn't want her trying to fight his battles. That Tommy Horst was twice her size. One-on-one, Ross could take care of himself—he just had to make sure a gang of them never caught him alone. "Forget about it, okay? Let's go talk to your father."

In the kitchen, Mia locked the door and shuttered the windows. Her father paused in the act of dishing out the kimchi fried noodles. "Do my noodles smell so bad you have to protect the neighbors?"

"No!" Ross said. "They smell great."

Mia laughed. "It was a joke, Ross."

He didn't want to say that he never joked about food. Especially when it smelled as good as Dr. Lee's noodles. They both took plates and began to eat.

"Dad, we need to talk to you. Ross—"

Ross hastily tried to swallow.

She flicked her fork in his direction. "I'll tell him my part first. You go ahead and eat."

He was halfway through a plate of noodles when she casually repeated Tom Preston's remark about having worked for Voske. He almost spat out a cabbage leaf. "What?"

"It's common knowledge," said Dr. Lee, and Mia nodded. "It's just not talked about much. About eighteen years ago, Voske sent Tom Preston to Las Anclas as a spy, in preparation for a takeover. He lived here for a month, and at the end he went back, told Voske all the wrong things, and then warned us. He brought two of his friends—Sera and Omar—who'd been Voske's bodyguards too. When Voske attacked, the three of them fought on our side." At Ross's incredulous look, he added, "It *has* been eighteen years. It's old history."

"So about the book..." Mia began.

"What's in it?" Dr. Lee asked. "I see why it's valuable in general, but why does Voske need it?"

Ross pushed aside his empty plate. "People say a couple years ago, one of his prospectors found an artifact that lets Voske know everything that happens in his town, and even other places."

Dr. Lee nodded. "Yes, we've heard that."

"They say that's how he's been able to take over all those other towns. He knows their weaknesses. Maybe it's true. When I found my claim, there was no sign of anyone else. I didn't blast my way in, or even build a fire. But Voske's people were there the day after I made my first find. How did they know?"

"Good question."

"People say he even knows what's said in closed rooms." Ross glanced at the adobe walls and timbered ceiling. He lowered his voice. "If he wants my book that much, it might have something in it that's just as useful to him."

"But what is in it?" Dr. Lee repeated.

"Weapons!" Mia cut in excitedly. "There aren't many drawings, and the writing's in Japanese, but it has schematics for weapons we can build ourselves. And you know how hard it is to make gunpowder, Dad—this is a manual for weapons that don't need it."

"Imagine what Voske would do with that," Ross said grimly.

"This is quite interesting. And also dismaying," Dr. Lee said. "I'm glad you two filled me in. There would definitely be people here who'd keep the book and throw out both you and the bounty hunter. Especially since it's impossible to disprove a mind-control accusation. A lot of folk will be only too ready to believe that you can force people to like you."

Ross laughed, but not happily. "I wish!"

"So where is this book?" asked Dr. Lee.

"Hidden," Mia assured him. "Once the bounty hunter showed up, I designed a special hiding place. If he wants to steal it, he'll need hours and hours of searching. And a welding torch."

Ross frowned. "I wouldn't put it past him. I should move it. I'm sure he's seen me go in your cottage."

"It would be quite difficult for him to get in without being seen," said Dr. Lee.

"He's not just a thief. He's a killer." Ross rubbed the scar on his side, sick with the idea of bringing danger to the Lees. "Maybe I should take the book and go."

"You have to stay!" Mia exclaimed. "We're having a dance for you! I already started airing out my mother's pink dress."

Ross had no idea how to respond. Luckily, her father rescued him.

Dr. Lee smiled at Mia. "I think she'd like that. Ross, there's no point in leaving now. The bounty hunter will catch you outside of town, and then the book will go straight to Voske. Let me handle this. Mia, I'll have to tell Tom Preston you were eavesdropping."

"Go ahead. It wasn't like I meant to," she said. "But when they started talking about Ross that way—well, too bad for them."

Dr. Lee's smile turned grim. "I imagine the rest of the council will be interested to hear that Defense Chief Preston—formerly employed by Voske—recognized a current hireling and let him into town without telling us. The bounty hunter will be gone by morning. You can rest easy, Ross."

"As for you." He patted Mia on the shoulder. "Get out your dancing shoes."

Ross must have made a face, because as soon as her father left, Mia said, "Dances are fun! Everyone wears their best

clothes, and families decorate tables and cook their best reci-
pes, and some people go as couples. But you don't have to," she
added hastily.

Ross studied his borrowed shirt.

"We can get you a nice one."

He wondered if Mia was trying to suggest that he go with
her. He wondered if Jennie was going with anyone. It wasn't
clothes that worried him. Dancing! Another thing he didn't
know how to do. Another way for him to feel stupid. Like he
didn't belong anywhere around people.

Mia seemed to be waiting for an answer, but he couldn't
remember what question she'd asked. The room was too hot,
the ceiling too low, and he was suffocating.

He pulled at the door. It wouldn't open. He shook the handle.

Mia reached over and flipped the latch.

He threw the door open and bolted.

He didn't know whether he was sorry or relieved that she
hadn't followed. Trying not to think of dances and couples, he
ran across the town square toward the darkest buildings. *I'll
take the book and leave,* he thought. He'd seen Mia's face when
he ran out of the kitchen, and it made him feel even worse.

Dr. Lee was right. He couldn't evade the bounty hunter a
second time. He could burn the book and then leave—if he
could bring himself to destroy such a marvelous artifact.

But if he left, he'd never see Mia again. He'd never spar
with Jennie. He'd never get the chance to learn more of the
science that explained why things worked, or read more than
short and simple words. He'd never eat any more of Dr. Lee's
delicious cooking. Even little things like hot baths and clean
clothes would be hard to give up.

If he stayed, he'd have to face all of those people every day.
Half the town seemed to hate him, and even the ones who
liked him were overwhelming when he had to deal with them
all the time. He'd have to live under ceilings. Even when he

slept outside, nightmares about the singing tree followed him. Each left him more tired and edgy than the last, until his bones ached from exhaustion and every sudden movement felt like an attack.

He wanted to keep running, but he was surrounded by walls.

At the far side of the town hall, he came to a stop, breathing hard. The sentries were on wall patrol, lanterns swinging rhythmically above him. The generator had broken down again. He knew what Mia would be doing tomorrow.

Maybe he should apologize. But he had no idea how.

He pushed off the wall and ran until he ended up in the empty yard of the darkened schoolhouse. The sky was a canopy of blazing stars pierced by the black spear of the bell tower.

He remembered the pretty redheaded girl at his last trade fair, who'd flirted with him and invited him into her caravan. He'd been glad when she asked, but once he was inside, alone with her, he'd felt trapped and fled. Later, lying alone under the stars, he'd wished he'd stayed, and promised himself that next time he would.

Here he'd had a next time, and he'd done the exact same thing, all the way down to regretting it afterward. What was wrong with him?

Ross paced back and forth, trying to sort it out, until he heard footsteps. He spun around, reaching for the knives that weren't there. He couldn't hold one in his left hand anyway.

Sheriff Crow's yellow eye glowed like a cat's in the darkness. "Come with me."

21

Felicité

THE PARTY WAS GOING PERFECTLY. EVERYONE Felicité invited had come, including Jennie and Indra, wrapped around each other in a slow dance. Carlos Garcia was happily waltzing with Faviola Valdez.

Nasreen Hassan, who had been watching them, tipped her punch glass to get the last drops.

"I'll get you more," said Felicité.

She joined Brisa and Becky at the punch bowl.

"Maybe I should switch to rat training." Brisa gestured with her glass; Felicité stepped out of the line of fire. "I know, I know, I'll be twenty-five before I stick with an apprentice-ship long enough to finish. But I like so many things! And I love watching Trainer Koslova. Did you know that she talks to the older rats in Russian?"

"Sheriff Crow speaks Russian," Becky murmured. "She learned it from her mother."

"I didn't know that until yesterday." Brisa squeezed Becky as if she'd said something clever. Then she turned, her pink ribbons swinging. "Felicité, where is Wu Zetian? It's funny how she runs around town so much on her own. Kogatana sticks to Yuki like a burr."

"Wu Zetian is a free spirit," Felicité said airily. "I could never cage her in. She loves to explore, but she always comes back to me."

"I wish I had a pet who loved me," Becky said enviously. "Neither of our cats will come indoors."

Felicité handed Nasreen a glass of punch as the slow song ended.

"Your votes, please," Felicité called, standing at the small table that held two dishes of stones and a decorated box. "Green stones if you liked the song, red if it was boring."

Her guests lined up. Felicité counted the votes in the box: eighty percent red. She returned the stones to their dishes as the band struck up a fast tune, with a strong, steady beat. Everyone ran to dance. Brisa did a backflip, narrowly missing stepping on her own hair ribbons. Felicité winced, wishing she hadn't had to invite Brisa. But Becky was so happy.

Felicité had promised herself to stay away from Indra unless he approached her first, but she couldn't help eyeing him and Jennie. There was something about the way they were dancing . . .

Indra grabbed Jennie's hand and spun her toward him. Before they could collide, she twirled away, laughing—and Felicité had it. Jennie moved and laughed exactly the same way when she sparred with Ross Juarez. As if they existed in an intimate bubble of space.

Felicité's mother came in quietly and drew her aside. "Felicité, I am sorry to interrupt your party, but you are required to record a meeting. The sheriff called it. And that is all I can say." She beckoned to Sujata. "Sujata, how lovely you look tonight. May I request you to take over as hostess? Felicité will return as soon as she can." Her mother gave a gracious smile, and the door closed behind her.

Felicité let out a sigh.

"It's got to be about that claim jumper," said Carlos, mopping his forehead.

"Or the bounty hunter," Faviola suggested.

"My cousin said she heard someone at the stable say that the bounty hunter can turn into a ghost and walk through walls. That's how he gets people." Nasreen gave a dramatic shiver.

"I haven't heard anything about ghost powers," said Felicité. "And if I haven't heard it, it can't be true." *And Daddy would never be that friendly with a Changed man,* she thought. "But I'll know more soon. Sujata, here's the list of songs. Remind people to cast their votes, and keep track, will you?"

Felicité found both of her parents in the parlor. "I'm ready."

Her mother shook her head. "You'll be going alone, darling. Elizabeth Crow claimed sheriff's privilege to hold a closed interrogation, and I claimed mayoral privilege to have it recorded."

This was the first time she would serve as scribe at a meeting that her parents didn't attend. Felicité didn't know what to think.

Her daddy patted her hand. "You're there to make sure the sheriff doesn't beat a confession out of anyone."

Her mother tsked. She was not amused by jokes about council business.

"You can come back to your friends afterward, Felicité," her father said. "I'm glad to see Jennie Riley among them. That's a good friendship to cultivate."

He had never talked about the Changed like that before. He always added, "for a Changed person . . ." and occasionally, "for one of those mutants . . ." He was talking about Jennie as if she were a Norm.

Her mother nodded. "Having a solid friendship eases a working relationship."

"I see a bright future for that girl," said her daddy. "I wouldn't be surprised if she ends up defense chief."

Felicité kept strict control over her face, but the urge to shudder was so strong that she had to bolt to her room to conceal it. She fetched her writing materials, put on her second-best walking shoes, and hurried to the sheriff's. The backup generator hummed and the electric lights were on, which meant this meeting was even more important than she'd realized. Making sure her hat was tilted perfectly, she opened the door.

"Here's the scribe," Sheriff Crow said. "Let's get started."

Ross Juarez and the bounty hunter sat at opposite ends of the table. The bounty hunter loomed over Ross, sinister and grim. Ross eyed him with that intent expression Felicité had seen when he sparred or practiced throwing knives. How could anyone who fought that well be scared of parties?

The sheriff gave Felicité a nod to begin. "According to new information I've obtained, both of you lied to me. Ross, you're still on probation. If I say you go, you go."

As she recorded that, Felicité pressed her lips together to hide her smile.

The bounty hunter said calmly, "I told you I worked for a private individual."

"Kings are not private individuals." Sheriff Crow pushed her hair back so Felicité was forced to see the stretched skin and jutting bone of her face. "The fact that you're working for Voske is good reason to kick you out of town. But if you have a legitimate basis to take the boy, let's hear it."

"Ross Juarez is a claim jumper."

Ross's head snapped up. "I am not!" His voice cracked.

The sheriff gestured to him to be quiet. "You'll get your turn."

The bounty hunter's voice was even deeper than Mr. Riley's. "Ian Voske told me that Juarez stole a valuable item from a claim staked by one of his own prospectors. I was hired to retrieve the item and to bring Juarez back alive."

"So he can kill me and put my head on a pike," Ross said.

The bounty hunter shrugged. "What Voske does with you afterward is his business."

"I'm not a claim jumper!"

Sheriff Crow slammed her hand on the table. The two of them shut up. "What's the item?"

"A book," replied the bounty hunter. "I wasn't told what's in it."

The sheriff addressed Ross, whose right hand was so tightly clenched that his knuckles had paled. "What's in this book?"

Felicité had to lean forward to catch the mumbled "I can't read it."

So even after weeks in school, he was still illiterate. He might be tough, but he wasn't bright.

"Tell me what happened after Voske hired you," said Sheriff Crow to the bounty hunter.

"First I cornered him at the Joshua tree forest. I figured he'd surrender. But no. He crawled through the entire thing."

Sheriff Crow said what Felicité was thinking: "Can you *do* that?"

Ross muttered, "The thorns start two feet up the trunk. Mostly."

Grandmère Wolfe had taught that Joshua trees had root and branch systems that made the entire forest one big tree, two miles around. Was Ross brave, or a coward? From what Felicité knew of Voske, she supposed that she, too, would rather crawl through two miles of thorns than face him.

The bounty hunter continued. "He went so deep into the desert, I figured he'd die of thirst, get eaten by a coyote pack, or run into a hive cactus. But no. Eventually I cornered him in a gully that dead-ended in a cement wall. He got away from me there, too."

"How?" asked Sheriff Crow.

"He sank a knife into me and dove into a grove of singing trees."

Felicité's pen jerked, spattering the page. She'd heard

about the shard Ross had cut from his arm—which was brave enough, but getting within range of those trees on purpose? After she'd seen a singing tree kill a deer, she'd had nightmares for weeks. If the choice was Voske or singing trees, there was no question: she'd prefer Voske.

"Your turn, Ross," said Sheriff Crow. "How did you get the book?"

"It was in my claim, and I have it marked on a map. Here." Ross pulled a rolled hide from his backpack. "It was in open territory. Voske's soldiers jumped my claim."

The bounty hunter took out his own map. "Here's the borders of Voske's kingdom. And there—well inside the border—is the claim."

The sheriff compared the maps. "I see that his kingdom is significantly bigger than it was a year ago. And much bigger than the boundaries marked on Ross's map. It isn't his fault that Voske has conquered a number of towns and laid claim to enormous parcels of open territory since the map was made."

The bounty hunter shrugged and refolded his map.

"It's my claim," Ross insisted. "This is my grandmother's map, with her claims marked on it. She left it to me when she died. But when I started excavating my claim, Voske's gang jumped me."

"What happened then?" asked the sheriff.

"They stole my burro and everything he was carrying—my shotgun, my trade goods, my tools, my food and water—and gave me the count of thirty to run before they started shooting."

"How did you get away with the book?"

"I snuck back at night and took it. It was mine!"

"Do you dispute the bounty hunter's account of how you got here?"

Ross rubbed his side. "Except that he didn't mention that he shot me, no."

The man smiled. "I notice you didn't ask about his Change yet, Sheriff."

"What?" Ross's voice cracked again.

"It's not relevant," the sheriff said.

The bounty hunter leaned in, his voice persuasive. "Isn't it? You're feeling sympathy for him right now. You believe him. Weren't you seeing him as a harmless little boy you want to take care of? That's what he does."

Felicité noted the brief look of doubt that crossed the sheriff's hideous face. Ross looked appalled, but that was an easy expression to fake.

"I wouldn't call him harmless." Sheriff Crow cast a meaningful look at the bounty hunter's bandaged arm.

As she wrote, Felicité realized that she, too, had been sympathizing with Ross, or at least imagining what she'd have done in his place. What if the bounty hunter was telling the truth? And what if Ross could read minds as well as influence them? The idea of anyone digging into her thoughts was horrifying. She hoped the sheriff would order him to leave right then and there.

"Ross, let's see the book," Sheriff Crow said.

"I hid it in the desert." Ross opened his backpack. "Search if you want."

Sheriff Crow gave him a wry look, her one eyebrow lifted. Then she shrugged. "Fine. Without proof that you stole it, the book is your property." She turned to the bounty hunter. "Is this book worth Voske sending an army to retrieve it?"

"He doesn't need an army. He sent me."

Sheriff Crow's eyebrow went up again. "I see. Ross, go back to the Lees'." She cast a sarcastic look at the bounty hunter, and Felicité could hear the quotation marks in her voice when she spoke. "'Bounty hunter.' Why don't you go to Jack's Saloon and have a beer while the council meets? Felicité, please bring the council."

Ross was out the door before Felicité had capped her ink
bottle. If he could influence people, why didn't he make
Tommy and his friends quit throwing rocks at him? Why
didn't he convince that bounty hunter to let him go?

Somebody here is lying, she thought as she slipped out
into the night.

An hour later, her father stood before the council, arms
folded. "With all the new information we've learned, it seems
that this situation is no different than Voske's demand for
tribute five years ago. Giving him what he wants will only
make us seem weak. It'll make him more likely to attack us,
not less."

Judge Vardam nodded. "Since this bounty hunter cannot
prove that Ross Juarez stole the book, I am little inclined
to believe him. And since he was hired by Voske? Not at all
inclined. In fact, I don't even want him in town." Felicité
couldn't mistake the angry glance the old woman gave her
daddy.

Judge Lopez also glared at him. "I'm sure I speak for all
of us when I say that you cannot withhold important information from the rest of the council, Mr. Preston. You had no
right to keep that man's secrets."

Felicité's father didn't lose his cool. "I made a judgment
call. Maybe it was the wrong one. Anyway, you all know now."

"Let us have a vote," her mother said quickly. "Who wants
the bounty hunter to leave town empty-handed?"

To Felicité's surprise, it was unanimous. Then she understood: her daddy was going to lose anyway, so his vote
demonstrated that he was willing to compromise.

Sheriff Crow said, "I'll see to it that he's out of here by
sunup."

Her parents always stopped talking about Voske whenever
Will walked into the room, but Felicité knew all about his
kingdom festooned with the heads of his enemies, the towns

he'd conquered to expand his empire, and his Changed children, who had been promised kingdoms of their own when they came of age. She wanted Ross gone, but she would be glad to see Voske's man gone too.

As Felicité headed home, her father's praise of Jennie echoed in her ears. She couldn't stop seeing Jennie and Indra presiding over the council.

It will not happen, she promised herself.

By the time she returned to her party, she knew exactly what to do. She scattered compliments on Jennie's dancing, her party dress, and her teaching skills, all in Indra's hearing. *Clink! Clink! Clink!* When Jennie headed for the door, Felicité thanked her for coming. *Clink!*

Before Indra could follow, Felicité said wistfully, "I envy Jennie! So good at everything she does. She and Ross Juarez are amazing to watch at the schoolyard every morning. Their sparring looks like they're dancing together." Then she gave Indra her politest smile and moved away.

After the guests departed, her father called her into his office. The council record book was open on his desk. Felicité glanced at the upside-down pages, and recognized the sheriff's interrogation of Ross and the bounty hunter.

"Darling," he said. "You're grown up enough to help out with investigation. If there is any sign that Ross is Changed—if you see anyone behaving as if they're influenced by something outside of themselves—I want to know. And if you see that book of his, tell me."

Felicité smiled. "Leave it to me."

22

Jennie

JENNIE CIRCLED ROSS, LOOKING FOR AN OPENING ON his left. She'd found that he learned faster if she didn't encourage or explain.

She feinted, jabbed, ducked under his kick, and swept low to take out his left knee. He pivoted. Down rammed his right arm, strong as whipcord and steel, to block her kick. She glimpsed a fleeting smile that sparked a sunburst in her heart. He was getting it, all on his own. Even if he never recovered the full use of his hand, he was slowly filling the hole in his left-side defense.

He attacked. She let him step in, then moved close and grabbed his left wrist. He instinctively turned it to try to grab back, but his fingers couldn't grip. She twisted his arm into a joint lock and swept his feet. He hit the ground, his hair fanning around his head. She pounced, pinning his arms with her hands and his body with her weight. Ross tapped out.

He was learning, but he wasn't there yet. And he knew it.

He grinned up at her, muscles loosening under hers. It was nice to see, though she knew he'd soon tense up again. She'd never seen him relaxed except during or right after a match.

Jennie rose and offered her hand to pull him up. Then she remembered: he didn't like being touched once they were done sparring. She was about to step back when his fingers gripped hers. A grunt, a tug, and he was on his feet again, his breathing even, the steady pulse above the curve of his collarbone visible at the loose collar of his shirt. He was still far too thin.

"I'm thirsty." A voice broke the magic circle.

It was Z, standing with the other students in the schoolyard.

She sensed something amiss, but everyone was where they should be—and then she noticed Indra, perched on the fence post. That was odd. He usually spent his mornings with his family, or in private lessons with Sera.

"Good session, don't you think?" she called, giving him a wave. Then she turned to her students. "Practice is done. You'll find your assignments on your slates."

She turned to ask Indra about shield side defense, but he was gone. Odd.

Ross was squeezing his left hand in his right.

"Give it time."

"I know." Now that he wasn't fighting, he was falling into his habitual slouch, as if closing into himself.

Jennie hated seeing that as much as she hated seeing the dark smudges under his eyes. Nasreen had whispered that they were the shadows of his incredible eyelashes, but she knew better; Mia had mentioned finding Ross asleep in her yard.

He had agreed to go to the beach with the two of them and the kids, so maybe he wanted to socialize but didn't know how. "Come to Luc's with me tonight," she suggested. "I think you'd really like Sera Diaz. The Rangers are friendly, I promise. And they love to talk about sparring."

At the word "Luc's," Ross's shoulders had tightened. "Thanks. Maybe another time." He shot through the school door as if escaping a firing squad.

Beach is fine, Luc's is not fine. Too crowded? Too noisy? Too many reminders of Felicité calling him a mutant? Jennie sighed, then turned her attention to the day's work.

She was still thinking about Ross during Ranger practice. Could the obstacle course help strengthen his hand? She was so distracted that she didn't register how quiet Indra had been until he approached her afterward.

"Walk with me to Luc's?" he asked.

"Don't we always?"

Indra gave her a quick, odd glance, his braid swinging. Golden light from a longhouse highlighted his face as he said softly, "You never gave me an answer. About moving in. Let's talk about it after Luc's, okay?"

Jennie's stomach clenched as she nodded. She'd known this talk was coming, but each day she'd thought, *Not yet.* Now she'd spend the entire evening dreading it.

"Indra? Jennie?" Frances called. "We're stopping by Sera's."

They caught up with the Rangers at Lisl Plaza, the square of adobe houses where Sera and Paco lived. Windows were opened to the balmy summer air, sending out the delicious aromas of fried onions and garlic and cilantro. Families sat around tables at the evening meal. Jennie could hear one of her eight-year-olds retelling the legend of Orion, which she'd taught during today's astronomy lesson.

Teaching. Stories, true and imagined, passed from one to another. Hearing it made her feel good.

When Sera opened her front door, Yuki and Paco looked up from the couch, startled. Paco's bandaged leg was propped on a footstool.

"Am I interrupting something?" Sera inquired with a smile. The Rangers behind her hid theirs. Jennie had guessed that the guys had been secretly dating, but Yuki was so private that she hadn't even asked Meredith.

"Yuki was trying to get me to go to Luc's," Paco explained.

"My treat." Yuki brandished a handful of scrip. "Come on."

"Yes, come," said Sera. "We're all going. Unless you two would rather have your own table?"

"I don't want to go at all," said Paco. "Luc's is where I play. Where I dance. I don't want to go to Luc's and *sit.*"

"You want to go and eat tacos," Julio suggested.

"Who cares about tacos? Doc benched me for a whole month. He says when I'm onstage, I play with my entire body, not just my hands. All I'm allowed to do is go to my apprenticeship and cut glass," he finished miserably.

"You do play with your entire body," Frances pointed out.

"Yes, but Doc Lee wasn't supposed to know that." Paco retorted. He added gloomily, "Somebody ratted me out."

Sera shook her head. "Paco. You don't lie to the doc. You know what he can do. You might end up a hundred and twelve years old."

"That's not funny," said Paco, though everyone was laughing.

"Okay, let's move. Rangers!" Sera pointed to Paco. "Mission: Luc's!"

Six Rangers swooped down and hoisted him into the air. Those beneath his bad leg were careful to keep it straight. He protested unconvincingly. Jennie grabbed his crutches as the Rangers began marching down the path. Someone called the count; someone else laughed.

Sera and Yuki—with the cushion—followed. "You two are dating, aren't you?" she asked, with a grin. "You can admit it. I promise, the Rangers won't tease you."

Paco glanced back. "Cat's out of the bag, Yuki. Yes, Mom, we are."

Julio immediately made a loud kissy noise. Yuki rolled his eyes, but a smile flickered at the corners of Paco's mouth as he rapped Julio on the head.

The smile vanished when they entered Luc's and he saw the empty stage. The Rangers assured him the month would fly by and they knew people who'd had worse injuries, but Paco winced, as if sorry he'd come.

They meant well, but who likes being told to be grateful it wasn't worse—that it doesn't really matter—that it's not as bad as you think it is—when you've been hit with a huge disappointment? Jennie was trying to think of something that would actually be comforting when Sera started confiscating everyone's lemonade and ale glasses and lining them up. Jennie had no idea what she was doing, but Yuki seemed to; he flashed a quick grin as he handed Sera a spoon.

Ah, Jennie thought as Sera began tapping on the glasses. Each one rang with a different note. When she hit a sour one, she made a face, and took a sip out of that glass—Julio's, Jennie thought. Then she hit it again. The note was still flat.

Paco tilted his head, listening.

"He did that on crystal once, when I was visiting the glazier's," Yuki told Jennie. "It sounded like chimes."

Sera tapped at the glasses, trying to play a melody.

"Here," Paco said, after the third sour note. "There's an exact measure. Don't tell me you don't remember from school. Everybody has to do this experiment."

A chorus of "I forgot!" and "We did?" rose up as Paco tapped a glass, his slanting brows furrowed. He took a careful sip. When he had gotten the glasses tuned to a full octave, he sat back, satisfied.

Sera began tapping out the opening notes of "Hijo de la Luna." Yuki picked up his fork and thumped on the table, heavy on the downbeat.

With two knives, Paco began beating out a counterpoint. Jennie started to sing, and everyone joined in. Paco played the table and plates and glasses like a one-man band.

Except for their skin and hair color, which were the same shades of brown and black, Paco and Sera looked so different— Sera with her straight brows and softly rounded features, Paco with his wickedly slanting brows and sharp nose, cheekbones, and chin. But their expressions were the same, focused and intent on the rhythm.

A huge platter of tacos appeared, and Paco ended the song with a crescendo that threatened to crack his plate. Everyone clapped. Jennie was glad to see him take his share, and he joined in the talk as they demolished the entire platter.

When they got up to go, Paco said softly, "Sorry, Mom. I didn't mean to be a jerk."

Sera snorted. "If Doc Lee ever benches *me* for a month, you'll have to roust out the entire town to cheer me up." She smiled at Jennie and Indra. "That reminds me. The Kawakamis are moving to Sunset Circle, so there'll be an empty apartment at Jackalope Row. If you move fast, you could nab it."

"What?" Jennie exclaimed.

Indra threw his arm around her. "We talked about this, Jennie."

She stopped herself from saying, *But I didn't say yes.* She would not have this conversation in public.

After they left Luc's, she and Indra walked silently through the crowded streets until they reached the relative privacy of narrow Primrose Path.

Jennie said quietly, "When did you talk to Sera about us moving in together?"

"At lunch, I guess. What difference does it make? We've been over this." Her ears, sensitive to every shade of his voice, heard a quickness to his speech. Like he was defending himself.

"Not really. You brought it up." Jennie watched her boots hitting the hard-packed earth. "And I said I wasn't ready."

"Jennie, you are ready." Indra caught her hand again. She let her fingers stay in his as he said, "We're not kids anymore. You're an adult twice over, with two jobs. Too bad you can't vote twice, like Preston used to."

She smiled at his attempt at humor. "Too bad I can't keep both jobs." She took a deep breath. "We've only been dating for six months. I'm still not ready to move in with you, and I wish you hadn't talked about it with Sera."

"Why not?" Indra asked, turning to face her.

"For one thing, it would hurt my parents to hear about this from other people, instead of me."

He dropped her hand and made an impatient gesture. "Your parents are the mellowest people in the entire town."

"That doesn't matter. Every big decision is talked out in my family. It's the way we do things."

"Then let's go now." He reached for her hands. "I know they believe in the sanctity of marriage. If it's living together that bothers you, let's get married first. We could have the biggest wedding in Las Anclas."

His face was so open and filled with longing, and his hands were so warm in hers. She could see herself marrying him. She'd have a beautiful wedding gown sewn by Mrs. Callahan and embroidered by Grandma Riley, whose needlework was the best in town. Mia and Meredith could be her bridesmaids. Everyone would toast the happy couple, and there'd be feasting and dancing. Indra would be so handsome at her side. And then, on the wedding night, everyone would walk them to their room, carrying candles and singing . . .

But marriage wasn't about the wedding. Jennie had grown up hearing that, and now she understood the truth of it.

"Listen to me, Indra. If I'm not ready to move in with you, I'm not ready to get married, either. We're too young."

It hurt her to say those words, but there was more she wanted to do, and more things she needed to see, before she could settle down. She owed Indra—and herself—the truth.

"Lots of people get married at our age," he protested.

"I know. Pa married Olivia Lee as soon as they turned eighteen. And they were divorced before they were twenty."

Indra pulled his hands out of her grip. "Is there someone else?"

How did he know? Then Jennie caught herself: there was nothing *to* know. She had no reason to feel guilty. "Are you serious? Of course there isn't!"

"What about Ross Juarez?"

An incredulous laugh escaped from Jennie's lips. "Ross?

He practically leaps through a window if you so much as try to shake his hand!"

"That's not what I saw this morning."

Jennie had never heard that tone before.

This is jealousy, she thought. She stared at her boots, on the verge of dizziness—like she was waking up from a dream. But this was no dream. Nor a romantic song. There was nothing romantic here.

"Think, Jennie," said Indra. "Could he be using his Change power to make you like him?"

Jennie took a deep breath. "Ross has no Change power. Or at least not that one. He'd be having a very different time at school if he did. But Ross is not the issue here. The issue is that I'm not ready for this."

"What's 'this'?" Indra asked, flinging his arms wide. "Marriage? Moving in?"

"Both."

"So, what, it's time for 'We said we could see other people,' is that it?" He clenched and unclenched his fists, then shook out his hands as if he was trying to shake off his anger. "I don't want to 'see' anyone else."

Embarrassment prickled Jennie's skin. Two feet away, the entire Cohen family was busy weeding their kitchen garden. She was certain they were listening.

"Let's go inside, okay?" She pointed toward her house.

Indra caught her arm. "I don't care who hears." His voice rose angrily. "What do you want, Jennie?"

"I want this to be a private conversation," she said, her own temper rising. "Like it should have been in the first place."

"Too late now." He turned on his heel. "Have fun with your claim jumper."

He walked away, leaving her standing alone in the middle of the road.

23

YUKI

YUKI'S BED JERKED, JOLTING HIM AWAKE. HE CLUTCHED the mattress, thinking he was at sea. No; it was an earthquake. The windows rattled gently, but nothing fell from his shelves, and Kogatana stayed curled at his feet. It was only a small quake, then. From the dimness of the light, he had some time left to sleep.

Then his mind leaped from memories of tossing on the ocean to the sea caves. This quake might have been the one to jar something loose—something he could prospect.

Moving silently, so as not to awaken his mother or Meredith, he dressed and headed out, Kogatana padding at his heels.

The streets were nearly deserted, silent except for the chirping of crickets and morning birds. Yuki felt as if he had the entire world to himself. But by the time he reached the gate, it had already opened for the farmers and hunters and fishers who started work before dawn. He knew two of the sentries from school, and hurried past before they could ask where he was going. No doubt they'd mention it to their friends, and those friends would tell their friends, and he'd get interrogated by a dozen different people before the end of the day.

The earthquake woke me up, he rehearsed to himself. *I felt like taking a swim.* Neither of those were lies.

The fishers had long since launched their boats, so he had the beach to himself. He walked along until he reached the sheer cliff pocked with caves, some above water, some submerged. He didn't see any new ones, but you never knew what might lie beneath the waves.

Years before he'd come to Las Anclas, an earthquake had shifted some of the cliff face, revealing an ancient building. But that had been mostly above the waterline, and had long since been picked clean. Other ancient houses must still be buried beneath the tons of stone. He checked the cliffs after every one of the occasional earthquakes but had never found anything but seaweed and mussels.

He stripped down to his swimming trunks, braided and tied up his hair, secured a collecting bag around his waist, and put on the goggles that Mr. Ahmed had made for him.

He patted Kogatana. "Stay."

Yuki took a deep breath, then dove into the chilly, blue-green water. He swam rapidly along the cliff, scanning the familiar stone walls and avoiding grasping strands of kelp. Phosphorescent fish glimmered in the darker depths, and he dove to avoid an eel wreathed in crackling blue lightning.

The world beneath the waves was both familiar and strange, like an old shirt altered to fit someone else. He'd learned to swim before he could walk, but the environment of the deep ocean was completely different from that of the shoreline. Once, his mouth and nose stuffed full of the oxygen-rich breather moss that the *Taka* had grown in hydroponic tanks, he'd been able to explore for over a quarter hour at a time, but no one around Las Anclas had heard of it, not even the traders who sailed the local coasts. He was limited to the few minutes he could hold his breath.

He was about to surface when he noticed a new crack in the brown rock. He kicked hard. The opening was narrow, but he could squeeze through. He peered at the slice of water illuminated by the pale filtered light. The crack led to a larger space, but all he could see was water with strands of kelp floating in it. No. Not kelp, cords. He'd found a ruin!

Yuki swam up and floated, filling his lungs and thinking. He'd been told to report any new cave and not to explore it alone. But he'd grown up diving deeper than any citizen of Las Anclas; whoever accompanied him would be more likely to get in trouble than he would. Or, worse, they'd forbid him to go in at all—and then he'd lose what could be his first real claim.

This was his cave—in his territory. Anything could be inside.

He took a deep breath, then dove and eeled his way into the crack. Rough stone scraped his chest and belly as he pulled himself through. Then the stone dropped away beneath his hands, and he was in.

It was nothing like the tunnels of stone and coral that he'd explored as a child. This was a labyrinth of fallen walls and tilted staircases, jammed with tattered skeletons of furniture and chunks of rubble, illuminated only by the dim light that filtered in. The dark water was choked with floating cords, bits of cloth, and coiled springs and wires. A few fish were the only living things in sight: until an hour or so ago, this had been a sealed environment.

Excitement tempted him to start exploring. But his old training and discipline held him in place.

Without gravity to orient you, it was easy to swim down when you meant to swim up, or left when you meant to swim right. The few times Yuki had ever seen anyone explore a cave in Las Anclas, they'd used ropes to find their way out. But on the *Taka* they'd warned him that ropes got tangled in wreckage and rocks, trapping divers until their air ran out. Divers could be lured into relying on their ropes rather than on their mental map of their surroundings. But ropes could get broken or bitten through. Ropes killed.

The crack is that way, he told himself, quickly building

a map in his mind. *That way is up. That way is down. That way is away from the crack.*

He spotted dishes and machinery amid the rubble, but the ground was covered in a layer of silt; if Yuki disturbed it, visibility could drop to zero in an instant.

Avoiding the hanging wires, he swam around a tilted wall, into darker waters. The pressure in his chest was starting to hurt, but he ignored it. He knew exactly how long he could hold his breath. Then he spotted a glimmer of metal, brighter than the corroded stuff he'd seen before, within the still-upright remains of a broken cabinet. A silver statuette lay partially buried in a mess of rotting wood, slivers of glass, and chunks of brick.

Yuki didn't have much air left. He gently eased out the statuette and tucked it into his bag.

As he began to swim out, he felt a ripple in the water. He turned in time to see the cabinet hit the ground. A huge puff of silt rose up like smoke. Now he could see nothing but swirling darkness.

Fear jolted through him. He shut down the instinct to gasp for breath, and made himself recall his map. He knew where he was. He didn't need to see. He retraced his path, swimming for the crack.

A hard, thin object scraped his leg, then snapped around his ankle and pulled tight, trapping him. He must have put his foot in one of those coils of wire.

Don't panic.

He reached down and untangled himself, his fingers clumsy. He was running low on oxygen, and it was affecting his coordination. He got the wire off, then swam on. Something soft wrapped around his face. Yuki slapped it off. Where was the crack?

He stretched out his hand, and touched a solid wall.

Was he too high, or too low? Or had he gotten turned

around entirely? Wild thoughts of trying the other direction raced through his mind.

No. That was how divers died. He would not panic and second-guess himself. He had swum down to retrieve the statuette.

So he swam upward, trailing his fingers along the wall. His head throbbed, and his lungs ached. The impulse to breathe clawed at his throat.

Was he even going up? Or had he gotten so disoriented that he was going down, or sideways? His ears rang, and he knew he wasn't thinking straight.

Then he touched the rough edges of the crack. He pulled himself through, fumbling and clumsy, the pain in his lungs excruciating, until he saw blue light ahead and tumbled out into the open waters. He was kicking his way toward the surface when everything went black.

He woke to the shock of cold air. He sucked in a breath and grabbed for something solid to hold on to. Then he remembered where he was. He floated below the cliffs, sucking air, too dizzy and weak even to be relieved.

Sick fear wrung his entire body. He'd nearly drowned. If he'd blacked out even seconds earlier, he'd have breathed in water before reaching the surface.

Exploring a ruin wasn't like exploring a reef. He'd thought he'd been careful, but he'd missed the signs that should have either told him not to touch the statuette, or how to do it safely.

It was true: prospecting was dangerous.

He made it to shore and stretched full-length on the sand, eyes closed, chest aching. Kogatana scampered up and started licking his face. Gradually strength trickled back into his limbs. Still on his back, he pulled out the treasure that had almost killed him.

It was a dancer poised on one foot, her arms outstretched

and her hair coiled around her head, forged of some silvery metal. Yuki examined the absorbed, inward-turned expression on her face, and the finely detailed straps on her shoes. It had to be hundreds and hundreds of years old, and now it was his. He could feel the weight of all those years in his hands, connecting him to its long-dead owner. He or she must have cherished it.

The cave was probably full of treasure, but as with the ancient city with its barrier of crystal trees, there might be no way to reach it. Yuki didn't know enough to dive in the cave safely, but neither did anyone else. He'd rather keep it a secret than have the entire town learn he'd had yet another prospecting disaster. Maybe he'd just tell Paco.

The sun hadn't even risen yet; he'd only been underwater for a few minutes. As he walked home, he wondered if Ross knew how to swim.

24

Jennie

SERA FACED JENNIE ACROSS THE KITCHEN TABLE. "I can't tell you how sorry I am."

Of all the sympathetic comments Jennie had endured since the breakup, this one hurt the worst. Her throat constricted.

"But I have to ask," Sera said. "Can you maintain discipline around Indra without letting your emotions get in the way?"

"Of course I can," Jennie said firmly, though her stomach churned. Was she about to be thrown out of the Rangers?

But Sera gave a brisk nod. "I knew it. And Indra says the same. You aren't the first and won't be the last Ranger couple to get in this situation. Training and working the way we do, it's natural for people to pair up. Sometimes it doesn't work."

"Thanks." Jennie couldn't help wondering if Sera had ever paired with another Ranger. Rumors had always flown about her and Mr. Preston, including that he was Paco's father. But Sera had never mentioned it, and Mr. Preston didn't treat Paco like a son.

Sera pushed back her graying hair. "It'll be hard for a while, but I think you'll get to be friends again. You were close long before you started dating."

Jennie smiled. "That's the first thing anyone's said that's actually made me feel better."

"Good to hear." Sera slung her rifle over her shoulder and went out.

Before the door could close behind her, Felicité appeared,

carrying a basket. The basket handle, Wu Zetian, and Felicité all wore matching spring-green ribbons.

"I'm so, so sorry about you and Indra," Felicité said earnestly. "You seemed so perfect together. I was taking some scones to Grandma Narayan, and Mother and I decided to pack some for you, too. Pastries won't mend a broken heart, but they're better than nothing, right?"

Jennie forced a smile and a thank-you, feeling more than ever like she was trapped in a supporting role in some awful play.

Felicité didn't leave. Waiting for her cue?

Jennie wondered if she was supposed to invite Felicité to stay. And what? Talk about Indra? She gritted her teeth.

"I'll go deliver the rest." Felicité patted the basket. "Oh. Daddy wanted me to convey his sympathies, and his disappointment."

Jennie winced inwardly. She hadn't even thought about how Mr. Preston would react. She felt like she'd let down the entire Ranger team.

Felicité concluded, "But of course your own feelings must come first." She gave a sad little wave as she left.

It's the hands, her ma had once said. *People talk more truly with their hands.*

Jennie remembered Indra's hands that horrible night, how he'd flexed them, his fingers stiff. Today, Sera's callused hands had gripped and twisted.

Felicité had said all the right things, and her expression had been sympathetic, but her hands had been relaxed, and that pat she'd given the basket had been downright satisfied. She wasn't a bit sorry.

Jennie was tempted to throw the scones on the mulch pile, but that would be a waste of good pastry. They would be delicious; the Wolfes' cook had been hired away from Jack's.

She'd take them to the picnic. Ross would enjoy them.

■ ■ ■ ■ ■

Z, Dee, and Nhi ran ahead up the trail, their clear voices blending with the calls of the seagulls. Jennie and Mia followed them, with Ross a few paces behind.

Jennie stepped aside at the top of the bluff. "Ross, meet ocean."

He didn't seem to hear her. The wind tossed his hair and rippled his shirt, but otherwise he was completely still. The water below sparkled like a million bits of mica, creating new patterns of glittering movement every time Jennie blinked. Toward the shore, wavelets painted white lines across blue-green water; at the horizon, blue-gray water merged with deep-blue sky. A flight of pelicans soared on the sea breeze.

Jennie breathed in the salty air, trying to imagine what it must be like to see the ocean for the first time. From the joy and wonder that illuminated Ross's face, she knew she hadn't even come close. "Worth the trip?" she asked.

Ross started, and she was rewarded with a rare smile. "Yeah, I think it is."

"Oh, I should have brought you sooner," said Mia.

The Terrible Three reached the waterline. Z waded in, poking a driftwood stick into the surging tide. Nhi and Dee flung themselves down on the dry sand, and Dee began burying Nhi's feet.

Ross pointed at a hazy gray-brown hump on the horizon. "What's that?"

"Catalina Island," Mia said.

"Where the Changed people went?"

Mia nodded. Jennie turned away, remembering those ships full of refugees sailing into the empty sea, the Rangers watching to make sure they left. Rangers were sworn to obey, regardless of their personal feelings, but how had they really felt? What would Jennie feel if she was ever ordered to do something like that, to people like herself?

My Change is a gift, she told herself fiercely. *It doesn't matter what anyone else thinks. My Change is a blessing from God.*

She reached out with her mind and pulled a bleached stick of driftwood into her hand. Ross flinched.

Jennie's heart sank. How many times had someone whom she'd known her entire life, whom she'd always thought was fine with the Changed, let some comment slip that showed that they weren't fine with it at all?

She whacked the stick against her thigh, and Ross flinched again. Jennie twisted the stick in her hands, hiding her relief. He'd seen her use her power before; he'd only been startled by the sudden movement.

She wanted to apologize, both for doubting him and for making him jump, but that would only make the awkward moment worse. Indra was so easygoing and relaxed, but except when they were sparring, Jennie felt like she had to step very carefully around Ross.

Indra *had* been easygoing.

Z let out a shrill squawk. "Help! Help! It's got me!"

Ross took off like an arrow. Mia and Jennie ran after him.

Z thrashed around in knee-deep water, struggling to escape from a strand of kelp that had seized her arm and was coiling up toward her shoulder.

"What's that?" Ross gasped. Water splashed around his boots.

Z giggled, drawing her knife. With a dramatic slash, she sliced through the kelp and brandished the still-wriggling strand. "Want a belt? It'll keep your pants up nice and tight!"

The Terrible Three fell in a heap on the sand, laughing.

"Let's eat," Mia said, kicking at the tendrils of kelp groping for her toes.

"What is that stuff?" Ross asked.

Mia took the kelp from Z. "You girls harvest while we set up the picnic. I want a couple thicker strands, too, to take home to my dad for tourniquets. Don't worry," she said dryly, "we'll rescue you if the big ones get you." And then, to Ross, "It stays alive in seawater for a week or so. Dad cuts it up fine to use for sutures."

She opened the picnic basket. Jennie filled the empty jugs with seawater, and the girls dropped in handfuls of writhing strands. Ross hovered, watching.

Jennie pushed the basket toward him. "Would you mind setting out the food?"

She watched covertly as he unwrapped each item. It was like he was opening Christmas presents, and each gift was better than the last.

Finished, he eyed the cliffs like they were yet another present. "What's in those caves?"

"We'll show you!" Dee offered instantly. "After we eat," she amended, digging in.

"Okay, thanks." Ross took a huge bite of tamale.

"Have you prospected in caves, Ross?" Z asked, winding a strand of curly hair around a finger.

With what Nhi clearly thought was enormous subtlety, she edged closer to him. "Was it dangerous?"

Mia stuffed her knuckles into her mouth, and Jennie smothered a snicker. Ross kept on eating, oblivious to the girls' flirting, so they took the opportunity to scoot even closer.

A pork bun vanished from between Jennie's fingers. She glanced around. A few squirrels had ventured onto the beach, lured by the picnic, and one of them was nibbling away at her bun. Before she could react, a plum dumpling disappeared from a plate and reappeared in another squirrel's paws.

Jennie threw a handful of sand at them. "Shoo, you thieves!"

The squirrels scampered off, but not before they'd teleported away the last of Felicité's scones. They were welcome to them.

Nhi put her hand on Ross's arm. "Would you like another cinnamon roll?"

He jumped up. "What about those caves?"

Z tugged Dee up. "Let's show him."

Nhi licked icing from her fingers, then poked Dee. "Hey! Maybe we'll find Princess Cloud!"

Dee shook her head. "I don't think she'd have run this far."

The girls led Ross toward the caves, sand kicking up behind their heels.

"Who's Princess Cloud?" Mia asked.

"One of our kittens, I think," said Jennie. "I bet a hawk got it. Well, let Dee think it found another family."

She watched the trio point out the caves while Ross stayed out of touching distance. Though the bounty hunter had been gone for a few days, the shadows under Ross's eyes had darkened, and while he'd always startled easily, it seemed to take less and less to make him jump. Something was wrong with him, something she wasn't seeing.

"I wanted to ask you." Mia's next words came out in a rush. "Do you think Ross lied, and he's Changed, like the bounty hunter said?"

"What makes you think that?"

"He might be making me feel things. I mean, mentally controlling me so I feel things." Mia nervously clicked the beads on her belt abacus.

"What things?"

She snapped her slide rule in and out and in again, then mumbled, "Making me like him."

Jennie tried not to laugh. "Mia, he doesn't need a Change to do that."

"I keep catching myself standing at my work table, not doing anything, just thinking about him. That's weird, right?" Before Jennie could reply, she added, "How can you tell if a feeling is real?"

Jennie bent down to avoid her friend's eyes, and picked up a pebble. She tossed it into the ocean, way beyond the waves. Unfortunately, her own feelings didn't get thrown away with it. Now that Mia had brought it up, Jennie had to admit to herself that there had been some truth in Indra's accusation. There was a spark between her and Ross.

But it was so soon after her breakup, she wasn't sure if she wanted to do anything about it. And more important, Mia liked Ross—Mia, who had always wanted to fall in love. Jennie would never respect herself again if she poached Mia's guy.

"Jennie?" Mia asked. "What's love supposed to feel like?"

"I'm still learning myself."

"No, you're not. You have tons of experience. Compared to me, anyway." Mia added glumly, "Everyone has tons of experience compared to me."

"Oh, that's not true. Meredith doesn't either, as she's the first to point out. Anyway, Ma and Pa say that everyone's got their own way of loving. There's no such thing as 'supposed to.'"

Mia's shoulders relaxed.

"But I do think he likes you," Jennie added.

"If he does, why did he panic when I mentioned the dance? He actually jumped up and ran away. Like he knew I was about to ask him to go with me." Her face crumpled unhappily.

Jennie gave her a hug. "I don't think he had any idea. He doesn't know anything about how to be with people. Seriously, from everything he's said, he's only ever been around three people in his entire life, and two of them were trying to kill him."

Mia didn't even smile. "Yeah, Dad gave me a talk about that. He said I should only approach Ross from the front, and if I want to touch him, I should do it slowly so he can see it. And I shouldn't stand between him and the door." She glumly dug her fingers into the sand. "Everything I've done with him has been wrong."

"I don't think so," Jennie said. "You're the only person who can touch him and not have him pull away or freeze, even if he does flinch at first."

"You touch him too, when you spar with him. He seems to like that."

Jennie nodded cautiously. "Maybe the only kind of touching he's used to is fighting practice. But that makes the way he is with you more special, right?"

"Hey, I have an idea—since he likes sparring with you, why don't you teach him to dance? You're so good at it."

Jennie swept up another stone and tossed it, watching until it splashed into the sea. But when she bent to pick up another, fingers closed around her wrist.

Mia's gaze was intense behind her glasses. "Do you like Ross too?" Jennie hesitated. Mia might not have much experience with boys, but she could read Jennie like a newspaper. Her brows lifted. "You do like him. Why didn't you tell me?"

Jennie had hoped that she would never have to have this conversation, but now that it was actually happening, it was a relief to be honest. "I didn't want to get between you."

"There isn't any 'us' to get between." Mia squared her shoulders. "You can ask him. I bet he won't run away from you."

"I don't know about that," Jennie said.

"Of course he'd want to go out with you. Anyone would. You're so pretty and strong and you're good at everything. And you know how to kiss."

Jennie put up a hand to stop her. "I'm sure he likes you. I'm not so sure what he thinks about me. I mean, besides as a teacher and sparring partner."

Mia peered down the beach. In the distance, Ross was keeping the Terrible Three out of a half-submerged cave.

She turned back to Jennie. "If Ross likes us both, I wouldn't mind. I mean, because it's you, I wouldn't mind. At least, I think I wouldn't. What do you think? Would that be okay with you?"

Jennie struggled with her own tangle of feelings.

He's the only guy in town who appreciates Mia, and she lights up like a bright-moth whenever he's around. How can I risk taking that away from her?

Sparring with him is like dancing, and every time he trusts me enough to tell me something, it feels like a gift.

Why did it have to be either/or? Wouldn't it be better if none of them had to choose?

Mia's round face was turned hopefully up to Jennie, framed by the same bowl haircut and slipping-down glasses she'd worn since she was eight. And yet Mia had been the one to cut through the dilemma that Jennie had seen no way out of without hurting someone. Which one of them was really more mature?

"How about if we ask him to go to the dance with both of us?" Jennie suggested. "If he says yes, we can see if we're having a good time or if it feels weird."

Mia flashed the same warm smile that Jennie had loved when they were two little girls on a dusty playground. "Okay!" She added quickly, "But you ask him."

Two days later, Jennie walked into Luc's, breathing in the toasty aroma of baking biscochitos. The light was dim, and a fan blew cool air over the jam-packed interior. Laura Hernandez played with the band, competing with the clinking of forks and the clamor of voices. Jennie waved.

Her heart thumped when she heard a familiar voice.

"Jennie! Come join us!" It was Sera.

The nine other Rangers had squeezed shoulder to shoulder at the biggest table. Indra gave a polite nod. Sera elbowed to make space, and the people on her bench scooted over until Julio nearly fell off the other end.

"Hey," he protested. "Is that any way to treat your future captain?"

"Might not happen if you can't hold your seat," cracked Sera, straight-faced.

Julio promptly scooted back, launching a turf war that only

concluded when the table started to tip. Jennie squeezed in, half her butt hanging over the edge. Indra was three people over, but she felt as if she could measure every inch of the space between their bodies. She could hear every breath he took, and smell the faint, sweet ghost of the coconut oil he used on his hair.

"What if Jennie had tried to skirt around the pit mouth?" Julio asked, going back to the discussion they had obviously been having.

She was startled to hear her own name. They had cleared a space on the table, and were re-creating her disastrous patrol. Julio was moving the riders (blue corn chips) away from the rattlesnakes (knives) and around a napkin that apparently represented the pit mouth.

"With a bunch of panicking kids?" Frances used a knife to flick several chips onto the napkin, accompanied by gobbling noises. "She would have lost a couple."

Sera nodded, her gaze on Jennie. "Paco said he didn't know which were scarier, the snakes or the thirteen-year-olds. Personally, I'd rather face the snakes."

Frances absently munched a chip. "There's nothing much you can do in the heat if your patrol doesn't obey orders."

Sera added dourly, "They're too young to be shot for insubordination. Unfortunately."

The Rangers laughed as Luc appeared with a tray of tacos: crispy carnitas, chicken, rabbit, fish, and potato for Indra, who didn't eat meat. Jennie relaxed. At least this part of her life had gone back to normal, even if she couldn't help being very aware of him. From the studious way he ate his tacos, she suspected the feeling was mutual.

Afterward, as she headed home for Ross's dance lesson, memories arose with each puff of dust under her feet. Indra had walked her home every day for the past year, when they had both been students and Ranger candidates. They weren't yet talking again, but at least they could work together.

Everything she'd believed had been resolved now seemed open-ended and complicated. Did she want Indra to still care? Did she want to get back together? What did it mean that she was excited about going to the dance with Ross and Mia?

In her room, she pulled out one dress after another, but nothing seemed right.

Just pick something. She put one on, barely even noting which it was. Mia had been so sure Jennie had all the answers, but all Jennie had were questions.

25

Ross

ROSS'S STEPS SLOWED AS HE APPROACHED THE RILEY house, which seemed to be two adobe longhouses built in different styles and joined together, with extra rooms jutting out at random points. Ross couldn't figure out which was the front and which was the back, let alone where to go in.

A clamor of voices emerged from an open door, along with the smell of braising onions and sweet peppers. "No, I did not forget to latch the henhouse." A blue-green light flashed in rhythm with the boy's voice. "I know better than that!"

"Well, someone let another chicken loose." Ross recognized the deep, measured tones of Mr. Riley. "Or let something into the coop. Chickens don't teleport."

"So you kids know what your job is." The cheerful woman had to be Mrs. Riley. "Scat! Go find the missing chickens, or else find what got them."

"Whoever finds them gets to pick tonight's bedtime story," her husband added.

Ross was nearly knocked down by a mass of little kids shouting, "Here chicken, chicken, chicken!"

"Hey, Ross." José waved at him. "Come on in."

He looked for a place to put his shoes, then saw that everyone inside was wearing theirs. He stepped into an enormous kitchen. Mr. and Mrs. Riley, José, and a couple of teenagers sat at a long table. Their plates were scraped nearly clean.

"Hungry?" Mr. Riley asked. "Unfortunately, tonight's chicken stew is missing an ingredient—chicken! But there's plenty of vegetables and gravy."

"Thank you." Ross tried to remember the proper manners for declining a meal—not that he did it often. "I already ate. With Dr. Lee. And Mia."

Mrs. Riley smiled. "You must be here to see Jennie. I'll let her know before I go to work."

José offered him a platter of thumbprint cookies. "Did you feel the earthquake? There was another aftershock this morning."

Ross bit through buttery shortbread and tart prickly pear jelly. "Yeah. The chimes woke me up again."

"Chimes?"

"From the crystal . . ." Ross trailed off awkwardly at José's blank look. He'd thought the earthquake had made the singing trees ring out so loudly that they could be heard in town, but that must have been part of his dream.

"Dishes, guys." Mr. Riley snapped his fingers. "It's your week to wash. Ross, would you like a glass of barley water while you're waiting?"

"I'm here." Jennie appeared at an inner doorway.

Ross had been about to say he'd like the barley water, not because he was thirsty, but because he liked this warm room scented with hanging strings of herbs and garlic, and he liked the easy give and take of Jennie's family. Though the ceiling was low and the kitchen was crowded, he didn't feel trapped.

She beckoned to him. "I've finished my lesson plans, so we have the whole evening."

She'd taken her hair out of its usual braids, and it stood out around her head like a black dandelion puff. Instead of the comfortable shirts and pants she taught and fought in, she was wearing a bright red dress with a skirt that ended above her knees.

She was as pretty as ever, but that dress, the color of blood—
the color of the singing tree—he hated that color now. Dr. Lee
had said his nightmares would fade with time, but, if anything,
they were getting more and more vivid.

As they walked down a long hall, a gust of wind rose from
beneath a closed door, rippling Jennie's skirt and startling
Ross.

"Good work, Yolanda!" called Jennie. Another gust
answered her.

"Yolanda lives here?" he asked, surprised.

"Yes. Lots of kids do. Paco Diaz lived with us when Sera was
on Ranger missions until he was old enough to be left alone.
Sometimes we take in Changed kids to teach them how to use
their powers, or at least get used to them. But Yolanda . . ."

Jennie's voice stayed even, but Ross was used to watching
for subtle alterations in her face when they sparred. Her eyes
were narrowed in anger. "She Changed, and her parents dis-
owned her. She says she won't go back even if they change
their minds, so I guess we'll adopt her. She's already begun
calling herself Yolanda Riley."

Jennie's room was almost as big as Mia's cottage, but otherwise it was completely different. Framed pencil drawings of
her family hung on the walls. The only things on the bed were
pillows and an embroidered quilt. Plants grew in a box fitted
into the window; the room smelled of sharp herbs and sweet
flowers rather than of oil, metal, and chemicals. Both rooms,
however, were full of pages from old books—Mia's lay in drifts
on every flat surface, while Jennie's were neatly stacked on her
desk, and there were even a few bound books on a shelf.

"Here." She dropped a pile of folded clothes into his arms.
"When Paco grew out of these, he donated them to us. Try
them on. If they fit, you could wear them to the dance."

Ross eyed the polished floorboards. Now that Jennie had
mentioned trying the clothes on, which meant he'd have to

take his own clothes off, he was too embarrassed to even look at her.

"I'll go make sure the play yard is empty. We can have our dance lesson there." She opened her wardrobe. A full-length mirror hung on the inside of one door, and a crossbow, a sword, and two daggers were mounted on the other. "I'll knock before I come back in." She whisked herself out.

The room held so much of Jennie's presence that he instinctively glanced around to make sure she was gone. It even smelled like her. She must put the herbs from the window box in with her clothes. He thought his mother might have done that.

He set his backpack down, making sure the book was tucked out of sight. Mia had encouraged him to show it to Jennie, and it would be fun to see her excitement—but he was uneasy enough having the Lees know. He'd already put them at risk. He might be endangering the Rileys as well.

He was as unused to thinking about these things as he was to borrowing clothes. But Jennie was waiting.

With a quick glance at the closed door, he shook out the garments. The black linen pants were embroidered down the outer seams, and the white shirt down the front and around the cuffs. The blue jacket was beautifully cut. The whole outfit was worth several months of work in trade, or a winter's worth of food. He could hardly believe that anyone would trust him with something so valuable, even for an evening.

Ross barely recognized the guy in Jennie's mirror. He looked tired, but not hungry. His hair was clean and brushed. Though the cuffs of the expensive shirt came down to his knuckles, the equally expensive pants fit perfectly. He looked ... prosperous.

A knock at the door made him jump. "All dressed?" called Jennie.

Ross almost said no. He liked the thought of her seeing him in these fine clothes, but it also made him nervous. He forced himself to straighten up before he spoke. "Yeah."

Jennie came in, red skirt swinging. Trying to avoid the sight of it, he watched her face instead, and was rewarded with a delighted grin. "You look great, Ross. Like it?"

"I'm afraid something will happen to it," he admitted. "I might tear it, or spill a drink on it."

"The nice thing about clothes is, you can wash them," Jennie said with a chuckle. "But wear it with your own jacket, not Paco's. That should turn some heads."

"My leather jacket?" It fit well and gave reasonable protection against cold and sharp objects, but it was hard to imagine it being an object of admiration. "It's old. It's patched. It's been through a million fights."

"The fights are what make it cool. Most of the guys here would trade their younger sibs for it." She smiled at him. "Speaking of a million fights, the kids keep wanting me to ask you about them. About what you've seen in the world. The whole town is interested in you. Most of us never get farther than our fields. Could I write a newspaper article about you?"

The thought of the entire town knowing things about him made his neck tighten.

Jennie said quickly, with another smile, "I don't mean now, but someday. Later on." She indicated his old clothes. "Do you want to dance in those, or stay in what you're wearing?"

"I don't want to get these sweaty," he said, glad she'd changed the subject.

Ross felt an odd mixture of relief and regret as he put on his old clothes. Then he stashed the dancing outfit in his backpack and followed Jennie into an empty yard fenced with juniper bushes. The hard-packed dirt was pale gold in the fading light.

"How much you do you know about dancing?" she asked.

Ross had come to hate all questions that began with "How much do you know," but not as much as he hated the answers he had to give. "Nothing." Of course.

"It's easy. Think of it as very slow set sparring. I move, you back up. You move, I give."

She took a step toward him. He slid backward, his shoes moving smoothly over the even ground. He watched for the frown that would mean he was doing it wrong.

Instead, she smiled. "Good! Now you come forward. Step, don't slide."

Ross took a step, and Jennie glided away.

"Forward."

She stepped toward him. This time he retreated, matching how she placed her feet. Then she beckoned and he stepped forward. They repeated the sequence. As she'd promised, it was easy, not that different from what you'd teach someone first learning to fight.

She added in a sideways sway and began guiding him around in a circle. After all their sparring, it felt natural; he'd gotten used to the way she moved, though it was strange to go so slowly.

Jennie stopped, and he stopped with her.

"Okay, that's the basic step. Everything else is variation. Shall I show you some?" He nodded. "The first is the waltz. That's a dance for two. Put your right hand here." She patted her waist.

Ross had touched her before, but rarely for longer than it took to strike or block. After that first match, he'd never managed to take her down again. The tree-red dress clung to her body, outlining the dip and curve of her hip.

"Slow sparring," she said encouragingly. "Very slow."

He put his hand on her waist. The cloth slid under his palm, and he had to press firmly to keep his hand in place. He could feel the warmth of her skin, and his hand slipped again as she inhaled.

The normal rhythm of her breathing was briefly interrupted, and a tiny muscle tensed in her jaw. If they had been sparring, he would have thought it had occurred to her that he could win.

She reached for his left hand. His fingers twitched, locked, and refused to close. The scar pulled and ached. But she molded her hand to his. Forcing his muscles to relax, he coaxed his fingers into clutching a little tighter. Her hand was cooler than her waist, with ridged calluses and scars on the striking surfaces of her knuckles.

She lifted their linked hands to shoulder height. "Move in place, step-two-three, step-two-three."

Ross moved, unable to concentrate on anything but his right hand on the curve of Jennie's waist, his left hand holding hers, and the weightless touch of her other hand on his shoulder. Back two-three, forward two-three, and one step sideways. Linked together, they moved in that back-and-forth circle, close enough for him to feel her breath as she counted aloud.

So this was dancing. He relaxed into the pattern, inhaling her scent of dried flowers and herbs. Her half-closed eyes caught the ochre rays of the sinking sun, and tawny sparks glinted against deep brown.

"Ready for the fun stuff?" she asked.

"Sure."

She took a big step, whirling him outward. He stumbled, then caught the rhythm. They spun and turned around the yard, step-two-three, step-two-three, until the house and the juniper bushes blurred around him, and her cloud of hair tickled his cheek.

After a while, she slowed and began to speak. "Paco wore that outfit for folklórico—that's a group dance. If you want to learn it, you'd have to ask him once his knee heals. But I can show you some different ones."

She taught him some simple moves, then returned to the waltz. Unlike sparring, dancing wasn't so tiring that you were forced to do it in brief rounds or collapse from exhaustion. He wondered how people knew when to stop, but didn't ask for fear that she'd demonstrate. Maybe they could keep moving forever, step-two-three, step-two-three, just him and Jennie and the broad sky above them.

She finally brought them to a halt. Ross expected her to move away, but she didn't, leaving him conscious all over again that he had his hands on a girl's body. Two instincts fought in him: to pull her in and hold her close, and to run. He tensed with the effort of doing neither.

Jennie let go of his shoulder, twirled under his hand, and stepped back. It was natural to let their hands drop then, and he surreptitiously wiped his clammy palms down his jeans.

"And also we have solo dances!" Her words came faster than usual. "I forgot about those."

"Dancing alone? With people watching you?"

"You don't have time to learn one anyway," Jennie said hastily. "But I can show you one of mine. No one's seen it yet. You'll be the first." She clapped her hands in a fast beat. "Can you keep this rhythm?"

Ross's left arm ached too much to clap, so he slapped his right thigh instead. She stamped her feet while her arms moved with piston-like precision, mapping patterns that were almost too fast to see: her left arm executed a set of five gestures, her right did a different set of eight, and all the while her hips swung to make her skirts fly out and her feet pounded a counterpoint to his beat.

All those difficult movements were done with the same beauty and power she brought to her martial arts. Ross could have danced with her forever, but he could have watched her forever, too.

With a quick grin, she leaped high into the air and threw herself backward in a spectacular series of flips, landing on her hands just before she would have crashed into the junipers. She balanced upside down, her skirt over her head, long dark legs in scarlet shorts stretched out elegantly, toes pointed toward the sky. Then she brought her legs down slowly, showing off her strength and control, until she was bent over backward like a bridge, her palms and soles pressed to the ground. She stood with a flourish, as if it had all been easy.

"I was thinking of doing that one for the dance." Ross could tell exactly how easy it hadn't been by the lines of sweat trickling down her face. "What do you think, Ross? Do you think people will like it?"

He couldn't even begin to put into words how much he thought they would. Finally he settled for "Yeah." Then he added, "I think I'm actually looking forward to the dance now."

Jennie smiled. "Would you like to go with Mia and me? We talked about it, and we'd both like to go with you."

"Sure," Ross spoke before he thought. Thinking about it, he added, "Yeah. I'd like that."

He wondered how Mia danced. Would she have as much strength and grace as Jennie? Or would she be awkward and shy, like he had been? Either way, it was something he wanted to see. He had an image of himself at the dance with Mia and Jennie beside him, and he almost believed it would happen.

Jennie had trusted him with those fine clothes, and with the first look at her new solo dance. And Mia trusted Jennie. Ross slowly walked to his backpack.

"I have something I'd like to show you. But it could be dangerous to know about it. Do you want to take a look?"

"Yes. Let's see it." Jennie took the book as carefully as if it was a newborn pup. First she examined the binding, then reverently turned the pages. Unlike Mia, who had focused on the diagrams, she drew her finger down the lines of writing.

To his surprise, she looked at him and laughed. "So all this time, you've been walking around in borrowed clothes with a king's ransom in your pack! No wonder that bounty hunter was so determined."

"Mia said it's in Japanese."

"Yes, I think she's right. You could get Yuki Nakamura to read it." She glanced at him mischievously. "You'll have a perfect opportunity at your riding lesson tomorrow."

Ross grimaced. "I nearly killed his rat, and I was worthless during the snake attack. I'm sure he's still mad at me. I'll figure it out on my own."

"It's too bad you and he got off on the wrong foot. I think you have a lot in common." Before he could protest, she added, "But I won't say a word unless you give me permission."

"Good." Now that she knew, he decided to take an even bigger risk. "Can you hide it for me? I don't think the bounty hunter has given up, and he knows where I'm staying."

Jennie's smile vanished. "Sure. I'll put it in the schoolhouse, up on the rafters. No one ever looks up there, and they wouldn't see it or be able to reach it if they did." She indicated a diagram. "This looks like an alarm system. We could use—"

The door latch rattled. He lunged for the book, but Jennie was faster, flipping a fold of her skirt over it to hide it.

Tonio burst through the door. "Jennie! Pa wants you right now!"

"Tell him I'm coming." Ross followed her back to her room, where she hid the book in a drawer, under her clothes.

His hand dropped to the empty loops in his belt, and then he reached toward the daggers in Jennie's closet. "Can I?"

"Go ahead."

They ran out, Ross patting the borrowed knives as he kept pace. He wasn't sure what he was supposed to do if it was a family crisis. But if it was a wild animal attack, he was set.

They found the rest of the Rileys gathered outside around a sobbing Dee, who was crouched on the dusty ground.

Jennie sat down next to her sister. "Dee? What's the matter?"

Dee lifted her tear-streaked face. "I've Changed."

"But honey, you wanted to Change." Jennie put her arm around Dee's shoulders.

"Not like this. I wanted a cool power like yours or Pa's. Look what happened to me!"

She blew on the powdery dirt between her feet. A puff of dust rose up, formed itself into a dust devil no bigger than a man's finger, spun for a moment, and then died.

"That's it?" José exclaimed. "That's pathetic."

As Dee let out a fresh howl, Mr. Riley said, "José. You do not put down other people's powers. They are a blessing from God, and you know it."

Dee wailed, "But you only get one blessing. Now I can't get anything good! You can see for miles and Ma can talk to horses and Jennie can grab things and José can make earthquakes and even Tonio can light up dark places, and all I can do is make stupid little dust things!"

"Maybe it'll get stronger, Dee," José said doubtfully.

Mr. Riley jerked his thumb over his shoulder. José went back inside, followed by the other kids.

Lowering his voice in the hope that only Jennie would hear him, Ross said, "I think I'd better go."

To his alarm, he only attracted Dee's attention. She lifted her head. "Right, Ross? Isn't this the most useless power you've ever seen?"

He thought about it. "No. I met a guy once who could make little horns grow out of his forehead. Now, *that* was a useless power."

Dee managed a smile.

Jennie patted her on the arm. "You know, Dee, when I was a toddler, I couldn't lift anything bigger than a pebble. It's like baby steps. José was right. If you keep practicing, you should get stronger."

"Great," Dee muttered. "Someday maybe I can make a big dust devil."

"That would be very useful in a fight." Her father scooped her up and set her on her feet. "Dee, this is your Change Day, and you know what that means. José and I will get the food ready for your party. Wash your face and invite your friends. And be quick. It's getting dark."

A sharp twinge in his wrist made Ross realize that he had been rubbing his scar. He didn't want to get stuck at a party full of little girls, but he didn't want to head back to the Lees', either. Since he didn't seem able to sleep, maybe he could try napping in the day, like Mia. That might trick the nightmares into staying away.

"I'll start the pie first," said Mr. Riley. "What kind do you want?"

Dee scrubbed at her face. "Lemon meringue."

"I think we've got enough chickens left to round up some egg whites. Lemon meringue it is."

As Dee scampered back into the house, a tiny dust devil swirled after her, collided with the threshold, and collapsed.

"Baby steps," said her father.

26

Mia

MIA PACED ALONG THE IRRIGATION ROWS IN THE Vardam orchard, followed by Mr. and Mrs. Vardam, and Sujata, all holding lanterns.

Small, deft hands had dug a channel from the east canal, diverting a stream of water into the uncultivated woods along the wall. All around the wet earth of the channel were what looked like baby handprints.

"See, Mia?" Sujata said. "They're stealing our water again!"

They followed the diverted stream into the woods, where it led to a moat crossed by miniature bridges of bundled twigs and sticks. At the center was a typical raccoon city of lean-tos, tree houses, and walkways of swinging vines. Many pairs of red eyes stared at them from within.

"Clever little things," Mia said. "Isn't it amazing what they can do with nothing but the ability to tie knots?"

"And plan," Mr. Vardam said. "Plan their devilry." His chameleon skin had turned black in the dim light.

Mrs. Vardam patted his arm, leaving the brief impression of her brown fingers. "Dear, I think devilry is a bit strong. Mischief."

"It's devilry if I have to dig it all up." He swung around. "Mia, can you figure a way to keep them out? I know you've done your best, but this is the third time in six months."

She was already sifting through ideas, from traps to electrified fences to chemical repellents. Mr. Vardam cleared his throat. "Not sure right now," she said hastily. "I'll work on it."

"For every month you keep us raccoon-free, there'll be as much fruit as you and the doctor can use." Mrs. Vardam held out her hand.

"Deal," Mia said, sealing it palm to palm. She hoped she wouldn't be faced with apricot–goat cheese kimchi—though if she was, she could always feed it to Ross.

As she walked into her yard, she wondered how the dancing lesson was going. She sat on a tin washtub, checking to see how she felt. What if Jennie and Ross were still dancing? What if they were . . . doing something else?

Mia glared at a chunk of pipe. So what if they were? Did that take anything away from her? She'd watched her classmates fight over who got to date whom, as if the people themselves had no say about it. She'd even seen lifelong friendships break up. Mia had always promised herself that she would never do anything so silly, assuming she ever found anyone she wanted to date who was willing to date her. Anyway, Jennie wouldn't go behind her back.

Mia decided to work on her flamethrower near her window, so she'd see Ross if he walked by. At first she glanced up every few minutes, but then she became absorbed in her work. She was soldering the igniter safety catch when a flicker of movement caught her eye. The front door of the surgery opened, and out walked Ross.

She glanced at her clock. Two a.m. Was he coming to sleep in her yard? She hoped he'd want to talk to her first. She turned off the electrical current and set her tools and flamethrower aside to cool down. But the knock didn't come. She went to the door to look out. Across the square, moonlight glowed pale on Ross's shirt. He was walking away from her, toward the town hall.

Should she go after him? If he'd had a nightmare, would he want company? Maybe he would if he saw her.

Mia hurried after him, debating whether to call out. He didn't seem to notice that anyone was behind him. To her surprise, he walked inside the town hall. No one would be there at this hour, and it had a strong slate ceiling. He wouldn't want to sleep under that. Maybe he'd stashed his book there, instead of giving it to Jennie for safekeeping.

It was dark inside. She felt for the flint beside the door, and lit the lamp. Ross was nowhere to be seen. But the basement door stood open.

That shouldn't be possible. There were only four keys: the sheriff's, the mayor's, Jack's, and her own. She checked; hers was still on her key ring. Then she remembered Ross's lock picks.

The blanket hanging from the old wagon had been thrown back, exposing the open tunnel.

No one was supposed to know about that tunnel but the town council, the council scribe, and Mia herself. It was the most carefully guarded secret of Las Anclas, a means of escape should the town be captured—or a means for an enemy to slip inside, if the secret got out.

Was Ross a thief after all? Was he an agent of Voske's? Maybe the bounty hunter had told the truth.

Horrified, Mia thought, *I offered him guest privilege, and Dad backed me up. Whatever Ross does is our responsibility.*

She did not believe it. Did not want to believe it. But she had to know.

Mia descended into the tunnel, ran till she reached the ladder, and climbed up into the mill. She could hear her own heart beating in the silent, empty space. For the first time in her life, she was outside Las Anclas after the gates closed for the night.

If she went out with the lantern, the wall sentries would

see her. If Ross was waiting outside with invaders, the sentries would be her allies. But if there was some innocent explanation, she didn't want them involved—and she didn't want anyone to know about the tunnel if she could avoid it.

Mia doused the lantern and waited until her eyes adjusted to the darkness. Then she slipped between the rows of corn until she reached the trail that ran along the ridge. Ross was far ahead, a lone figure moving south.

He's running away, she thought, coming to a halt. *It's all my fault! I made Jennie ask him to the dance with both of us. He'd rather leave everything than go to the dance with me.*

Sickened, she watched, uncertain what to do. In the distance, coyotes howled. She was sure he could hold his own with the coyote packs. That was no excuse for running after him and trying to drag him back to a life he clearly didn't want. But those were animals. And what about that bounty hunter? Mia didn't believe he'd really gone. Ross had lost his first fight with the man, and he still couldn't use his left hand effectively. She should at least try to talk him into staying until it healed.

She ran after him. She'd tell him he didn't have to do anything he didn't want to do. He could go to the dance with anyone. He didn't have to go to the dance at all. She'd never mention the book again. She'd give him back all the diagrams she'd copied from it.

The fire-bright glow of the singing tree brought her to a sudden halt.

He was heading straight toward it.

Mia tucked her head down and ran, shouting, "Ross! Stop!"

He stumbled, swayed, then turned. "Mia?"

"Ross, get out of there!" She started down the slope, skidded on a patch of gravel, and fell. She was fifteen feet from the tree, well within range of the lethal shards. Ross was much closer. She didn't know why the pods hadn't exploded already.

Leaves clashed together, ringing out a final threat. She was too close to get out of range and too far to reach him, but she jumped toward him anyway.

Ross turned from her and lunged at the tree. His fingers spread over the crystalline trunk. The chiming stopped.

Mia gave a sob of relief. "Ross?" Why wasn't she dead? "Get out of there!"

The tree shivered, chimes rising in pitch with the rise of her voice. She froze, watching hm in silent agony. He stood very still, hands and cheek pressed against the tree. Then he whispered, "Back up, Mia. All the way."

"You're not safe."

"Yes, I am. Back away. Go up to the road."

One step at a time, without taking her gaze away from Ross, she climbed back up the slope, until she was twenty-five feet away, and he was the black shadow of a boy against a pillar of crimson light.

Then, while she watched, he too slowly backed away, step by step until he stood next to her, breathing hard.

"I did it. It wanted to hurt you. But I stopped it." He sounded bewildered. "How did I get here?"

"You walked out. I followed you."

"I . . . what? The last thing I remember was trying to fall asleep. I dreamed that it called to me." He began to turn away, but stumbled and nearly fell. Mia caught him by the shoulders.

"Come on. Let's go back."

For once, he didn't pull away. "Yeah. Let's go."

As they headed home, she asked, "What happened? How did you stop that thing?"

"I think it's like you said. It's my tree. Those dreams—I think it was trying to talk to me. Trying to get me to talk to it."

"Talk, how? Aloud?"

He shook his head. He was staring sightlessly up at the sky. She had to steer him to keep him on the path.

"I don't have the words," he said at last. "I'm so tired."

"A little farther. Here, between these rows of corn. We don't want the sentries to see us."

Inside the mill, Mia relit the lantern and led him into the tunnel.

Ross ran his fingers along the dirt walls. "This is amazing."

"Yes, but you can't tell anyone about it, ever!" she said urgently. "It's the town's last resort, to get the kids out safely if we're ever invaded. How did you even find it?"

"Jack took me into the basement once. That's what prospectors do—find hidden things. I meant to ask you about it." He yawned again. "I forgot."

"Well, forget you ever saw it."

"Okay."

Back in her cottage, they sat on the floor by her bed, and she poured out hibiscus tea. "You should get Dad to look at you. Make sure you're okay."

He shook his head, nearly spilling his drink. "Tomorrow," he mumbled. His head tipped back, and his hand sank toward the floor.

She caught the jar before he could drop it, and put it on the floor. When she straightened up, she found that he was leaning against her, fast asleep. He was warm and his hair was soft against her neck. She stroked his cheek gently, then curled herself into him and closed her eyes.

27

YUKI

YUKI SHADED HIS EYES AGAINST THE FIRST RAYS OF dawn. Mr. Riley and the others on the day's patrol waited outside the stable, but Ross was nowhere to be seen. The teenage sentries peered down at them from the sentry walk. Everyone was watching, amused or pitying, as if Yuki had been stood up at a dance.

Mr. Riley leaned down from his seat on Spot, the pinto mare, his dreadlocks swinging. "When did you last speak to Ross about his riding lesson?"

"Yesterday morning, at school. He knows he's supposed to be here."

"We can't wait any longer. The two of you will have to catch up with us."

As the patrol rode out, Henry called down from the wall, "Hey, babysitter! Did your baby toddle off and leave you alone?"

Yuki's mother clapped her hands. "Back to work, sentries."

"Yes, Ms. Lowenstein!" Henry said with exaggerated respect and an unnecessary salute.

She turned her baleful yellow eyes on him. "Or do we need extra drill after your watch?"

"Shut up, Henry," said Sujata. They all scrambled into position.

Yuki took one last look around, but he saw only the kids in the training corrals, the grooms with the tired horses from the night patrol, and Mrs. Riley soothing a mare in heat.

Gritting his teeth, he returned Fuego and Snow to their stalls. Ross was the one who had shirked his duty, but Yuki was the one who had been made to look like a fool. He regretted having told him off after the rattlesnake attack. If he'd kept his mouth shut, Jennie would never have given him this assignment.

He wished he were with Paco, who had been assigned sit-down duty until his knee healed. Making arrows at the armory was tedious, but it wouldn't feel that way with Paco there. . . .

"Stay, Kogatana," he ordered. She leaped up on to Fuego's saddle, and began to clean her whiskers.

Yuki set off for the surgery, expecting to see Ross running toward the stables, or to meet someone who would explain that he had been taken ill or sprained his ankle or been sent to run some crucial errand. Not even a ten-year-old—not even Henry—would simply not show up for an assigned task.

At the surgery, he yanked off his boots, then hurried inside, surprising Dr. Lee.

"Where is he?" Yuki demanded.

"Yuki! You startled me!" Dr. Lee was filling a jar with some pungent liquid. "Where is who?"

"Ross was supposed to meet me for a riding lesson."

"Ah. His room is at the top of the stairs. Knock first."

Yuki took the stairs three at a time. He slipped and caught himself painfully against the banister. He banged on the door, then threw it open. The room was empty.

"He may be at Mia's," called the doctor. "Knock first. Actually, let me come with you."

Yuki jammed his feet back into his boots and stalked out, Dr. Lee following him. He forced himself to rap more politely on the door to Mia's cottage.

No answer.

He tried again. Nothing. He opened the door.

Ross was asleep—asleep!—on the floor, leaning against a sleeping Mia. Their backs rested against a bed piled with machinery and loose pages. Between them rested a jug of . . . something.

Yuki's expectations of Ross had been low to begin with, but this was unbelievable. He was even more surprised by Mia, who was responsible, if a bit absentminded.

The sound of laughter startled him. Dr. Lee leaned against the door, wiping his eyes.

Yuki didn't find it the slightest bit funny. While Mia and Ross had been having their drunken party, he'd helped Paco with a series of painful exercises to keep his knee flexible. Ross hadn't actually shot Paco, but he'd contributed to that disaster. Getting drunk enough to miss his riding lesson was not only selfish and irresponsible, it showed a total lack of respect for Yuki as a person and his role as Ross's teacher.

"Wake up!" he shouted.

If he hadn't been so angry, the way the two jumped would have been hilarious. Ross kicked the jug over—Yuki was surprised to discover it was full of hibiscus tea, not liquor—and Mia flailed her arms, then dived for her glasses, knocking them under her desk. She scrambled after them, sending a flurry of papers across the floor.

Ross's next reaction was even stranger. He clutched at his ankles with both hands, then fumbled behind his back and whipped out a wrench, which he brandished like a weapon.

"What are you doing?" Yuki demanded.

Ross squinted at the wrench, then put it down again, flushing a dark red-brown all the way to the tips of his ears.

Mia had found her glasses, and was busy shoving the papers away from the pool of hibiscus tea, her hair falling into her crimson face. "Dad? What are you doing here?" She cast Yuki a nervous glance. "What are *you* doing here?"

"You're late," he said to Ross. "You have a riding lesson. Remember?"

From the look on Ross's face, he clearly had not remembered.

"I'm sorry. I'll get dressed." He glanced down at his grubby jeans and shirt. "Never mind. I'll go now."

Yuki walked out in a rage. Ross caught up, wincing every time his feet hit the ground. He looked terrible. His hair was stringy, the shadows around his bloodshot eyes were as dark as if someone had punched him, and he moved as if the air hurt his skin.

"What did you two put in that hibiscus tea?" snapped Yuki. "Dr. Lee's preserving alcohol?"

"Let's get on with the lesson."

At the armory, Yuki picked up two saddle swords and his bow and arrows, then waited impatiently as, one by one, Ross tested the balance of four knives. The guy could weigh himself down with all the knives in the world, but they'd never make up for the fact that he couldn't wield a sword or shoot a bow.

Ross recoiled when the bright morning sunlight struck his face. He backed up and leaned against the doorway.

That was the last straw. Yuki folded his arms. "You don't want to learn? Fine. We're done here. Go nurse your hangover."

Ross looked up in confusion. "I don't—I do want to learn."

"You're not acting like it."

"I'm here, aren't I?"

Someone cleared their throat loudly from the sentry walk. Yuki looked up into his mother's narrowed cat-eyes. "Do your job, Yuki," she ordered. "Do you want your life to depend on someone you didn't teach to ride?"

Then she turned her yellow gaze on Ross. "As for you, it looks like you've already punished yourself. If you don't like working with a hangover, don't drink more than you can handle."

Ross opened his mouth, then closed it. He gave Yuki's mother a quick nod.

"Let's go." Yuki mounted Fuego slowly, so Ross could see how it should be done.

He was still brooding on his mother's words as they rode toward the gate. He knew his life might depend on anyone in Las Anclas, down to the little kid assigned to ring the bell. But he couldn't conceive of trusting them with his life. He imagined himself in some pitched battle, certain that the person at his back would protect him, as he was protecting them. He could imagine Paco in that position, and Sera. He could imagine Meredith, and his mom. That was it.

He certainly couldn't imagine trusting Ross, who couldn't even manage the reins correctly. Yuki raised his hand to demonstrate. "Hold them like this."

He knew that Ross had an injury to his left hand, but this was the first time he'd paid attention to how Ross used it. Leaning over the saddle, Yuki watched Ross struggle to close his fist. The muscles in his forearm bulged and the scar went from white to pink, but he couldn't get his fingers to touch his thumb. There was no way he could grip the reins.

Yuki took a deep breath, trying to set his anger aside. He had a job to do. As long as Ross was willing to put in minimal effort, Yuki would do whatever he could to ensure that he learned how to ride competently, if not well.

"Grip with your thighs. You don't really need the reins to ride. See?" He tucked his reins under one knee, raised his empty hands, and urged Fuego forward. "I'm telling him which way to turn by shifting my balance and nudging him with my knee. Horses are very sensitive. You don't kick them. You don't jab them. And you don't yank on their mouths. Press with your right knee. Gently."

Ross gave him a doubtful glance, then obeyed. Snow circled the yard. His suspicious look changed to a tentative smile, but the smile vanished when he reached Yuki again. "Okay. What next?"

"Let's catch up with the patrol. I can explain more on the way." Yuki nudged Fuego to move, and Snow followed.

Outside the gates, he started to ride in the patrol's tracks, which led to the left.

"Whoa!" Snow was plunging, ears back. "Why's she doing that?" Ross asked through gritted teeth, clinging to the saddle.

"Something's spooking her. *You're* spooking her." He followed Ross's fixed gaze to the left, toward the cornfields and the ridge beyond. Then he remembered how Fuego had balked at the blood-red singing tree.

"If you're scared of something, it'll scare your horse. They're sensitive, remember? They tense up if you tense up." Yuki jerked his thumb over his shoulder. "Turn right. We won't catch up with the patrol anyway. Let's practice balance."

The sunlight brightened as they passed the squash fields, and a flock of hummingbirds zoomed past, signaling to one another with bright flashes of their reflective wings. Kogatana tapped Yuki with her paw. He whipped up his bow and nocked an arrow.

A coyote scout tilted its tawny ears toward them from behind a bush. It yipped twice quickly, and then a third time. The bushes rustled as the rest of the pack retreated.

The coyote packs never gave up hope that they might catch a rider off guard, so they sent scouts to check out most patrols. Yuki glanced at Ross, expecting him to be fumbling for his sword atop a skittish Snow. Ross held a knife by its blade—something six-year-olds were taught not to do—but the angle of his wrist and the way he gauged distance suggested that he knew what he was doing. Snow stood perfectly still, without even a toss of her head.

"Think they're gone?" Ross asked.

Kogatana was cleaning her whiskers. "Yes. Kogatana would still be alert if they weren't."

Ross flipped the knife into the air and caught it by the hilt. It was a classic show-off move.

Yuki was not impressed. "Let's try the trot." He demonstrated how to rise and settle into the saddle, matching the horse's rhythm.

Ross didn't do as badly as Yuki expected, and he decided that Ross probably wouldn't fall off if he held a sword. Yuki was about to give the order when Kogatana squealed in warning. Fuego plunged down and nearly threw him, and a dark shape leaped for the horse's neck.

Yuki fought to regain his balance and rip his sword free. Before he could, a tarantula fell away from Fuego. The huge spider curled up in the dust, furry legs thrashing. Red-streaked liquid oozed out around the hilt of Ross's knife.

Fuego tossed his head and struggled to pull up his leg. Yuki leaped down. Fuego's hoof was caught in a sticky web trap. Yuki cut him free and checked his leg. To his relief, the horse was unhurt.

Ross clambered down, and used his saddle sword to flick his knife away from the dead tarantula.

"The blood is poisonous. Don't touch it," Yuki said, then regretted the words—Ross clearly knew what he was doing.

Ross cleaned his knife in the sand and didn't reply.

"Thanks," Yuki said. "That was a good throw. But why did you hold it by the blade?"

"Depends on the balance. This one's weighted toward the hilt." He handed over the knife. Yuki tried holding it by the blade. It felt incredibly awkward. Ross repositioned his fingers. "Like that."

With Yuki's hand in his, Ross moved to aim at a distant cactus. Then he slid the knife from Yuki's hand and threw it.

The knife thudded into the cactus. Spines shot out in all directions and pattered down on the sand. Ross stepped around them to retrieve the knife. "Just practice," he said, returning it to his boot.

Now Yuki understood why Ross had grabbed at his ankles when Yuki had woken him up—he'd been reaching for knives. No wonder Dr. Lee kept warning him to knock.

All his training had failed to give Yuki reflexes like that. While he'd been drilling endlessly and occasionally fighting animals, Ross had been seeing the world and surviving real dangers. And he'd apparently done it all on foot, with no weapons other than those little daggers.

"I wish I'd had a bow when that bounty hunter was after me," Ross said. "I mean, I wish I knew how to shoot one."

"Just practice," Yuki said. But he didn't say it mockingly. "We better move on. We should get the horses to the stream before it gets too hot."

Heat waves shimmered in the air. It was a relief when they finally reached the stream at the bottom of a gully. A shadow flickered over their faces as a hawk rode the air currents above.

"Damn." Ross pulled up his mare an instant before Yuki saw a man's silhouette step deliberately to the edge of the cliff, blocking the sun.

Ross gripped one of his knives, and Yuki reached for his bow. The man leaned against his rifle, which was pointed upward, not at them, and stood silently, watching as the horses descended toward the stream. Ross turned until he was almost backward in the saddle, his gaze unwavering, until the bounty hunter was out of sight.

The smooth rhythm of Fuego's walk had broken. Yuki deliberately relaxed his muscles, breathed evenly, and told himself to be calm. Eventually, Fuego calmed down too. "He could have shot us," Yuki finally said.

"He could have shot me." Ross kept glancing back. "He wanted me to see him."

"If he doesn't want to kill you, then what does he want from you?"

Ross's gaze shifted away. "Nothing."

Yuki had heard the rumors, from the plausible to the ridiculous: Ross was a claim jumper, he had a dangerous Change talent, he'd stolen King Voske's crown, he had a map to El Dorado, the Lost City of Gold. But no bounty hunter chased people across the desert for nothing.

At the stream, the horses lowered their heads to drink, and they dismounted to refill their canteens. Yuki splashed water on his face.

"When, um, when I first saw Kogatana, you did this." To Yuki's amazement, Ross sketched the kanji for *kogatana* in the air.

"You remember that?"

"Where did you learn it?" Ross dipped his canteen.

"On the *Taka*," Yuki replied. "The ship where I was born."

Ross straightened, water dripping from his fingers. "You were born on a ship? What kind of ship?"

Everyone in Las Anclas knew about his past, and most of them had learned not to ask questions. Even Paco avoided certain topics. Yuki was about to fob Ross off, mostly out of habit, but the quiet, nonjudgmental curiosity prompted him to break habit and speak.

"It was an 'aircraft carrier.' Like a floating city. It came from a country called Japan, hundreds of years ago. We sailed in the deep ocean. Every day, we were somewhere different." Yuki sketched *kogatana* in the air. "Kogatana.

The first character is 'small,' and the second is 'sword.' Little sword: pocketknife." His fingers reached up, drawing another pair of kanji: "*Taka*. That was my ship. It means 'hawk.'"

Memories flooded his mind, washing away the desert, the bright-blue sky, and Ross's curious face. He remembered the smell of deep-sea brine. He remembered riding dolphins and fishing with a spear gun. He remembered the lush greenery of the hydroponic tanks. He remembered the flavors of rice, of sweet red beans, of green tea. He remembered violins playing at twilight. He remembered stepping through the sacred gates to pray to the spirits of rice and wind and ocean. And he remembered his first mother.

He blinked, and the desert was back.

"How did you get here?" Ross asked.

"The *Taka* was conquered by pirates. My parents put me on a raft, but they had to stay."

"Why?"

"Because my mother was the queen." Yuki turned away, schooling his face. "If you've heard people call me a prince, that's why."

Ross looked baffled, and Yuki wished he hadn't brought it up. "They came out of a storm and took the *Taka* by surprise." Memory assaulted him: flames shooting skyward from the superstructure, the crack of artillery fire. The others rowing him away on the raft while he yelled for them to go back, to wait for his parents.

And, finally, washing up on the beach near Las Anclas. He hadn't understood until much later that he was the only survivor because the others must have pretended to drink, and had given him all their water.

He dug his nails into the back of his hand, shutting the door on those memories. He wasn't on the raft and he wasn't thirteen. He was eighteen, in Las Anclas, in the desert, right now. With Ross staring at him.

Yuki felt as if he'd been cracked open like an egg. Then he remembered that Ross supposedly could manipulate people's emotions. Yuki had begun the ride furious, but then he'd started thinking the guy wasn't that bad. So maybe it was true.

On the other hand, Ross had saved Fuego. And if he really could make people like him, Tommy and his Norm friends would have stopped hassling him by now.

Ross blurted out, "Could you teach someone to read Japanese?"

Once again Yuki was taken by surprise. He lowered his canteen. "I guess. Was that why you were asking me all that stuff?"

"I don't know much about reading," Ross said to a nearby cactus. "Is it harder than English and Spanish?"

Yuki almost laughed. Ross's face and body gave away everything he felt, as if he'd never learned how to conceal his emotions. Maybe he *had* stolen Voske's crown. It was easier to believe than his being a sneaky manipulator.

Yuki almost hated to break the bad news to him. "Japanese has two syllabaries—those are like alphabets—with forty-eight characters each. The hard part is that it also has about three thousand Chinese characters."

"Oh."

Yuki hesitated. Ross *had* saved Fuego. "If you'd still like to learn, I could teach you. But it could be years before you could read anything difficult, like a book."

"Thanks." Ross sounded discouraged. "But I won't be here that long."

I won't either, was on the tip of Yuki's tongue. But he wasn't sure he wanted to get into a discussion about prospecting yet—especially now that Yuki had a claim of his own. What if the price of learning from Ross was sharing the sea cave? "Can you swim?"

Ross's brows drew together in confusion. "No. I've never been around that much water." No competition for the cave, then. Then he blurted out, "Listen, Yuki. I didn't want to make excuses. But we really didn't drink anything. I mean, besides hibiscus tea." Keeping his eyes on the ground, he added, "I had a bad night. I—I didn't feel good. That's why I forgot about the lesson. It won't happen again."

It was clear that Ross was telling the truth, and it was also clear that he wasn't telling all of it. But he didn't owe Yuki any explanations. Probably the missing part had to do with the romance he was obviously having with Mia Lee, which was none of Yuki's business.

"If you're sick, you should say so. I would have postponed the lesson. We're done anyway. You can practice riding without reins on the way back."

He mounted Fuego, and watched Ross clamber up on to Snow. To Yuki's amusement, the mare turned her gray head, as if asking Yuki for permission to move. He clicked his tongue, and they set off.

After all his suspicions about Ross, and all the wild claims of outlawry and mind control, Yuki thought that the truth was probably simpler: he was a young prospector with trouble in his past, who'd spent his life by himself and wasn't used to having to explain himself to others.

Probably.

In any case, there was no point quizzing Ross now. He looked dead on his feet. Yuki would schedule one more lesson. If Ross showed up promptly and tried his best, that would go some way toward proving that he was trustworthy.

As the gates of Las Anclas came into sight, Yuki's thoughts

drifted back to his childhood. The *Taka* was so much smaller than Las Anclas; had it seemed bigger because it had been more sophisticated and mechanically advanced? Or because he'd been so young? If the pirates had never attacked, would he have gazed at the ocean's vastness one day and felt trapped within his own kingdom?

28

Ross

ROSS TRUDGED AWAY FROM THE STABLES, HIS HEAD throbbing, the afternoon sunlight almost blinding him. Then a shadow fell across his face, and his body automatically snapped into a defensive stance.

Mr. Preston loomed up. Ross hastily lowered his hands, heat creeping up his neck.

"You're fast," the defense chief said. Definitely the first human words Ross had heard from the guy. But then he reverted to his usual menace. "I'd like to take a look at that book of yours."

"I already told the sheriff, I hid it in the desert."

Mr. Preston shook his head. "You don't understand. I'm considering buying it from you. But I can't make you an offer sight-unseen."

Ross stared at him. Mr. Preston used to work for Voske, and had conspired with the bounty hunter. Maybe they were still plotting together. If Ross accepted his offer, what was to stop Mr. Preston from taking the book, keeping the payment, and turning Ross over to his friend?

"I hid it in the desert," he repeated.

Mr. Preston's pale gaze narrowed. "Do you think someone else here can make you a better offer?"

"It's not for sale." Ross bolted for the surgery, his head pounding sickeningly.

He'd flopped onto the floor to pull his boots off when Mia pounced. "Ross! You're back! How did it go?"

He groaned.

"That bad?" Mia helped him to his feet. "Dad fixed something for you to eat. We didn't think Yuki would bother packing a lunch."

"You got that right." Somehow he made it to the kitchen, and sank gratefully into a chair. The Lees let him eat in silence, but he could feel their attention. Three fat burritos, two dishes of shrimp-and-cabbage kimchi, two peach dumplings, and three glasses of cucumber water later, he took a breather.

Mia sat across from him, elbows on the table. "So, how did it go?"

Ross shrugged. "Okay, I guess. Once we got going. We saw the bounty hunter in the hills. He made sure we saw him too."

Dr. Lee pursed his lips. "I'll make sure the sheriff knows."

"I'll bet she already does," Ross said.

"The Rangers certainly do," Dr. Lee predicted.

And Mr. Preston, thought Ross.

"What's the use of making sure he saw you?" Mia asked. "I thought he wanted to kidnap you."

Dr. Lee nibbled on a pickled shrimp. "He probably wants to intimidate Ross into surrendering the book."

Ross nodded. "I think so too. But it won't work."

Mia shot him a significant look. He knew she wasn't thinking about the bounty hunter, or even about the book. She was thinking about the crystal tree. He got up and served himself another burrito, even though he was too full to eat it. He could feel Mia's gaze burning into his back.

Then Dr. Lee spoke. "Ross, Mia told me that your nightmares aren't only based on memories—that you have a connection to the singing tree beyond the cornfields. How are you feeling?"

"Like something scraped my skull from the inside." Ross

pictured crystal roots winding around bone and crystal shards piercing flesh, and shuddered.

"Is it a Change, Dad?" asked Mia. "I'd have thought Ross was too old for that."

Ross sat down, the untouched burrito before him. He closed his eyes.

"Not necessarily," said Dr. Lee. "Though it's more common to Change at the beginning of puberty, it's possible for a Change to occur in men at any time before puberty ends. I've heard of men Changing as late as their early twenties. Ross?"

Reluctantly, he opened his eyes. "What?"

"Do you know if you've grown at all within the last year or so?"

"No." Ross indicated his worn jeans. "I've had these for years, and they still go down to my ankles."

"It's probably not a Change, then. In any case, Change is genetic. This seems to be caused by a specific incident."

"So you think it's a sort of symbiosis?" Mia sounded as happily intrigued as if Ross was a machine she was designing. "The tree grew from his blood, so it has a mental link with him?"

"That's what I'd guess. It's also possible that tiny fragments of the shard, too small for me to see, remained in his wound, so—"

"I don't care how it got there," Ross interrupted. If there were still fragments inside his body, couldn't they start growing again? "How do I get the thing out of my head?"

Mia and Dr. Lee looked at each other.

"Once I get a better range on the flamethrower, I'll burn it for you," she offered.

A high, eerie note reverberated through him. "No!" He clapped his hands over his ears.

Mia's eyes were wide behind her smudged glasses. "Is it listening to us right now?"

Ross pressed his fingertips to his temples, but that didn't shut out the piercing echo.

"We can talk about it later," Dr. Lee said. His voice was calm and soothing. "I think first, Ross could use my headache elixir."

"Ugh, that stuff tastes bad," Mia said. "But it works, Ross. Drink it fast."

He would have drunk tarantula blood if it would ease the pain. He gulped down the bitter liquid without a complaint. Soon most of the headache receded, but he still felt as if the chimes might sound again at any second.

A bell rang. Ross's hand jerked, knocking over his glass. A few drops of milky liquid spilled on the tablecloth.

"I believe I have patients to see." Dr. Lee left the kitchen, closing the door softly behind him.

Ross righted the glass and took a deep breath. "I have to go back to the tree."

Late the next night, Mia returned from retooling the ironmonger's generator. "It's quiet out there," she said to Ross, who sat on the floor of her cottage, practicing his reading. "If you want to go, maybe we should do it now."

Ross laid aside the page. He hadn't been able to pay attention to it anyway. "I don't want to go. But I think I have to."

"What's your plan?"

He let out in a long sigh. "I'm going to try telling it to leave me alone. Are you sure you want to come?"

She nodded. "You might need some help getting back."

"All right. But if anything goes wrong, don't try and help me."

"Okay." Mia sounded as scared as Ross felt.

They started off across the dark town square. When Mia's fingers collided with his, he didn't pull his hand away. The next

step, her knuckles brushed against his hand again. On purpose? He snuck a sideways glance, just as she snuck a sideways
glance.

He promised himself that he wouldn't flinch if she took his
hand. Her warm fingers closed over his. Once the first shock
of contact was over, he liked the feel of it: small but strong.
Calluses in the right places. It made him feel light-headed, but
it wasn't bad; just intense. As they walked, he could barely feel
his feet hitting the ground.

They slipped into the town hall and, from the darkened mill,
watched the sentries stroll by in pairs. Ross and Mia worked
out their timing, then ran through the corn to the road.

The ringing he had begun to hear in the tunnel was much
louder now.

"Something wrong?" Mia whispered.

"It's the tree," he said. "Do you hear chimes?"

"No," she whispered. Her fingers clutched his tightly. Ross
felt the tree before they saw it, moonlight reflecting crimson
off its gemlike facets. He knew where it was like he knew his
own left hand. He could even sense how far the shards could
reach. And he knew it wouldn't loose those shards at him.

"Stay here," he whispered.

Mia dropped his hand and waited.

He slid down the ridge. As he approached cautiously, the
chiming stopped. His footsteps sounded loud in his ears—
almost as loud as his heartbeat.

The tree waited, bright as the blood that had poured from
his arm and almost taken his life with it. Approaching it was
harder than it had been to run past a whole grove of singing
trees.

He forced his right hand against the trunk.

As he had in the previous night's dream, he saw himself as
if in a distorting mirror: a small figure made of red and yel-

low light, which he sensed indicated fields of heat. He felt his roots digging into the soil, searching out fragments of crystal to add to itself . . . Himself. Farther out were several more figures in yellow and red—one standing on two legs, and a cluster of smaller ones on four. The small ones might feed him if they came closer, but the tall one was not food. That one shouldn't be . . . harmed.

The "figure" was Mia. Then Ross was back in his own body, dizzy, nauseated, disoriented.

He jerked his hand away from the tree and stumbled away. It was very dark. He scanned for heat, then remembered that a human couldn't sense that.

"Ross?" Mia called softly.

He wondered how much time had passed. It had felt like seconds.

"Ross, are you okay?"

"Yeah. Give me a little more time. I don't think I've gotten through to it yet."

"What are you trying to say to it?"

"Get out of my head. Stop giving me nightmares. Stop calling to me. Stop—"

"Why don't you pick one?" She sat down in the road to wait.

He hadn't had one good night's sleep since he'd been wounded. *Stop giving me nightmares* seemed a good place to start. He remembered what Yuki had told him about communicating with horses: you had to focus on one thing and really mean it.

He pictured himself lying in bed, peacefully asleep. No, that wouldn't make sense to a tree. How had the tree seen the world? He would have to figure out how it was reaching out to him before he could tell it how to stop.

Ross laid his hand against cool crystal . . .

This time he listened as well as saw. The tree's perceptions weren't only of physical things. It had feelings. Mia wasn't

merely a human who shouldn't be harmed, she was a person
it cared about.

How could a tree care about a person? The tree felt the
same way about Mia that Ross did. But if the tree had emotions, why was it torturing Ross?

He tried to listen for its feeling about him, but all he "saw"
was that distorted mirror again. When he tried to listen more
carefully, he found himself remembering, almost reliving the
desperation and the will to survive that had allowed him to
drive a knife into his own body. Those feelings had gone into
the shard. And now they were in the tree.

It's me, he thought. *The tree is part of me.*

*It's not trying to hurt me. Trying to shut it out is like trying to
cut off my own arm.*

He tried to convey his intention the way that he had con-
veyed his intentions to the mare: *Humans need to sleep at
night. You have to be quiet.*

The tree understood quiet. Its leaves went still and its scarlet pigment drained into the roots, leaving every part of it
above ground absolutely transparent.

That wasn't exactly what Ross had meant, but at least he
was communicating. He'd gotten that far by listening, so he'd
listen harder.

Not listen harder, listen wider. Ross stretched out his—the
tree's—senses.

The world became a chorus of shimmering sound. Beyond
the range of human hearing or vision, the trees sang to one
another. His tree could hear music all the way out to the borders of the ruins, and see signals of light. What were those
other trees saying?

Not listen harder, not wider, but deeper.

Ross imagined himself diving into a well, swimming deeper
and deeper into black water, searching out a spark of light.
The light was blue. He reached for it. Pain seared through him,

like when the shard had been growing inside his arm, but now it was everywhere. Crystal daggers expanded in his chest, crushing his lungs, piercing his heart.

He hit the ground, gasping for breath. Someone was calling in a low voice.

"Ross. Ross. If you don't answer me, I'm coming down there to get you."

His throat ached as if he'd been shouting. "Don't come near—no—no. Wait." He glanced up. Ruby veins glowed in the leaves silhouetted against the night sky. "No, it's okay. It won't hurt you."

Mia hesitated. Then, moving jerkily, she skidded down, grabbed his arm, and hauled him to his feet. His legs were so shaky he could hardly stand, and his vision swam.

"You were yelling. Or trying to. It sounded like you were being strangled. What happened?"

"I think I felt somebody die."

"What?" she squeaked, then cut herself off. The wall and its alert sentries were not that far away.

Ross struggled up the slope, leaning on Mia. He was relieved that a little of his strength was returning, though he was still dizzy.

"I think it was a prospector," he whispered. "A prospector who got made into a tree. I felt her death. I think the last memories of the people they killed are in those trees. And my tree . . . it's got some of mine."

"Seriously?" Mia whispered back. "Wow. That's the most amazing scientific discovery I've ever heard of. Can I tell Dad?"

Hesitantly Ross said, "I guess. If he'd promise not to tell anyone else."

"Never mind. I can't. You're not even supposed to know about the tunnel. If I tell him we were out here, he'd have to tell the rest of the council."

"Then don't say anything. I still need to come out here. I've got to figure this out."

"Okay. Sure. Look, it's late. How about we go back now? You don't look so good."

"I don't feel so good," he admitted.

As they walked up the road in silence, Ross wondered what he'd dream about that night.

29

Felicité

FELICITÉ MADE CERTAIN THAT SHE WAS EASY for Indra to find. She arrived at school early every day, although that meant she kept getting stuck doing drill. She exercised without protest, grateful that the overcast sky kept the air cool, so she wouldn't get sweaty and smelly. But he never returned to the schoolyard.

She considered various graceful speeches. All began with showering golden coins upon Jennie, moving to sympathy, and then to the dance—and her own lack of an escort. Should she be humorous? "Oh, how funny, here I am organizing everything, and I forgot to organize a date for myself!" But that wasn't funny, it was pathetic.

When Indra's braid brushed against her chair at Jack's, was that on purpose? At Luc's, when she walked past him, she distinctly heard his breathing change. Was he admiring the fit of her dress, her graceful walk? Each tiny gesture was examined for hidden meaning when she retired at night, but the light of day brought dissatisfaction.

Pursuing him was undignified. A Wolfe should not have to ask.

The dance was four days away. She sadly regarded her exquisite lace dress embroidered with silver starflowers. There was no use pretending Indra's tiny gestures had any secret meaning. Couldn't he see how perfect they were for each other? How long could he hold on to a grudge over a single slip of the tongue?

She'd give him one more day, and then she'd have to settle for Tommy Horst, who at least was a reasonably good-looking Norm from the Hill.

Her mother called, "Felicité? Someone is here to see you."

Felicité raced out, her heart beating fast.

But there was no dark braid on the guy waiting below, no warm brown skin. She didn't recognize the black tunic embroidered with silver starflowers or the tight-fitting trousers. And his hair was blond—

He turned. To her astonishment, it was Henry Callahan. He bowed—formally, not mockingly. "I came to show you what you'll get if you'll be my escort to the dance."

Her habitual "no" was shaping her lips, but it stayed unspoken. She realized that she was looking up at him, even though she was wearing heels. When had that happened? Henry had always been one of the shorter boys, with those unfortunate freckles shining unpleasantly under the aloe salve that Dr. Lee handed out to fair-skinned families.

He'd asked her out before, but never in a way that would make any girl want to say yes. Once he'd sworn that he'd die if she didn't date him, and when she politely declined, he'd clutched his throat and dramatically collapsed to the ground, making the entire school laugh. And that was typical.

But here he was, alone, almost unrecognizable. How had he gotten so stylish? If it weren't for those freckles, and that floppy hair the color of old straw, he'd almost be . . . kind of cute.

"You match my dress for the dance," she said. "But no one's seen it yet."

"My mother made that dress, and I asked her to make me something that matched. I hope that wasn't too weird." He shifted uncomfortably.

Mrs. Callahan would be a horrifying mother-in-law, but

Henry wasn't proposing—only asking her to a dance. On impulse, she said, "I would love to go with you."

Henry had been glumly eyeing the carpet. His head lifted. "You're joking."

Felicité clasped her hands. "I never joke in matters of the heart," she said mock-soulfully. He laughed, as she'd known he would, and she held up a finger. "But you have to promise."

"What?" Henry said suspiciously.

"No heroically rescuing me—and by that I mean no more roaches."

He raised his hand as if taking an oath. "I swear."

Felicité felt much better when she came to breakfast the next day, and was even happier to find her parents alone. "Good morning, Daddy. Good morning, Mother."

"What have you learned about Ross Juarez's book?" her father asked.

Simultaneously, her mother said, "How are you progressing with the dance?"

They smiled at each other across the table.

Someday Felicité wanted to sit across from her own husband. They would smile at each other just like that, perfectly in tune.

Her daddy said, "You first, Valeria."

"Darling? Is there anything you need?"

"Everything's nearly ready." Felicité hadn't breathed a word about the presentation. It was to be a surprise for her mother and the whole town, to start the dance on a memorable note.

"I'm proud of you." Mother took a last bite of fried turnip cake and set her chopsticks on their rest. "I must go, dears. The guild chief is waiting." She kissed Daddy, and Felicité watched as she left. How did her mother make walking out a door look so elegant? Felicité straightened her spine, and arranged her arms more gracefully. Control, every moment.

Her father laid down a half-eaten scallion pancake and turned to her. "Have you discovered anything regarding Ross since your last report?"

Felicité couldn't think of a positive way of saying "Still nothing," so instead she focused on details. "He spends a lot of time alone with Mia Lee."

Her father smiled, but his tone changed. "I don't need a report on his love life. I want a report on his book. Beginning with its location."

Felicité was thrilled. He was asking her to spy for him! "Should I search Mia's hut?"

Regretfully, he shook his head. "That would be going a bit far. Just keep watch. If you visit Mia and spot it lying in the open, let me know."

She daintily dipped a cruller in warm soy milk as she wondered how she could manage that. Wu Zetian had not been much help when it came to Ross, nor had the bounty hunter. Before he was ordered out of town, he'd spent all his time in Jack's, talking to people, especially the sheriff. Felicité was sure he'd been mining for information.

"I'd need some business for Mia," Felicité said. "We're not friends, you know."

Her father laughed. "Mia might not be your first choice for your drawing room, but she's a fine mechanic." Then his smile faded. "Maybe I'm old and suspicious, but it occurs to me that she has access to the entire town. I've seen people do things they never would have done, except that they thought they were in love."

Felicité had never considered that angle. How many times had her parents told her to look beneath the surface?

She nodded, disappointed with herself. "I'll do my best."

Once again, Felicité watched Ross sparring with Jennie. She'd seen engaged couples dance less sensually. Teachers weren't allowed to date students. But he wasn't really a student—he wasn't even a citizen—and she'd only been appointed temporarily.

Good; that meant Jennie was distracted from Indra. Felicité did wonder what Mia thought, though; even her father had assumed Mia and Ross were dating.

After school, Felicité followed Ross as he dragged a wagon all over town, collecting smelly used vegetable oil. He spoke to no one. Then he had dinner with the Lees. She strolled past the window and spotted Dr. Lee demonstrating some surgical technique on a fried flounder. Ross and Mia looked as fascinated as Felicité was repulsed.

Then Mia and Ross went to Mia's cottage. Felicité followed, tired and hungry and incredibly bored. But Daddy had given her a mission, and she meant to carry it out. Still, she told herself, at the first sign of lip-locking, she'd call it a day.

She ducked around an untrimmed shrub, disturbing a flight of glowing bright-moths, and wedged herself between the wall and the bush, her knees pulled up under her chin. Felicité signaled to Wu Zetian to keep out of sight and fetch her if anyone approached the cottage.

For the next two hours, Felicité heard nothing but clanking, scraping, and an excruciatingly dull discussion about electrical wiring. Then Ross said he needed to study, and for another hour, there was only clanking. Felicité remembered that Mia often stayed up all night. Surely her father wouldn't expect her to do the same?

Ross broke the silence. "I think tonight I should go alone."

Crash! Some metal object dropped to the floor.

"No way," Mia said. "It's not safe."

That sounded interesting. Felicité's discomfort and hunger were forgotten. She was wondering if she should risk a peek when she felt the tap of a little paw: *Someone is coming.*

There was a knock on the door. From the way things crashed and tinkled inside the cottage, Mia and Ross were not expecting visitors.

Felicité was surprised to hear her cousin Julio's voice. "Mia, we've got an emergency. That winch on the front gate is jammed and the gate's stuck open. Mr. Horst and Mr. Nguyen each sent a couple of workers over, and Jack's bringing coffee. This could be a late night."

"Oh. The gate." Mia sounded alarmed, which was odd; normally she seemed to love burrowing into greasy machines. "Um, you go ahead. I'll catch up with you."

"I can wait."

There was a series of clatters that Felicité couldn't help hearing as exasperated. Then Mia said, "Ross, don't study without me. It's important; you need a study partner. Wait for me to get back!"

It was the most suspicious-sounding thing Felicité had heard in her life. Her father was right. They were definitely up to something.

She waited until Mia and Julio's footsteps faded, then sent Wu Zetian to keep an eye on Mia. If Ross left, Felicité would follow him herself.

She inched upward, glad she'd thought to wear a black hat and dress. She tilted the brim to shadow her face, though she knew that people in lit rooms couldn't see out. Pins and needles prickled her legs as she peered inside.

Ross sat on the floor with a book. The book? No. Felicité recognized the reader she'd studied when she was five. He rubbed his eyes, then leaned back against the bed and stared at the ceiling.

She sank down, sighing.

The moon had emerged when the light in the cottage

went out. Felicité rotated her shoulders, wondering if Ross was going to sleep. Wouldn't she have heard him move the engine off the bed?

The door creaked—he was leaving!

After a count of twenty, she skirted the junk in the yard until she could see the town square, which was empty except for him. To her surprise, he entered the town hall.

She darted in after him, shrouded by darkness. The lamp was gone from its usual place on the side table. When her eyes adjusted, she made out a black square in the gloom: the basement door. Open. She ran into the basement. Empty. There was only one way out: the tunnel.

The tunnel she had only learned about this year, when she'd been appointed council scribe. The only people who knew about it were the council, the scribe, the teacher . . .

And the mechanic. Mia had broken one of the most important laws of Las Anclas.

Felicité had to get her father. At once. But then they might never know what Ross was planning.

She slipped into the tunnel and felt her way to the mill. She thought of calling the sentries, but what if Ross heard, and bolted? She had to be the one to find out what he was up to. Yes, she was breaking the rules too—but it was for the good of the town. When she looked at it that way, it was secretly thrilling.

Once she got to the trail along the ridge, Ross was easily visible, starlight gleaming off his white shirt. Then a flash of scarlet startled her. She'd forgotten about that gruesome crystal tree below the ridge.

He walked straight toward it without even slowing down. Was he sleepwalking? It was already too late to warn him. She held her breath, bracing for the horrifying clash of chimes and pop of breaking glass that would signal his death.

She rubbed her eyes. Ross was standing beside a singing tree, and nothing had happened.

He had to be Changed, but not like the bounty hunter had said. His Change kept him safe from those killer trees. But that didn't explain what he was doing. He stood beside it with his arms clutched tight across his chest. Then he lifted a hand, and laid it against the crimson trunk.

Chimes began to tinkle softly. In an eerie echo, more joined in from the hills, and from far beyond the mill. She had never heard anything like it before. It was almost as if the trees were talking to each other.

Ross let out a cry of pain. Felicité jumped. But every tree had gone silent, and none of the pods that contained the deadly shards had shattered.

He staggered a few steps away, then crumpled to the ground.

At first she thought he was dead; then she heard the sounds he was making. He was crying. Ross lay there sobbing in the dust, like Jack had sobbed after Sheriff Crow had lost their baby.

Felicité took an uncertain step toward him. Then she thought, *What would I say?*

She backed away, then tore down the road. She didn't breathe easy until she emerged into the town square.

As she ran home, her panic eased, leaving her hungry, thirsty, and tired. Ross's Change seemed more a danger to himself than anyone in Las Anclas. But it was illegal of Mia to have shown him the tunnel, and illegal for him to use it this way.

She arrived home still wondering what to report. Maybe it would be clearer in the morning. Felicité slipped into the kitchen to get a drink. At the first crank of the pump, a light flared, and in came her father, carrying a lamp.

"I waited up for you." He gave her a glass of water,

standing silently by until she had finished. "Were you out investigating?"

"Yes, Daddy."

"I like your dedication. Just what I expected. So what did you find?"

She hesitated, then began at the beginning.

But the more she talked, the guiltier she felt over what she was about to do to Ross. Not that she cared about him personally, but when she remembered him sobbing in the road, she couldn't help feeling sorry for him. But how could she fail to tell her father that the town defenses were vulnerable?

Felicité opened her mouth. Then she imagined what would happen after she spoke. They couldn't just exile Ross: he could come back through the tunnel with enemies. They would have to kill him. Her father would not hesitate if he thought it was necessary to protect the town. She imagined Ross lying dead in the dust, as he'd lain in the road, but with his white shirt soaked crimson.

Felicité closed her mouth. She couldn't bring herself to cause his death. She'd solved the mystery: she knew he was Changed, and she knew what his power was, but he clearly had no intention of using it to harm Las Anclas. All he seemed to be doing was harming himself. She could file this away with the other secrets she kept in her mental lockbox, with the mayor's seal stamped in gold across its fine wood.

"I watched him for hours," Felicité concluded. "He didn't do anything but flirt with Mia and study. I never saw the book."

Her father patted her cheek. "Sometimes learning that nothing is going on is as important as discovering information that seems more exciting. Good work, darling. Now, go get some well-earned rest."

30

Mia

MIA DIDN'T NEED A LIGHT TO KNOW THAT ROSS WAS gone and her cottage was empty.

She dropped her tool bag, then picked it up in case it contained something she'd need. Then she put it down again. What she really needed was a weapon that might work against the tree. At first her mind went blank, and then she knew what to do. It was exactly like her old master, Mr. Rodriguez, always said: "Desperation equals inspiration." She picked up a jug of oil, a bow and arrows, and a heavy jacket, and fled.

She was inside the town hall before she remembered that a lantern would have been helpful. She felt her way into the basement and through the tunnel. When she found the lamp waiting at the mill, she knew Ross was still out there. It was a relief—but scary, too. Something was obviously wrong: sunrise was only a few hours away.

Mia held the jug tightly against her stomach and ran her fastest, the bow slapping against her back. She was out of breath when she spotted a body lying a few paces from the tree.

"Ross?" she called as loud as she dared.

There was no response.

"Ross, wake up."

He didn't move.

She didn't see any blood, but if the tree had attacked him, it would surely attack her, too. She set down the jug and the bow, pulled on the jacket that wouldn't even stop a knife, let alone a crystal shard, and forced herself to take a step down the slope.

Tears stung her eyes as she slid the rest of the way. There was no warning chime from the tree, which gleamed bright as arterial blood in the starlight.

Ross lay on his stomach, curled into himself. She couldn't tell if he was breathing. She reached out, but stopped herself. When she was a child, she'd gone to pet her oldest cat and found it cold and stiff under the fur. She'd run away without telling her dad, as if so long as nobody else knew, it might turn out to be a mistake.

As long as she didn't touch Ross, he might still be alive. Once she touched him, whatever she found would be real and irrevocable. Gritting her teeth, she forced herself to lay her hand on his shoulder.

Crystal leaves rang out a warning. She shielded her face with her hands.

"Mia?" Ross mumbled.

A sob of relief nearly choked her. "Ross. You're alive."

He rolled over and stared up at the sky. "I'm so . . ."

"Sick? Hurt? Tired?"

". . . dizzy."

"Let's get you out of here."

She dragged him back up the slope. He wasn't bearing any of his own weight, and she had to set him down in the cornfield. He lay as still as he had when she'd found him. She checked him over thoroughly, as her dad had taught her. He didn't seem to have any injuries, but there were signs of shock: clammy skin, shallow breathing, rapid pulse. She took off her jacket and wrestled him into it. A hand-me-down from her father, the jacket was baggy on Mia but tight across Ross's shoulders.

She put a hand on his chest to reassure herself that he

was still breathing, then ran out to retrieve her bow and jug. When she got back, he was struggling to sit up, panting as if he'd run for miles.

Mia pushed down gently on his shoulder. "Take it easy. We've still got a few hours before dawn."

He lay back down with a long exhalation of relief.

"What happened? It wasn't this bad last time."

"It started out like last time," he said slowly. "I could see like the tree sees, in patterns of heat. I could see animals. A person—probably the bounty hunter."

"Do you think he saw you?" Mia asked.

Ross continued as if he hadn't heard her, as if he were trapped in a dream. "I tried to make a deal with the tree. Built a wall in my mind, so I could shut it out when I need to. Put a door in the wall, so I could let it back in. I tried going deeper. I could hear every tree. From here to the nearest ruins. They all remember how they grew. From the deaths of animals and people." He drew a shaky breath. "No, I didn't hear the trees. I felt them. I felt all those deaths."

He was shivering as if it were winter. He looked more pale and ill than when she'd first seen him, unconscious on her dad's operating table.

Mia said fiercely, "I'll destroy that thing."

"You can't."

"Oh, yes I can. I figured it out. It's growing in a hollow in that gully. Liquids flow down. If I pour oil down the slope, it'll pool around the trunk. Then I light an arrow and shoot it into the pool, and that thing burns."

"No." Ross grabbed her wrist. "You can't! If you kill it, I think you'll kill me. That tree is part of me, don't you get it?"

Mia took refuge in the comforting process of logic. "Okay, Ross. You said you could hear the trees—sorry, *feel* the trees all the way up to the edge of the ruins. But no far-ther than that, right?"

He nodded.

"So that's the farthest edge of your range. Everything has some kind of range. You go far enough, you can't hear voices, and you can't see light. Changed people who can feel emotions or sense things can only do it up to a certain distance. So if you go far enough away, you won't feel that tree anymore."

Her throat hurt too much to go on. She'd always known that Ross might leave, but this was the first time she under-stood that he might not even have a choice.

"I'd have to stay away," Ross said slowly.

His life is more important than my feelings, she told herself. "I'll get you a gun. That'll even things up with the bounty hunter. Your hand is better now, right?"

Ross reached out and put his left hand on hers. "Yeah." Then, with a grunt of effort, he sat up, bracing his right hand on the ground. His hair hung down around his face. "I feel sick. But better. I think I can walk."

He didn't look like he could. "Let me help you. I'm put-ting your arm around my shoulders, okay?"

He nodded. Mia hooked the oil jug to her belt, slung the bow and quiver on her back, pulled Ross's arm over her shoulders, and put hers around his waist. He didn't flinch, but that didn't make Mia happy. It meant he felt so terrible, things that would normally bother him barely even registered.

He leaned heavily on her as they walked, making her glad she spent so much time lifting engines. She was strong enough to prospect, and like Jennie said, prospectors were basically specialized engineers. Maybe she could go with him when he left, to explore the desert and blast their way into amazing ruins. But she hadn't walked two more steps before reality intruded. Ross would probably run away from her if she suggested it. And she couldn't imagine leaving Las Anclas without its engineer, let alone leaving her dad and Jennie and her relatives and the cats.

They were halfway down the road when Ross said, "I'm not leaving."

Mia was too scared to hope. "But nothing's been fixed. You can't live if you can't sleep."

"I'll figure it out." They walked a few more steps, then he added, "I might have gotten through to it this time. I'm not sure. I'll have to see."

She stopped, and braced herself. "Ross. You have to promise me you won't ever, ever go back there alone. I don't know what I can do, but maybe I can do something. I was worrying the whole time I was fixing the winch. It probably took much longer because I was distracted." She shut herself up by biting down on her lower lip. "Promise."

"Okay." He lifted his head to look into her eyes. His nose was two inches from hers. The starlight bleached his face of color, but she could see the strain. "I promise."

They trudged up the road, matching their steps, hips bumping, his fingers gripping her shoulder, hers tight around his waist.

When they passed the gardens in the town square, instead of heading for her cottage, she steered him toward the surgery.

Ross dug in his feet. "I don't want to go to my room."

"We're not going to your room. We're going to the infirmary."

"What will we say? You can't tell about the tunnel."

"We don't need to say anything. Dad's a doctor. He'll take one look at you and put you to bed."

31

Jennie

JENNIE WAS GLAD TO SEE DEE SKIPPING ALONG, spilling grain out of the bucket as she went to feed the chickens. She might not be happy about her dust devil power, but the coming dance had certainly cheered her up.

"... and Z thought Yuki should dress like a prince." Dee tilted her head. "What does a prince wear? In that book with pictures, they wear metal armor. Did he wear metal armor on his ship? How could he dance in metal?"

"I'm sure he won't wear metal anything," Jennie said.

"Oh! Hey! Is Ross out of the infirmary yet? It would be so sad if he had to miss his own dance. And never see my dress."

Jennie smiled. "I haven't seen him yet, but Mia said Dr. Lee would let him out this morning. And I know he was looking forward to the dance."

"Do you think he'll dance with me?" Dee gave an extra skip.

"If you ask him nicely, he might. Actually, try asking him nicely and giving him a slice of Pa's buttermilk pie."

Dee hefted the feed bucket and started to step into the chicken coop. Without quite knowing why she was doing it, Jennie grabbed her by the shoulder and jerked her back. Grain flew everywhere.

"Hey!" her sister protested. "What did you do that for?"

Jennie held out her arm to stop Dee from trying again. "I don't know," she said slowly. "There's something wrong. Let me take a look first."

Her sister sighed impatiently. "You haven't fed the chickens for weeks, that's all. They're just bigger—the ones that are left, anyway. C'mon, we have to get our decorations set up!"

"That's next," Jennie reminded her. "We promised Ma—"

"I know, I know. Animals come first." Dee fiddled impatiently with the grain pail as Jennie studied the coop. One thing was obvious: the chickens seemed spooked. They were all on perches or up in their nests, not pecking around in the dust like usual. Maybe a predator had just left. But the wicker door was still latched.

She unhooked it and peered in, looking for drops of blood or paw prints. The dirt was absolutely untouched, without even a chicken track to disturb it.

Dee shifted the pail again, muttering, "Jennie, can you move?"

There was something familiar about that perfectly even layer of dust. Where had she not seen prints where there should have been—?

"Dee, get back. Now!"

Jennie grabbed the rake leaning against the coop and prodded at the nearest lump of hay. A wad of white fur fell out.

It was an animal's pelt, but there was no blood on the inside, only a smooth membrane. It was more like a snake's shed skin than the remains of a kill. She used the rake to spread it out on the ground, trying to get a sense of its original shape.

Dee shrieked. "It's Princess Cloud! Something ate her!"

Jennie examined the pelt. "What kind of animal was Princess Cloud?"

"I don't know," Dee sniffled. "She was little and cute."

"Where did you find her?"

"On patrol."

"But you haven't been—" She stared at her sister. "You know you don't bring wild animals inside the gates."

"But Yuki and Meredith knew."

The pieces of the puzzle snapped into place. The last time

Dee patrolled had been the snake attack. So one more rule had been forgotten that day, and by Yuki and Meredith, of all people.

Jennie picked up the rake in both hands. "Get behind me."

She struck down at the too-smooth dust. The entire floor of the coop crumbled away, and the smell of rotting meat wafted up. Chickens rocketed into the air, sending feathers in all directions, and one settled at the bottom of the gaping hole. A fang gleamed white, and the chicken was dragged squawking into the dust.

"A pit mouth!" Dee howled. "A pit mouth ate Princess Cloud!"

Jennie turned on her sister. "The pit mouth *is* Princess Cloud!" Dee ran screaming, the grain swirling in tiny whirlwinds behind her. Jennie ran after her, into the kitchen. "José! I need you to guard the chicken coop. Make sure no one gets near. There's a pit mouth in it."

José choked on the plum he was eating. "In the chicken coop? Seriously?"

Jennie glared at him. "Yes. Now go!"

She yanked on the fire bell beside the door. Everyone tore into the kitchen. "Where's the fire?" asked Yolanda. A gust of wind rose up in emphasis.

"It's not a fire. There's a pit mouth in the chicken coop."

Every face stared back at her with the same disbelieving expression.

"Yes!" she shouted. "A pit mouth! Never mind how it got there. Everybody, out of the house. Tonio, Dee, go warn the neighbors, and stay with them when you're done. Yolanda, go tell the sheriff and the watch commander. I'm getting Mia, because I know what they'll want done." She glanced at her grandmother.

Grandma Riley nodded. "Good plan. I'll tend the little ones."

Jennie ran.

When she reached Mia's cottage, she flung open the door without knocking, and stood on the threshold trying to catch her breath.

Mia stood in the middle of the room in a dress that seemed composed entirely of pink ruffles. She had a smear of black dust across the tip of her nose. A bewildered-looking Ross was perched on the bed, between two engines.

"It looks nice?" he was saying.

While Jennie caught her breath, she noticed that he looked much better: eyes bright, body relaxed. Like he'd actually gotten a good night's sleep. "You better take the dress off," she said. "I have something for you to blow up."

"Wow!" Mia clapped her hands, then rubbed them together. "A dance and an explosion on the same day! What is it?"

Jennie was already sick of the reaction she knew she was going to get. "There's a pit mouth in our chicken coop." And she was not disappointed. Both Mia and Ross gave her *that* look.

"I'm on it." Mia fluffed at her skirt, sidling a desperate glance at Ross, then at Jennie, who jerked her thumb at the door.

"Oh. Right." Ross ducked out, and then stopped. "Need any help?"

Jennie laughed. "With the dress?"

"With the explosion?" Mia said. "Sure!"

"The dress looks great," Jennie called as she closed the door behind Mia. "Ross, so do you. Feeling better?"

"Yes." He glanced at the people bringing decorations and dishes to the tables set up around the square. "I needed a little time to, um, rest."

Mia's door banged open while she was still buttoning her overalls. "I'll need my wagon, and . . ." She stopped. "Did you say it was in the chicken coop?"

"What's happening?" Ms. Salazar rushed up from the table she had been decorating, leaving a trail of sparks in her wake.

Before Jennie had a chance to speak, Sheriff Crow strode to the front of a gathering crowd. Everyone was pelting Jennie with questions, at least half of which she could have answered with, *Yes, the chicken coop.*

The sheriff clapped her hands. "We'll hear the story once. At the site. If you have business there, come along. Otherwise, back to whatever you were doing."

Hordes of people trailed behind them by the time they got to the Rileys', where they found an aggravated José fending off busybodies with the rake.

"Glad you're here!" he said. "Aunt Flora went to get Ma."

The onlookers scattered at the sight of Sheriff Crow. Soon Mr. Preston arrived, leading helpers from the armory who pulled Mia's demolitions cart.

"Now's the time," Sheriff Crow said. "Jennie, what happened?"

Jennie gave her report. The sheriff listened closely, then said, "What was it that you noticed first?"

"In retrospect, maybe that no chickens were on the ground. They didn't even jump down when they saw us coming with the grain. Though I only realized that now."

Sheriff Crow gave a firm nod. "Excellent observation. You were right to trust your instincts."

"Observation?" Mr. Preston shook his head. "You had a pit mouth in the chicken coop, eating your chickens for weeks, and nobody noticed until now?"

José said politely, "Mr. Preston, the pit couldn't have been there for weeks. I was inside the coop feeding them yesterday morning."

"It must have built the pit overnight." Jennie eyed the coop. "But the pelt I saw was small. My guess is that it was hiding in the straw or even buried in the dirt during the day, and coming out to eat the chickens at night. Until it metamorphosed."

Mia waved her hand wildly. "Where is that pelt? Can I have it?"

"If you want it. I sure don't. Where did it go?"

José lifted an overturned bucket, revealing the crumpled lump of fur. "It was giving me the creeps," he said apologetically.

Mia picked up the pelt with a pair of tongs and tucked it away in a gunpowder bag. "Dad will want it. The first ever pit mouth specimen! Too bad it's only the skin."

Jennie's pa pushed through the crowd, pulling a drooping Dee with him. "Sheriff, I believe my daughter has something to tell us all."

Dee unhappily explained how she'd found "Princess Cloud."

"Where are Yuki and Meredith?" the sheriff asked.

Meredith stepped forward. "I'm here."

"Go fetch Yuki," Sheriff Crow ordered. Meredith ran.

Mia and the demolition team, assisted by Ross, began to set up their equipment. Jennie watched the two of them having an intense discussion over the explosives.

"What's he doing here?" snapped Mr. Preston.

Mia and Ross both started. Mia said, "Ross has experience with explosions in confined spaces, when you don't want to bring down other parts of the structure. I've only blown up things out in the open."

Ross pointed at the house with his slide rule. "The chicken coop is pretty close. Since we don't know how deep the pit mouth is, we have to use enough explosives to make sure we get it, but direct the blast so the house doesn't come down."

"Please!" Jennie exclaimed, not caring if it sounded like she was begging. "Let him help! We've lived in this house for generations."

Mr. Preston waved his hand. "I'd forgotten that prospectors use explosives. Back to work."

Meredith had returned, with Yuki in tow. Both of them looked apprehensive. "Did you see Dee pick up a strange animal on patrol?" Sheriff Crow asked.

"Yes," they said together.

"We meant to make Dee take it to quarantine, but the snakes attacked, and I forgot all about it." Meredith elbowed Yuki. "You forgot too?"

He gave a brusque nod, his mouth a tight line.

Mrs. Callahan spoke up. "This is why we have quarantine rules. *My* children are trained to obey—"

Sheriff Crow clapped again, the sound sharp and loud. "Everyone who doesn't have business here is dismissed."

Mr. Preston frowned, but didn't object. The crowd began to disperse in twos and threes, still chattering.

The sheriff glanced from Yuki to Meredith. "You two will help the Rileys fix any damage caused by the explosion."

Meredith and Yuki agreed fervently.

"Dee!" Sheriff Crow continued. "I'll leave your punishment to your parents. This is why we've raised the age for patrols. It's too easy for little mistakes to grow into big ones." She glanced from the tuft of white fur sticking out of Mia's bag to the chicken coop. "In this case, literally."

Then she glanced at Mia, who waited beside the plunger. "Ready, Mia?"

When Mia nodded, the sheriff ordered everyone farther back.

Jennie fought the instinct to yell "Wait!" so she could run inside and get just one thing, but she didn't even know what that one thing would be.

Mia counted down from ten. Nothing moved except for the shadow of a passing hawk.

Jennie closed her eyes. The shock wave rocked her backward. Bits of dirt stung her face and hands. There was a moment of silence.

Then her pa's arm slid around her shoulders. "It's okay, Jennie. We didn't lose the house."

She opened her eyes. The chicken coop had been replaced by a giant hole, but the house stood. Three bedroom windows had shattered, and the wall next to the shed had a crack in it, but it stood. The only real wreckage was the supply shed that had been between the house and the coop.

"Our decorations!" Jennie exclaimed, remembering what

that "one thing" was. "Our table for the dance! Everything was in the shed!"

She ought to be happy that the house was safe, but all she could think of was the work that had gone into the Riley table: her ma's playful carved animals, her pa's crocheted place mats, her own embroidered pillows for the benches . . .

Dee began to sniffle. "My doilies! I decorated each one!"

Her father patted her comfortingly. "Tom, I'd like to make certain there's no structural damage to the house."

"I'll tell Julio to send an alternate team on the afternoon patrol," said Mr. Preston.

"Rileys!" her father called. "Nobody goes inside until the carpenters and I have made sure it's safe. Not even to get your dancing clothes."

Jennie ruefully plucked a feather from her overalls.

Brisa ran up. "I'll get you replacements!"

As she tore off, Dee wailed, "I don't care about replacement chickens!"

Mrs. Callahan said loudly, "I doubt the Preciados have any chickens to spare."

Meredith and Yuki came up next. Neither of them could look Jennie in the eye.

"I'm so sorry," said Meredith.

"It's okay," Jennie replied, trying to mean it.

"It's not okay," said Yuki glumly. "I wish there was some way we could make it up to you. Besides cleanup."

Meredith smiled. "Why don't you take a look at my new dress? It's not finished yet, so you can alter it to fit yourself. It's dark red cotton. I think it'll be gorgeous on you."

32

Ross

MIA TWIRLED IN THE MIDDLE OF HER COTTAGE, HER skirts flaring out. Ross liked the contrast of the petal-pink of all those ruffles with the blue-black silk of her hair.

"Still looks good," he said.

"You look good too." She peeked out the window. "While we're waiting for Jennie, tell me what happened while you were in the infirmary. Every time I looked in, you were asleep."

"That's because I slept the whole time, except when your father woke me for meals."

"I meant with the singing tree. Did your deal work? Did you have nightmares, or did it leave you alone?"

"No," said Ross, after a pause.

"No, which?"

"I didn't have nightmares, but it didn't leave me alone. Not completely." It was hard to put feelings, intentions, and images into words. "I did dream about it, but it wasn't scary or awful. Actually, it was kind of interesting. I guess while I was figuring out how to talk to the tree, it was figuring out how to talk to me."

"That's amazing," Mia said. "And a little bit creepy."

"It's a lot less creepy than what was going on before." For the first time since he'd come to Las Anclas, he felt as strong as he had before Voske's soldiers jumped his claim. His left hand still couldn't grip, but he was getting used to that, and working around it. He wasn't tired, he didn't hurt, he had more than enough to eat and drink, and when the dance ended tonight, he wouldn't be afraid to fall asleep. It was such a relief that he couldn't bring himself to worry about what his dreams might mean.

Jennie knocked and came in. Her dress was the color of red wine—and it had obviously been made for someone much smaller. Every beautiful curve strained the seams, especially in the low-cut front.

"You look great," Ross managed, knowing he shouldn't stare, or at least not at the places where he was staring. He tried to keep his eyes on her face, on the matching threads she had woven into her braids.

Jennie sighed, stretching the dress even tighter across her breasts. "It's Meredith's dress. I altered it, but—"

"It looks better that way," Ross blurted out. "It's great."

Mia burst into giggles. A beat later, Jennie joined in. Embarrassment burned through him, but then he realized that neither of them was laughing at him. Or, at least, not in a mean way.

"Can you breathe?" Mia asked.

"It's a challenge," Jennie admitted. "Come on, let's go dance!"

She and Mia each held out an arm and waited, smiling. Ross slowly stepped into the space between them. He slid one hand into the crook of Jennie's sleekly muscled arm, her skin like silk. His other hand tucked into Mia's arm, which was as light-boned as a bird's wing.

They set out, easily falling into step. As much as seeing his tree for the first time had been a nightmare come true, walking arm-in-arm with Mia and Jennie felt like a dream. He couldn't help smiling as they entered the square.

Under bowers of vines, streamers, and hanging baskets of flowers, elegantly dressed people sat at beautifully decorated tables. The biggest and most elaborate was by the town hall, where the mayor and defense chief and their family sat, with

Henry Callahan sitting beside Felicité. But though the entire town seemed to have turned out—except for the unlucky handful stuck on sentry duty—none of them were Rileys.

"My family must still be trying on other people's clothes," Jennie said with a rueful glance at the bare table that was obviously theirs. "Let's go visit yours."

Mia's relatives applauded when they walked up.

"That's your mother's dress, isn't it?" her aunt asked wistfully. "It looks beautiful on you."

"All three of you are beautiful." Grandma Lee smiled. "Have a seat!"

"Dante just dropped off his contribution." An uncle indicated a covered platter. "I'm not sure what it is, exactly."

Mia cautiously lifted the lid. The platter was covered with fist-sized balls of transparent gelatin that had fish and flowers of colored gelatin suspended within. "I don't know what they'll taste like," she said dubiously. "But they're pretty. And they haven't melted or exploded or burst into flames. Yet."

The tables laden with food filled the summery air with delicious smells. "Do people share their food?" Ross asked.

Mia grinned. "That's the best part! You're expected to at least taste as many dishes as you can, and still dance. Try not to explode."

Ross swallowed. "When do we start eating?"

"Not until the dance officially begins," Jennie said. "I know this one opens with a presentation, because I've heard Felicité rehearsing it before school. Oh, there's my family!"

The arriving Rileys, in fancy but poorly fitting borrowed clothes, waved back as they made their way to their barren table.

Yuki hurried up, formally dressed in a black suit. "I owe you for the pit mouth. Take this."

He held out a silver statue of a dancer. Ross instantly recognized it as an ancient artifact.

"Where did you get that?" Jennie asked.

Yuki pushed the statue into her hands. "It's the best thing I have."

"It's beautiful." She admired it, then returned it to Yuki. "I can't take this. If you help us rebuild the shed, that's good enough."

Yuki gave it back to her. "Just take it for the evening. As a decoration."

Jennie smiled. "I would love that. Thank you."

Yuki walked away.

Ross leaned close. "I wonder where he got it. It's worth everything else here put together."

As Jennie went over to carefully set the statue on the Riley table, Mia reached for a dish. "Can I give the Rileys our chili noodles? They're Mr. Riley's favorite."

"Of course," said Grandma Lee.

"And the fish soup," said an uncle.

"And some *panchan*." A cousin handed Ross a platter laden with small bowls of kimchi, potato salad, and stir-fried vegetables.

As they set the gifts on the Riley table, they were joined by Jack Lowell with goat stew and corn tortillas, Anna-Lucia with a peach pie, Ms. Lowenstein with beef brisket, and a sparkling woman with an embroidered tablecloth. Two women in their sixties, one with a crown of white braids and one who looked like she was related to Sheriff Crow, brought a basket of flatbread. Across the square, people rose from every table to offer food and decorations.

Ross took a step back in alarm as Felicité came up with an enormous bouquet of white roses. She couldn't expect him to be part of the presentation, could she?

But she didn't give him a glance. "Jennie, I'm so sorry about the shed. But you look marvelous. Have you seen Brisa? We should have started by now."

Jennie shook her head. "She ran off right after the explosion. She said something about replacements."

Felicité headed for the Vardams' table. Between its canopy of colorful streamers and his embroidered tunic, Mr. Vardam's chameleon skin made him into a rainbow man. She greeted him, and then turned to Sujata. "Brisa isn't here. Can you take her place?" she asked. "I can write out her poem."

"I hate recitations," Sujata replied. "Especially unrehearsed. Can I do anything else?"

"I'll cut the poem down to two lines. Please?" Felicité said winningly.

Sujata caved in. "Oh, okay." They walked away, leaving Ross breathing in relief. It seemed that the visitor's dance would leave the visitor in peace.

Grandpa Lee hushed everyone. "It looks like we're starting. Finally."

The musicians played a fanfare. Felicité, Becky, and Sujata walked to the center of the square, each carrying a large bouquet. Felicité's white bouquet and Becky's pink one matched their dresses and the straw hats; Sujata was the odd girl out, in a crimson sari and a clashing yellow hat. She held a bunch of yellow roses.

But the one Ross felt sorry for was Becky, who stood stiffly, her gaze fixed on the ground. Her lips moved, but though the entire town was quiet—the only sound a distant cry of birds— she was completely inaudible.

Sujata was next, balancing a slate behind her bouquet. She read so fast that Ross couldn't catch anything but "glorious history" and "glacier," or possibly "gracious." At least it was short, he thought gratefully as his stomach growled. He heard snickering from a far table.

Felicité spoke clearly. "With these poems—"

"What poems?" a boy called.

To Ross's surprise, Henry half-rose from the mayor's table, hissing, "Shut up, Basil."

Felicité lifted her chin. Her voice wobbled slightly as she began again. "We salute the grace of the past with the promise of the present, by presenting these bouquets to our esteemed and honored mayor, Valeria Wolfe."

She curtseyed and handed her bouquet to the mayor. The other girls did the same.

The bandleader nodded, and the musicians began to play the opening waltz. The mayor and Mr. Preston walked into the square, followed by other town leaders.

Henry bowed smartly to Felicité. Ross waited for a frog to jump out of Henry's pocket, but no such thing happened. He held out his hands to Felicité, and they began to dance.

"You know this one." Jennie smiled at Ross.

Mia bounced up. "Hey, three can waltz as easily as two."

Holding hands with them, Ross stepped and twirled, spinning inward until they were surrounded by couples and, here and there, larger circles of dancers. He felt self-conscious, but everyone was too busy having their own fun to pay any attention.

The second dance was easier. He didn't even mind when somebody spun a girl so fast that she staggered, then collided with Ross, knocking them both down.

Jennie pulled him up. "Let's show them how to do it!"

Ross and Jennie gripped hands. Instead of dancing, they began to spin like two children on a playground. Faster and faster they spun, falling into each other's rhythm the way they did when they sparred, until all he could focus on were Jennie's bright eyes and smile against a whirling background. Her braids stood straight out behind her.

Ross became aware of clapping and cheering, and they slowed to a stop.

"That was great," Mia said. "Do it with me!"

Jennie laughed. "Ready?" Her strong fingers closed around Mia's wrists, and the two girls began to spin, slowly at first, in time to the dance. Jennie sped up, and Mia struggled to match her, laughing.

Then Jennie shifted her weight and lifted Mia off the ground, whirling her through the air. Mia let out a shriek of delight, and the people around them clapped. Several other couples started spinning.

Soon Jennie slowed, letting Mia sink until her feet touched down.

She began to stumble, but Jennie held her up, spinning her into Ross's arms. He twirled Mia, though he didn't lift her off the ground; he didn't trust his left hand. When they stopped, Ross was slightly dizzy.

"Let's sit down," Mia said.

"And then let's eat," he suggested.

"Pa's back!" Jennie ran to the Riley table.

Mr. Riley was in clothes he had obviously borrowed from someone shorter.

"What's the report on your house?" Sheriff Crow appeared out of the crowd. Ross was startled by how different she looked in a clinging black dress.

"We've checked the back half," Mr. Riley said. "It looks fine, but the rest will have to wait for daylight. So . . . time to eat. Sheriff, I see your mothers brought their famous fry bread."

Sheriff Crow offered the basket to Ross first. He took a piece of the hot flatbread drizzled in honey, and started to raise it to his lips. The smell of the bread and the oil it was fried in seemed strangely familiar. He'd had it sometime—many times—long ago, when he'd lived in a town.

"I think my father used to make this," he said.

"Oh?" Sheriff Crow licked honey from her lips. "What's his tribe?" Ross closed his eyes, trying to summon more of the memory. "Or did I jump to a conclusion? My mother Tatyana made half the fry bread, and she's not Indian."

"No . . . No, I think you're right. But I don't know how I know that. All I remember is this bread."

"Maybe more will come back to you," she said kindly. "But first, eat it before it gets cold."

Ross took the hint, then sat sifting crumbs between his fingers. The bread brought a flood of memories he hadn't known he had. Nothing terrible: Squirming away from his mom as she dried his hair with a towel. Watching dust motes dancing in a ray of sunlight. Petting a black dog with a graying muzzle. He hadn't even remembered that they'd had a dog.

"Are you okay?" asked Jennie. He nodded. "Then come try Anna-Lucia's peach pie."

"And Aunt Olivia's fish dumplings." Mia already had a pile of them.

There was more food than Ross had seen in his entire life. He filled his plate, then squeezed in between Mia and Jennie. Despite the noise and the movement, he felt safe and relaxed. Jennie and Mia chattered to each other, talking across him, as he ate slowly, enjoying the flavors and textures.

Jennie's scent of herbs and flowers, and Mia's of soap and olive oil, drifted pleasantly from either side of him. Mia's ruffled skirt had fallen across his lap, and he could feel Jennie's bodice rise and fall against his side as she breathed. For the first time in his life, he felt lucky.

33

Felicité

FELICITÉ TRIED TO ENJOY DANCING WITH HENRY, who was surprisingly graceful, but she couldn't help reviewing and re-reviewing the humiliating failure of her presentation. What in the world had happened to Brisa?

Indra waltzed past her—with Nasreen again. This was their third dance! Nasreen was supposed to be her friend, but she hadn't said a word about going with Indra. It was all part of the general disaster that her celebration had become: Nasreen keeping secrets from her; Brisa standing her up—

As if summoned, Brisa came dashing into the square in filthy, oil-spattered work clothes, and triumphantly presented an armload of dusty cloth to Jennie. "I brought you some doilies!"

Felicité forced a smile as Henry burst out laughing. She would be poised and gracious if it killed her. "I'm glad nothing happened to you."

Brisa put both hands to her face. "Felicité! Oh, no! Did I miss the presentation?"

"Where have you been?" Brisa's mother exclaimed, the sheriff right behind her. "I told Sheriff Crow you were missing!"

"Replacing the Rileys' decorations," said Brisa blithely. "From when we won the prize for the Year of the Dog festival. First I rummaged through the pantry closet, then I searched the garden shed, and then I remembered the boxes up in the attic. And there they were! But I tripped coming down the ladder, and some stuff in the attic fell on me. But I got the doilies!"

The sheriff laughed. She was wearing high-heeled shoes and an elegant black gown cut on the bias, which flattered her form. From one side. Did she actually think she was still beautiful?

"That is a lovely gown," Felicité managed, too upset to hear the *clink*.

Sheriff Crow nodded her thanks, but did she say anything about the decorations or the music? No! Everyone was laughing about Brisa's doily hunt, as if that was more important than the poems and the presentation.

Brisa hurried toward Becky. "I'm so sorry, Becky. I lost track of time."

They were so close that Felicité could hear Becky's tiny voice saying, "These things happen. Don't worry about it. Meredith and I escorted each other."

"I know these things happen," Brisa said unhappily. "I've watched them happen to you all the time. I wanted to be the person who didn't do that to you." Then she leaned in and kissed Becky softly, nothing touching but the two girls' lips.

"Come closer," said Becky, reaching out.

"I'm all moldy!"

"I don't care." Becky took her by her mold-covered shoulders and threw her arms around Brisa, hugging her tight. When they parted, Becky was the one to offer a kiss.

A romantic song began to play. Sheriff Crow held out her hand to the circle around her. "Who wants this dance?"

Five or six men pushed forward. Half of them weren't even Changed. Felicité was appalled when Jack Lowell stepped up front. How could even Jack, who was known as the nicest man in town, want to slow-dance with his cheek pressed up to that . . . skull? The crowd looked on, some admiring, some clearly envious, as the two began to dance.

Felicité had begun the evening so happy, under a lovely starlit night, exquisitely attired from the crown of rosebuds on her hat to her new dancing shoes. She'd planned a treasure trove of graceful compliments with which to shower the townspeople when they praised and admired her for her hard work. And it had been hard work.

But nobody noticed. Henry was busy laughing with Tommy and Carlos. She walked past the table where Sera and Ms. Lowenstein were pulling apart a loaf of braided challah bread, and Yuki, Paco, and Meredith were demolishing a steamed fish. Everyone was having a great time—except for the person who made the whole thing happen.

Felicité reached the Wolfe table, which was decorated with her stupid bouquets. She threw the nearest to the ground—it was that or cry. And she would not cry.

A waft of verbena, the rustle of silk, and there was her mother. "Are you all right, dear?"

Daddy was right behind her. "Great job, sweetie. You made us proud."

"It was not," Felicité said, trying to keep her voice low. "You heard. You saw. The presentation was horrible. And no one cares how much work I put into it—into everything."

Her mother smiled. "Everyone is having such a good time, they won't remember the awkward start. That is what I call a success."

"But nobody appreciates what I did!"

"They might not say so, but look at how much fun everyone's having. Here is something you must learn about political leadership: Most of the time no one notices a good job. They only comment on things they dislike, or when you've handled an emergency. But we noticed."

She kissed Felicité's hot forehead. "Will you excuse me? I promised to speak with Constanzia."

Her mother walked up to the Changed woman, ignoring the haze of sparkling light that surrounded her.

Felicité's father sat down beside her. "Your mother is the most perfect woman in the world, but sometimes she can be too kind."

Of course he meant how her mother was kind to Changed people, but right now Felicité didn't care. "I tried so hard."

He patted her on the cheek. "Here's something I learned back when I was bad and bold: no battle plan survives contact with the enemy."

"Enemy?" she repeated, and gave an unsteady laugh.

"But we know who planned and executed the attack. Shall we pick up these fallen soldiers?" He began gathering up the flowers.

34

ROSS

ROSS WAS ON HIS FOURTH DISH OF APPLE CRUMBLE and Mia on her third when Jennie and Brisa took the square for a dance battle.

Jennie did a different routine from the one he'd seen, powerful but less acrobatic. She finished with a single backflip, and landed balanced on one hand. Then she bounced to her feet. Everyone applauded.

"I've seen her do four of those in a row," he said.

Mia chuckled. "Not in that dress, she can't. She's lucky she did one without it tearing at the seams."

Ross couldn't help wishing it would. Just a little bit.

Brisa strutted up. She'd changed into clean pants and a shirt, and had a rainbow of ribbons tied around her pigtails. With a mischievous look at Jennie, she launched into a series of spins on the ground, now on her back, now on her hands, and, briefly, on her head.

When she leaped up, one of her ribbons had come loose. Jennie tried to catch Brisa's attention, but she had already launched into a series of backflips. On the third, her heel caught the trailing ribbon and jerked her head back. She fell with a yelp, her foot twisting beneath her. The drummer continued for another beat, then stopped.

"Ow," Mia said, leaping up. "I felt that, just watching. Where's—oh, here he comes."

Dr. Lee hurried up, with Becky and Brisa's parents close behind him. He said wryly, "You can see Becky outside of the infirmary, Brisa. You don't need all these excuses to go there."

Brisa gave a watery giggle. Her parents made a chair of their hands and carried her off, Becky trotting anxiously at their heels.

The musicians started up again. "Want to dance?" Jennie asked. "Can't sprain your ankle in a circle dance."

Mia was on her feet in an instant.

"After I finish." Ross pointed to his plate.

He settled in to watch, letting the beat carry him away. Jennie looked as strong as she was, but Mia's size and delicacy were deceptive; Ross knew that she could lift him. Jumping, laughing, pink ruffles fluttering, she clearly was dancing purely for her own fun. Jennie's style was more polished; she had obviously practiced the steps, while Mia was simply following along. Catching Ross's gaze, she put some extra swing into her hips, and made her entire body ripple like water. He had to gulp for air.

The circle dance ended, and a waltz started up. Sheriff Crow and Jack Lowell glided expertly past.

"It's good—" Jack began.

"I think—" Sheriff Crow said.

He laughed. "You first."

Ross had never before seen the sheriff get flustered. "Oh, it was nothing."

"It matters to me," Jack said in a low voice. It was clearly a private moment. Ross started to get up.

"It reminded me—" the sheriff began.

Dr. Lee ran up, interrupting them. Ross had never before seen him so angry—or angry, period.

"What is it, Dante?" Sheriff Crow asked.

"My house has been searched!"

"Vandalized?"

"No. Searched by a professional. Nothing out of place."

"How do you know?" Jack asked.

Dr. Lee addressed the sheriff. "If someone went through your weapons and ammunition stores, wouldn't you know?"

"Yes. It has to be that bounty hunter." She glanced around quickly, and beckoned. "Ross?"

He got off the bench, his heart pounding. Very quietly, she asked, "Where's your book?"

"Hidden," Ross said. "Not at the surgery."

Mia and Jennie hurried up. "What's going on?" Jennie asked.

Sheriff Crow tapped her foot. "Even with a skeleton crew on the walls, that man should not have been able to get inside. I need to know how and where he got in. Let's go find him."

"I'll guard the book," Ross started. "No, I can't—"

The sheriff gave a short nod. "He's probably waiting for you to lead him to it."

Once Ross had been more afraid of that man and his rifle than of an entire grove of singing trees. If he'd known then what he knew now, he'd have climbed out of that gully and faced the bounty hunter with nothing but his knives. He'd have faced him with his bare hands. "I'll help you search."

"I'll deputize you," the sheriff said. "Let's go to my office, and I'll return your weapons."

"Can you deputize me, too?" asked Mia.

Sheriff Crow gave her a puzzled look, then nodded. "If you like."

Dr. Lee pointed at Mr. Preston and Mayor Wolfe, who were waltzing across the square. "I'll go report this to Tom and Valeria."

Jennie tapped her foot thoughtfully. "The bounty hunter doesn't know anything about me. I'll guard the book."

35

Felicité

THE REEL ENDED, AND TOMMY HORST ESCORTED
Felicité back to her table.

"That was nice." He sounded nervous. Was that because
she'd finally danced with him?

She gave a smile calculated to be sweet but not encourag-
ing. She'd promised herself to dance with anyone who asked,
but those clumsy feet would not mash her toes twice.

"Hey, Felicité, I've been to every table." Henry's cheerful
voice came from behind. "And I can definitely say that you've
got the best eats. The best flowers. The best everything." He
held out his hands. "Now that there's a bit more room to
move, let's show them the best dancing."

"Let's." Felicité wasn't sure Henry was actually the best,
but at least she was free of Tommy.

She was amazed—Henry turned out to be an excellent
dancer, spinning her among the other couples. Felicité nearly
lost her hat, and her hair streamed behind her. She laughed,
exhilarated. For the first time that night, she was enjoying
herself. She was glad she'd rearranged the bouquet. Her
family did have the best table, and the best food. Her dress
was the most beautiful in the entire square. And this dance
was—

Splat.

A cold drop hit her cheek.

She jerked out of his grip. Henry laughed. "Tripped over
a raindrop?"

"It can't be raining. The stars are out. It never rains this time of year."

"What do you call those?" He pointed at the thunderheads fast obscuring the full moon. "Flying cows?" He laughed.

Purple lightning flashed. Henry's voice was drowned in a clap of thunder, and in an instant, Felicité was drenched in rain.

She yanked her hands free, and pulled her straw hat down over her ears. "My hair!"

Behind her, Meredith's laughter rose above the pelting rain. "Run! Run! Don't let your hair melt!"

"Come on, Felicité, let's dance in the rain." Henry splashed after her.

She picked up speed. Mud splattered her ankles and the hem of her dress. Henry's footsteps died away. She ran on alone, faster than she ever did in training, and didn't slow until she saw her house.

Felicité darted to the side door, raced up into her room, and locked the door behind her. Then she pulled the curtains. She unpinned her hat, tossed it aside, and turned up the lamps on her dressing table. Her mirror was at least six generations old. Family legend claimed it as a treasure from China, handed down from mother to daughter.

The mirror had never reflected anything like her before.

Her face stared back at her, framed by intricately carved wood. Her hideous, mutant face.

Nictitating membranes slid across her eyes, distorting the elegant uncreased eyelids she'd inherited from her mother. On both sides of her neck, gills gaped red and wet as open wounds. She forced herself to keep breathing with her nose, like a normal person, until the skin finished growing across her nostrils and the gills took over. The grotesque frog-like webbing on her hands was still limited to the first joints of her fingers, but it would grow if she got any wetter. She could feel it between her toes, too, the stretchy itch she utterly despised.

She tore off the dress and flung it away. Over her breasts and belly, her smooth brown skin had grown a layer of silvery scales. That was all it took: a few minutes of moisture, all over her skin. If she ever pressed her naked body up against the naked body of a sweating man, her Change would surely begin.

There would never be "the One."

No man would ever accept her monstrous body. If she wanted to keep her secret, she would have to be alone forever.

She was lucky to even have that choice. She still had nightmares about that first Change, alone in her own bathroom when she was thirteen, but she knew how very lucky she was. Imagine if it had happened in public! She was lucky to have a bathroom with a lock, and parents who didn't insist on her swimming or training hard or playing any sports where she'd get soaked in sweat. She was lucky to have Wu Zetian to help her keep her secret.

She whistled. Wu Zetian sleepily emerged from her rat house. She was the only living being ever to see Felicité in her monster form. Felicité cuddled her and sniffed back tears, afraid they would leave scaly tracks across her face.

She put her rat down and grabbed a towel from her bathroom, and rubbed it over her hair and her monstrous body until her skin burned and turned red, and she felt the Changes fading. When she faced the mirror again, there was Felicité Wolfe, future mayor.

Norm.

The rain poured down outside. She opened her closet and took out the gloves, the scarf, and the hat with a veil that she always wore whenever there was any chance of rain. Some of the girls snickered when they saw her like that, but as long as they were laughing at her "obsession" with her hair, they would never suspect the truth.

She put on a dry dress and closed-toe shoes. Then she picked up the scarf, careful to arrange its rich, soft folds right up under her ears. She pulled on the gloves. Last the hat, with the golden ribbons tied firmly under her chin. The veil covered her face.

She sat down on her bed, Wu Zetian by her side, and waited for the rain to end.

36

Mia

MIA, SHERIFF CROW, AND ROSS WERE HALFWAY TO
the jail when the storm hit.

By the time they reached it, they were all soaked. Mia
hoped her mother's dress would survive. It squeaked at
every step. Embarrassingly, the loudest squeaks were at her
armpits, where it was impossible to stop wet silk from rubbing against wet silk.

The jail was deserted, its four cells empty; no drunk-
and-disorderlies were sleeping it off for the night, though
the dance would probably end there for a few.

Sheriff Crow led them into her office, where she unlocked
the weapons cabinet. Ross was clearly relieved and happy
to finally get his knives back. As he undid his belt to slide
the sheaths back on, Sheriff Crow beckoned Mia.

She had never seen the sheriff's bedroom before. Purple
lightning flared, briefly revealing a plain bed, a night
table, and a clothes press. Sheriff Crow shut the door and
started to peel off her slinky dress. Mia obligingly turned
her back.

"Are you sure you want to go along with us?" the sheriff
asked.

The transition from the noise and cold of the storm to
the hot still air of the bedroom was suffocating. "Yes. Well.
I think—"

"What, Mia?" Sheriff Crow rustled around, pulling on
her sturdy work clothes. "I know you can hit a target, but

what I'm trying to figure out is what you bring to an actual fight if that bounty hunter gives us one."

"I have to protect Ross," Mia blurted out.

"*You* have to protect *him*? From what little I know about Ross Juarez, the one thing that seems clear is that he can take care of himself."

If she had seen what Mia had seen, at the base of that blood-red tree . . . Mia crossed her arms. Silk squeaked. "I have a flamethrower."

"It's raining."

"I have a crossbow that shoots six arrows."

"Simultaneously?" Sheriff Crow stopped knotting her rawhide laces. "When did you make this? Why haven't you told me before?"

"Um. Well. I only tested it yesterday."

When she'd test-fired it, the recoil had knocked her down, and every arrow had gone wild. She'd felt tiny and weak then, and she felt tiny and weak now, especially in the same room as the strongest person in town.

Sheriff Crow was giving her a very suspicious look. "Does it work?"

If Mia confessed that she couldn't use it herself, there would be no reason for her to come along. But if she waited till they were at her cottage, maybe Sheriff Crow could take it, and she'd be so pleased with it that she'd let Mia come with a regular crossbow. "Oh, it definitely works!"

Ross called, "Could I borrow a shotgun?"

The sheriff gave Mia another suspicious look as they returned to the office. She got a gun for Ross, and took out her own rifle. The two swiftly loaded their weapons.

"Okay." Sheriff Crow tucked her rifle under her arm to protect the touchhole from the rain. "If you're that determined, Mia, let's go get your miracle crossbow."

They set out into a wild wind that drove stinging rain

into their faces. When they neared her cottage, Mia was surprised to see golden light in the windows. "Did I leave the
light on again? I'm so absentminded—"

Two rifles whipped up, pointing at the door. Waving the
others back, the sheriff kicked the door open.

A tall man in a long black coat sat on Mia's bed, one elbow
resting on the engine as he browsed one of her manuals. His
face was scratched from forehead to neck.

"Stand up," Sheriff Crow ordered.

The bounty hunter laid the manual aside, then stood,
hands held away from his body. "I figured you'd show up
sooner or later."

"Who've you been fighting?" the sheriff demanded.

"Cats." The bounty hunter jerked his thumb toward the
surgery.

Mia gasped. "You didn't hurt my cats?"

"Boot's on the other foot." His lips thinned in what might
have been a smile.

A sheet of purple lightning brightened the windows to a
mad glare. Spheres of light leaped along every metal object
in the room. The bounty hunter took a fast step away from
the bed, where the engine briefly glowed with lurid light.
The cottage vibrated in a blast of thunder.

When the rumbles began to roll away, he said, "This is
not a natural storm. That purple lightning and St. Elmo's
Fire? I've seen it before. Voske's oldest daughter Changed
last year. Deirdre's a stormbringer. If she's here, Voske's outside your gates right now."

Ross's voice cracked. "You're a liar. You're working for
him. This is some kind of trick."

"Any particular reason we should believe you?" Sheriff
Crow inquired.

Mia quietly felt along the stacked boxes until she found
the comforting shape of her flamethrower.

"Take a look," said the bounty hunter. "You won't have seen the army approaching because Deirdre uses mist to settle the dust from the horses' hooves. But I bet you can see them now."

"And you're telling us, why?" Sheriff Crow held the rifle loosely, muzzle pointed at the floor. Mia knew how fast she could bring it up. She wondered if the bounty hunter did.

He had seemed perfectly cool before, even when St. Elmo's Fire burned on the engine inches away from him, but now his lips tightened. "Voske didn't send anyone to warn me he was coming. I think he's planning to kill me along with the rest of you."

Mia was ready to rush out and take a look for herself, but the sheriff said calmly, "And why would that be?"

The man leaned back against the wall, equally calm, as if they were having a casual conversation over drinks at Jack's. "Voske hired me to fetch the book, preferably along with the boy who stole it. He also gave me the option to kill the boy."

Mia edged closer to Ross.

He went on. "When I tracked him here—well, Tom Preston and I know each other. I tried to get the book and the boy by legal means. When you wouldn't surrender them, I tried to intimidate the boy into handing it over. When that didn't work, I tried to steal it. I take off my hat to you, Juarez." He tipped an imaginary hat to Ross. "I still don't know where that book is."

"Sounds to me like you did your best for your employer," said Sheriff Crow. "What went wrong between you?"

"I think Voske got paranoid," the bounty hunter replied. "He hired me for a job that should've taken a couple days. It's been over a month. If he's been spying on me, maybe he saw me talking instead of fighting, and thought I was throwing in with you folk."

"I don't suppose you know how he spies on people?"

He shrugged. "No idea."

Ross scowled. "Don't believe anything he says. He claimed I could control people's minds!"

The bounty hunter's mouth twitched in amusement. Mia suspected that the lie had come under the heading of "legal means."

The sheriff seemed to agree. "That was to turn Preston against you, but this story makes sense. Voske's tried to take Las Anclas before, and we know that he never forgives what he sees as betrayal. If he thought you double-crossed him, and he knew we were planning a dance tonight . . . Yes, I can see him deciding it was the perfect opportunity to take the town, and get the book, the thief, and the traitor along with it."

The bounty hunter nodded. "So here I am. If I'm going to be fighting him anyway, I'd rather have some backup."

The sheriff tucked her wet hair behind her ears and turned her entire face to the man. "Are you asking me to deputize you?"

"Yes." He returned the sheriff's cool gaze with unblinking black eyes.

"All right," she said. "Let's go."

37

YUKI

YUKI SAT SHOULDER TO SHOULDER WITH PACO, watching the mud fight Henry had started. Laughing kids competed to see who could slide the farthest, while his friends slow-danced in the rain.

"I thought I'd hate watching everyone dance when I can't," Paco said. "But it's okay. I'll be able to dance next time. Maybe I'll teach Ross folklórico, since he's got my old outfit."

"Yeah, you should." Yuki leaned his head against Paco's shoulder. He couldn't remember ever feeling this relaxed.

The tower bell rang.

Yuki snapped upright.

The bell kept ringing, tolling out a pattern so unexpected he almost couldn't place it. The bell was ringing for Battle Stations—without even going to Lockdown first. It had to be a prank. But Henry, the only person who might even consider it, looked as poleaxed as everyone else, a forgotten mud ball dripping in his hands.

"It's real," Paco said. He started to get up, then fell back. "Ow—damn! Where's Dr. Lee?"

"Dr. Lee! Dr. Lee!" Brisa's high voice came from behind them, accompanied by the thump of crutches. "You've got to heal us!"

The doctor came splashing through the puddles. "I just left Tom Preston. There's an army at the gates."

Paco grabbed his arm. "You have to fix my knee. I don't

care how much it shortens my life. I'm not sitting here while my town is attacked."

"Me either." Brisa raised clenched fists. "They'll need us!"

Yuki held his breath as Dr. Lee glanced from one to the other. "Brisa, your ankle would have healed in a few weeks anyway. It'll be fine as long as you don't kick anyone. But Paco, even if I did heal you—and you're right, that would take months off your life—you'll still have a limp, and it'll still hurt. You need to do rehab—"

Paco waved it all away. "I don't care. As long as I can walk."

"Do it, Dr. Lee. They're both on my bow team." Even as Yuki spoke, he found it hard to believe this was actually happening.

"All I'll take is one month," Dr. Lee warned, motioning Brisa to sit beside Paco. "And you, a week. Go on, Yuki. They'll catch up with you. Go."

He ran through the pelting rain. A crowd had converged at the armory, party clothes dripping. Judge Lopez supervised the children and old people in the supply lines, passing along weapons and ammunition.

"Your weapons are on the wall," Josiah Rodriguez called to Yuki. "They're sending the kids to collect everyone's armor from the schoolhouse. Stay low!"

Yuki vaulted over the corral fence and ran to the wall, where he found Meredith checking her arrows. As the leaders of the best two student bow teams, they were positioned on either side of the front gate, with the best adult shooters on the gate itself.

He took up his position behind a shield, glad to see a bow and a full box of arrows waiting. His mother was already on the wall, incongruous in her brocade party dress, issuing orders as calmly as if this were another boring drill.

What finally convinced Yuki that it was real was how

chaotic it was. Unlike the way things happened in the smoothly organized drills, half the people who should be there weren't, others were in the wrong places, and no one wore armor. His own team members were hastily removing bracelets and embroidered vests, elegant hats and high-heeled shoes, and tossing them into the basket held up by Grandma Callahan.

Julio Wolfe splashed up. "Can you see them?"

"Not in this rain." Yuki's mom peered into the darkness.

His heartbeat raced. He'd rather know it was bad than not know at all.

A fork of purple lightning lit the entire sky. In its glare he saw the army lined up in rows, some mounted.

Henry gasped, serious for once. "There's thousands of them."

Yuki's mother's voice cracked out. "There are not. He's spread them out so it looks like there's more than there are."

"Get ready!" Fast, splashing footsteps on the sentry walk brought everyone's attention to Mr. Preston, his embroidered tunic dripping. "They'll try to blow up the gate."

Yuki gripped his bow, wishing he could see better. He wiped his eyes; it didn't help. The rain was too thick, the clouds heavy overhead.

Then the rain stopped instantly. Clouds parted with unnatural speed. The light of the moon was so bright that it seemed like another lightning flash. He saw enemy soldiers grouped around bulky objects wrapped in shiny oilcloth. Those must be their explosives.

"Mr. Preston!" Yuki's mom called out. "Do you think this is Voske's army?"

"It has to be. What I wish I knew is if Ian Voske is out there himself."

A horn blared a series of notes, and tiny flames arced toward the wall. Yuki ducked as fire arrows flew overhead.

"Here they come," Mr. Preston said.

Yuki wished he felt as calm as Mr. Preston sounded.

With a ripping sound, Voske's soldiers sliced off the oil-cloth, revealing barrels.

The barrels began to move. Some were pushed by heavily armored fighters, but one rolled by itself, obviously propelled by some Change power.

"Teams One through Three," Yuki's mom called. "Aim for the pushers. The rest of you, on my mark, light your arrows, and hit the barrels before they reach the gate. Everyone, hold for my command."

"They're too close," Henry muttered. "We should shoot now."

Yuki clenched his teeth to stop himself from snapping, *They're still out of range, idiot!*

The smell of sulfur eddied on the air as the arrows were lit. Arrows flew overhead, this time lower. Someone at the far end of the wall let out a scream.

Yuki peered around his shield, trying to see how the enemy armor was jointed. He heard his mom's voice in his mind, crisp and clear: "Remember! When your enemy is wearing armor, don't shoot at their bodies. Aim for elbows, knees, armpits, neck. Anywhere the armor has to gap. They'll be doing the same to you."

The figures and their barrels of explosives moved closer. Behind them, the line of soldiers also approached.

Another wave of arrows flew overhead from the attackers. Down the wall, a bow twanged. An arrow flew out—and clattered harmlessly off the helmet of one of the attackers.

"Henry. Step out of line, and join the supply team." Yuki's mom's voice was sharp.

"But I hit the guy!"

"You know what 'edge of range' means. Even if he hadn't been wearing a helmet, that arrow would barely have had enough velocity left on it to scratch him. Now, get off the wall."

"You're pulling me off the wall, when I nearly got the first kill?" Henry protested.

Mr. Preston's voice rang out. "Henry Callahan, get off the wall *now*."

Yuki's mom called, "Aim!"

Yuki hefted the bow, picking his target: A big soldier, whose armor shifted, exposing his knees as he lifted his foot out of the mud.

"Shoot."

The air filled with the hiss and hum of arrows. Curses and some barks of laughter rose from the attackers. The line wavered slightly, then pushed on. None were hit. Yuki felt a spurt of anger and disappointment when his arrow thumped against the soldier's armored leg.

"If you can hit them, they can hit you," warned Mr. Preston.

Yuki hastily ducked behind his shield. Seconds later, another wave of arrows clattered off the shields and the upper part of the wall with a sound like hail.

"Aim." The whispers ceased. "Shoot!"

This time, Yuki's man staggered, a hand clapping to the arrow in his knee. He stumbled back, but his team pushed the barrel on. Over the field, four other figures writhed, and two lay still, arrows sticking up.

On the wall, someone screamed, and there was a sob. Yuki's mom ran, bent over, to see what was going on. "Take over, Meredith."

Meredith's voice was steady. "Aim! Shoot!"

Flaming arrows hit two barrels, but Voske's soldiers yanked them out before the fire spread.

"Aim! Shoot!"

"Rifles at the ready!" Julio Wolfe shouted.

Yuki's mom ran back. "Where are the dried cow patties?"

From below, Mr. Rodriguez said, "They've been rained on, Ms. Lowenstein. Shall we dip them in oil?"

"Do it," she called. Behind her, Meredith yelled, "Aim! Shoot!"

Yuki leaned out, shot—and the arrow pinned someone's hand against a barrel. The soldier let out a stream of curses.

"Ew, they're sticky!" Sujata cried. "And they stink!"

"Quiet on the wall!" Yuki's mom's voice was calm but carrying.

"Aim! Shoot!"

"Team Ten, in pairs, launch those patties."

An acrid smell singed Yuki's nostrils as two people from Team Ten bent low and passed behind him, heading toward the gate. Another pair followed.

"Aim!" Meredith called, then screamed.

Yuki spun around. His sister was down on the ground, with bright blood on her face and hair.

Their mom appeared out of nowhere, her yellow eyes huge. "Take the archers." She thumped his shoulder, then ran toward Meredith, keeping low, a shield angled to cover most of her body.

Yuki tried to speak, but his throat had gone dry. He worked his lips, slapped an arrow to his bow, and yelled, "Aim!" He paused to pick a target, wishing he knew which of them had shot his sister. "Shoot!"

A dozen soldiers fell or staggered. Yuki sneaked a quick peek along the wall, but he couldn't see either Meredith or his mother.

"Aim!" he called, when he remembered everyone was waiting. He nocked an arrow. "Shoot!"

Flaming cow patties arced into the air, falling on soldiers and barrels alike. A few stuck and burned. Attackers leaped and lunged, trying to put the fires out. Yuki felt a fierce laugh building at their howling and their clumsy dance. Then he remembered that he was exposed, and yanked his head back. An arrow whistled past his cheek.

An explosion rocked the wall, making Yuki clutch at his shield. "Aim!" He pulled an arrow up. "Sh—"

A flaming arrow hit the barrel below him, which exploded in a fireball.

Everything went white. His ears rang. Someone tugged his arm insistently. "Are you all right? Yuki, are you all right?"

"I'm fine," he said automatically. He was flat on his back. He sat up and felt around until he found his bow; he couldn't see anything but pulsing light.

"Good. Keep it going."

"Aim!" Yuki cried. He didn't know if anyone was listening. "Shoot!"

"Duck!" A hand thrust his head down.

Two more barrels exploded. He kept his eyes shut. When he opened them, he could see better, though lights flashed every time he blinked. The fires were so bright, and the attackers were so close he could see the details of their armor. It wasn't bullock armor plates, but something covered with metal links. Why wasn't his armor here yet?

"Are you hurt?" Meredith crouched beside him, her hand still on his head. Her head was bandaged and blood covered her face, but she was alive.

"Aim! Shoot!" The voice on his left belonged to a man.

Yuki rubbed his burning eyes against his shirt. His face was filmed with oily, smelly fertilizer residue. Mr. Preston knelt at the next shield over, peering intently down. He raised his pistol and shot. An attacker threw up his hands and fell into the mud.

"Are the barrels gone?" Yuki's mom called

A shuffling and a rustle behind Yuki, and there was

Yolanda Riley, her spiky hair flattened to her skull. "Armor, Yuki." She dropped it and crawled back along the sentry walk, her own armor creaking.

"Two remaining," Mr. Preston shouted, his voice strained. "They're almost close enough to blow the gate!"

They couldn't aim directly below without making themselves easy targets. Yuki yanked his armor on. He couldn't figure out why he was having so much trouble until he noticed his hands shaking.

Quick footsteps pattered down the wall. Brisa ran past in a low crouch, her pigtails swinging at each step. She was already armored, and carried a rock in either hand.

At the edge of the wall, next to the gate, she readied herself, then stood up. An arrow bounced off her breastplate, and another scraped her side. But her arm whirled in an expert throw as she hurled first one rock and then the other at the barrels below.

The explosions came almost on top of each other. Flaming bits of wood and chunks of dirt rained down all around them. Yuki tried to blink away the flashing lights and jagged shadows that distorted his vision. From the wild cheering, he knew that Brisa had been in time: the gate still held.

More arrows clattered against the shields as Yuki's mom knelt down. "You okay?"

"Yeah."

"They're not mounting another attack," said Mr. Preston. "That's covering fire."

Arrows whizzed out, and they all ducked. Several hit the shields, and one clattered off the wall inches from Yuki's foot.

"It's a distraction." Mr. Preston turned his head. "Julio!"

"Here, Chief."

"I think Voske's out there himself. That means a secondary plan, probably already in motion, and a backup readying."

"Secondary?" Julio's alarm echoed Yuki's own. He'd thought it was all over. His stomach lurched.

"The target has to be the back gate," Mr. Preston said. "They're probably moving in a wide circle so we won't see them until they charge. Take four teams to reinforce the back wall. Trainer Crow?"

"Here." Sheriff Crow's mothers, the town rat trainers, stood below the wall. Kourtney, a black-and-white rat, rode on Trainer Crow's shoulder, and Al, a brown rat, rode on Trainer Koslova's. Four others waited alertly at their feet.

"Please place your best teams on each wall, and at the town hall. But I want you at the back wall, and you, Trainer Koslova, here at the front gate."

Yuki and Kogatana were one of the best rat-and-human teams. He hoped they wouldn't get stuck at the town hall.

But when Trainer Koslova began, "Yuki, go fetch Kogatana," Mr. Preston said, "Not Yuki. I need him." His blurry profile peered out at Voske's lines, then Yuki felt his gaze. "Yuki, do you have to go to the infirmary?"

"I'm fine." Well, he would be, soon.

"Good." Yuki could hear Mr. Preston's relief. "Take your bow team and follow Julio."

Yuki's head ached, his ears rang, and his mouth was desperately dry. He could barely see anything but bright afterimages.

"Yuki." It was his mom's voice.

She pressed a canteen into his hand. He took a deep drink, then held it out, though he could have drained the whole thing. Someone else took it, and he heard the water slosh as they gulped.

"Brisa?" Yuki asked.

Brisa chirped, "Present!"

Yuki hadn't seen him yet, but if Brisa was here . . . "Paco?"

A steadying hand came down on Yuki's shoulder. "I'm here."

"Paco, is the rest of our team here? My vision's coming back fast, but I can't see faces."

"Half your bow team is in the infirmary," said Mr. Preston. "And so is Meredith's, so combine. Meredith, you and your team are under Yuki. Go as soon as he's got his sight back."

"We're ready," Yuki replied.

38

Jennie

JENNIE FOLDED MEREDITH'S DRESS, NOTING THE seams she'd have to repair before she gave it back. It was a relief to be back in her Ranger night-training clothes. She'd enjoyed seeing her cleavage nearly make Ross walk into a wall, but she enjoyed breathing more.

She opened the schoolhouse weapons chest. The bounty hunter was a big man, and carried a sectional staff as well as a rifle. She'd avoid the worst danger from the rifle by staying away from the windows. He'd only have one shot before he had to reload, and if that shot hit the book, it would be worthless confetti.

Ms. Lowenstein had drilled them in gun versus knife. No one believed it until they saw someone with a dye-soaked sponge race twenty feet and tag the person armed with a dye-loaded water-shooter without getting shot.

She shrugged into her sword harness, making sure the straps fit snugly over her shoulders, and belted it across her ribs. Then she reached over her shoulder to check that the sword was loose in its sheath.

The bells began to ring Battle Stations.

She took a step, then stopped. The back wall was her battle station, but the bounty hunter was already inside. The bells meant that he was at large and fighting people—he might even have backup. She needed to be right where she was.

Jennie added a pair of fighting knives. Why give him even

twenty feet? She'd take her position right inside the door.

Standing in the shadow of the doorway, dagger ready, Jennie waited. What a great story this would make for the *Heraldo*! Maybe Ross would let her write about the book.

The porch steps creaked. Jennie flattened herself against the wall. The door flew open. She leaped behind the silhouetted figure and pressed her knife up against his throat.

A very female scream ripped the air.

"Felicité?" Jennie exclaimed, yanking her knife away.

"Jennie!" Felicité gasped.

Jennie glanced past her to a cluster of little kids, every face bug-eyed and scared. She had forgotten that Felicité's Battle Stations job was to escort the under-tens to the school-house.

She forced her voice to be calm. "Good job, kids! You were quiet as mice, exactly the way you're supposed to be. I didn't even hear you! Now, come sit in your places." As the children trooped inside, she whispered, "Did they really think that guy would attack little kids?"

Felicité's veiled hat tilted upward. "Voske might attack anyone."

"Voske?"

Crash! They spun around. The smallest children had started wandering. Some were rummaging through the weapons chest. Even worse, others peered out the windows, presenting perfect targets.

"Get away from the windows!" Jennie shouted.

"Stop messing with the weapons and get back to your seats!" Felicité cried.

The kids running away from the windows collided with the kids leaving the weapons chest. Some laughed, while others shrieked. A few started crying.

Felicité began grabbing kids and pushing them toward the

benches. Their yelling rapidly changed to cries of "That hurts! Let me go!" and the inevitable "I want my mommy!"

Jennie strode to the front of the classroom. A slate flew across the room and smacked into her hand. She slammed it down onto her desk.

Into the instant quiet she said, "Sit. Down. Now."

The kids sat down.

"All right. Felicité is in charge,"

"Right. Yes." Felicité came up beside her, her dress ghost-pale. "You have to do your jobs, and that means being quiet. If Voske's army gets past the walls, do you want them to hear you yelling?"

Voske's army? Jennie thought.

"No," several said, and heads shook.

"So we'll sit here in the dark, quiet as mice." Between the dark room and her veil, Felicité's face was completely invisible. Jennie could hear a tremor in her voice, but her tone stayed firm. "Everyone who does exactly what I say may come to the mayor's house for a party when this is over. Would you like that? Put up your hand if you would."

Hands shot skyward.

Jennie slipped up next to Felicité. "Voske's army?"

"It's at the gates."

Jennie's hand went to her sword hilt.

The bells rang again, in a pattern Jennie had only ever heard in drills: Inner Perimeter. The walls were in danger of being breached, and everyone but these children and their caretakers had to go defend them.

Jennie turned to the kids. "Follow Felicité to the town hall. Whoever she says is the quietest and the quickest will get a special prize at the mayor's party."

As they swiftly formed a line, Jennie whispered to Felicité, "If you hear the last bell, you know what to do."

The veiled hat nodded violently. Then Felicité took her place at the front of the line, her voice more like spun sugar than ever. "Remember. Quiet and fast!"

The kids streamed out the door behind her.

Jennie surveyed the empty schoolroom, moonlit in silvery blue squares. The book would have to remain where it was. Her place was on the wall at the back gate.

39

Mia

MIA COULDN'T DECIDE WHICH HURT MORE, HER FEET or her lungs.

Sheriff Crow and the bounty hunter ran easily along the sentry walk, sending water splashing. A few steps ahead of her, Ross was breathing hard; he'd only been out of the infirmary for one day, after spending the last four flat on his back.

The sheriff called over her shoulder, "Come on!"

Now Mia wished she hadn't found so many excuses when Jennie wanted to practice. The crossbow seemed to get heavier with every step. If she had a chance to redesign it, she'd figure out some way to use less metal.

Ross slowed down until she could catch up. "Want me to carry that thing for you?"

"I'm thinking . . . toss it in the bushes," Mia panted.

She hadn't even had a chance to explain that she couldn't use it herself. Once the bells had rung, they'd headed for the front wall. Sheriff Crow had told Ross, who had no Battle Station position, to come as her aide, and had waved Mia along.

At the time, Mia had been delighted. But now, with the crossbow banging into her back and a stitch stabbing her side, she wished she were anywhere else.

The moment they'd reached the wall, the bounty hunter had said, "I've seen Voske take towns this size before. Half his army is missing."

"Then we'd better find them," the sheriff had said.

Since he had Changed vision, Mr. Riley was making a circuit of the sentry walk to the west. The four of them were doing the same thing, heading east.

The rain stopped. A hand came down on her shoulder, and Ross said, "I can carry the crossbow."

She handed it over, and hastily polished her glasses on a wet ruffle. The result was smeary, but at least she wasn't squinting through raindrops. They'd reached the back-gate command post.

The sheriff peered into the darkness. The sentries clutched their weapons, scanning the barely visible fields. All the adults looked worried and grim.

Mia said, "The rain's lifted, and my cottage is close. Should I get my flamethrower?"

Sheriff Crow gave a decisive nod. "I'll wait here for Mr. Riley's report. Bring it here to the back gate."

"Can I go with her?" Ross asked. "I can protect her in case anyone got over the wall."

The sheriff smiled briefly, an eerie sight in the moonlight that shone through the rapidly vanishing clouds.

They trudged through the mud to her cottage. When she turned on the lights, they cast a golden glow on Ross standing in the doorway, his hair hanging in wet black threads, his dancing clothes clinging to his body and displaying every curve and angle of muscle and bone.

She'd never really studied the shape of his shoulders, though she'd had her arms around them. Or his hips. What was that little hollow called, right above the hipbones? Whatever it was, the wet cloth clung to it without a wrinkle. If Mia put her hand there, it would feel like skin on skin. Ross was clear on the other side of the cottage, but she imagined touching him so vividly that she was half surprised that he hadn't already run away.

So this was what people meant by fiery, swoony passions. Mia really did feel as if she was about to burst into flames and pass out.

When a familiar blush began to darken Ross's face, she wondered in panic if she had spoken her thoughts out loud. He carefully set down the crossbow in midair. It clattered to the floor. He recoiled. Mia realized that he'd meant to put it on a nearby box.

"I'll wait outside," he said.

"What for?"

Ross informed the floorboards, "In case you don't want to fight in it. The dress, I mean." He bolted, the door slamming behind him.

Oh.

Rummaging wildly, she found a sheet of aluminum and tilted it to get a reflection. While the ruffles hid most of her breasts, every other contour of her body was outlined in wet pink silk.

The aluminum crashed on top of the crossbow.

She carefully extracted herself from the dress and hauled her shirt and overalls over her damp underwear with unprecedented speed, then searched for a place to stash the dress where it wouldn't rust anything and wouldn't get stained, and where Ross couldn't see it. She finally moved the engine off her bed and hid the dress beneath the quilt.

"You can come in now."

Ross opened the door a cautious inch as she tied her bootlaces. She grabbed the flamethrower, glad to have something to look at besides Ross's transparent shirt. "Let's go."

"Wait," he said. "Do you know what you're getting into?"

For once he wasn't furtive, studying his hands or the ground or the ceiling or his weapons. He gazed straight at her, black eyes reflecting the hanging light.

"I've never been in a battle before," she said. "But neither has anyone else our age."

"I haven't, either. I mean, not armies fighting. But I have fought with people. It's not like fighting animals. Not at all." The rapid flow of words stopped abruptly, and he clenched his right fist; his left half-closed.

"You've killed people before." Mia had meant to phrase it as a question, but once the words were out, she already knew the answer.

Ross nodded, neither pride nor regret in his level gaze. "I'd rather run. But sometimes you don't have a choice. You do, though, don't you? The sheriff didn't order you to fight."

"No. I asked her if I could come."

"Can you fight?" He flushed again. "I've never seen you train. I know you fought the snakes, but that was with a flamethrower."

"I take my turn at sentry duty and patrol, like everyone else," she said, trying not to sound defensive. "I'm a good shot."

"But can you fight?"

"You mean hand-to-hand? I've been trained, but I've never been great at it." He didn't need to know that she regularly lost to fourteen-year-olds. "But like I said, I'm a good shot, so that's what I'll be doing."

Ross flicked a glance sideways, then back at her. "Look, Mia. It's a mistake to think you'll only shoot. You don't know what you might have to do."

Mia wished she'd trained harder, she wished that the work she had put in had gotten better results, and she wished Ross would stop looking at her as if he was certain she'd get herself killed. But she couldn't change any of that now.

He nodded sharply, as if he'd come to an agreement with himself. "Okay. This is the most important thing I know about fighting. Don't think too hard—actually, don't think at all. Just let yourself react. Can you do that?"

She'd heard this before. Every time she'd lost a sparring match, it was because she'd stopped to consider her next move or her opponent's next move, or because her attention had drifted. But she didn't want Ross to be distracted by worrying about her.

"Absolutely."

She suspected that he didn't believe her. He ran his hand through his hair, clearing it from his face. "Do you own any weapons besides that crossbow and your flamethrower, or do you check them out?"

"I check them out."

He opened his mouth as if to say something, then shook his head. "Where do you keep those explosives you're always warning me about?"

"Oh, those aren't ready, but I have something better." She pulled out a box of bottles from under her worktable. "Help me fill these with oil. We'll cork them with rags, so we can light and throw them."

They quickly prepared the bottles and loaded them onto her cart. At the back wall, they found Sheriff Crow, the bounty hunter, and Mr. Riley with a group of sentries, all peering intently to the northwest.

Then the archers showed up. Normally so neat and organized, they arrived at a staggering run, armor hastily strapped over their party clothes. Meredith had a bloody bandage around her head, Paco limped, and Yuki was covered with dark gunk that Mia hoped was soot rather than dried blood. Trainer Crow came last, with a rat riding on each shoulder and another pair trotting at her heels.

Julio pushed past Mia. "Is Voske's army out there? Do you see them?"

Mr. Riley shaded his eyes. "I spotted soldiers out there once the rain cleared. But we don't know how many there are."

"What's he doing here?" Julio pointed at the bounty hunter.

"He's with us," replied Sheriff Crow.

"How did he get here?"

"My question exactly." Everyone turned. Mr. Preston was at the base of the ladder, Jennie by his side. Though she knew Jennie couldn't fight a whole army, Mia immediately felt safer.

"Evening, Tom," the bounty hunter said. "A climber doesn't have to worry about eater-roses on your walls anywhere but forty feet along the gates."

Mia stared at him in alarm. "If he could sneak in, could the rest of the enemy do it too?"

Glancing at her, Mr. Preston said, "It's much easier for one man—one very skilled man—to get over than for an entire team." He eyed the bounty hunter with a mixture of annoyance and respect. "The Rangers just made a sweep, and no one else got in. What disturbs me most is the timing of this attack."

Sheriff Crow waved a dismissive hand. "We can worry about that later. Mr. Riley spotted a flanking movement coming around the west side."

"We can't leave the mill unguarded," Mr. Preston said immediately. "It's too valuable."

Because that's where the escape tunnel comes out, Mia thought.

Julio smacked his fist into his palm and gave a laugh that reminded her of when he was their schoolhouse leader. He was the one who'd convinced the council to let thirteen-year-olds go on patrol. "Hey, Uncle, I've got an idea," he said, his white teeth flashing. He sounded as happy as if the dance was still going on. "Give me the Rangers. We'll go covert and take out Voske himself."

Mr. Preston sighed. "And he would be where, Julio?"

"Do you know where Voske is?" Julio asked the bounty hunter.

The man spread his hands wide. "He could be anywhere. He likes to shift around for exactly this reason. Wherever he is, he'll be surrounded by an elite team of bodyguards."

Mr. Preston said, "Julio. You're better off defending the mill. Jennie will pick up the rest of the Rangers." He spoke directly to the bounty hunter. "My guess is that Voske will keep his ammunition directly behind his lines, ready for a fast move, rather than at a distance."

"You would be right," the man said.

Mr. Preston turned back to Julio. "This flank attack will probably hit the wall where the stream enters. Place your best bow teams to guard the mill, and circulate. Keep everyone on task. No enemy must get over the walls. I'm sending the Rangers on a mission. They'll keep the ammunition guards busy, and Jennie's team will blow up their ammo."

Mr. Riley put his hand on Jennie's shoulder, and she briefly leaned against him. Jennie was scared? Fear made Mia cold and hot at the same time. Nothing scared Jennie.

"Pick a team," Mr. Preston said.

Jennie stepped away from her father. She was suddenly all business, but Mia wondered how much of that was real. "Yuki, do you mind if I take Brisa?"

Brisa bounced up and down, then uttered a soft "Ow."

"Go ahead," said Yuki. "But I'll need a replacement. Mia, will you come with us? You're a good shot."

Mia swallowed, proud to be picked, but fear made her stomach clench. "Um, I need a crossbow."

Sheriff Crow raised an eyebrow. "You have a crossbow."

Mia hastily unstrapped it, too embarrassed to meet the sheriff's eyes. "Someone stronger than me needs to use it. The recoil knocks me down."

She shoved the six-arrow crossbow at Yuki, who took it and examined it curiously. "Thanks." He strapped it across his back.

Mia tried not to look at Ross, but she felt him shifting from foot to foot beside her.

"And I want Ross," said Jennie.

He put his right hand on his dagger. "All right. Mia, stick close to Yuki and Meredith, okay?"

Mia forgot her own fears and stared at him in dismay. The eastern perimeter ran right past that singing tree. If he got close, it might grab control of him again. "No!"

Everyone was staring at her. "Um, I need Ross with me"—thinking fast, she added—"to help with the explosives." She pointed at the cart of bottles.

Jennie's lips parted, her expression puzzled.

"You and me against the world," Mia said softly, then flushed with embarrassment. Couldn't she think of anything better than that stupid motto they used when they were eight?

But Jennie turned a serious face to Mia, as if she'd said something very important. "Of course. If you need him, take him. Can I have some of your explosives? Then I won't have to go back to the armory."

"Take them all." Mia avoided the perplexed looks everyone gave her. The memory of finding Ross at the base of that tree was too vivid. She said firmly, "I need Ross."

"Hold it," said Mr. Preston. "Mia, that's not your decision to make. I'm not sure I want this boy on anyone's team."

"Voske wants to kill me," Ross said. "I'd rather fight back than hide inside somewhere."

Mr. Preston gave him an irritated look. "I don't care what you want. You can't fire a crossbow with one hand. I'm not sure *what* you can do with one hand, other than get in the way."

To Mia's surprise, Yuki spoke up. "Mr. Preston." She had no idea how Yuki was doing it, but he seemed to tower over them all. "I want Ross on my team." Still speaking in that commanding voice, he ordered, "Ross, show him what you can do with a knife."

Ross immediately drew a knife, glanced up, and threw it. A stormchaser fell out of the sky, its carapace hitting the ground with a crack. Mia's jaw dropped. Those huge flying beetles moved like lightning.

Mr. Preston didn't show his surprise, but he nodded at Ross. "Go get your weapon back. You're on Yuki's team. Jennie, take off. We need Voske's ammunition gone."

40

Jennie

"DAD WOULD LET ME GO!" RICO'S VOICE WAS SHRILL. "I'm fifteen!"

Jennie didn't care that he was small for his age, but not only did he look twelve, now he was acting it.

His mother, Ms. Salazar, obviously thought the same thing. "Rico, fifteen is too young."

"Same age as Yolanda Riley, and she's going! Just because I'm shorter—"

"Yolanda is very responsible—" Ms. Salazar began.

"I'm the only firestarter in town. They need me!"

His mother's aura began to flash in an agitated pattern. Jennie suspected that they were both thinking the same thing: Rico would be essential if Brisa was taken out. If Brisa was killed.

"If you let me take Rico, I promise to personally protect him," Jennie said.

"Mom . . ." Rico whined.

Jennie briefly closed her eyes. Collecting him along with Yolanda and José had seemed such an obvious idea, but he was reminding her of the kids who'd gone berserk on the snake patrol.

Ms. Salazar's aura flared like a welding arc. "I hold you responsible, then, Jennifer Riley." She began sorting weapons, her hands shaking, her profile grim.

"Yes!" Rico pumped his fist in the air.

Sera gave Jennie a sympathetic smile. "And that's command in a nutshell."

After all the trouble she'd gone to in order to get Rico, Jennie now wished she could change her mind. But that would cause an even bigger stir—and she was out of time. She tried to ignore the sick sense that she'd made a huge mistake.

All the Rangers were poised to go. The sight of them geared up eased her tension, as if she had been traveling alone and had finally come home to her family.

"Armor off," ordered Sera. She turned to Brisa, José, Yolanda, and Rico. "We have extra gear in that trunk. Change fast, or you stay behind."

The Rangers swiftly removed their weapons and helped one another out of their armor, leaving them in black night-training pants and shirts. They needed to be fast and silent.

There was a shared rhythm of movement, almost of breathing, habitual from years of drill. Jennie had found her own place in that pattern. She didn't forget the danger of the mission, but there was comfort in the unity of purpose.

As Sera unstrapped her leg armor, she asked softly, "You see Paco? Or is he with Doc Lee?"

"Dr. Lee must have healed him. He's out with Yuki's team."

Sera made a rueful face. Jennie knew she didn't like Paco's talking the doctor into shaving months off his life, but Sera silently straightened up and dusted down her black clothes.

"Ready," everyone said. Rico hastily rolled up his pants; Brisa yanked out her ribbons and tossed them on top of her dancing clothes.

"Weapon up," Sera said.

As the Rangers swiftly rearmed themselves, Jennie handed each of her charges a backpack loaded with Mia's explosive bottles, carefully wrapped in cloth.

José pulled on his pack. "Now you're one of the team," he told Rico.

"Do I swear an oath now?" he asked hopefully.

"Ask again in three years, when you've finished Ranger training," said Indra.

Jennie checked her weapons with damp hands. Her tension was mirrored in her companions' faces—except for Rico, who grinned happily. *He doesn't really realize that this isn't a drill*, she thought, *where people get up at the end, wash off the red dye, and go to Luc's to cool down. This is the real thing.*

"Let's go," Sera said.

They took off along the east wall. The sentries backed up against the shields to let them pass. Rico and Jennie fell in last.

Jennie put her hand on his shoulder. "Rico, this is not a game. One mistake, and Voske's soldiers will kill you. They don't care if you're fifteen, or five. Get it?"

"I got it, I got it," he said impatiently.

Indra fell back, looming deliberately over Rico. "Forget Voske's soldiers. If you make one sound, or one move that wasn't ordered, *I* will kill you." His hand dropped casually to the machete hanging from his belt.

Rico's eyes rounded.

Indra's voice dropped to a menacing whisper. "Understand?"

Rico nodded, clearly too intimidated to speak.

As Rico hurried to catch up with José, Indra fell in step beside Jennie. It was good to feel the heat of his body so close beside her. Nasreen must have felt that same heat at the dance. Jennie pushed aside a flash of jealousy. She had made her choice, and she wanted Indra to be happy.

His braid swung over his shoulder as he grinned. "Having fun?"

"Absolutely."

"I see you staged an invasion just to escape the schoolhouse and go out with us."

"And it worked!"

Indra laughed. Jennie joined in, enjoying the excitement and satisfaction of doing an important job with a companion she could trust. Their feelings might not be completely resolved, but right now it was unimportant. They were living in the moment, running side by side.

At the easternmost point of the wall, the Rangers stopped. One dropped down a rope ladder.

Sera beckoned to them all. "We'll go covert as soon as we're down. Jennie's team, that means no talking. If you hear our signals, obey them, but don't try to do them yourself. Listen up:

"Tom and I invented these for the Rangers. This is 'I'm here, where are you?'" She whistled the call of a nightjar. "This is 'Get ready.'" She put her fingers in her mouth and made the rasp of a cicada. "This is 'Retreat.'" She hooted like an owl. "And this is 'Execute mission.'" She yodeled like a coyote on the run. "Hit the ground," she said. And then, quietly, "Let's move."

Rico had to show off by leaping from halfway down the ladder, but when everyone ignored him, he quietly fell in behind José. Sera brought up the rear.

Tom, Jennie thought as the team ran in twos through the rows of corn, heads low. She had never understood the bond between domineering Tom Preston and deadpan Sera Diaz and the jolly man everyone had called Uncle Omar. Jennie remembered how Mr. Preston and Sera had looked at each other at the news of Omar's death in a bandit ambush.

Now Sera was leading a team against Voske, the man they had all once worked for. She and Preston never talked about those days, at least not to anyone born in Las Anclas—but she wondered what they said in private.

The smell of the air changed; they'd reached the soy fields. She'd been running on instinct, relying on the Rangers' lead, but now she began listening. The team barely made a rustle as they ran low.

When they passed the bridge southwest of the singing tree, Sera pointed three fingers toward the gullies. Three Rangers peeled off to catch the tarantulas they meant to use as a distraction, using baskets and dead chickens as bait. The rest shifted toward the road; they were entering the area of maximum danger, for they had to be directly east of the attackers.

A thrashing of bushes spiked Jennie's nerves. Her hand closed on her knife. Rico faltered, looking around.

There was a crunch, followed by a soft thud. Whatever had attacked the Ranger pair in front was no longer a threat. Jennie flipped her thumb up. Rico shakily returned it.

They ran on. Twigs rattled again. This time she saw the threat, a charging javelina, moonlight glinting on its tusks and bared teeth.

Indra was nearest. He whipped out his machete, sidestepped, and brought the steel down on the back of the javelina's neck.

The line skirted the fallen beast and ran on. Soon afterward Sera halted them, indicated Jennie, and pointed toward the enemy: *time to scout.*

Jennie ran on, placing her feet carefully. She could hear voices. The danger was no longer from animals; it was from the humans themselves.

Twinkling lights—partly shaded lanterns—were visible a hundred feet ahead. She dropped and crawled over the crops that Voske's soldiers had trampled, her hands and knees sinking and sliding on pulped squash. About fifty feet away, she belly-crawled. Slimy pumpkin bits worked their way into her clothes and slid unpleasantly across her skin.

Glints and shadows resolved into a line of posted guards behind close-packed barrels and boxes: ammunition.

She fixed the scene in her mind, then began to inch backward. A roving guard, swinging lantern in hand, skirted a barrel less than twenty feet away. Jennie froze, not even breathing, as the footsteps crunched steadily by.

After they faded, she resumed her crawl, wriggling backward until she no longer could see individual barrels or guards. Then she got to her hands and knees, retreating…retreating…where were they? Had she missed the team? The thought of crawling alone into the desert, with its cougars and acid lichen and singing trees, was terrifying.

She licked her lips and whistled the nightjar call. Sera's nightjar whistled back. They were about thirty feet to her left. She reached them in a burst of speed.

Sera held up her hand. Jennie couldn't see her expression, but her attitude was one of expectation—and release. She could hear Sera's voice, after countless drills: "Over to you."

Jennie pointed to her four, breathing steadily to keep her frantic heartbeat under control. Steady, steady. Smooth. Just like drill. Rico's eyes were wide, his mouth solemn.

She pointed at the barrels. She and her team crawled toward the enemy.

41

YUKI

YUKI'S HEAD ACHED, BUT AT LEAST HE COULD SEE again.

The moon shone clear and bright, flooding the desert with silver, as he followed Julio beyond the yellow nimbus of the wall lights.

The rest of the team caught up, panting. Paco was limping badly, his face drawn with pain. Yuki pulled him aside, and kept his voice low. "You should go back."

Paco gave what passed for a reassuring smile. "It's fine. I'll hold this position."

"Start counting paces from here," Julio called. "Bow team captains, station a fighter every twenty-five paces. On my signal, lie flat. When you hear my next signal— when the enemy is within range—attack. Yuki, place your team first."

Meredith poked Yuki as they began counting. "Don't forget to test-fire Mia's crossbow. Nothing worse than a completely new weapon in the middle of a fight."

He held up six arrows: he hadn't forgotten. She watched as he loaded the crossbow, braced himself, aimed at a scrub oak, and fired.

The bow slammed into his shoulder, knocking him to the ground. He scrambled up and dusted himself off. "Good thing I brought a regular one, just in case."

"It tore up that oak," Meredith said. "Too bad you can't use it."

"I could if I was up against a wall." He slung the bow across his back.

"I hope it doesn't come to that." His sister adjusted her glasses with difficulty; the bandage kept getting in the way. "Can you see the enemy?"

He peered toward the tent of hazy light above the town, and shook his head. The stridulation of crickets drowned out any other sound. "Wonder how Mom's doing."

"Oh, I'm sure she's fine. I think I scared her half to death, though."

"You scared *me* half to death."

"I was startled," she protested. "It was wet. I slipped."

"Twenty-five. Meredith, here's your position."

He began counting again, moving until his entire team was placed. Then he took up his own position as Julio's people moved off into the darkness.

He stood gazing at the distant walls, outlined by tiny lights. Even after all the fighting, the whole battle felt unreal, as if he might wake up at any moment to the dull, peaceful routine of Las Anclas life.

A coyote yipped twice in quick succession, followed by a long howl. Julio's signal. Yuki dropped to the cold sand. Now everything felt real. He shivered.

Then Julio blew his horn. The enemy—already? Yuki leaped to his feet. As battle cries rose up all around him, he gave voice to his own, and charged.

42

Mia

ALL AROUND HER, PEOPLE SCREAMED AT THE TOP OF their lungs.

What am I supposed to yell? Mia thought.

Just like Ross had warned, she was thinking too much. He'd said not to think at all. How did you not think at all?

Flames glowed on faces, armor, upraised swords. Now that Voske's secret attack was ruined, his people had lit their torches. The mass of running soldiers resolved into individuals.

Clutching her crossbow, she calculated distance versus velocity. Ten steps more, and she could shoot . . . *five* . . . *four . . . three . . . two.*

She aimed and shot. The man stumbled to his knees, clutching his shoulder. He wasn't wearing armor. She slapped another arrow into the crossbow and cranked hard. There was someone, thirty degrees to the west. *Five* . . . *four . . . three . . . two . . .* She shot. The arrow hit the woman's chest and bounced off, not even slowing her. That one wore armor.

Load, calculate, shoot. Load, calculate, shoot. She shot too quickly, and the arrow flew over the next soldier's head. But Meredith dropped him when he was just ten feet away. *Teamwork!* Mia exulted. She could do this. It wasn't that hard: load, calculate, *aim*, shoot.

She grabbed another arrow, fingers sweaty; she nearly dropped it. Into the crossbow. Load, calculate, aim, shoot—

That arrow and two others hit a soldier. But the next woman over ran straight toward her—too close to shoot.

She flung down her bow and yanked out her short sword. Ross was right. It had come to hand-to-hand. Exactly what she wasn't good at! And thinking that she wasn't good at something was a thought, which was what she wasn't supposed to have. And thinking that thinking—

Something slammed into her, knocking her flat on her back. She stared up as a man loomed over her with a sword—

She flung herself to the side. The blade sank into the earth where her head had been.

From the ground, she saw the joint at his knee gape open. Using both hands, she drove her sword into it. The man screamed and fell.

Mia scrambled to her feet. It had worked! She'd fought without thinking. Of course, now she was thinking again. Looking around wildly, she saw that there was no one left to fight. The enemy had retreated.

43

Ross

ROSS DUG INTO HIS AMMUNITION POUCH, HOPING TO find one more bullet. It was empty. He hefted his shotgun to use as a club, then saw the enemy soldiers falling back. He spared a glance for Mia. She'd been holding her own with her bow, but when the fighting got fierce, he'd lost sight of her.

"We did it!" Julio exclaimed. "They're on the run!"

His people cheered. Ross finally spotted Mia, moonlight glinting off her glasses. To his relief, she seemed unhurt.

"Fall back!" A familiar voice roared out. "Fall back now!"

It was the voice of Voske's lieutenant, the man who had jumped Ross's claim and stolen everything he owned but the clothes on his back.

A cold anger burned through him. One of Voske's men sprawled nearby, a sword near his lifeless hand. Ross dropped the shotgun and grabbed it. The sword was heavier than he was used to, but it would do.

Yuki panted up. "Come on, we have to—"

"Voske's lieutenant!" Ross pointed at the burly, red-headed man. "I'm going after him."

"Go for it. I'll get my team and follow you." Yuki whistled sharply.

The moon had descended, riding above the hills. The retreating soldiers were silver-outlined silhouettes, led by the silhouette with glinting red hair. Ross put on a burst of speed. The man had slowed as he scanned his soldiers. Counting them. There was a hissing sound, and one of Voske's men fell with an arrow between his shoulder blades.

Ross didn't look back for the bow team. He was still running as he pulled his belt knife. He slowed to take aim, then threw.

The lieutenant whipped up his shield. The knife bounced off. But it delayed him long enough for Ross to close the distance. He hefted his sword, and brought it down with all his strength.

The man's sword came up in a vicious underhanded arc. Sparks flew as the steel blades met. The shock jolted Ross's arm to the shoulder, forcing him back as his opponent slashed for the kill. Ross dropped low and pivoted, using his momentum to snap a side blow to the rib cage.

The man blocked with the shield, then lunged, trapped Ross's blade in a bind, and tried to wrench it from his hand. But Ross had seen it coming in the twist of the man's wrist. He waited, then yanked back with all his strength.

The lieutenant was too strong to drop his blade, but he stumbled, lowering his shield. Ross side-stepped. If he'd had a knife in his left hand, he could have driven it into the man's side—but his arm was useless for anything but balance. He started to bring his sword around; the man raised his shield, and the opening was gone.

Then the man lunged, blade whirling in a complicated feint and strike. Ross blocked, using his left wrist to support his right hand. The man threw his shield; Ross barely managed to dodge it. As he ducked, the lieutenant's free hand swept down, and though Ross hurled himself away, one fingertip brushed his neck.

There was a flash of blinding white light, and an impact like the time his burro Rusty had kicked him in the head. When he opened his eyes, he was flat on his back, his ears ringing. Most of the bow team stood around him, looking down, Yuki wincing and wiping his eyes.

"Did you get him?" Ross tried to sit up. His right palm stung when it touched the ground, as if the hilt of his sword had burned him.

"No," said Yuki. "And we won't catch up now. He's gone."

Mia pounded up, weapons clattering, and dropped down beside Ross. "What happened?"

"Voske's lieutenant has some kind of Change power. Don't let him touch you."

He wrung and flexed his fingers. His muscles and joints felt watery. Mia offered him her hand. So did Yuki. But he was tired of looking weak, so he managed to pick up his sword and himself without anyone's help. He planted his feet wide so he wouldn't wobble, as Paco, the last member of the team, grimly caught up, dragging his bad leg.

Yuki pointed with his sword. "We're not far from the west wall. Let's get over there. The sentries will pull us up. We'd better report."

44

Jennie

IN THE FLICKERING LIGHT OF THE ENEMY'S TORCHES and lanterns, Jennie could make out Brisa and Yolanda on one side, Rico and José on the other.

The diversion had to be soon. It was time to place the bottles.

She slid her backpack off, and the others swiftly followed suit. Rico and Brisa began to hand their packs to Yolanda and Jennie.

As Yolanda took Brisa's pack, a bottle clinked. Yolanda froze.

"I heard a noise!" cried the nearest sentry.

Jennie pulled a throwing knife from her belt, and readied it as the sentry raised his lantern high, cocked rifle held loosely under his armpit. In her peripheral vision, she spotted José about to lay his palm on the ground. With her free hand, Jennie grabbed his wrist and shook her head. It was still possible—

"Tarantula!" someone yelled.

"Another one over here!" Guns fired.

The Rangers had been forced to start their diversion early. The sentries turned, and the one with the lantern took one step, directly toward Brisa. Two.

The air filled with the ululation of the Ranger charge, and the sentries ran to meet the attack.

Jennie gave the signal. She, Yolanda, and José crawled toward the nearest barrels, leaving Rico and Brisa behind. From the tightness of their mouths, she knew they understood the danger: if the three of them were killed trying to place the bottles, the other two would complete the mission.

She slid bottles from her pack as she knee-walked the last few feet. With trembling hands, she shoved a bottle between barrels, and kept going, placing the bottles one by one.

Soon both backpacks were empty. José was done. Yolanda placed her last bottle between a barrel and a big box, and began crawling back. Jennie and José followed—

A shadow moved. "They're at the barrels!"

Jennie leaped to her feet, drawing her sword.

"Retreat!" she yelled, hoping the sentries would think they'd repelled an attack.

As someone shouted, "Retreat? Where?" and a deeper, sharper voice snapped, "Who said that?" Jennie whispered fiercely to her team, "Go, go, go!"

They ran, José and Jennie closing in behind the others.

"Now?" Brisa panted.

"Edge of your throw," Jennie muttered.

Brisa glanced over her shoulder, almost unfamiliar without her ribbons.

Ten feet, fifteen . . . fifty. The sentries, blinded by their own lights, did not spot the black-haired team in their black clothes. Jennie exulted. It was working . . . it was working . . .

"Here!" Brisa whispered.

Rico shut his eyes and clenched his fists. Yolanda took up a defensive position, sword high in her right hand, left outstretched to summon the wind. Jennie and José flanked them as the sentries began to close in.

The sentries stumbled as the earth shifted beneath their feet. Before they could recover their balance, Yolanda's fierce wind sprayed mud into their eyes. Jennie reached out with her mind and yanked a pistol from one man's hand, then jerked so hard at a woman's belt that she went sprawling to the ground.

Brisa's arm whipped back, then out. A rock hurtled through the air. It hit a barrel, bounced off, and exploded. Flames flickered from the bottles, one by one, lighting up the barrels.

A man yelled, "Sabotage! Put out the fires!"

Most of the sentries dashed back toward the ammunition, then staggered as José loosened the earth beneath their feet. Brisa hurled another rock. It hit a barrel and exploded.

"Flat!" Jennie yelled. Her voice was lost in the blast.

She wasn't aware of hitting the ground. She blinked up at the stars, then sat up, struggling against dizziness. Rico, Brisa, José, Yolanda: everyone was present. Everyone was alive.

She got to her hands and knees as another barrel exploded, rocking her backward. Then another. Flames shot skyward, lighting the faces of her team. Brisa laughed. Rico grinned.

Silhouettes appeared from beyond the blaze, coming straight at them.

"Run!" Jennie commanded. Her ears rang. She wouldn't hear a signal if Sera was giving one.

But in the light of the fires, she saw that the fighting continued between the Rangers and far more soldiers than she'd seen protecting the ammo dump.

The plan had been for Jennie to retreat first with her team, and for the Rangers to close in behind her. Their mission was complete, so there was no reason for them to stay and fight. But the Rangers were not retreating, even though they were vastly outnumbered. Something was wrong.

Jennie raised her hand, then dropped it. She was too far from the fighting to be able to use her Change power. But she was able to catch Sera's eye.

"Jennie!" Sera shouted. She pointed her sword at a man with clipped silver hair. "That's Voske!" Then an ax swung at her head; she whipped the blade around to deflect it, then in to strike. The ax fell at her feet, followed by its wielder.

The silver-haired man—Voske—was surrounded by soldiers, so many that Jennie kept losing sight of him in the crowd.

Sera pressed toward him, backed by the other Rangers. Her voice rose above the clash of metal and crackle of flames. "Take him down! They'll fall apart!" She had worked for Voske. If she thought his army would scatter if he was killed, she had to be right.

"Did the plan change?" asked Yolanda. "Should we go fight?"

Rico tugged at Jennie's arm in silent inquiry.

She had sworn to his mother that she would protect him. The only way to keep her promise was to follow the original plan and escort the kids back to town. The chance to win the battle right now didn't change that. The fact that the Rangers desperately needed help didn't change that. She couldn't abandon the kids.

Jennie counted seven Rangers. Someone was already down. She couldn't abandon them. The captain could give independent orders—but one rule was absolute: you never abandoned your team.

She turned to José and Brisa. "You two get the kids to safety. I'm staying here."

José gave a quick nod. "You heard her," Brisa told Yolanda and Rico. "Run!"

Jennie drew her sword and dove into the fray. The trees were on fire. Burning leaves drifted down, and acrid smoke stung her lungs.

Light flashed off steel. She ducked, kicked her attacker in the knee, then whirled her sword in a lethal figure eight, forcing a path toward Sera.

"Where is he?" Jennie shouted.

Sera sidestepped a small fireball. It hit a branch and set it aflame. "There." She began to gesture with her dagger, then shouted, "Duck!"

Jennie dropped. An arrow flew past; she heard it hum through the air. An ax swung down at her head. Still on the ground, she brought her sword up horizontally, blocked the ax, and used both her physical strength and her power to twist the blade. The ax flew out of the enemy's hand. Jennie rolled to the side, and the blade buried itself in the dirt.

She leaped up. Five paces away an archer raised a crossbow. Jennie extended her fingers and jerked the bow out of the woman's hands. But the fighting was in such close quarters now that she didn't take a shot; instead, she smashed the bow over the back of a soldier's neck.

Her shoulder stung, and she slapped out a burning leaf.

On her left, Indra staggered. He'd lost his machete, and was fighting two opponents with a pair of knives. A man behind him raised a sword.

Jennie lunged, her free hand reaching out, and mentally yanked at the sword. The man hung on, but it swung away from Indra. Jennie took out the man's knee with a side kick, then brought her sword down on the arm of the next attacker.

"Jennie," Indra panted. All down one side his black clothes gleamed wet.

With her power, she wrested a knife from the hand of his last enemy. It pinwheeled toward her. She ducked, swept it from the ground, and threw it back.

A cool wind filled the air with glowing cinders and tumbling leaf-shaped flames. Jennie shaded her eyes and searched for the man with silver hair. She spotted him, closer now, though still surrounded by guards.

Voske seemed strangely familiar. Jennie squinted, her eyes burning with smoke and sweat. A sword swept toward her. She dropped her hand and jerked it down until the tip hit the earth, then cut down her opponent while his weapon was still trapped.

Again she searched. This was the first time she had seen Voske, but she knew that sharp-featured face.

A flare of light and a shock wave knocked her back. A tree branch lay a few feet away, burning furiously. Jennie lunged up, swept her hand out, and knocked several weapons askew. The smoke was making her dizzy. Her head pounded, and she staggered.

Voske was farther away now, surrounded by protectors. His silver hair glinted in the firelight as he spoke to someone.

"Around me!" Sera shouted. "We'll make a—"

She grunted. A blurry shadow shifted away. The Ranger captain yanked a knife from her arm and hurled it at the shadow.

Jennie threw her own knife in the same direction and heard a cry. A woman appeared where the shadow had been, a blade in her thigh. Frances tackled her from behind.

Voske was still out of reach, but firelight fell bright across his face. And she had it: he was a taller, paler image of Sera's son, Paco.

But Jennie had no time for distractions.

Sera pressed toward Voske, the remaining Rangers forming an attack wedge around her. Jennie couldn't see Indra, so she leaped into his usual place behind Sera's left shoulder.

She was back in the rhythm, deflecting attacks as they worked forward, one step at a time. On her right, a Ranger pulled his pistol and shot a soldier, who dropped. He clubbed another one with his pistol grip.

Sera fought off two men with her sword, then ran a few steps. Jennie picked up her pace, leaping over a fallen enemy. They were doing it! It was working! The battle would end right here, because Voske didn't share command, he was the only force keeping his people together—

"Take her down!" a voice shouted.

Two, three shots rang out. Sera staggered, then her sword lowered, her head bowed. Another shot knocked her back, and she fell.

Frances dropped to one knee, pressing her hand to her side. Blood spurted between her fingers.

The enemy advanced, weapons raised. Jennie reached with her free hand and her mind toward the sword swinging at her. Her mental pull exerted so little force that her opponent didn't even seem to notice. She stumbled backward, barely avoiding the strike, and tried again. Like an overworked muscle giving out, her power failed entirely.

"Retreat." Even her voice was gone.

But the others had the same idea. Desperately warding off the pressing attackers, the Rangers hauled up their wounded. Jennie blocked, swung, and kicked her way to Sera's still form. She picked up Sera's sword, using both weapons to drive back the enemy.

It was over. They'd lost, but she would keep fighting until . . .

She swayed, almost losing her balance. The attackers in front of her tripped and fell as a narrow crevasse opened beneath their feet. Jennie thrust the sword through her belt and bent over Sera. Four shots. No one survived four shots, but Jennie checked anyway. No breath, no pulse. Sera was gone.

Jennie pulled Sera over her shoulder. She was so light—

"Come on," José said in her ear. "I'll take her."

She couldn't speak. He dropped to his knees and laid his palm on the ground. Once again the earth rumbled, and a wave rolled through the dirt, knocking Voske's soldiers off-balance.

José rose, and took Sera from Jennie.

You never abandon your team.

She glanced back, and a few steps later, she scanned again. Someone was missing . . .

I'm looking for Sera. I want her to be alive.

Indra dropped to his knees and pitched onto his face. Jennie ran to him and turned him over. His eyes were closed. But when she put her hand on his chest, she could feel him breathing.

Sobbing, she hauled on his arm, but he'd become a dead weight. She finally managed to wrestle him over her shoulder, but when she tried to stand, her knees buckled. Kneeling in the mud with Indra's blood running down the back of her shirt, she thought, *I can't leave him. We'll both die if I stay, but you never abandon . . .*

All I have to do is move him. It doesn't matter how. She laid him down, got a grip under his arms, and began to drag him.

The Rangers struggled with their burdens into the darkness. Jennie forced herself to match their pace, though she could barely lift her feet and her lungs labored. Indra stirred, trying to get his feet under him. Jennie halted, sucking in air.

Brisa's whisper made her jump. "The kids are safe. Sorry I couldn't make it back sooner."

She held out a wad of cloth. Jennie tore it into usable pieces, her hands trembling, then pushed up Indra's shirt. Brisa's breath hissed in. It looked like he'd been hit with an ax; in the merciless moonlight she could see splintered ribs.

Jennie did the best she could with the makeshift bandages, then she and Brisa got Indra to his feet and his arms around their shoulders. At first he tried to take his own weight, but soon they were dragging him. His hands were icy cold. *His fire's gone out,* Jennie thought. The absurd thought kept circling in her mind, crowding out everything else, until they reached the wall.

"They're back," someone said.

"Let down the rope."

First they handed up Sera, then those too injured to climb. Jennie hauled herself over the wall. She was here. She was safe. She'd completed the mission.

"Someone tell Dr. Lee we're coming," she croaked.

"I will!" cried Rico. "I'm a Ranger."

Jennie walked from one moment to the next. Here was the pasture, pungent with clover, grass, and cow. Here were people saying words that she couldn't hear. Here were cow patties, black circles among the silver-edged grasses. She could feel a shivery bubble of laughter rising up, but she kept it inside. If she let it go, she knew it would tear her apart, turn into tears . . .

There was the Hill on the right. Here were her feet, dragging across the ground. There was Brisa beside her. There were people carrying Sera. She had to report, she had to . . .

A hand reached past Jennie, and someone slid a hand under Sera's shoulder. "Here," someone else murmured. "Let me help."

Jennie's vision swam, her ears roaring. No—a cheering crowd had gathered around them, more running along the path. Lanterns swung, highlighting faces with moving shadows as people yelled, hoarse and shrill, angry and triumphant.

"You did it! You did it!"

"Hurray for the Rangers!"

"Rangers! Rangers!"

They're cheering us, Jennie thought. *They're cheering us.* Euphoria expanded inside her chest, making her feel so buoyant her tiredness was forgotten, and she walked a little easier as two, then four people pressed in to help carry Sera, then more. Someone said, "Everybody lift!" Now they bore her high on a forest of hands.

Jennie's eyes blurred. The torchlight glimmered over the horrible looseness of Sera's hands, her upturned profile. Behind them came another group carrying the wounded. As the growing crowd approached the town hall, the sentries on the roof lifted their weapons and shouted.

Sera, whom Jennie had known all her life. Sera the strong, the capable. Sera, the fastest runner in town before the sheriff Changed. Sera the quiet, with her penchant for deadpan humor.

Her graying hair had made her look old, but Sera had been younger than Jennie when she'd first come to Las Anclas. Sera had visited Paco and the Rileys every time she was on liberty from the Rangers, patiently teaching him weaponry and riding in the hope that he'd be a Ranger too. Though he had the skills, he loved music, not fighting . . . and once Sera realized that, she had talked to the Old Town Band and arranged drum lessons for Paco.

Paco, whose face Jennie had seen on the man who was trying to destroy their town.

As they entered the town hall, people shouted in triumph.

But Jennie blinked back tears as she watched Sera laid with respectful, tender care on a party table still covered with an embroidered tablecloth.

Ms. Salazar glowed like a bonfire, her mouth crooked with joy and sorrow, as she crushed an exasperated Rico against her. Jennie's euphoria broke like a soap bubble, leaving behind a residue of exhaustion, grief, and guilt. She couldn't bear to hear Ms. Salazar's words of gratitude and relief—because Jennie hadn't protected Rico. She'd left him in the care of the other kids she was supposed to be protecting. They could so easily have been cut down along the way. And her choice had been wrong, because she hadn't killed Voske.

She hadn't saved Sera.

People were calling them heroes, but nobody had ever taught her the real cost of being a hero: if you survived, how did you deal with the guilt?

45

Felicité

FELICITÉ WATCHED IN HORROR AS DR. LEE'S helpers carried Indra to the far side of the town hall, which they'd screened off to make a field hospital. Indra couldn't be dead. He couldn't.

She had to find out.

She left her mother's side and pushed past the women guarding the entrance. Inside, people rushed back and forth, carrying basins and cloths. One of them collided with her.

"Sorry," she said, biting back an impatient retort. "I have to see—"

The man didn't wait to find out what she wanted. She skirted the table where she had uncrated bottles of antiseptic alcohol, and spotted the wounded laid out on folded blankets. No Indra.

He was on a table. Grandpa Horst cut his shirt open, while Becky held a strand of ropethorn. Dr. Lee ran up, covered in blood. He braced himself against the table with one hand, hair hanging around his haggard face, then pushed himself upright and laid his other hand on Indra's chest.

Felicité squeezed past someone with an armload of bandages, peering to see if Indra was still breathing.

"Where are those towels?" Dr. Lee asked impatiently.

"Is he alive?" she asked. "Will he be all right?"

He shouted—actually shouted at her—"Get out!"

Grandpa Horst took her gently but firmly by the shoulder

and steered her away. "Felicité, please give us room to work. Anna-Lucia, bring those towels!"

She ran out of the field hospital. She almost tripped over Jennie, who was crouched on the floor. As Felicité stared at her, too stunned to think, Jennie held out her hand. A pebble rolled from the corner of the town hall, then jumped up and flew across the room.

Jennie caught it with a sigh of obvious relief. Felicité couldn't believe she was sitting there playing with her Change power. Was she wounded too? There was blood on her clothes and in her hair. Maybe a blow to the head?

Daddy came in, leading a stream of people all talking at once. Felicité headed toward them—he would find out how Indra was doing. But he didn't even seem to see her. He went straight to Jennie. "Give me your report."

Jennie got slowly to her feet. "We blew up the ammunition. All but a few barrels. But Voske and his bodyguards were nearby. Sera tried to take him out. She's . . ." Jennie's chest heaved, and she shut her eyes. "We failed."

He repeated, "But you blew up the ammunition?"

"Yes."

That set some of the eavesdroppers cheering. Jennie winced, her lower lip trembling.

Sera is dead. Indra might be too. They couldn't kill Voske. It's not a successful mission to her.

Felicité's father rubbed his jaw. "Now we might have a chance. We need to—"

"Coming through." Yuki pushed through the crowds, princely even with his hair covered in soot and blood. More archers followed, plus Ross, with Mia trailing behind, flame-thrower strapped to her back.

"We routed that army from the back," Yuki told her father. "But the leader got away. Ross says he's Voske's lieutenant, a big redheaded guy."

Her father grimaced. "I know who you mean. He's probably reporting our north side numbers right now. We can expect another attempt—"

A huge explosion shook the building, then another. Some bottles fell off the makeshift shelves they'd made from stacked benches.

People started gabbling questions.

"Quiet!" Daddy shouted. "That's got to be the gates."

Mother was at Felicité's side, still smelling of verbena and sun-dried sheets, though her forehead was taut with strain. She had been overseeing everything, but now everyone milled around in confusion.

"Tom," she said. Felicité looked from one parent to the other as her mother asked, "Is it time?"

Felicité knew what she meant: *Is it time to use the tunnel?*

"Not until they're breaking down the door," he said. "Wait."

People parted like blades of grass as a black-and-white rat raced in. Trainer Koslova worked the crumpled paper out of its harness. There were no words, just a smeared scrawl: a line, with a big X in the middle, and then a smaller X through the line an inch or so away.

"They've blown the gates," Felicité's father said. "And part of the south wall, from the looks of it near the south forge."

"Felicité, let us take the children into the storeroom, where it's quieter." Her mother's glance was full of meaning.

She was about to agree when Daddy shook his head. "Wait, Felicité. Valeria, you go ahead." He pulled Mother up against him and kissed her fiercely. Then he turned away. "Yuki. Take your team. Find the sheriff. Tell her to protect the south generator and the armory. You've got to collect everyone you can and hold the gate. Voske must be sending everything he has against us now, since he's lower on ammo than we are. If they get inside the town, we've lost."

"Got it," Yuki said. He drank from the canteen someone had started passing around before he ran off.

Felicité's father beckoned to Jennie and the few Rangers with her. "Put together a team. I'll pull everyone from the east wall. Half will reinforce those on the roof here." The crowd looked upward, as if they could see the sentries. "The rest will join us in a flanking move from the east. Hit them from behind. Our target will be the breach by the south forge. I need the best fighters up front."

"Can we have Ross?" Jennie asked.

"Whoever you want. Just do it fast." He took Felicité's arm. "Darling, I want you to stay with me. I might need you to run an errand, and I need someone I know I can trust."

Her stomach clenched with fear. She knew perfectly well that he would only take her with him if he believed that the town hall wasn't safe. "Of course. Let me get my things." She reached for her hat.

"Your bow? Good thinking. Do we have any extra arrows?"

"Yes, my bow," Felicité said belatedly. She picked it up from where she'd left it after handing the children off to Judge Vardam. The quiver was empty, but there was no point adding to her father's worries. She picked up her veiled hat and tied it on firmly, and made sure her scarf was wrapped tight around her throat.

"No! No, she can't—" someone yelled, and then cut himself short.

Dr. Lee put his hand on Paco's shoulder. Paco jerked away and ran into the hospital. Dr. Lee went after him.

Felicité followed, as if pulled by a magnet. She had to see, to know.

Paco stood rigid at the table where they had laid his mother. No one had covered her face, or the faces of any of the dead; all the blankets were needed for the living.

Daddy walked across the room to Paco, who looked older,

his chiseled features gone blank and numb. Yuki lingered in the background, looking uncertain.

Felicité's eyes stung as her father pressed his own rifle into Paco's hands. "We need you, Paco. We need everybody, so no more of our people die. Take my weapon. Help me defend the town."

Paco's jaw tightened. "Okay, Mr. Preston." He stuffed the powder and ammunition into his shirt.

Felicité tried to spot Indra, but she couldn't see him, and though she wanted to ask about him, the words stuck in her throat. She walked out and found Jennie leaning against a wall, with Mia and Ross hovering around her, as concerned as if she were one of the wounded.

All of Felicité's feelings surged up. She meant to keep control, but she couldn't bear it. Sera dead, Indra maybe dying, after a mission led by Jennie. But Daddy still thought that mutant could do no wrong—he was making her a team captain. *The* team captain. When all she'd done was get back alive.

Jennie got forgiven anything because her Change was invisible. As long as Daddy didn't have to see it—as long as Jennie wasn't a monster—he could pretend she wasn't Changed at all. If Jennie had been the one who grew scales and gills like some hideous fish creature, he would have never let her into his Rangers, never trusted her, never smiled at her. Never treated her like she was his own daughter.

The words came out as though someone else spoke. "This is your fault, Jennie."

"I know," Jennie said, closing her eyes. "I know."

46

Mia

MIA HEARD A VERY FINAL-SOUNDING CLICK AS THE town hall doors locked behind her.

She could see clearly by the light of the torches and the full moon. Mr. Preston was already halfway down the main path, Felicité by his side, still in his dancing boots and embroidered greatcoat; Felicité wore the blue-trimmed white dress she'd had on the day Ross arrived, with the same matching veiled hat. Mia felt as if she were dreaming.

She ran to catch up with Ross and Jennie. He seemed to have recovered from getting shocked by Voske's lieutenant, but Jennie looked terrible, her braids unraveling and stuck together with blood, and a blank, fixed look in her eyes.

"Are you all right?" Mia asked cautiously. "I know you and Sera were—"

"Mia, I cannot talk about that now. I still have to fight." Jennie strode faster, her long legs distancing her from Mia and Ross.

"Did you hear what Felicité said to her?" Mia whispered to him. "Why would she say something like that?"

"Jennie's Changed. Don't you remember Felicité calling me a mutant?" Without waiting for a reply, he hurried to catch up with Jennie.

Mia had wanted to make them feel better, but she seemed to have said exactly the wrong things. Ahead of her, they matched strides, their backs straight and their heads held high.

"Anyone need any extra arrows?" Henry pounded up the

path, brandishing a full quiver with an air of happy anticipation. It was comforting to see one person acting exactly the
same way he did when things were normal.

"I could use some." Sujata caught up, grubby and blood-
streaked, her arm bandaged.

"Well, you can't have any." Henry held the quiver out of
her reach. "One shot, one kill. *My* kill."

Jennie pointed to where Preston and Felicité had vanished behind the lemon trees. "Let's catch up."

Mia found herself running once again, the flamethrower
banging painfully into her spine. They reached the wall; sentries helped them get over. The moon had vanished behind the
mountain, yet it was still easy to see. In fact, it was easier—

"Dawn soon," someone said as they ran through the
trampled corn.

They heard the battle before they saw it. Smoke drifted
on the air, obscuring struggling figures. There was the hole
blown in the wall, near the south forge. Fires smoldered;
Mia hoped the timber grove wouldn't catch, and that the
animals in the big barns were safe.

With a roar, Preston led the charge toward Voske's army,
which was trying to get past the defenders at the crumbled
wall. Mia lagged, her feet dragging. She was low on ammunition, but arrows lay scattered all over the ground. She
began collecting them. Not far away Felicité, her veiled hat
bobbing, had gotten the same idea.

A shout went up. Running figures broke past the defenders, who scrambled to surround them again. Mia found
herself in the middle of knots of fighting people.

The defenders and attackers struggled too close together
for her to use her flamethrower. But she could use her crossbow, if she aimed very, very carefully. She crammed the
arrows into her quiver and sought a good shot.

Jennie fought against a man and a woman both taller

than she was, her sword slashing quicker than Mia's eye could follow. Mia couldn't get a clear shot at either the man trying to club Jennie or the woman jabbing green-glowing fingertips at Jennie's eyes.

Close by, Ross fought hand to hand against a man with two short swords. Ross's knife moved so fast that all Mia could see were blurs and streaks of silver. He struck high, then low, and the man toppled, one of the swords ringing on the rubble. Ross looked around, beads of sweat flying from his hair, then threw his knife.

The woman with green fingers had sneaked up behind Jennie. She fell with Ross's knife in her throat; the light jittered, then abruptly went dark. Two more soldiers leaped over her to attack Jennie. Ross stooped to pull another knife from his boot.

Jennie and Ross fought side by side, blocking the way to the forge. No one could pass them to get into the town. Now Mia knew why everyone had given her such funny looks when she'd said she'd protect Ross. What had she been thinking? But as skilled as he was, he was still a day out of the infirmary.

She kept her crossbow ready until he skidded backward, leaving her a clear line of fire at a girl with sparks flashing between her fingers.

Calculate, aim—shoot.

The bolt hit Ross's attacker in the knee. Her lightning went out, and she toppled.

Ross abruptly spun around, left arm held out for balance, right hand ready with his knife. There was no one in his line of sight.

On the ground behind him, a man rolled over and lurched to his feet. He rushed Ross, sword raised to kill.

47

Ross

ROSS HAD BEEN HEARING CHIMES EVER SINCE HE'D reached the wall. He'd tried to reinforce the barrier in his mind, but it was impossible to do that and fight at the same time.

He did his best to ignore the shimmering sounds as he fought beside Jennie, whose strong right arm helped cover his weak left. Tired as he was, when he caught her eye, he couldn't help but grin. He won a faint smile back.

A teenage girl charged him, sparks flashing as she threw lightning back and forth between her hands. Ross brought up his knife, then remembered how Voske's lieutenant had shocked him. He skidded backward, knife lowered. The girl smirked, molding her lightning into a crackling sphere. Ross waited. Let her move first.

An arrow slammed into her knee, and she dropped, moaning. Her lightning flickered out.

"Listen up. We've found a way in."

It was the voice of Voske's lieutenant, as loud as if he'd spoken directly into Ross's ear. Ross spun around, expecting an attack. There was no one behind him. Someone crashed into him, sending him stumbling. When he turned back, a man lay in the mud at his feet, an arrow in his neck and a sword by his outstretched hand. But no lieutenant. Ross spotted Mia reloading her crossbow.

Chimes rang an impossibly high note in his head, over a voice too soft to hear. This was no memory or waking nightmare. His tree was trying to tell him something. He had to get out of the fight so he could listen.

He took a quick look around. Jennie had run to reinforce one of the Rangers. Mia aimed at someone in the smoky fray, her glasses reflecting the fire at the town gates. Mr. Preston ran by, rallying a group of people who'd become silhouettes in the swirling haze.

The smoke had thickened, but Ross could have found his tree with his eyes closed. He passed Felicité, still in her fancy hat, giving someone an armful of arrows.

He crouched beside a boulder and closed his eyes. He visualized his inner wall, a huge concrete structure like the one he'd crawled through to get to Las Anclas, with a small metal door.

He pushed open the door. Now he could hear the voice, sharp and clear: "... and grab as much ammo as you can carry. We'll move covertly alongside this ridge. It runs parallel to the town walls. Then we'll cut across and get over the wall between sentries, find either Preston or the mayor, and take them out. Then we get the rest of the town council."

Ross opened his eyes. Mia was inches away, peering worriedly into his face. He jerked backward.

"Sorry," she whispered.

"I've got to find Mr. Preston," Ross said.

48

YUKI

YUKI RUBBED HIS STINGING EYES ON HIS SWEAT-soaked shirt.

The townspeople stood shoulder to shoulder in a defensive line, but there were fewer of them. Too many people he knew lay on the ground. He didn't know if they were dead or unconscious, and he couldn't stop fighting long enough to check.

A horn blew a hoarse note. Giving a huge outcry, the enemy rallied at the smoldering hole in the gates, and charged.

Sheriff Crow and the bounty hunter raced by, and smashed directly into the front row of attackers. Her crimson-streaked sword hummed and struck, hummed and struck. His staff blurred as he blocked and attacked.

People whom Yuki had never even seen in training were fighting. Grandma Callahan stood in a shadowy alley, carefully sighting a crossbow. Jack was down on one knee, defending himself with a butcher knife. Grandma Riley darted from person to person, touching necks, hands, any bare skin. Sweat froze instantly, shocking the enemies so her partner, Flora Riley, could knock them flat with a blow from her singlesticks.

Enemies charged, but once again the town threw the attackers back. Laura Hernandez, weaponless, slashed out with her claws, sending soldiers stumbling backward, bleeding. Mr. Riley swung his rifle like a club.

Yuki ran to Meredith's side, his sword whirling directly over his sister's head. He lopped off the hand of a huge guy trying to smash her down.

He heard crossbows twanging, but no gunshots—everyone seemed to be out of powder.

Nearby, Grandma Callahan lay still on the ground. He ran to pick her up. The crossbow fell from her hands. Meredith reached out to help. Their mother came up behind, limping badly, as they retreated to the doors of the armory.

"She's dead, Yuki," she said softly. "You can set her down."

He straightened up, gripping his sword. This was it. This was the end.

The enemy leader began to shout a command, then dropped when the bounty hunter's staff slammed into his head. Sheriff Crow ran to back him up, sword in hand, but even her strength was giving out. She was moving no faster than an ordinary woman.

A burst of light flashed from beyond the front gates. Another explosion? But no sound followed. The enemies froze in the process of reforming their lines, then scattered, some ducking. Someone bellowed to rally them as a small figure appeared around the edge of the twisted, smoke-blackened command post and lifted gnarled hands toward the gates. White-hot flame roared, igniting the ruined doors in a spectacular conflagration.

Yuki stared in astonishment. It was his former schoolteacher, Grandma Wolfe!

Her shrill cackle reached the defenders, who cheered. Once again she sent fire after the enemies, though this burst was much smaller. Her third try was no more than a candle flame. She staggered, but Sheriff Crow sprang to her aid.

Over her shoulder, the sheriff cried, "Keep it up! Keep it up, they'll be charging again. Don't let them break the line!"

The crack of a rifle snapped Yuki's attention toward the stable. Paco leaned against the wall, hair in his eyes as he leveled Mr. Preston's rifle, aimed, and shot. An enemy dropped in his tracks. Before the man hit the ground, Paco was reloading with a speed he'd seldom showed in training, his face uncharacteristically grim. He fired again, taking down another attacker. Then another. And then he stopped: out of ammo. Yuki swore to himself. The quiver on Paco's back was empty too.

Paco hefted the rifle, ready to use it as a club. But he was braced against the wall, all his weight on one foot. His knee had obviously given out. One exchange of blows, and he'd be taken down and killed—if someone didn't shoot him first.

Yuki raced for the stable, bending low to avoid fire. Arrows whistled past, but none hit. He fetched up beside Paco, and hastily unstrapped Mia's six-arrow crossbow.

Curiosity momentarily smoothed the tense angles of Paco's face. "Does that thing work?"

"Watch." Yuki jammed his back hard into the wall, and waited.

With an enormous roar, the enemy stampeded through the gates. Half of the attackers seemed to be headed straight for them. Yuki waited till they were in range, then shot. A tremendous impact slammed into his shoulder, jarring every bone in its socket. But six attackers fell, and the unified charge broke up around them.

Yuki hastily reloaded, then shot again. The crossbow again took out a swath of attackers. It didn't simply shoot six arrows at a time—it shot them at a lethal velocity, knocking people down even if they struck armor.

As long as he had ammunition, he could hold the line that kept the enemy out of his town. Once the defenders' line broke, they were finished.

He had enough arrows for two more shots.

On the *Taka,* they'd had a saying: "Die on deck." In Las Anclas, they said "Die with your boots on." Yuki had never imagined that he'd die on dry land, surrounded by people who didn't even speak his native language. He'd lost his kingdom, and he'd renounced his title. But at least he'd go down fighting, as his first parents had. He hoped they'd be proud of him.

Paco shifted his weight, then staggered. Yuki caught and steadied him. Their faces were inches apart.

"Are you mad?" Paco asked, his voice husky with exhaustion.

"Mad?" Yuki echoed.

The enemy line had retreated and gone into a huddle. He watched them, bracing for a charge.

But Paco wasn't looking at Voske's people. He glanced toward the town hall. "You've always wanted to get away. Now you're defending a town you never managed to leave."

Yuki glanced over Paco's shoulder at his mother and sister, who were counting the little ammo they had left, and turned back.

"I'm defending the people I love," he said. "It seems like a good way to go."

The tension eased a little in Paco's face, though his mouth trembled before he compressed it to a thin, determined line. Not caring who might be watching, Yuki kissed Paco—and Paco kissed him back, even more fiercely.

But over the roar in Yuki's veins came the noise of the enemy. They were reassembling for their next charge. He tucked the crossbow against his shoulder, and set his back to the wall.

49

Ross

MR. PRESTON RUBBED HIS FOREHEAD, THEN WENT BACK to loading the last of his powder into his pistol. "Are you sure?"

"From where I was standing, I could hear every word," Ross said firmly.

"I could too," Mia piped up, to his surprise.

"I'll have to pull people out to deal with it." Mr. Preston spoke as if talking to himself. "The first few soldiers will walk straight into that singing tree. If it doesn't chime and warn them, it'll kill those few, but the rest will scatter and reform. I'll put my Rangers—"

Though Mr. Preston was so smoke-grimed it was impossible to see his expression in the snapping firelight, Ross knew what he had to be thinking: most of his remaining Rangers were wounded.

"I'll put a group on either side of the ridge to ambush them while they scatter. All right, that's the plan," Mr. Preston said decisively as he shoved the pistol through his belt, and bent to pick up his sword. "Where are the rat—no, there's no time. You stay here. I'll be back."

And he was gone, into the smoke.

Ross whispered, "Did you really hear it too?"

"Of course not." Mia pushed up her glasses in a defiant gesture. "It was Mr. Preston, so I figured you'd need backup."

Tired and aching and worried as he was, Ross felt a brief warmth behind his ribs, almost like a laugh, except that it hurt in a way that nothing to do with physical pain. He wanted to hug Mia, but flexed his hands instead. His left had gone numb except for occasional flashes of tingling pain.

"Who can Mr. Preston find?" Though a fragile light blued the eastern sky over the hills, the gate was lost in a cloud of black. "If he pulls anyone from the front gates, Voske's people might get inside."

"He'll have to take the defenders from the town hall," said Mia.

"Where the wounded and the little kids are." Ross felt sick.

They were losing. Even with his ammo gone, Voske had the advantage—an army of professional soldiers up against towns-people used to drill, not war. If his lieutenant's team got over the wall, there would be no stopping them.

Flakes of ash drifted on the wind, dusting Mia's hair. Ash had been falling the last time Ross had seen his parents. He remembered sitting on the floor of Mia's cottage, telling her how they had died. How they might have lived, if it hadn't been for him.

If he and his book hadn't come to Las Anclas, maybe Voske wouldn't have attacked. The citizens here had protected Ross from Voske's bounty hunter.

There was one thing he could do for them. If he could take out the lieutenant and his soldiers, that might turn the tide.

Ross knew exactly how terrifying and painful it was to have a shard growing inside you. He even knew, though he flinched away from the memory, how agonizing it was to die that way. But if he wanted to save Mia—if he wanted to save Jennie, and Jennie's family, and Dr. Lee, and the kids in the town hall—he didn't see another way.

"I thought of something." Once he said the words, there would be no taking them back. "Like Mr. Preston said, I think my tree will kill the first soldiers who go near it. If I can get it to hold back until they're all within range . . . it could get all of them."

"Can you do that?"

Ross shrugged. "No idea. I can try."

Mia started to reach out toward him, then pulled back. "Ross. If it does work, what will that do to you?"

He closed his eyes, but the images were in his head, where he couldn't get away from them. Mia had seen the outer effect when she'd had to half-carry him to the infirmary. What she couldn't understand was how it had felt—and those deaths had only been memories caught in crystal.

He wrapped his arms tight around himself to stop shaking. "Probably knock me out? Maybe I can get far enough away that it won't." He forced out the words. "Or. I do have that wall I built in my mind. But it hasn't been holding up very well."

"I don't think we should count on that." Mia hefted her flamethrower. "If you do it, I'll cover you."

Ross turned away. His throat hurt and his eyes stung. She had spoken so easily, without knowing what it felt like to hear those words for the first time in his life. *I'll cover you.*

He would do anything to save her life.

He wiped his eyes on the ruin of his embroidered sleeve, feeling a pulse of regret. Paco had raised a hand in salute at the dance, clearly pleased to see Ross making use of his outgrown clothes.

Voske will not put their heads on pikes, Ross resolved.

If he was going to do it, he had to do it now. The moon had vanished. The blue light of impending dawn outlined the mountains, melding the landscape into shadow. But Ross knew exactly where the tree was.

He ran, leaping over the dim shapes of rocks and bushes. As he got closer, the sounds of Mia's footsteps and his own, of her harsh breathing and his, even the clanking of her crossbow against her flamethrower, were all drowned out by chimes. Ross could hear each individual note. He even knew by the quality of the sound how big the leaves were and whether they struck against other leaves, or against branches or seedpods.

They reached the ridge above the tree. The air was still, and no leaf moved. The music played in his mind alone.

"Wait here." He raced to where the tree stood silently, ruby lights glimmering within.

He took a deep breath, and laid his hand on smooth, cool crystal.

50

Felicité

"HERE I AM." JULIO RAN UP TO FELICITÉ'S FATHER, breathing hard. Dan Valdez and Ms. Segura followed him, with Felicité right behind. "Is this everyone?"

Daddy glanced around. "I hope not. Let's give it another minute."

Purple lightning flashed from the wall to the sky. Clouds formed, roiling in a vortex. Rain began to patter down. Felicité's veiled hat and clothing briefly protected her, but as rain soaked through her clothes and blew against her veil, the flesh of her neck began to itch and crawl. Her gills were forming.

She backed away and reached for her scarf. Her fingers touched the bare skin of her exposed neck. Felicité's mouth went dry with horror. The scarf had fallen off, probably when she bent to pick up those arrows. She could feel her gills gape as she pulled her hair forward and tried to tug the veil down to her shoulders.

The smoke vanished under the rain, and the fire that had begun to lick at the trees died down to steaming embers. For the first time they could see the entirety of the hole blown in the wall, and the number of people trying to break past it. Moonlight shone on the silvery hair of a teenage girl surrounded by guards. She stretched her hands to the sky.

"Deirdre!" shouted a woman beside her. "That's enough! The fire's out. You can stop now!"

The girl clenched an upraised hand into a fist. Her clear

voice rose above the rain. "Daddy thinks I'm weak! He'll see. I can do it. I'm stronger than the storm!"

Red, green, and orange lightning flashed across the entire sky, followed by thunder so loud it rattled through Felicité's teeth and bones. The rain intensified. Then it stopped, just as abruptly. The girl crumpled to the ground.

Several of the guards bent over her, checking for signs of life. In the sudden stillness, the female guard's voice carried clearly. "She pushed herself too hard. Deirdre's dead."

Felicité yanked her wet hair forward, plastering it against her neck as hard, cold triumph burned inside her. The enemy girl had died just in time. Another minute of her storm and Felicité's nose would have closed off, forcing her to breathe through the gills. What if someone talked to her?

She took a good long look at the dead girl, who lay still, silvery hair covering her face in locks like dead snakes. That was what the Change did. It made people use you, it made Norms hate you, it turned you into a monster, and if you gave in to it, it could kill you.

Her father was right to hate the Change.

The guards began squabbling over the body. "I'm not telling the king his daughter's dead," said the woman. "You tell him."

The man backed away. "Not me!"

Bellowing a battle cry, he charged at the forge workers who stood in a line, pipes and hammers in hand. Mrs. Horst let fly a bolo that tangled his legs. The woman who had guarded the girl took his place, and the fighting resumed.

Felicité's father took aim at an attacker and shot, but his pistol clicked. He pulled up his powder bag, shook it, then flung it down. The last of his powder was ruined.

Jennie ran up, followed by Henry, Mr. McVey, Mrs. Torres, and Ms. Gboizo. Henry and Jennie seemed unhurt, but the others wore makeshift bandages.

"That makes ten of us." Her father turned toward the ridge. "I guess this is as good as it gets. Let's go."

As Felicité trotted behind him, she thought of the Change that had ruined Sheriff Crow's face and killed her baby. Even Changes that didn't physically warp you could break you inside, like Ross and his bond with that deadly tree. She wondered what he was planning to do. She'd seen him talking to Mia, and then the two of them had headed straight for it.

After about fifty yards, her father pointed south. Three people ran off. Another twenty yards or so, and he pointed north. Jennie and two others headed for the cornfield. Only Julio and Henry stayed with Felicité and her father, Henry running by her side.

"Are you all right?"

"Yes." She tugged her hair closer to her face.

Henry patted the hilt of his sword. "Isn't this exciting? Did you see how many I killed?"

"I hate this," Felicité said.

His face became serious. "I'll keep you safe."

She didn't want the protection of anyone who thought bloody chaos was exciting. She leaped over a small cactus, hoping to get a little distance. Dawn was coming.

She glanced at her father, whose face betrayed exhaustion and tension.

That was a mistake. He sent a searching gaze her way, reaching his free hand to give her a comforting pat on the cheek. His eyes narrowed—she could see them clearly in the pale light.

"Did you hurt your neck? Let me see." He reached for her veil.

Felicité's hands darted up to block his. "No, it's nothing. It's just my hair."

"No. I see something. Sometimes you don't notice a bad wound until it's too late. Let me—"

Felicité backed away, then stopped. If she ran, he'd know she was hiding something. He reached out again. As soon as he lifted her veil, Daddy would know she was a monster, and he would never love her again.

She spun around and pointed toward the ridge. "Ross is Changed. He can control that singing tree. He's doing it right now. I'll show you."

"What?" Her father's bloodshot eyes widened. "He's *what?*"

Felicité started running. His footsteps were right behind her, Henry and Julio flanking him.

Mia stood on the ridge, peering down. Below her, Ross leaned against the singing tree, pressing his face and right hand into the crystal trunk.

Her father stopped beside Felicité, staring in horror. "What's he doing?"

The tree's brilliant coloring began to fade, starting at the tips of its branches and draining downward. It went pink as a rosebud, then transparent as dusty glass, and then so clear that Ross appeared to be leaning on air.

"Felicité's right," Julio whispered, his eyes wide with shock. "He's controlling it."

Ross stumbled away and scrambled on hands and knees up the ridge. When he neared the top, Mia grabbed his hand and hauled him up. Before anyone could say anything, the two of them bolted, Ross staggering as if he was wounded or utterly exhausted.

"Get back," Felicité's father warned.

As she obeyed, she wormed her fingers under her veil. The desert air had evaporated most of the rain. Daddy was watching Ross and Mia flee. Felicité stealthily rubbed her neck dry until she felt her gills close up under her fingers.

51

Mia

MIA HAULED ROSS INTO THE RELATIVE SAFETY OF the cornfield. He was already reeling, and the tree hadn't even done anything yet.

"Did you do it?" she gasped.

He didn't speak, and she thought maybe he couldn't. Then he whispered, "Yes."

A heartbeat later, she heard the distant sound of shattering glass.

Shouts of surprise and fear echoed across the ridge. Ross doubled over. Mia pulled him upright. He sagged against her. All the color had gone out of his face, except for where he'd bitten his lip till the blood ran down.

The far-off cries turned one by one into screams. His plan had obviously worked, but Mia didn't feel any relief, let alone triumph. She didn't know which was worse, listening to Voske's soldiers dying in agony, or listening to Ross sobbing with pain beside her.

She dragged him farther into the field, but he only made it a few steps before he tripped. Mia bent to steady him, but the flamethrower swung around and nearly hit his head. She had to let go of him to block it, then shoved it back impatiently as Ross sank to his knees, hands over his face.

Mia put her hand on his shoulder. "Come on, I'll help you walk."

He didn't move. She unstrapped her flamethrower and

put it on the ground. Obviously she'd never get to use it, and she might have to carry him.

Ross screamed, then recoiled as if he'd been shot. He fell on his back, arms outflung. Mia dropped down beside him.

Jennie pounded up, mud splashing, braids flying, eyes wild. "Where's he hit?"

"He's fine. He's only fainted."

"What?" Jennie knelt next to Ross. "He's been shot. I saw it. Just like Sera. Just like—"

"He's done this before." It was unnerving to see Jennie panicking. "He'll be all right. See?"

She laid her hand on his chest. The ribs molding the thin shirt were still. She waited, but her hand didn't move. She leaned over and put her ear against his mouth. She heard no hiss of breath, felt no puff of warm air. Mia felt as if the earth had crumbled beneath her and she was falling through cold and empty space.

Jennie cried out, "He's dead. Mia, he's—"

"No, he's not," Mia insisted, willing it to be true. She put two fingers under his jaw. Nothing. She pressed harder, her own heart lurching, and found a faint pulse.

His heart was beating. But if he didn't start breathing soon, it would stop, and then there'd be nothing anyone could do.

Dad had taught her how to make people breathe. He'd told her it had worked for him twice, years before she'd been born, once on a choking baby and once on a woman struck by lightning. But everyone she'd ever seen him try it on had died.

Mia drew a deep breath and gently exhaled into Ross's mouth. It felt as if something was blocking her, and she didn't see his chest move. Then she realized that she'd skipped the first step.

Though every nerve burned with impatience, she forced

herself to go through each step, exactly as she'd had been taught. She tilted his head back. Pinched his nose shut. Made sure her mouth was sealed over his.

And tried again.

This time she felt his lungs fill with air. As she breathed for him again, she kept her mind on her father's lessons, visualizing everything he'd showed her and carrying out each step without variation, as if she were following the directions in a manual.

Three breaths. She tasted salty iron—blood from where Ross had bitten his lip.

Four. She should have let Ross go, that night after the rattlesnake attack.

Five. She should have made him go.

Six. That look on Jennie's face, when she'd said Ross had fallen just like Sera.

Seven. How long could they stay here before someone attacked them?

Eight. If she checked his pulse again, what if she couldn't find one?

Nine. She had to stop thinking. She couldn't stop thinking.

Mia was taking the tenth breath for herself, her head buzzing weirdly, when she heard a gasp. Ross coughed, then sucked in his own breath of air. And another. He breathed in ragged, shuddering gasps. But he was breathing.

Jennie was guarding them, sword drawn, gazing out toward the ruddy, dawn-lit ridge. Tears ran down her cheeks, glinting in the peachy glow of the rising sun. Her mouth trembled with grief.

"Jennie." Mia's voice was hoarse.

Jennie didn't move.

Mia made an effort and put more force into her voice. "Jennie, he's all right. Look."

Jennie slowly lowered her head, then sheathed her sword and dropped down beside Ross. She put one arm around him, and pulled Mia down with the other. Mia gripped her tight and laid her cheek against Ross's hair, which was as soft as a cat's. Now she was crying too.

The screaming had stopped.

Mia lifted her head at the sound of running footsteps. Enemies approached, silhouetted against the pink-streaked sky. Mr. Preston's sharp voice rose as he drew a small group of defenders together into a line.

One of Voske's men ran to the edge of the ridge. He took one look, then backed up hastily, nearly falling. "They're dead!" His voice was clear in the still dawn air. "They're all dead! There's crystal growing out of them."

The enemy line faltered. Then a tall man stepped out, facing Mr. Preston. He was too far away for Mia to be able to see his face, but his hair glinted silver in the strengthening light.

"That's Voske," Jennie said, her voice flat. She stood up, drawing her sword.

The sweet sound of crystal chimes rose delicately on the air. From farther away came more chiming, faint with distance, but joining into the same intricate melody. All the way out to the ruined city, the deadly trees rang out their warning. Mia tightened her grip on Ross.

"Retreat!" Voske shouted. "Sound the retreat!"

One of his soldiers blew a horn. The line of enemies began to back away, all except Voske. He lifted a rifle to his shoulder and aimed at Mr. Preston. Mr. Preston shoved Felicité behind him, and started to raise his sword.

Julio leaped to shield his uncle, but Mia was already on her feet. She dove for her flamethrower, snatched up the nozzle, and slapped the plunger. A huge tongue of flame roared out in a spectacular burst of orange and red.

It sputtered out immediately, but it was enough to distract Voske, whose hand jerked as he pulled the trigger. The bullet smashed into a sapling oak beside Mr. Preston, and a spindly branch fell.

Voske stared at Mr. Preston, who stared back. Then he slapped his pockets; he'd run out of ammunition. He wheeled about and took a couple steps, loping to rejoin his retreating soldiers.

52

Jennie

FOR THE FIRST TIME IN THE FOUR DAYS SINCE THE
battle, Jennie's hand didn't hurt when she fixed her hair. Though
the bruises were fading, her memories stayed sharp and bright
as knives.

In the mirror, she saw an unfamiliar figure, an intruder in
someone else's room. But her room was exactly the same. She
was the one who had changed.

She touched the weapons mounted by the mirror, then let her
hand drop. There would be no morning drill.

There hadn't been any in those awful days when she helped
bury the dead, enemy and friend, then searched for more beyond
the walls.

She'd been so dazed and exhausted that she had felt as if she
were sleepwalking. Adding to the dreamlike sense were the
fields of wildflowers that had sprung up after the rains: brilliant
orange poppies, yellow mustard flowers so bright they stung her
eyes, purple sage, sun cups, desert stars. Glitter-lizards scuttled
among them, creatures they usually saw only in early spring.
She'd had to push aside spires of blue lupine to find the bodies.
But there hadn't been as many enemy dead as she'd expected,
and Voske's people had taken away their wounded.

"They'll be back," her pa had said as they stood on the south
wall, staring out at the new grove of obsidian singing trees.

But he was laughing as Dee made a sugar dust devil whirl
into his coffee mug. Paco sat by José, his leg stretched out and
resting on a chair.

Her pa leaned back in his chair. "There's no need to decide yet whether or not you want to keep the house, Paco. You're always welcome here."

"If you move in with us, you can help with my chores," José said, and wiggled his arm in its sling. "Between the two of us, we make up one guy."

"Thanks," said Paco, as if the joke hadn't even registered. She was glad to see that he was even speaking. Those first few days, he hadn't talked at all.

Jennie tried not to stare at his prominent cheekbones and angular jaw, so much an echo of Voske's. Paco didn't know who his father was—he'd sometimes talked about it when he lived with them. She wondered if her parents knew. They must. A lot of the older people in town had to have figured it out.

In this town where everyone knew everything, for once, a secret had been kept. As far as Jennie was concerned, she would take it to her grave.

Paco met her eyes, and she realized she'd been staring. His forehead puckered inquiringly.

"Any ideas for a headline?" It was the first thing that came into her mind. "I want to write an article for the *Heraldo*."

He shook his head, his expression closing off.

Her ma had been watching him too. "You don't have to write about the fighting, Jennie. Everyone knows what happened."

"That's true," Jennie said. "But people keep saying, 'Did you know my uncle was a hero? My dad, my mom, my cousin?' Mr. Tsai told all of us contributors that it's important to record the brave things people did."

And maybe if she filled her ears with other people's stories, she'd be able to drown out her own.

Paco bent his head over his plate.

Jennie took a square of corn bread. "But you're right, Ma. That can wait. I've got to give the students the big news, so I'd better get moving."

As she passed the infirmary, she glanced at the curtained windows, as she had every day since they'd carried in Ross's limp body. Mia had reported that he was getting better, but Dr. Lee wouldn't let anyone see him. "Not even me," she had said indignantly. He wouldn't let Jennie visit Indra, either. With so many seriously wounded patients, Dr. Lee had been forced to ration his Change power, healing them only enough to save their lives.

Jennie tried to picture Ross and Indra walking out of the infirmary, healthy and strong. She couldn't do it. She tried to bring back good memories, but all she could see was Ross falling, lying so still in the mud with blood around his mouth, and all she could feel was her failed struggle to lift Indra, his impossibly heavy weight, and the deathly chill of his hands.

She stamped her foot, hoping the jolt would drive away the memories, and walked faster when she saw the students milling around the schoolyard.

Yuki leaned against a fence, Kogatana on his shoulder. The bruising from Mia's crossbow was still visible around his collarbone and upper arm, but it had faded from black to purple.

He seemed pleased to see her. "Hi, Jennie. Mom sent me to invite you to dinner tonight. It's Shabbat, so the food will be extra-good."

The adults had decided that Yuki was done with school. Like Paco, he wasn't getting a formal graduation. The excuse was that there was too much rebuilding going on, but Jennie knew that Paco had refused to have a ceremony. Yuki had too. She wondered if it was to draw attention away from Paco's choice.

"Thanks," Jennie said. "Tell her I'll be there."

"I asked Paco, too, but he said no." Yuki paused, and Jennie wondered if he too was remembering how the Rangers had carried Paco to Luc's, over his halfhearted objections, and they'd all sung "Hijo de la Luna." "I'm worried about him."

"I am too. It must be terrible to lose—" She was afraid she'd start crying if she even said Sera's name aloud. Belatedly, Jennie remembered that Yuki had lost both his parents, years ago, and felt even worse.

"It is." Yuki reached up to stroke Kogatana, who was nuzzling him. "You'd think I'd know what to say to him. But I don't."

The image of Voske's face seared Jennie's mind, nose and chin and cheekbones sharp in the flickering firelight. She forced it away, and it faded, leaving her heart hammering as if she'd been running.

"Do you feel like the battle changed you?" she asked impulsively.

Yuki hesitated, then down came his chin in his characteristic clipped nod. "You know Paco and I were defending the front gate. He could barely stand. We were both out of arrows. I was sure I was going to die, and I'd never get the chance to leave Las Anclas. But I wasn't afraid or angry. Then I remembered being on the raft with Miyazawa-san and Fumi-san and Yoshida-sensei. I'd always thought they sacrificed themselves for me because I was their prince. And I'd wondered if they would have regretted that if they'd known I'd never be a prince again."

Jennie recalled the solemn, haughty boy whose first, broken words in English had been to demand that he be addressed as "Prince Yuki." How glamorous she and the other girls had thought him, and how disappointed they'd been when he'd finally told everyone that he was no longer a prince. But she'd never known the names of the people whose bodies had been found with him.

He went on, "Here's what I realized after the battle. Maybe they didn't give me their water because I was their prince."

Jennie glanced out at the schoolyard. Rico was tearing after Will Preston, yelling, "You didn't tag me! You're still it!"

Guilt choked her. She forced the words out. "You were a kid. They would have protected you no matter who you were."

Yuki shook his head. "That wasn't what I meant. At the end

of the battle, when I was nearly out of ammo, I was willing to die for the sake of the people I loved. So maybe they were too."

Jennie had never before heard Yuki talk so openly. The battle really had changed him. But not as it had changed her. *He* hadn't done anything wrong.

Jennie had to say something, before he could ask her if she, too, had been changed. "Do you still want to leave Las Anclas?"

He studied the ground. "Yes." Then he pushed away and walked off. She suspected that he regretted having shared that much.

In the schoolyard, students stood in a knot, arguing.

Rico exclaimed, "Ross's power is so cool!"

"It is not cool," Felicité retorted.

Brisa put her hands on her hips. "Ross saved the whole town. Where I was standing, we were losing. Then those chimes started ringing, and Voske called the retreat. That's because of Ross."

"Where I was standing, we were doing fine." Henry thumped his chest. "I was with Mr. Preston. We could have taken out Voske's best team. I was all ready to kill Voske myself when Mia got in the way with that flamethrower. Though that blast was pretty great."

Felicité's hands were gripped together, the nails white. "It was awful. You didn't see it, Brisa."

"What was it like?" Carlos asked.

Jennie wondered if Felicité was haunted by her own memories. They hadn't spoken once since Felicité had said, "It's your fault." Now her words were as brittle as falling ice. "I was right there beside Daddy when a man staggered up the ridge, screaming, and fell down at my feet with crystal growing through him."

A girl's voice rose in a shout. "You don't know what I had to do in the field hospital! Don't tell me all the horrible stuff you saw outside!"

Jennie turned, almost not recognizing Becky Callahan's

face, scarlet with rage. Jennie hadn't even known she was capable of yelling.

Felicité's voice, too, rose angrily. "That's what your hero's precious Change power did. Ross is a monster!"

So that's what her real voice sounds like, thought Jennie. *But what does she have to be angry about? Everyone close to her is fine.*

Sujata shoved past Henry and confronted Felicité, face-to-face, almost nose to nose. "How dare you call Changed people monsters! Monsters like my father died to protect this town."

Felicité stood there, her hands rigid by her sides, and Jennie stepped between them. "Take your seats. Now."

Sujata's hand was already raised to slap Felicité. Jennie caught her eye and shook her head. Slowly Sujata lowered her hand.

Felicité flinched as if the slap had landed. "Jennie. I should not have said that." And when Jennie didn't speak, there was the sugar again. "Ross did save the town."

But Jennie was waiting for the apology for that monster crack.

Felicité's throat worked, then she turned, shoulders straight, ribbons fluttering on her hat, and stalked into the schoolhouse, followed by Henry and the others. Brisa put her arm around Becky's shoulders.

Sujata murmured, "I don't know what's got into Felicité. Maybe *Daddy* has been raving about monsters, but she better not say anything like that again, mayor's daughter or no."

"I don't think she will," Jennie said, though she wasn't sure of anything anymore.

"Nobody is like themselves. Oh, yes—Indra asked after you. Dr. Lee says you can go see him this afternoon."

"Thanks, Sujata." Jennie stepped into the schoolroom, studying all the faces. Some angry, others curious, some off in their own worlds. A few of the smaller kids surreptitiously kicked one another under the desks. Henry grinned as he took the seat by

Felicité, who sat with her head bowed, so all Jennie could see was an enormous feathered hat and a beautifully worked lace scarf.

She drew in a deep breath, her eyes stinging when she took in the empty desks. Some belonged to people who'd been hurt. But two were empty because the fifteen-year-olds who'd once sat there were dead. Estela and Ken had ignored orders and run into the thick of the battle, meaning to help. Another empty desk was covered with curlicues and flowers, scratched on by sharp black claws. Laura Hernandez had followed her orders, and held the line till the end.

"I have an announcement," Jennie began, and she didn't have to ask for quiet. "There will be no school until further notice. No!" The cheering that had begun stopped abruptly. "It doesn't mean you're free. Some will help with the harvest, others will be sentries, and you older ones will be on patrol until the wounded heal. Everyone will be training, because sooner or later, Voske will be back."

She wanted to end on a less grim note, but couldn't. "The memorial is at sundown. You're dismissed."

When everyone was gone, Jennie glanced up at the rafters, where she had hidden Ross's book. She wondered how important that book really was.

There was one person who'd know: the bounty hunter. If he was still around, the sheriff would know where.

Jennie walked to the sheriff's office, then stopped on the threshold when she discovered the bounty hunter leaning against the wall, eating a saucer of apple crumble. He seemed even taller and more formidable in the light of day.

A headline popped into her mind, making her smile for what felt like the first time in months: "Mysterious Bounty Hunter Eats Breakfast with Heroic Sheriff!"

"Morning," he said.

Sheriff Crow beckoned her in. She wore her hair in two

braids, the way she had before her Change, leaving her entire face bare. "This is Jennie Riley."

"So," Jennie said. "You're"—*On our side? Spying? Still here?*—"staying in town?"

He put down his fork. "Tom Preston invited me to join the Rangers."

Jennie tried not to show the flinch that she felt right down to her bones. But Sera's empty shoes had to be filled. She straightened, and looked him in the eye. "Can I ask you why Voske attacked us? Was he after Ross's book?"

"I think the book was more of a bonus," Sheriff Crow replied. "He's after the town. He's tried before, you know."

The bounty hunter gave a nod.

"But how did he know to attack on the night of the dance?" Jennie asked. "Or was that an accident?"

The man shook his head. "There are no accidents with Voske." He flicked a glance at the walls, and Jennie scanned the room uneasily.

"Jennie, that's not for the newspaper, or the schoolyard," said Sheriff Crow. Jennie nodded. Her throat hurt. Then the sheriff faced the bounty hunter. "I was meaning to talk to you about names.

"My name isn't really Elizabeth Crow. Crow isn't a last name at all. It's the name of my tribe. Way, way back when—sometime after the world changed—my people saw everything being forgotten. The one thing they were set on remembering was that we are Crow. So we used it as our name, because that is the one thing you can never forget."

Jennie was surprised that the sheriff would tell this story—a story she had never heard—to a man who had so recently been an enemy.

Sheriff Crow went on. "Funny thing is, a couple years ago, a trader visited Las Anclas. He told me that way out east there's a whole town of us. They don't call themselves Crow. They have a word in their own language. My own language—a language I don't know. But they are my people. I thought about changing my name, and taking one of theirs. But then I thought, *This is what my people are here.* In Las Anclas, I'm Elizabeth Crow. So what I'm asking you is, what do you want to be called in Las Anclas?"

The bounty hunter hesitated, then said, "Furio Vilas." He paused again, before adding, "It's my real name."

Jennie wanted to ask more, but the way the two were looking at each other made her feel like a third wheel. She backed out and went home.

She spent the day writing articles. There was something comforting about pinning down all those memories with ink on flat paper, just the facts.

Midafternoon, she put on her best church skirt and blouse and went to the infirmary. She walked past the sleeping figures and curtained-off beds in the men's ward until she found Indra gazing at the ceiling. He smiled when she sat down beside his bed.

"I'm sorry about your father."

His smile went out like a snuffed candle. "The doctor said he couldn't have felt anything when the wall blew up under him. I guess that's something to hold on to."

Sera had died quickly too, but Jennie couldn't take that as comfort.

"Jennie?" Indra interrupted her thoughts. "I wanted to thank you for saving my life."

"I didn't." Grief seized Jennie by the heart, strong as pain. Stronger.

"You did," Indra insisted, half-sitting in his effort to infuse his breathy voice with force. "Dr. Lee said you got me here just in time."

She didn't want to argue, but she couldn't help saying, "I couldn't lift you."

"I know. It didn't matter. You got me out anyway."

"You remember?"

"I remember it all," Indra murmured, sinking back again.

"I do too."

"There were so many of them."

"Yeah."

"They'll be back, you know." When Jennie nodded, he added, "I'm so glad you're one of us. We need you."

Jennie barely stopped herself from saying, *I got Sera killed.* She knew she hadn't, or at least hadn't been any more responsible for Sera's death than any of the other Rangers, but it felt true.

"We need *you.*" She patted his hand. His hot skin felt less real under her fingers than her memory of how cold he'd been. Unnerved, she put her hands in her lap. "I hope you get better soon."

"Jennie—"

"Did you know the bounty hunter is joining the Rangers?"

Indra's eyes widened. "Nobody told me that."

"Yuki told me yesterday that his staff work is an art form." Jennie kept talking, keeping the flow of words unbroken. Nothing about old hurts, no old questions to open up feelings like wounds.

He fell asleep while she was talking. She'd seen that sleeping face sharing her pillow so many times, but he seemed so vulnerable this time. She leaned down, then pulled away before she could kiss him on the mouth. She couldn't do that anymore. Instead, she brushed her lips across his forehead and tiptoed out.

Mia was in the front hall, in a pair of her father's baggy black pants and a baggier white shirt. They began walking toward the town hall.

"I didn't see Ross in the men's ward," Jennie said.

"His bed's curtained off," Mia replied. "Last time he landed in the infirmary because of his power, he got better after he got some rest. Dad's hoping that'll work again, so he doesn't want anyone disturbing Ross."

So you've known about his power for a while. Jennie didn't resent that. What hurt was that neither of them had told her.

As if she had spoken aloud, Mia said, "I only found out by accident. I would have told you, but it wasn't my secret. He would have told you eventually. He trusted you enough to give you his book! But he didn't even know what was happening to him at first."

"Okay." It did make Jennie feel better.

"Dad says he thinks Ross will make a complete recovery." Mia sounded like she was trying to convince herself.

Maybe Mia, too, felt as strange as Jennie, but hadn't mentioned it for fear that she was the only one. "Hey, Mia, is there anything from the battle that you can't stop thinking about?"

"Most of it was horrible. I had nightmares for three nights straight. The worst part was when I thought Ross was dead, and there was nothing I could do to fix it." Mia's somber expression transformed into a joyful smile. "But then he started breathing again, and I realized that I *had* fixed it. It was the best thing I did in my life. Every time I think about it, it makes me happy."

"You should be happy," Jennie agreed. She tried to call back the relief she herself had felt, but it slid out of her mind, as if she were trying to clench a fistful of water.

At the town hall, they squeezed onto a bench near the front row. The mayor, the council, and the town's religious leaders were on the dais. Even Rabbi Litvak had come down from his home on the mountain. His forehead was already creased with stress: the intensity of people's emotions must be pressing in.

When all of Las Anclas was there—the benches were filled, and many others stood along the walls—the memorial began. Jennie had been dreading this for days. As the rabbi led the prayers for the dead, she gripped her hands in her lap. She could hear the harsh breathing of people fighting emotion; a few benches away, someone gave a muffled sob. When the rabbi had finished, the Catholic members of town began the Rosary. Jennie tried to listen to the words, but instead she found herself picturing Sera falling. Ross falling.

When the prayers from the various religions were over, Mayor Wolfe began to read the names of the dead.

She paused after each as someone came up to offer words of eulogy. Ravi Vardam. Estela Lopez. Alice Callahan, Henry and Becky's grandmother. Ken Wells. Laura Hernandez. There were more sobs, which made it harder to hold back her own. Jennie shut her eyes and clenched her teeth. If she slipped even a little, she would never stop crying.

"Serafina Diaz," the mayor said, startling Jennie. She hadn't even known that Sera was short for anything.

Mr. Preston rose from the council bench. "Everyone here knows where Sera and I came from, though we never talked about it. The past was the past, we figured. We wanted to be judged on what we did here, as citizens of Las Anclas."

His gaze swept the room. "But I think Sera wouldn't mind if I told you what she said when we first saw this town. She was just seventeen years old. She took one look at the walls, and she said, 'There's no heads on pikes. How do they keep order?'"

There were a few mild chuckles. Henry Callahan let out a whoop, fiercely shushed by his mother.

"We saw how Las Anclas kept order—by rule of law, not rule of force. Sera decided that she wanted her child to grow up in a place where everyone was equal under the same law. And so she worked hard to help keep that law."

All eyes turned toward Paco, sitting between Jennie's ma and pa. Jennie was close enough to touch him, but his head was lowered so she couldn't see his face, his arms crossed tightly across his chest. She quickly looked away.

"Let me tell you about Sera Diaz." As Mr. Preston continued, Jennie pressed her fingers over her eyelids. It was the little things that hurt the worst: Sera's deadpan jokes; how she put so many chilies in her salsa that nobody else could eat it; how she'd raced Jennie down the main street, slipped in the mud, and squashed Dr. Lee's tomatoes; the time they'd all played "Hijo de la Luna" on glasses.

There would be no more of those moments. Jennie had spent years imagining the day she would finally become a Ranger under Sera's command. Her dream had come true, but Sera wouldn't give any more orders, or grin and ask for the last drop of lemon juice. Sera was gone, and all Jennie had left of her was a secret that she wished she'd never found out.

53

Mia

MIA OPENED THE SURGERY DOOR, HOPING HER DAD had fixed something normal for lunch. She was hungry after a long session repairing the gate, and in no mood for turnip pudding.

"That you, Mia? If you want to see Ross, he's ready for visitors."

"Thanks, Dad!" Now she'd even forgive turnip pudding. She raced to her cottage, snatched up a diagram, then tore back to the surgery.

Ross's curtain was open for the first time. He sat up in bed, propped against a pillow. She had to stop herself from rushing up and touching him to reassure herself that he was all right. Instead, she spun around and yanked the curtain shut, then turned to meet his slightly puzzled smile.

"How are you feeling?" she asked.

"A lot better," he said. "What've you got there?"

He looked worn and thin, lost in an enormous nightshirt that was neither wet nor transparent, but Mia felt the way she had when he'd stood in her doorway, drenched with rain.

She clutched the diagram to her chest. "I was so sure you'd love this, but maybe you won't. I couldn't ask because Dad said you needed to rest and he wouldn't even let me come look at you. Not that I meant to spy!" She shut her mouth so fast her teeth clicked.

His eyes crinkled with amusement. "Hand it over."

Mia sidled up to the head of the bed so she could see both his face and the diagram, then remembered that he didn't like people lurking behind him and lurched back into his line of sight.

She stabbed at the diagram with a finger. "It's a gauntlet for your left hand. It'll be steel, lined with leather."

He touched the paper. "What's this sliding part do?"

"Well, I saw you fight, and I remembered my own lessons and I realized that if you can't make a tight fist, you can't really do anything . . ." Ross's jaw twitched. Mia hurried on, tapping the paper until it rustled. "The steel bars go over your wrist and forearm as a brace, which also functions as a shield. Once it's on, you can move the slide with your right hand to lock your fingers in place, in a fist or holding a weapon or even straight out if you wanted to do any open-handed strikes."

She studied his face, but she couldn't tell how he was taking it. "I wanted to make it so you could throw a knife, but I watched you do that with your right hand and it's a pretty complicated sequence of movements and you have to let go of it at exactly the right time and I couldn't figure out how to make it work. Sorry."

Ross was giving her a very strange look.

"You hate it. That's okay. I don't mind." She snatched the diagram and crumpled it behind her.

He whispered, "It's perfect."

"What?" Mia bent closer.

Ross lifted his chin. His eyes were so dark they looked black, framed by thick, curling eyelashes. Mia's bones caught on fire. She wasn't sure she could stop herself from kissing him, or possibly from passing out. She crushed her diagram into a sweaty ball.

Ross reached up with his good hand and touched the side of her face. The diagram fell to the floor. His hand was warm on her cheek, cupping it as gently as if she were some prospected treasure he had to be careful not to break.

She gave into the impulse she'd been fighting for so long, and stroked his hair. He didn't flinch.

Ross lifted his other hand and reached behind her neck. He pulled her in, and Mia had only an instant to disbelieve that it was really happening.

He kissed her.

She felt the contact all the way through her body, not just on her lips, hot and tingling like a mild electric shock. A good shock. Her fingers closed around a handful of his hair, then slid down the smooth skin of his back, bumping gently over his ribs. He stroked her neck lightly. Now she felt like she was on fire. But good fire. Then he clutched her shoulders, loosely with his left hand and almost bruisingly with his right, and kissed her harder. He didn't even let go when he had to tip his head back to take a breath. She let him breathe, then caught him by the shoulders and kissed him back. And then Mia couldn't analyze what she felt like, because she wasn't thinking at all.

Ross pulled her down beside him, and she lay with her head pillowed on his shoulder and his hair falling over her face. It smelled deliciously like the lemongrass soap she'd helped make for the infirmary. She wrapped her arms around him, half expecting him to freeze, but he drew her in even closer. He was so warm, and his skin was so soft, and he was holding her as if it would kill him to let her go. It made every awful, terrifying, miserable moment in the last month worthwhile.

Ross said quietly, "You have no idea how long I've been wanting to do that."

Mia blinked. "Oh, really? You too?"

He nodded. She leaned over and pressed her lips into the hollow of his throat.

"I see you've recovered, Ross," said Mr. Preston.

Mia recoiled in surprise—and fell off the bed with a crash.

When she scrambled up, Ross's face was at least as red as hers had to be.

"I could come back at a better time," Mr. Preston offered, sounding amused.

"No, no," Ross managed.

Mia nodded so quickly her glasses almost flew across the room. "It's okay!" The only thing that was worse than Mr. Preston catching them kissing was the thought that if he left, he would know they were kissing right then.

"Ross, I'm here on the mayor's behalf as well as my own. We wanted to thank you for what you did for our town."

Mia put a protective hand on his shoulder. She could feel his muscles tensing.

"You . . ." Mr. Preston hesitated, his mouth twisting. Then his face resumed its usual calm expression. "That's quite an impressive Change power of yours. I'd like to know more about it."

Ross started trembling. Mia said, "It almost killed him. You can't ask him to do it again."

Mr. Preston raised his heavy eyebrows. "I didn't realize it took so much out of you. Anyway, there'll be no problem with you becoming a citizen, if that's what you want. Your probation's over."

Ross stopped breathing, giving her a moment of pure terror. Then she felt him inhale. "Let me ask you something. Do you think Voske will try again?"

"I'm sure of it."

With an effort, Ross sat up straight, bracing his palms against the mattress. "I've decided—I want to sell you my book. I think the town needs it."

Mr. Preston actually smiled. "Thank you. We'll give you

good value for it. We can talk about the terms later. For now, I'll leave you to your . . . recovery." To Mia's embarrassment, he winked at her as he left.

When his footsteps had safely faded, Ross whispered, "I feel like I just escaped a collapsing mine."

"He's even scarier when he's trying to be nice," Mia agreed.

Ross nodded. "But his offer . . . Becoming a citizen . . ." He paused so long that she too forgot to breathe. "I'll take it."

"You will?" Mia heard her own voice rise up in a squeak. She threw her arms around him, almost as thrilled as she'd been when he'd kissed her. "You will! Great!"

"Your father and I had a long talk about it. He thought Preston might make the offer," he admitted. "So I had some time to think about it. I thought about it. I want to stay." For the first time, he sounded certain.

A thought came to Mia's mind, making her giggle. "Mr. Preston doesn't know he won't be able to read the book, does he? When are you planning to spring that on him?"

Ross laughed. "I thought I'd get Yuki to read it first. I'd like to know what it says."

"Shall I go ask him?"

He tugged her back to the bed. "How about later?"

54

Ross

ROSS LAY IN BED, STARING AT THE CURTAINS SO HE wouldn't have to stare at the ceiling. Indra had barely been able to walk when Dr. Lee let him go, and Ross could walk perfectly well. So why, after all this time, was he still stuck in the infirmary? He kicked at the covers. At least he'd talked Dr. Lee into bringing down some real clothes so he could get out of that nightshirt.

He wished Mia or Jennie would show up. It had been great to see Jennie the other night, but they'd barely started talking before she'd remembered that she'd forgotten some job and had to rush out. He picked up the newspaper she'd left on the bedside table and once again sounded out the headline: "Las Anclas Repels King Voske's Attack!" in huge letters, and below, in smaller type, "Town Celebrates, Mourns."

Then came the welcome sound of rustling curtains. "Come in!" Ross called.

Dr. Lee gave Ross a mock frown. "Next time you turn up here, I'm carving your name over the bed. See that I don't have to."

Ross grinned. "I'll try to stay out."

"You've got visitors. When they leave, you can too." When Ross started to leap up, Dr. Lee held out a warning hand. "Be sensible, and take it slow."

Ross nodded. "Thanks, Dr. Lee."

As Dr. Lee went out, Mia, Yuki, and Jennie came in. Jennie held a familiar shape wrapped in oilcloth.

Ross swung his legs over the edge of the bed. He'd had it with people standing over him. "You guys can sit down if you want."

Mia dropped down in an instant, rocking the bed, then scooted closer. Ross slid a half inch over, until their shoulders touched. He felt her let out a long sigh at the same moment that he did.

Jennie sat on his other side, a little farther away, and handed Ross the package.

He hefted it in his hands, then unwrapped it.

There it was, the book that had started everything. Ross touched the worn leather cover. He'd known how valuable it was when he'd first opened it, and had imagined what he might get in trade for it: a rifle and ammunition, new clothes, old maps . . . Things he could load onto Rusty's back and carry with him. Probably he could get all that from Mr. Preston. But it felt as if what he'd really gotten, before he even began negotiations, was a whole new life.

It was hard to let go, but he couldn't hold on to it forever. Ross handed the book to Yuki, who took it with the same reverence Ross felt. "Can you read it?"

Yuki sat down, took a pair of glasses from his shirt pocket, and put them on. He opened the book to the last page, read silently, and then looked at Ross. "Mia said this was a manual."

"Isn't it?"

"It's a diary. The page I just read was about how the writer had an argument with someone she worked with, and then she went home and found that her daughter had tried to cook something and spilled milk all over the floor."

"You need to start at the beginning," Mia said. "That's where the diagrams are."

"I am at the beginning," Yuki said. "Japanese reads from right to left—our books open the other way around. Let me see how it ends."

He leafed through the pages until he came to the diagrams, then kept going until he reached what Ross had thought was the first page. His expression didn't change, but he got up, turned away from them, and stood still for a while.

The others sat in silence. Ross took hold of Mia's hand.

Eventually, Yuki faced them again. When he spoke, his voice was husky. "I'd better read this to you."

Ross tried not to stare at him. Had he been holding back tears? Why?

Yuki began to slowly translate. "'My name is Yamaguchi Hina. I'm a professor of medieval Japanese history at the University of Tokyo. I came—'"

"What's the University of Tokyo?" Ross interrupted. "And what's 'medieval'?"

"She taught ancient history at a big school . . ." Jennie shrugged. "Somewhere in Japan, I guess."

"Its ancient capital," said Yuki, then went on. "'I came to America for a conference on medieval East Asian warfare. There was some kind of catastrophe—war or natural disaster—we don't know. Nothing electronic works anymore, and nearly everything mechanical has some electronic components.

"'I have only a few blank pages left in my diary, and even in a gathering of historians, I'm the only one who still uses paper and pen. I thought about recording what's happening now, but I'm sure others are doing that, so I decided not to waste this paper duplicating their work. Instead, I drew up the material from my presentation, from memory. It seems trivial, compared to everything else, but I hate to think of it being lost forever. Perhaps it will be useful or informative for someone someday.

"'Unless I can find a ship with sails, I don't think I'll ever get home. If anyone finds this and can take it back to Japan, please deliver it to my husband. His name is Yamaguchi Tatsuya, professor of modern Japanese literature at the University of Tokyo.'"

Yuki ran his fingers lightly over the words, his head bent.

"Thank you," Ross said.

"May I borrow it?"

It had been hard for him to even let Yuki see it. But he remembered Yuki's ship, and his lost expression when he'd told Ross his story. "Take it."

Yuki carefully rewrapped the book and started out. Then he turned back, one hand crushing the curtain. "I was wondering, Ross. Are you still going to prospect, now that you're staying in town?"

"Yeah. I figure I can go on trips, and come back."

"Would you consider teaching me how to prospect?"

"You want to prospect?" Ross asked.

Mia started laughing.

Jennie shook her head in mock dismay. "Yuki, all this time and you never even told him?"

Yuki gave them both an exasperated look. "I had to think about it."

"You mean, teach you in exchange for translating the rest of the book?" Ross asked.

Yuki shook his head. "I'll do that regardless. Just . . . would you teach me?"

Ross had never taught anyone anything, and it was unnerving to imagine Yuki's intense gaze while he tried to do so. But Yuki also seemed to feel like a stranger in Las Anclas, and Ross couldn't help sympathizing with that.

"Prospectors have to know how to make deals," Ross said. "Translate the book, and teach me to ride. Then I'll teach you to prospect. Deal?"

Ross held out his hand, and Yuki touched his palm with his own.

"Deal. And thank you." Yuki hurried out, clutching the book.

Ross caught Jennie making a furtive gesture to Mia, who replied with a nod.

"What's wrong?" Ross asked, instantly suspicious.

Mia patted his shoulder. "Nothing. Well, except that it's not just Mr. Preston who knows that you're the one who... did that thing. With the tree."

"Apparently Felicité overheard you talking to Mia about it and alerted everyone around," Jennie added. "And then after the battle she and Henry told the entire town. Sorry."

"It's okay," he said glumly. "I figured it must have come out."

Though he hated the thought of everyone knowing, that was nothing compared to how he hated knowing it himself. His first few days in the infirmary had been one long nightmare, endlessly reliving the last moments of all the soldiers he'd killed. He could still hear their screams rising up above the song of the trees if he didn't keep reinforcing the wall in his mind.

He stood up. "Dr. Lee said I could go. I'd like to see the sky."

The girls fell in step on either side of him as he walked outside. He stood on the porch in his bare feet, looking across the dark square. People were gardening by the light of hanging lamps. Inside the infirmary, he'd lost all track of time. He hadn't even known if it was night or day. Now he could look up and see the waning moon.

"There's something else," Mia said.

"Something bad?" he asked quickly.

Jennie grinned. "No."

On his other side, Mia wore a matching grin. "Would you mind closing your eyes and letting us lead you?"

When he'd first come to Las Anclas, he wouldn't have been able to do that even if he'd wanted to. Now he took a deep breath, then closed his eyes and held out his hands.

Mia's small hand folded around his left, and Jennie's larger one gripped his right. Both were warm and strong. The girls led him back into the surgery. He shuffled along, listening to their breathing. He could tell Mia was trying not to laugh.

"Stairs," warned Jennie.

He stepped up carefully. The girls stayed at either side, steadying him.

"Cat," warned Mia.

He gently pushed the furry creature out of his way with his foot. It meowed indignantly. "Sorry," he told the cat.

When they reached the top, he heard his bedroom door open.

"We hope this was worth keeping you in the infirmary an extra day or so," Jennie said.

They led him to the bed and sat down on it with him, still holding his hands.

"Open your eyes," said Mia.

They had taken out the ceiling and replaced it with glass.

"Paco helped us." Mia sat down beside him. "He's an apprentice glassmaker. We made a deal with him and his master."

"A lot of people helped," Jennie added. "It was a big job. Don't worry, we didn't tell them anything personal. We just said we thought you'd like it."

The stars shone as clear and bright overhead as if there were nothing there but the still night air. Sometimes when he'd stretched out alone on the desert sands, just as he was drifting off to sleep, he'd felt as if the world had turned over and he was falling into the sky. The stars he gazed at now were laid out in the same brilliant patterns across the same vast black sky, but Jennie and Mia sat warm beside him, ready to catch him if he fell.

RACHEL MANIJA BROWN (www.rachelmanijabrown.com) is the author of the memoir *All the Fishes Come Home to Roost: An American Misfit in India*.

She works as a therapist, specializing in the treatment of PTSD (post-traumatic stress disorder).

SHERWOOD SMITH (www.sherwoodsmith.net) is the author of many fantasy novels for teenagers and adults, including *Crown Duel* and the Mythopoeic Award Finalist *The Spy Princess*.

They both live in Southern California.

If you would like to be emailed when their next book comes out, please visit the following link: http://eepurl.com/Tzv25.